Praise for Pamela Britton

"This is the kind of book that romance fans will read and reread on gloomy days."
—*Publishers Weekly* on *Tempted*

"Keep the tissues handy for this heart-tugging, warm and brilliantly touching tale of possibilities with strong dialogue and beautifully etched characters."
—*RT Book Reviews* on *Rancher and Protector*

"Passion and humor are a potent combination… author Pamela Britton comes up with the perfect blend."
—*Oakland Press*

"Britton's characters are stubborn and flawed, and the supporting cast is wonderful and punches up the story."
—*RT Book Reviews* on *Mark: Secret Cowboy*

"It isn't easy to write a tale that makes the reader laugh and cry, but Britton succeeds, thanks to her great characters."
—*Booklist* (starred review) on *Seduced*

With more than a million books in print, **Pamela Britton** likes to call herself the best-known author nobody's ever heard of. Of course, that changed thanks to a certain licensing agreement with that little racing organization known as NASCAR.

But before the glitz and glamour of NASCAR, Pamela wrote books that were frequently voted the best of the best by the *Detroit Free Press*, Barnes & Noble (two years in a row) and *RT Book Reviews*. She's won numerous awards, including a National Readers' Choice Award and a nomination for the Romance Writers of America Golden Heart Award.

When not writing books, Pamela is a reporter for a local newspaper. She's also a columnist for the *American Quarter Horse Journal*.

Books by Pamela Britton

Harlequin American Romance

Cowboy Lessons

Cowboy Trouble

Cowboy M.D.

Cowboy Vet

Cowgirl's CEO

The Wrangler

Mark: Secret Cowboy

Rancher and Protector

The Rancher's Bride

A Cowboy's Pride

A Cowboy's Christmas Wedding

A Cowboy's Angel

The Texan's Twins

Visit the Author Profile page at Harlequin.com for more titles.

Pamela Britton

MARK: SECRET COWBOY & RANCHER AND PROTECTOR

HARLEQUIN® THE COWBOY COLLECTION

Recycling programs
for this product may
not exist in your area.

ISBN-13: 978-0-373-60145-5

Mark: Secret Cowboy & Rancher and Protector

Copyright © 2015 by Harlequin Books S.A.

The publisher acknowledges the copyright holder
of the individual works as follows:

Mark: Secret Cowboy
Copyright © 2010 by Pamela Britton

Rancher and Protector
Copyright © 2011 by Pamela Britton

Printed in U.S.A.

CONTENTS

MARK: SECRET COWBOY

This one's for Karli, who graciously allows me to write my books in her coffee shop every day. Thanks for the flowers in my "office," the double-shot Almond Rocha Mochas and most of all, your friendship. You're truly a light in my life.

CHAPTER ONE

SHE WAS THE one woman he could never have, and it drove Mark Hansen nuts.

Nicki Sable stood in the shadow of the announcer's booth, laughing at something Jesse Cody said, their words drowned out by the blaring voice coming from the loudspeakers. She didn't see Mark there, spying on her. He had to crouch to peer between the white metal pipes. He stood in a twenty-by-twenty pen, one that served as a corral when it wasn't being used by rough stock riders to store their gear, and seeing her there, watching her talk to Jesse, made Mark's stomach clench.

Damn that Jesse Cody, he thought, going back to rubbing rosin on his bull rope. The no-good son of a gun had it all—the best equipment, a supportive family and, most of all, Nicki Sable.

"You ready to ride?"

Mark glanced up, shocked to see Nicki on the other side of the fence, a half smile on her gorgeous face as she looked him in the eyes.

"Think so," he said slowly, glancing around him for a moment to ensure one of the other Cody brothers wasn't standing behind him and that maybe she was talking to him. Then again, they didn't all ride bulls. Only Jesse did. Mark's nemesis in more ways than one.

"You ever ridden Bandito before?" she asked.

Mark kept his gaze on his rope, trying hard not to let her see how difficult it was to remain unaffected by her presence.

Pure and simple, he wanted Nicki Sable.

Since the first moment he'd spotted her mutton busting when she was nine years old he'd been fascinated by her. Not that he'd wanted her back then, but the spark of interest had been there from the very beginning. As she'd gotten older, and grown into a true beauty with her honey-colored skin and stunning green eyes, his fascination had turned to something more. Trouble was, he worked for her father. And her dad hated his guts.

"I rode him at your dad's practice pen," Mark said. "I think he was hoping he'd toss me on my keister."

"Who?" she asked. "My dad?"

Mark smirked, which was about as close to a smile as he could get, what with his face all frozen like it was. "Yup."

She frowned. "Just what is it with you and my dad?"

Mark almost laughed. "You wouldn't believe me if I told you."

"Try me," she said, seeming to be genuinely curious.

Mark glanced toward the arena. They were still tie-down roping in there, the crowd suddenly cheering as someone—Mark didn't know who—jumped off his horse at the exact same moment a black angus calf fell to the ground, the rope that'd put him there stretched taut between the steer and the horse.

"How much time do you have?" Mark asked, once the sound of the crowd faded.

"All day," she said, tipping her head sideways, her long blond hair—Barbie hair, he used to call it when they were kids—falling over one shoulder. "I have to help my dad load stock once we're all done."

Today was the finals of the Dakota Days Roundup. In less than an hour, Mark would try to win himself some money at one of South Dakota's most popular rodeos. And so he should be focusing on the job at hand, not chatting with the biggest distraction on God's green earth.

"Let's just say he and I don't see eye to eye," he said. Specifically, Jonathan Sable would never forgive Mark for wanting to date his daughter. Years ago, back when Mark had first started working for the owner of Sable Livestock Company, he had made the colossal mistake of asking Mr. Sable's permission to date Nicki. That was the cowboy way—to ask permission before courting a woman. Mark would never forget the man's words: *The day you win the NFR is the day you'll date my daughter!*

"About what?" she asked, glancing toward the filled-to-capacity grandstands when the crowd let out another yell.

You, he almost answered.

"What I do for a living," he said instead, because he knew Jonathan couldn't stand the fact that Mark rode bulls and, yes, that was a total double standard. The man made his living breeding some of the finest bucking stock in the world, but he didn't want his daughter dating one of the cowboys who rode those bulls, because he felt bull riding was a dead-end career.

Whatever.

But there was another, more important reason why Nicki's father didn't like him around.

His name wasn't Jesse Cody.

Mark risked glancing up at her. Nicki was search-

ing his face intently, as if she were trying to pull apart
invisible curtains to catch a peek of what was going on
inside his head. "You don't really think that, do you?"
she asked. "That my dad feels you're not good enough
for me because you ride bulls?"

And there he went again, putting himself on the spot.
Lie to her and keep the peace between her and her father. Don't lie and stir the pot.

"I do," he said, because when it came right down to
it, he could no more lie to her than he could keep from
wanting her. She smelled so damn nice standing there.
Like some kind of flower. The scent was so at odds
with the potent smell of livestock that he could have
sat there and inhaled the unique fragrance all day. He
looked up at her.

Again, that penetrating stare. "Well," she said slowly,
having to pause for a moment because yet another cowboy had jumped off a horse, a sorrel gelding stopping
so hard it practically sat on the ground. "What if *I*—"

"Nicki!" someone yelled, a male someone.

Mark shook his head; he recognized the voice. Of
course he did. After nearly a lifetime of tension between them, he could ID Jesse Cody's husky baritone
from fifty feet away.

"Your father wants you," the blond cowboy said, his
rigging bag thrown over his shoulder.

Even in profile Mark could see Nicki's lips press
together, as if she was disappointed. "My father can
wait," she said.

"No, he can't," Jesse contradicted, shooting Mark
a glare. "He's trying to get some steers loaded. Wants
you over there ASAP."

Nicki glanced at Mark, sunlight turning her eyes the

exact same color as lime rinds. "You going to be here for a while?" she asked.

"Yeah," he said. Until they were done with the bull riding.

"Good. I have something to ask you, but I'll have to do it later. I'll be right back." She dashed off, just as she always did when her father summoned her. She might be twenty-nine years old, but she was still Daddy's little girl. Mark wouldn't be surprised if Jonathan Sable hadn't spotted her talking to him, and then invented a reason for calling her to his side.

"I see you're still mooning after her," Jesse said.

Don't react. Don't let him see how badly you want to punch him in the nose. Just keep rubbing rosin on your rope.

Mark squared his shoulders. "Just being sociable, Cody."

Jesse tipped his hat back, his wide blue eyes suddenly more pronounced beneath his white Stetson. "Yeah, right," he said, turning on his heel and heading for the entrance of the livestock pen, where all the other bull riders waited to ride.

White. What kind of hat was that? No *real* cowboy wore white. That was only for movie stars and wannabe rough stock riders—just like Jesse.

Then why does he beat you some of the time?

Mark just shook his head, trying to fling the thought out of his head. That was all he needed. To let Jesse Cody get into his brain right before jumping on a two-thousand-pound animal. Bad enough that Nicki had distracted him.

Nicki.

She wanted something from him, and whatever it

was, Mark doubted he'd have the willpower to say no.
When it came to Nicki Sable, he'd be willing to ride the
meanest bull this side of Texas for her. And everybody
knew it—including Nicki.

SHE'D ALMOST DONE IT, Nicki thought. She'd almost asked
Mark Hansen out. Shoot. Her heart *still* pounded at the
thought of what she'd been about to do.

Dad would be furious.

But she didn't care, she thought, walking toward the
livestock loading area. She was old enough to know
what she wanted—and to do it, too. She just wished
she didn't feel as if she had to sneak around behind her
father's back.

You are *sneaking around.*

"You seen my father?" she asked one of the other
rough stock riders, a kid who didn't look old enough to
pilot a car, much less ride broncs or bulls.

"Can't say that I have, ma'am."

Ma'am. As if she was twice his age or something.
Then again, with rodeo competitors starting their professional careers in their teens these days, maybe she
was close to twice his age.

"Thanks," she said, scanning the area around her.

The South Dakota rodeo grounds were nestled in a
shallow valley, one edged with golden mountains covered by tall pines. To be honest, it looked pretty much
like the hundreds of other rodeo grounds Nicki had been
to over the years. A combination of metal pipes—these
ones painted white—and wooden chutes used to load
the animals into livestock haulers. She followed her
ears—you could hear steers complaining from a mile

away—and found her dad by one of those chutes, his stooped form concealed by the wooden sides.

"There you are," she said.

Her father glanced up, and Nicki realized that he was going to burn in the afternoon sun if he didn't put his hat on. She could already see his scalp was pink where his gray hair was thinning.

"And there *you* are," he said. "Help me out here."

Nicki raised an eyebrow. Her dad had at least three other guys on site, although they were nowhere to be seen. He didn't need her, not really. Even though he was at least fifty pounds overweight, his belly hanging over his belt, he was still in great shape. Honestly, she wouldn't be the least bit surprised if he hadn't sent those other men off just so he could summon her to his side after spotting her talking to Mark.

"Sure," she said. "What do you need me to do?"

"Stay away from Mark Hansen."

That brought her up short. "Daddy—"

"I saw you talking to him," he said, hoisting up his pants, an ancient silver buckle catching the sun. He'd won it steer wrestling "back in the day." "If the idiot had a lick of sense he'd be ignoring you and focusing on the bull he's about to ride, not chatting with my daughter."

Nick lifted her chin and almost admitted the truth: that *she* had approached Mark. But she didn't want to rile her father even more. "That *idiot* works for you, Dad. You must not hate him too much."

"He works for me 'cause he's good at handling livestock, but I don't want him handling *you*."

"Dad!"

"I mean it, Nicki. Stay away from that boy."

For a moment Nicki felt like an actress in a 1950s

movie, one where the heroine wanted to date the man from the other side of the tracks.

Was Mark from the other side of the tracks?

He certainly came from a family that wasn't exactly known for its upstanding behavior. Well, all right, Mark's father was the one branded as trouble. Rumor had it that he'd frequently take his frustrations out on Mark. But Tomas Hansen had been dead for a few months now. Liver problems brought on by his alcohol addiction. Maybe that was why her dad didn't like Mark. She would bet he feared that the apple might not fall far from the tree.

"Dad," Nicki said. "I'm a grown woman. If I wanted to date Attila the Hun you couldn't stop me."

"I can as long as you live in *my* house."

Then maybe she would move out.

But she didn't say that. Instead she let out a sigh of frustration and went back to work. It was easy to let her mind wander when she worked with her dad. The steers weren't any taller than a wooden barrel, most of the brown-and-white animals so young they called out to each other nervously. In a matter of minutes they had them all loaded up in the two-story aluminum trailer used to transport animals between rodeos.

"Thanks," her dad said.

"No problem," Nicki replied.

"You going to watch the bull riding?" he asked, resting an arm on the upper rail of the pipe fence.

"I was planning on it."

After I talk to Mark.

Because no matter what her father said about Mark, the truth was she wanted to go out with him. There was something between them, although what it was, she had no idea. But every once in a while she'd catch him staring at her, and suddenly everything inside her would stop and the skin on her arms would prickle and heat would scald her flesh.

"Good. I'm sure Jesse will appreciate you rooting him on."

Jesse.

She almost shook her head. When would her father realize she wasn't interested in Jesse Cody? He was like an older brother to her. The *entire Cody clan* was like family. They might be some of the wealthiest people in Wyoming, but they were also the nicest, most generous, most loving individuals she'd ever known.

"Yeah, Dad," Nicki said. "I'm sure he will…just as Mark will, too."

It was like jumping out of a barrel in front of a bull. Her dad straightened, eyes narrowed. "What in the hell do you *see* in that man?"

Kind eyes.

It was the first thing that came to Nicki's mind. Whenever he was handling an animal he always did so with such a gentle touch. He was the first to jump in to do a job. The first to offer a helping hand when someone needed it. She liked that about him best of all. But even more importantly, *Mark Hansen was hot.* Of course, she couldn't tell her dad that.

"He's a nice guy," she said.

"So's Jesse."

"I'm not going to marry Jesse, Dad, so you can put that thought right out of your mind."

"I never said you were."

"But you've been hoping for a wedding announcement ever since we graduated high school."

He looked toward the arena. The crowd had erupted into cheers. Steer wrestling was just about over.

Nicki studied her dad's face. He looked old for his age. Years of hard work. That was what he'd tell her if she mentioned it to him.

"I just want what's best for you," he said at last, his gaze holding her own. "If you married Jesse Cody you'd be set for life."

"I don't care about money."

Jonathan shook his head. "What's wrong with having money?"

"Nothing," Nicki said. "I just prefer a man who makes his own way in the world."

Like Mark.

She knew her dad was thinking the same thing. "Nicki, if you knew how hard your mom and I struggled when we first met and married, you wouldn't say that. I swear sometimes it's why she left me."

They both fell silent, because the loss of her mother, even though it had happened years ago, was still an ache in both their hearts, although for different reasons.

"But she had your love, Dad," Nicki said. "That's all that mattered to her."

He looked away, and Nicki knew he was thinking the same thing she was; in the end, not even their love for each other had mattered. She'd still left him.

She went to him and gave him a hug. Despite getting up there in years he could still squeeze the life out of her. He did so now.

"Daddy," she squeaked.

He let go, then tipped her chin up with a work-roughened hand. "Love you, Nicki-doodles," he said gruffly.

Gone was the cowboy most men were intimidated by. The man known for his bluster. The crusty old rancher who could castrate bulls without batting an eye. This was her dad. Sure, he was a tough cowboy, but he had a soft center and she knew he was just looking out for her.

"I love you, too," she said.

But she would still ask Mark Hansen out.

If her dad wanted her to be happy, he'd get used to the idea.

There was just one problem.

She had a feeling Mark would turn her down.

CHAPTER TWO

BANDITO TRIED TO kill him before the gate even opened.

"Easy there," someone said, as the bull jumped up. Who it was, Mark didn't know. He was too busy trying to get out of the damn bull's way. With yet another snort and lunge toward the front of the chute, Bandito reared again. Mark was forced to jump off, but not before his black hat was knocked askew.

"She-ute," someone else said. "Got your hands full there, Hansen."

He didn't need to peer around to know who *that* was. Jesse Cody.

"Gonna have a good time trying to cover that one," his nemesis added.

He's just trying to rile you, Mark told himself, cramming down his hat. *Don't even give him the satisfaction of a look.*

"Let's tie him in," he heard Nicki's father say.

Mark finally looked up. Jon Sable had his eyes on his bull. Two of his ranch hands came forward. They strung a rope across the top of Bandito to keep him from rearing again. Mark sank onto the bull before Jon gave him the go-ahead.

The bull reared again—or tried to. The rope kept his head down. That seemed to piss him off even more, but Mark didn't care. Sure, his hands shook as he tightened his bull rope. Adrenaline. Happened all the time. Still, he adjusted his position slowly. Bandito seemed to take it personally that Mark dared to touch him in any way.

"Easy there," he murmured, as if that would help.

He tightened his rope even more, and his chest felt as though it was vibrating thanks to the way his heart pounded. Just a little tighter grip. That was all he needed. And, really, the purse he was up for wasn't all that big. If he blew it it was no big deal. This wasn't Oklahoma. Now *that* ride he needed to make.

"Good luck," someone muttered.

Mark nodded. The gate opened.

"Good luck" rang in his ears as Bandito jumped out of the chute.

Jesse Cody.

Concentrate!

Bandito's front feet hit the ground. Mark was flung forward.

His hand connected with the bull's neck.

Son of a—

He jumped off. He had no choice. He'd slapped Bandito.

Mark landed hard, fell to his knees for a moment and had to quickly scurry—more like crawl—out of the bull's way. The glove on his right hand filled with dirt. Bandito charged past, heading to the exit gate without a backward glance. When Mark stood up he spotted the orange flag.

Just as he thought: disqualified.

Good luck.

The words rang in his ears again.

Damn it!

Mark bent and brushed off his chaps, not really caring if they were dirty. He just needed something to do, a moment to collect himself, because out there somewhere Nicki might be watching.

"Stupid son of a—" He jerked his hat off his head, angrily swiped at a line of dirt on its brim before cramming it onto his head again. One of the clowns came by and handed him his bull rope. The woven cord with a cowbell at one end slapped his leg as he jerked it out of the clown's hands.

"Thanks," Mark muttered, heading toward the fence.

"Hey," someone called. "If you'd wanted to give that bull a high five, you should have done it in the chutes."

They might be in the middle of a rodeo arena, the crowd halfheartedly clapping at his attempt to ride Bandito, but he still heard the words. When he looked up at the chute he'd just exited, Jesse was there, peering down at him, hands on his hips.

"Nice flying dismount, though," he added, before turning away.

I should flying dismount onto his face.

But if he were honest, Mark was more angry at himself than anyone else. Jesse might be an ass, but he wasn't the first fellow competitor who had tried to psych him out.

Yeah, but this was the first time in a long while that it's actually worked.

"Tough luck," a female voice said.

He took a tight grip the top bar of the arena fence and pulled himself over, cowbell clanking.

His sister, Janie, sat on the top rail of an empty stock pen, watching him, and her look of sympathy instantly soothed his anger. She still wore her Navaho-style barrel-racing shirt, the fringe under the arms hanging limply by her sides. "You looked like you could have taken Bandito if you hadn't let Jesse psych you out."

"You heard that?" he asked.

"Of course," she said, turning toward the man in question. Jesse was about to get on his own bull, so they were now being ignored. Mark saw his sister stare hard at Jesse for a moment, anger flickering in her brown eyes, before turning back to him.

"Some days I wish I had a firecracker or two to throw in his direction."

"Yeah, well, I should know better than to let Jesse Cody get under my skin."

She nodded and slipped off the fence. "I blew my ride, too, if it's any consolation."

She'd swung wide on the last barrel. Mark had caught a glimpse of it as he'd prepped for bull riding. "Looks like we're both out of the money today," he muttered.

"And we could have used it, too," Janie said.

It was true, despite what Mark had told himself just before his ride. They could *always* use the money.

They exchanged commiserative glances. Their mom had been officially diagnosed with Alzheimer's four months ago, and the medication they'd put her on cost a small fortune. Sure, she had medical insurance through the state, but that didn't cover everything. And one day they'd have to hire someone to keep an eye on her, or send her to a special facility. They were trying to prepare for that by putting aside as much as they could, which wasn't much.

"You ready to leave?" Mark asked, the two of them pausing outside the cattle pen.

"Yeah. Chica's tired. Been riding her pretty hard lately."

They'd both been working extra hours, at their day jobs and on the rodeo circuit, but Mark's efforts were actually yielding results. For the first time in years he might have a shot at the NFR. If he rode his bull at the end of the month in Oklahoma, he'd make it all the way.

"How about you?" Janie asked. "You want to stick around and watch the end of the bull riding? Or do you want to take off?"

"Let's take off," he said. The two of them carpooled together to save on gas. "Just gotta pick up my rigging bag."

"Cool. I'll load Chica." Janie gave him a quick hug. "You're gonna make it this year," she said, squeezing his shoulders as she drew back, the turquoise earrings she wore flashing in the sunlight. "And I'll be there to watch."

He clutched the front of her hat, shook it gently so she resembled a bobblehead. He'd been doing that to her since they were kids, and she smiled at the familiar gesture. "You're gonna make it, too."

"Not this year, bro," she said, still smiling. "But that's okay. I've still got lots of years ahead of me."

"Ouch," he said, pretending to wince. It was her favorite taunt—that he was getting too old to compete. But even though the words were said in jest, she had a point. At age thirty-one, he knew his bull riding days were numbered. Already his bones ached from the many injuries he'd sustained over the years. A dislocated shoulder. Numerous broken ribs, and a few other bones to boot. At the rate he was going he'd be lucky to be in a walker when he was eighty, but that was the price one paid.

"You know I don't really mean that," Janie said.

"I know." He gave her a reassuring smile. "See you at the truck."

But as he unzipped his chaps he wondered what he'd do if he didn't make the cut this year. Probably go on a drinking binge.

No, he'd never do that.

Mark couldn't stand to drink. Too many years of stepping over his dad after he'd passed out on the family-room floor. And yet he still missed the bastard. His death a few months ago had left Mark shaken. They'd had a love-hate relationship Mark's entire life, but nobody had pushed him harder than Tomas Hansen when it came to riding bulls. It was only after he was gone that Mark realized just how much he'd come to count on his dad's support—if one wanted to call the constant badgering and belittling comments "support." Janie had been even more severely affected by the old man's death.

Mark rolled up his chaps and stuffed them into his rigging bag. His bull rope went in next. His mind was so far away that at first he didn't hear the familiar feminine voice.

"So," Nicki said. "About my dad."

He jerked upright.

She smiled. "What I was about to say before I was so rudely interrupted—" She glanced toward the chutes and stiffened. "Oh, wait, Jesse's about to ride."

Jesse. Mark tried not to let his irritation show.

"Here we go, ladies and gentlemen, one of the nation's top cowboys…"

Yeah, because he had money coming out his ears. The Codys didn't need to ride bulls or rope cows or wrestle steers for a living. For them, rodeo was a hobby.

Jesse's family had more money than the Vatican. And so he could afford to rodeo full-time. That always, *always* put him on top of the money list. Sure, things had gotten better ever since the PRCA limited the number of events an individual could compete in, but you were still at an advantage if you could compete every weekend, which Jesse Cody did.

"Looks like he's ready to ride," the announcer said.

The crowd cheered. Nicki stepped onto the bottom rung of the fence and pulled herself up to see better. Jesse came out of the chute an instant later. Mark told himself not to watch, but couldn't seem to stop himself. Granted, all he could see was Jesse's bobbing head, but he only had to listen to the crowd. Their cries grew louder with each stride Jesse covered. Four seconds, five…Mark counted them off. He knew the moment Jesse made it. So did the crowd, because they let out a roar that could be heard the next county over.

"He did it," Nicki said, her grin as wide as a dinner plate. "Right on."

"Yeah," Mark murmured. "Great."

Her gaze honed in on his own. "Try to contain your enthusiasm," she said with a teasing grin.

He shrugged.

Her gaze turned serious as she climbed down off the fence. Mark saw a few of the guys that had yet to ride glance in her direction. They all knew who she was, and more than a couple nodded a greeting. She nodded right back before saying to Mark, "Although I suppose you have every right to be disappointed, and a little angry, too. I heard Jesse razzing you before you rode."

"Jesse can razz me all he wants. It's my own damn fault for letting him get into my head."

"Yeah, but he didn't have to do it. I think he's mad at me, and he's taking it out on you."

"Mad at you? About what? And why would he take it out on me?"

"Because I told him this morning I was going to ask you out. And I don't think he liked the idea."

CHAPTER THREE

NICKI NEARLY LAUGHED at the look on his face.

"*You're* asking *me* out?" he said.

"Yeah," she answered. "Is that a problem?"

He scrubbed a hand over his face. "*You* want to ask *me* out," he said again, as if he couldn't quite trust his ears, which maybe he couldn't. The crowd let out a yell when they heard Jesse's score. Eighty-nine. High score so far.

"Look, I know how you cowboys hate women who make the first move, but I figured one of us had to do it, especially since you think you're not good enough for me or something."

"I didn't say that." Mark scooted a little closer to her. "I said that's what your father thought."

And as always whenever he was near, Nicki felt her body react to his presence. She felt ticklish inside. That was the only way to describe it. Her whole body erupted in goose bumps.

"Well?" she prompted, glancing behind him in time to watch Jesse climb out of the arena, a wide grin on his face. He took off his white hat and waved it at the crowd. She was nearly deafened by the roar.

"What did your father say when you told him you planned to ask me out?" Mark asked over the noise.

Nicki's smile faded. "Well, uh…"

"That's what I thought." Mark stuffed more gear into his bag.

"What I do with my personal life is no business of his," she said, tempted to step on Mark's rigging bag in a bid to regain his attention. Instead she waited for him to finish, watching as he gripped the zipper angrily, jerking the thing closed.

"You're right," he said, slinging the bag over his shoulder and straightening. "It isn't any of his business, but he'll make it my business, trust me. One date with you and I'd be fired faster than a calf runs to his momma."

"Then we don't have to tell him."

Mark froze.

She touched his hand. The tummy tickles turned into something that felt an awful lot like an adrenaline rush. Her lungs stopped working, a part of her thinking that if just *touching* him felt this way, what would *kissing* him feel like?

"I can't," he said, pulling his hand away before hefting his bag over the fence. It landed with a thud.

"Mark, wait—" she said, stepping in front of him.

"Whew, doggie!" someone cried. Nicki glanced beyond Mark's shoulder and spied Jesse about to drop into the pen. "Did you see that Nickelodeon?" he asked her. "Like stealing candy from a baby." He came up to her and jerked her to his side. "How about you and I go out and celebrate?"

"Jesse, I—"

"She can't," Mark said.

Nicki stiffened.

"Oh, yeah?" Jesse asked, the fire in his eyes so out of place on his face that for a moment it took her aback.

What was it with these guys? They were two of the kindest, most honorable men she knew, yet when they were together, they were like two opposing magnets, always at odds with each other. It drove her nuts.

"Yeah," Mark said, shuffling forward a half step. "Because she's going out with me."

Nicki's brows shot up. She couldn't stop her mouth from falling open, either.

"Hmm. Wonder what Mr. Sable will think when he hears about that?" Jesse asked.

But Nicki was smart enough to recognize a prime opportunity when she saw one. She had a feeling Mark would have kept saying no if not for Jesse's intervention. "He's not going to say anything," she said, "because you're not going to tell him, are you, Jesse?"

His eyes narrowed. She tipped her head and gave him a look of warning. Jesse was one of her closest friends, but that was all, *a friend*. She knew he'd have her back if it came right down to it.

"You know your dad's going to kill you if he catches wind of this."

When she glanced at Mark it was in time to see his own eyes narrow. Sure, he knew her dad didn't want him going out with her, but it had to sting to hear one of his biggest rivals echo the sentiment.

"But he's not going to find out, is he, Cody?" Mark asked.

Jesse didn't look too happy to be doing Mark Hansen any favors, but in the end his loyalty won out. "No," he said. "He won't, but that doesn't mean someone else around here might not spill the beans."

"Nobody's going to know but you," Nicki said, glancing around. Well, that might not be precisely true.

Someone else might have overheard, but she'd take her chances. Whatever there was between her and Mark, she meant to get to the bottom of it.

"You better treat her right, Hansen," Jesse said, and—good God—he puffed his chest out.

"Jesse, that's enough," Nicki said. "Mark will be a perfect gentleman."

Jesse glanced from one to the other. She saw his shoulders relax a little. "He better," he said, shoving his white hat down on his head before straightening.

"Oh, don't you worry, Cody," Mark said, stepping next to her and throwing an arm around her shoulders. "I'll be wearing my kid gloves."

Nicki almost elbowed him in the side, except that being pulled so close to him, her side fitting next to his almost perfectly, left her kind of breathless. He was all muscle. She could feel his strength now that they were body to body.

"See that you do," Jesse said before tipping his hat at her. "I'll catch up with you later, Nickelodeon. I'm off to pick up my winner's check."

"How do you stand that guy?" Mark asked, releasing her the moment Jesse was out of sight. And, wow, that did a lot for her self-esteem.

"What do you mean, how can I stand him? Jesse's great."

Mark didn't say anything and for a moment Nicki wondered if it might have been a mistake to ask him out. Sure, there was this…this *thing* between them, but there was also their differing opinion on the Cody family, too.

"Maybe to you," Mark said. "But to me he's the biggest pain in the rear I know."

"That's just because the two of you compete against each other."

"No," Mark said with a shake of his head. "There's more to it than that."

"Is that why you agreed to our date?" she demanded, placing her hands on her hips and glaring up at him. "As a way of getting even with Jesse? Or didn't you think I noticed the way you changed your mind the moment he arrived?"

Mark shrugged.

Men. She was half tempted to tell him she'd changed her mind. One thing kept her from saying those exact words: the memory of what it had felt like when he'd pulled her close.

"Look," she said. "Jesse's one of the hardest working men I know. He manages his dad's cattle operation, did you know that?"

"I was always under the impression he only worked when he had to."

She shook her head. "No. It's a full-time job. Keeps him busy pretty much 24/7, what with all the cattle they run. When he's not competing in rodeos, he's out riding the range, or working with ranch hands, or doctoring cattle. He's a hard worker, as hard as you. All the Cody brothers work hard. Each of them has a job to do on the Cottonwood Ranch."

But Mark didn't look as if he cared. Nicki could tell she fought a losing battle. "Okay, fine. Don't believe me. But you're meeting me at the entrance to the rodeo grounds in twenty minutes regardless of your feelings for Jesse Cody."

"For what?" he asked, appearing perplexed.

"Our date," she said.

"Tonight?"

She nodded. "On our way home. Just the two of us."

"I can't," he said. "I'm supposed to drive with my sister."

"Can't she find her own way home?"

"I suppose—"

Nicki didn't let him say another word. Instead she did something bold. She touched his lips with her fingers to silence him. To be honest, she'd been dying to do it since the moment she'd met him. He had such masculine lips.

It amazed her how soft they were. "Not another word," she said with a smile. "Twenty minutes. Be there or I'll tell my dad that you stood me up on our first date."

"Hey—"

But she didn't give him time to reply. "See you in a bit," she said as she turned away.

She just hoped she really *would* see him.

I CAN'T BELIEVE I'm doing this, Mark thought as he walked toward the entrance of the rodeo grounds. All it would take was for one person to spot him climbing into Nicki's truck and the word would be all over the circuit that he and Jonathan Sable's daughter were an item. Just what he needed.

He almost stopped and turned back.

But there she was. He could see her dark blue pickup truck from where he stood. Her blond head turned in his direction. She'd spotted him.

Pretend you didn't see her.

But he couldn't do that. Truth was, he'd wanted Nicki Sable for so long he could no more ignore her than he could avoid his own nose. But this was a bad time to let a woman into his head. A really bad time. Not to mention her father hated him. Those two reasons alone should have him running in the opposite direction. Instead he glanced over his shoulder, made sure nobody was around, then quickly headed to the passenger side of her truck.

"I thought for sure you'd change your mind," she said with a smile.

I almost did.

But he just shook his head as he slammed the door closed. "Let's get out of here before someone sees us."

"Scared?" she asked, glancing over at him.

"No. Just being smart. The last thing I need is your father chasing me off with a shotgun when I report for work on Monday."

She laughed. Mark felt his hands clench. Usually he tried to avoid getting close to her…for exactly this reason. Whenever she was near he felt the same way as he did when he jumped off a bull. Wild. Reckless. Full of adrenaline…and damned if he understood why.

"Believe me. My father's bark is worse than his bite," she said.

"Easy for you to say."

It was still early in the afternoon. Mark had to squint against the sun to stare at the Black Hills, because that was what he had to do. Look at anything other than Nicki Sable. They were in Rapid City, near the southern edge of town.

For some reason he expected Nicki to turn toward the heart of the city. She didn't. Instead she went in the opposite direction, toward the hills. Then again, that might be a good thing. The farther away from the rodeo grounds they got, the better. No one would spot them if they were off the beaten path. And he suspected Nicki knew that.

"This was a damn fool mistake."

"Excuse me?" she said, turning to look at him.

"Keep your eyes on the road," he barked when the truck swerved toward the shoulder just a bit.

She faced forward, but took a quick peek at him once again. "What's a 'damn fool mistake'?"

She knew. "Look," she said. "If you want me to turn back, just tell me now."

"Where are we going?"

She glanced at him again, this time without swerving the truck, thankfully. "That's a surprise," she said.

Barbie.

That was what he'd called her when they were kids. Nothing had changed now that she'd matured. She was one of those women who were so beautiful it was hard not to stare. Cowboys all over the Midwest had made a play for her, but she'd always turned them down. That made her something of a catch for most of the guys on the circuit, yet she still kept her distance. Except where Jesse Cody was concerned. Actually, she hung out with all the Cody brothers.

"So," she added, "are we going?"

Mark dropped his gaze to his lap. He'd changed since the bull riding event. The crisp blue jeans he wore were free of dust and grime, but he studied his legs as if they held a map to the universe.

"Yeah," he heard himself say. "We're going."

"Well, you don't have to sound so happy about it," she chided with a smile.

He couldn't help himself. Dating her was like being

in a minefield. He couldn't stand the Cody brothers. Well, that wasn't precisely true. Dex and Dusty were all right. It was Jesse—her closest friend—that Mark couldn't stand, and he had a feeling the root of their animosity toward each other had to do with Nicki.

"What do you see in him, anyway?" he asked.

"See in who?" She was frowning as she steered the truck around a corner.

"You know who."

She grinned. "So that's what has you all riled up. You're jealous of Jesse, aren't you?"

Mark shook his head.

But she didn't buy it. "What is it with your two, anyway? As far as I can recall, he's never done anything to make you hate him."

"I don't hate him," Mark said. "I don't hate *anybody*."

"Then what is it?" she asked as they reached an onramp. He had no idea where they were going, but that felt good. He was tired of the constant stress of the rodeo circuit.

The season's almost over.

Yeah, but there were still two months left. Two months of scrimping and saving in the hopes that he could make it to one more rodeo…and then another, and another. Traveling cost money. Sometimes he felt like a rat on a wheel. No matter how much money he won he had to spend it in order to make more.

"I don't know what it is about him that rubs me the wrong way. I just don't like him. Maybe it's the hat."

"The hat?"

Mark motioned to his head. "The stupid white hat he wears."

Nicki darted him a look, one he couldn't read. "He wears that hat for a reason."

"Oh, yeah?" he said. "Let me guess. He considers himself such a great bull rider that he wears a white hat to demonstrate how rarely he hits the ground."

She glanced over yet again, this time with sadness in her eyes. "You really don't like him, do you?"

"Well?" Mark pressed, ignoring her question. "Am I right?"

"You're way off base. Way, *way* off."

And something about the way she said the words made him sit up a little. He felt the same way he did in the emergency room after a bad fall. As if a doctor was about to deliver news that might not be good.

"What is it?"

They'd turned onto a winding road, Mark wondered just where, exactly, she was taking him. The farther they drove out of the city, the fewer places to eat there were. Guess they weren't having dinner.

"Do you remember a gal named Laurie Brandon?"

Laurie Brandon. Why did that name sound so familiar? "She went to high school with us," he said. "Had some kind of disease, I think."

"Hodgkin's," Nicki stated.

"That's right," he said, lifting his cowboy hat. "But I didn't know her well."

"Jesse did," she said with another glance in his direction.

"Okay. I remember now," he murmured. "They were pretty tight."

"Jesse wanted to marry her," Nicki said.

"I think I remember hearing something about that, too. But she died, didn't she?"

Nicki nodded.

And he put two and two together. "Don't tell me. He wears the hat for her?"

"Yup," she said, slowing down. They'd started to climb a little. "Always has," she added. "Originally, it was to help her spot him behind the chutes. Kind of a joke between them. But then she passed away…"

And he kept on wearing it. Nicki didn't need to say the words. It made Mark feel like a real jerk. "Damn."

"Honestly, there's more to Jesse Cody than meets the eye. More to the whole family, really. They're salt of the earth. You'd like them if you ever got to know them."

Fat chance that would happen. They traveled in different circles, with the exception of the rodeo circuit, the only thing they had in common. As the owners of a vast fortune, one with its basis in land and cattle and natural gas, the Codys had it all. That was how they could afford to rodeo full-time. They didn't have to worry about a mom with health issues or the recent passing of a parent.

Mark stared out the passenger-side window. Nicki seemed content to let him. He missed his dad, damn it, but not for the reasons most people might suspect. There'd been nobody better at getting under his skin than Tomas Hansen. One snarky comment—and his dad had been full of them for Mark's entire life—could get him hyped up as nothing else could. As twisted as it sounded, those snide remarks were how Mark had become one of the best bull riders in the nation. Sure, some people might call it verbal abuse, but for Mark it'd been much more than that. He would just about kill himself in order to stick his rides, all so he wouldn't have to put up with his dad's demeaning comments afterward.

"We're almost there."

Mark forced his eyes to focus again. They'd entered some low-lying foothills, the road winding left and right. When he glanced over his shoulder he was surprised to note how high they'd climbed. Rapid City looked like a Monopoly game board from this height.

"Well, I hope there's food where we're going."

"There is," she said.

A picnic, perhaps? That'd be something Nicki would do.

Something Nicki would do.

He was out with Nicki Sable.

Had he lost his mind?

"There it is," she said excitedly, lifting a hand from the steering wheel and pointing.

Mark saw it then—the sign. Actually, he'd seen those signs before. They were all over Rapid City.

Dakota Days: Where the West Can Be Won.

"You're taking me to a *cowboy theme park?*"

"Yup," she said with a wide grin. "We're going to pretend to be gunslingers for the rest of the afternoon."

CHAPTER FOUR

HE DIDN'T LOOK too thrilled.

"Come on," she said. "It'll be fun, although I won't be dressing up as a cowboy." Nicki drove beneath the massive wooden arch. "I see myself more as a Mae West."

"You're nuts."

"Am I?" she asked, telling herself to relax. But that wasn't easy, given that she was with Mark Hansen.

A man she'd fantasized about for most of her life.

But if her father ever found out she'd gone out with him, there'd be hell to pay. Was that part of his allure? she wondered. Was he the forbidden fruit? Or was there something more between them? Something more than physical attraction, she quickly amended, because there could be no denying that from the moment he'd climbed into the truck she'd been on edge. He had a unique scent. Sweet, almost musky, and every time she came near him it drove her nuts.

"This is too much," Mark said.

They'd crested a small hill, and Nicki found her own brows lifting in surprise when she saw what lay on the other side. She'd seen pictures, but still…

"This is incredible."

And it was. Someone with an eye for detail had constructed an old Western town. Or maybe they hadn't constructed it; maybe it was left over from the days when cattle rustlers had roamed the plains and women had worked their seductive wiles on a man in exchange for a couple of dollars. The town sprawled over what had to be at least an acre, probably two, complete with a saloon, blacksmith shop and two-story hotel. Nicki could see guests milling about, although where they had parked was anybody's guess. There was no sign of modern-day accoutrements anywhere in sight, just a wide dirt road between the storefronts, with horses, and yes, even a carriage or two, rambling around.

"Can you really spend the night here?" Mark asked.

"I think so." Nicki glanced over at him uncomfortably, because just like that she'd felt something shiver down her spine and settle in her stomach.

Awareness.

The thought of spending the night anywhere with Mark had her body tingling in a way that damn near made her squirm in her seat.

And could anyone blame her?

Mark had always been considered a bona fide rodeo hunk. More than a few of her friends had commented over the years about what it would be like to spend an evening with him. And now here Nicki was. She'd be spending the afternoon with him…and maybe even the night.

"I guess we follow the signs," she said, heading up yet another small hill, this one covered with a grove of pine trees indigenous to the area.

"That explains where the cars are," Mark said, glancing around.

They were at the top of yet another small hill, and just as he'd noted, there was a sprawling parking area on the other side. A single-story wooden building with a shake roof stood there—where they would pay their money and select their clothes, Nicki assumed.

"You don't really expect me to dress up, do you?" he asked as they passed a sign that said Park Admittance and Costumes, with an arrow pointing toward the structure.

"Hell, yeah, I do," she said, selecting a parking spot. "I don't think they'll let you in unless you're wearing something authentic."

She shut down the engine. Mark was staring at her, his brown eyes studying her with an intensity that made her uncomfortable.

Did he feel it, too?

"I'm already dressed like a cowboy."

He'd changed out of his bull riding clothes. His light brown, checkered shirt matched the caramel hue of his eyes. He still wore his black hat, its brim shading skin darkened by the sun. His five-o'clock shadow was firmly in place even though it was barely three.

"And I'm already dressed like a cowgirl," she said, gesturing to her own white, button-down shirt and blue jeans. "But I can't wait to wear a corset."

Something flared in his eyes and she knew without a shadow of a doubt that he was thinking of how she might look in that corset. Nicki blushed, but just as quickly as her embarrassment came, it faded, replaced by another current of sexual awareness. This was the first time she'd been alone with Mark Hanson, truly alone, and the knowledge that she was with him at last had her body heating in other places.

"Let's go," she said, because she knew that if she sat

in the truck a moment longer she might do something rash—like lean forward and kiss him.

Instead, she opened the truck door, feeling the coolness of the cab's air-conditioning waft around her for a moment before the warm South Dakota breeze took over. She didn't wear cowboy hats, but wished she was now, as the sun nearly blinded her.

"Lead the way," Mark said, coming around the front of the truck.

Nicki's whole body felt as hot as the air that pressed against her face. "Seriously, Mark," she said. "I really think you have to dress up in order to get into the park."

"No problem," he replied, his face in profile now as he gazed straight ahead. There was a bump near the bridge of his nose. Bull riding injury?

What was she doing, dating a bull rider? To be honest, that was part of the reason she'd never asked him out before. Everyone knew what it was like on the rodeo circuit. Even at the local level there were plenty of women who'd love to score a cowboy for a night. It was a rare man who could resist such temptations over and over again.

But Nicki had kept an eye on Mark in recent years. He wasn't the type to play around. Then again, maybe he just hadn't been tempted by the right woman....

Stop.

Whatever happened at the end of the day, it was meant to be. At least Nicki was doing something about the attraction between them.

The entrance to the park resembled an old-fashioned storefront, with an Admission sign next to the door. When they heard rifle fire in the distance, Mark glanced in her direction.

"Gunfight at the OK Corral?" she surmised.

"I guess so." He shrugged.

Nicki smiled. This was going to be fun. If nothing else, they would each be doing something they never had before.

Once they paid the entrance fee, they went their separate ways to select a costume. Nicki couldn't wait to see what Mark chose, but she knew immediately what type of costume she wanted for herself.

"Saloon Girl," she told the park employee.

The young woman, who looked to be barely out of high school with her braces and brown hair, smiled. "I know just the one. It'll look awesome on you."

What she pulled out made Nicki grin from ear to ear. The scarlet satin gown was perfect, with its corset-type bodice and wide, swishy skirts.

"Not many guests can fit into this puppy," the girl— Samantha, according to her name badge—said. "But if you do, I guarantee you'll have every man in town gawking at you."

Nicki wanted only one man to gawk. And maybe that was part of it, too. Mark was usually so standoffish toward women. Not just with her, but with everybody. She'd really like to knock his socks off.

She could tell the moment she emerged from the dressing area that she'd succeeded, but not because of the look on his face. No. His stare remained carefully blank. He was good at concealing his emotions, she realized then. But there were other indications that he was far from unfazed. His hands clenched, just once. And his body seemed to lean back, as if his mind formed the silent word, *Whoa.*

"How you doin', big boy?" she asked in her best

Southern accent. She rolled her bare shoulders, tipping her head and giving him a bold smile. She could feel the black feather in her hair, which she'd piled on top of her head, bob with the motion.

"You look nice," he replied, deadpan. She would have slumped in disappointment if she hadn't seen those tell-tale signs a moment before.

"You look great, too," she said. They'd dressed him in classic gunfighter attire. Black, low-brimmed hat, not curved up like a typical Stetson. Knee-length black jacket with matching trousers, and a white preacher's shirt topped with a finger-width tie. "But where's your holster?"

"Apparently you have to purchase your guns in town. At the general store."

She laughed. "That's perfect," she said, walking up to him and hooking an arm through his. "I say we go buy you some."

"Some?"

"Yeah, one for each hip."

"Good idea," he said. "I have a feeling I'll need them, to keep other men away."

Which was his way of saying she looked hot, Nicki hoped. It sure would make seducing him a lot easier if that was the case.

Was that what she wanted to do?

She glanced up at him again, thinking he had to be one of the best-looking cowboys she'd ever seen. And she wanted him. She didn't know why, had assumed her attraction to him would wane over the years. It hadn't. And so if things were to progress to the next level— beyond the polite words they exchanged on her father's ranch—this was it.

Seduction it was.

They exited the admission building and stepped into near-blinding sunshine. They would be taken to Dakota Town via an ancient-looking stagecoach. It had massive yellow wheels and a black exterior, and Nicki made a big production of being unable to get inside the thing without some help. If she were honest with herself, she'd have to admit she enjoyed playing the damsel in distress.

Mark seemed to know what she was up to. It was a well-known fact around town that she was something of a brain. She even did the books for Spurling Natural Gas, a locally owned company in town. But she enjoyed playing a vamp for Mark. The smirk he sent her as he helped her climb into the carriage nearly made her laugh. Then, too, the look on his face might have something to do with the three young men who eyed her up and down, one of them emitting a low whistle.

"Well, hello there," another one said.

"Hi," she replied brightly. When she turned to Mark to gauge his reaction, he was staring at them, his smirk having turned into a frown.

Ah. A reaction. At last.

"You boys come here often?" she asked, cocking a flirtatious brow.

Mark did a double take.

She ignored him.

"This is our first time," the one who'd whistled said.

They weren't much older than the girl who'd helped her dress, Nicki noted. Too young for her. But Mark didn't know that. She could feel him tense beside her. *Good.* She had a feeling that if she was ever to get him to make a move, she'd have to make him jealous. It had worked earlier, with Jesse.

"Ours, too," she said. "Maybe you could join us for a drink lat—"

"Nicki," Mark grumbled, tapping her elbow.

"What?" she asked innocently. When she looked into his eyes, she could tell he was perturbed.

"You know what," he grumbled.

She leaned toward him. "Jealous?" she whispered.

"No."

"Yeah, you are," she said, touched his upper arm. "You don't want to share me."

He just shook his head slightly before glancing out the window of the stagecoach. Had she gone too far? She thought for a moment that she might have, but then saw his jaw muscles flex as he gritted his teeth. Aha. He *was* jealous.

The coach set off. Nicki tried hard not to grin.

"Did you say drinks?" her young admirer asked.

"No," Mark answered, and the look he shot the youth made it obvious that any other attempt at conversation would not be welcomed.

Her new friend seemed to get the message. Nicki smiled at him in mock regret. She could have sworn she heard Mark's teeth click together, and she almost laughed. It felt as if she were taunting a bull, one that might charge at any moment, but she couldn't seem to stop herself. If she didn't act now, she might not get another chance to be alone with Mark, and suddenly it became vitally important that they connect today. *Now.*

They were headed toward town. The road was bumpy, and it seemed as if the stagecoach wheels found every hole. With each jarring movement Nicki found herself shifting closer to Mark. Not only that, but certain parts of her anatomy were in danger of breaking free.

"Maybe you should have chosen a different costume," she heard Mark say when, for about the tenth time, she had to pull her dress up.

"And miss out on driving you crazy? I don't think so."

Their eyes locked. He had an intensity about him, one that increased with every second he held her gaze. "You're playing with fire."

"I know," she admitted.

He frowned and looked the quintessential gunslinger in his black garb.

"Careful you don't get burned."

CHAPTER FIVE

MARK FELT READY to explode.

Between the way the idiots sitting across from them kept eyeing Nicki's cleavage, and the damn smell of her—roses, he thought... Hell, from the way his *own* damn gaze kept straying to the same part of her anatomy, his jaw ached with the effort it took not to bend her over his arm and kiss some sense into her.

Jonathan Sable's daughter.

That was who she was. He needed to remember that if he was to keep his hands off her—because that was what he was determined to do.

They couldn't arrive at Dakota Town fast enough, as far as Mark was concerned. He was so distracted he just about flung himself from the carriage once they arrived.

"Oh, Mark, look," she said as he offered her a hand down out of courtesy's sake. "It reminds me of the original homestead on the Cody property."

"I wouldn't know," he grumbled.

There was a line of people waiting to make the trip back to the admission building. Mark heard someone, a man, undoubtedly, let out an appreciative whistle as Nicki's leg emerged. Mark glowered in that direction.

"Are you sure we can't buy you a drink at the saloon?" asked one of the kids she'd flirted with earlier.

"Well, now, *I* wouldn't mind," she said, clutching

Mark's arm, her feather bobbing as she glanced up at him. "But I think my date might."

Mark gave the young man his best Clint Eastwood glare.

"Have a great time then," the kid said, turning away when the rest of his buddies emerged.

"You should really watch what you say to strangers," Mark advised.

But she was ignoring him. "I'm telling you," she said, turning toward what was obviously the blacksmith shop. A bare-chested man stood inside, pounding away at something. The metallic *ting-ting-tings* of his hammer could likely be heard all the way to the other side of town. "That looks just like the original Cody barn."

"I'll have to take your word for it," Mark murmured, guiding her toward one of the town's raised wooden sidewalks. Otherwise she probably would have stood there all day. "Right now, let's get out of everyone's way."

When he glanced around to get his bearings, he noticed a wooden sign indicating they were at the stagecoach stop. Beneath that was a sign pointing toward the saloon, hotel and general store. The store sounded as good as anything, because God forbid he should think about Nicki and the word *hotel* in the same sentence. Although if the truth be told, he could really use a drink.

"Haven't you ever been?"

The walkway was covered and Mark was grateful for the instant shade. "Been where?"

"To the Cody ranch."

He paused in front of the massive paned window of a barber shop. A few brave tourists were inside getting their hair trimmed.

"Look," he said. "Can you do me a favor and not talk about the Codys while we're on our *date?*"

How had she piled her hair up on top of her head like that? he found himself wondering. She looked so sexy in that getup. No wonder men had been eyeballing her.

"I just can't believe you've never seen their place— you know, out of curiosity or something."

"Come on," he said, hoping to find something to distract her, and resisting the urge to roll his eyes when another male guest doffed his hat in Nicki's direction. Talk about getting into the part! "I think I need a drink."

"Mark—"

But whatever else she'd been about to say was interrupted by gunfire. They both drew up short, Mark catching sight of someone running down the sidewalk across the street. On their side a figure in black garb and a black cowboy hat approached. An outlaw, Mark surmised. The man took one look at Nicki and made a beeline toward her.

"Look out," Mark warned.

"Sorry, ma'am," the man said. His face was covered by some kind of black grease that gave him a fake five-o'clock shadow. "I'm in need of your services."

"What—"

But then the stranger's arms were around Nicki's waist.

"Hey," Mark protested, but she was giggling.

"I'm warning you, Wild Bill," the outlaw holding Nicki yelled. The whole place came to a standstill. "Don't you take another step toward me. I'd hate for some harm to come to this pretty lady."

Mark saw the look on Nicki's face and realized she was actually enjoying this. He changed his mind about

going to her assistance, and hung back instead, crossing his arms with a smirk.

"Let the lady go," Wild Bill called, pointing a rifle
in their direction.

"Not gonna happen, Wild Bill," the actor said, drag-
ging Nicki back a step. His hand moved in the process,
nearly cupping Nicki's breast. "This pretty filly's mine."

Pretty filly? And was the man's thumb brushing the
swell of her flesh? It sure looked like it. Mark uncrossed
his arms.

"Not if I have anything to say about it," Wild Bill
retorted.

"Well, now," the bandit drawled, "we'll just have to
see about that." He pulled Nicki again, and, yeah, he
was definitely trying to cop a feel.

"Hey!" she cried, trying to push the actor's hand
away.

That did it.

Mark stomped forward, jerked Nicki from the man's
arms and knocked the fake gun from his grasp.

"Ow!" The actor rubbed his arm in pain, his expression one of dismay and disappointment as his weapon
skittered across the wooden deck.

"That's enough," Mark growled.

Wild Bill chose that moment to rush the bad guy,
crossing the street in a flash. Nicki's assailant didn't see
his coming, and Wild Bill's arms went around his neck
before he could do much more than blink.

"On the ground!" Wild Bill yelled.

The cowboy Mark had assaulted glared in his direction. "You heard the man," Mark said, tempted to pick
up the fake gun and point it at the jerk. "On the ground."

The actor did as instructed, even though it was apparent by the look on his face that he wasn't happy his show had been preempted.

Mark stepped back as Wild Bill moved to cuff the outlaw. "My thanks, cowboy," he said. Someone started to applaud. Others joined in. Nicki chose that moment to throw her arms around Mark's neck.

"My hero," she exclaimed, in a Southern drawl that would have done Scarlett O'Hara proud.

"Yeah, right," Mark said softly, but his words were interrupted when Nicki rose up on tiptoe and kissed him.

Hard.

SHE'D GONE TOO FAR.

Honestly, she hadn't meant to get so carried away. But then it had dawned on her that she was kissing Mark Hansen. She opened her mouth, felt Mark resist—but only for an instant. Within seconds he was kissing her back.

The applause grew louder. People whistled. They all thought it was part of the show, but for Nicki nothing had ever felt so real in her life.

Mark must have realized things were getting out of hand because he suddenly pulled back.

"Hey," she protested. Her whole body hummed. Her lips buzzed where Mark's mouth had touched them, and her body was on fire.

"Show's over," he said.

"We could have our own show if you want."

"Nicki…"

"I know, I know." She turned away. "You don't think it's a good idea. I can tell what you're thinking by the expression on your face."

He shrugged slightly. "Timing's wrong."

"Is it?" she asked, looking at him. "Why *not* now, Mark? You've had a thing for me for years. Don't bother to deny it—" she held up a hand to quiet his protests "—I know you have. Just like I've had a crush on *you* for years. So if one of us is waiting for the other to make the first move, I'll do it. It's never going to happen otherwise, because these things can't be planned. You know?"

She saw him look toward the man who'd "apprehended" the bad guy earlier. The pair were walking toward the jail.

"That was great," someone said, clapping Mark on the arm as they passed. Another man dressed in black, but he didn't look half as good as Mark.

"Thanks," Nicki answered, her eyes returning to Mark's.

"There are so many reasons why I should stay away from you right now," he said once the crowd had dispersed. "Why we should just get in your truck and leave."

"But we're not going to do that, are we?"

He took a long time to answer. "No," he said at last, but she could tell he wasn't happy about his decision. "We're here. We're in these damn monkey suits. Might as well enjoy ourselves for a while."

Because once they got home, things would go back to the way they were before. He didn't say the words out loud, but she had a feeling that was exactly what he was thinking.

"Come on," she said, determined to change his mind. "Let's go get that drink. I think I should buy *you* one after a rescue like that."

But the moment they entered the Dakota Saloon, he seemed to tense up. He didn't touch any alcohol, and neither did she. They ended up sitting at a table near the front window, sipping water. With the right side of his face illuminated by ambient light, and the other side left in shadow he looked more like a gunslinger than ever. "What's the matter?"

It was a big room, with twenty-foot-high ceilings, wood siding and floors, but next to nobody was inside. Most people were out of doors, enjoying the sights. Down the street another carriage rattled by. Mark still hadn't spoken by the time the passengers started to disembark.

"Mark?" she prompted.

"We shouldn't be doing this," he said at last.

Of course, she'd known he would say that. "We can take it one day at a time."

"Nicki," he said, his brown eyes fixing on her own. "You know your father doesn't like me. But I still respect him. When he finds out that I've gone behind his back and spent some time with you, he's going to kill me. This won't be your fault, it'll be mine, and that's okay. I'm man enough to take the blame, but your dad's my employer."

"And you're worried about losing your job."

He nodded. "I'm not like your pal Jesse Cody. I have to hold down a full-time job if I want to eat in between rodeos. I can't fly myself places. If I want to compete, I have to drive there. That means being on the road for hours on end."

She slowly stood, moved her chair around to his side of the table. "So I'm not worth the risk? Is that what you're saying?"

"No..."

"Then why would you let me go when it's obvious you care for me?"

She could tell by the expression in his eyes that'd she'd struck a nerve. "What the hell makes you say that?" he asked.

"You don't think I haven't noticed the way you look at me? Gosh, Mark, I've been waiting for you to ask me out, but you never have. You're afraid. Afraid of the way I make you feel."

"Nicki—"

"But I understand," she said, taking his hand. "I feel the same way. When your father died and I saw the sadness in your eyes, my heart broke for you. It actually ached. I knew then that my feelings ran deep. At the funeral, when I held you for a moment, you felt it, too, didn't you?"

She thought he might deny it, she really did, but there was one thing about Mark Hansen she truly admired: he was as honest as a cowboy could come.

"It doesn't matter," he said, standing suddenly.

She stood with him. "It *does* matter," she insisted. "It matters even more now that you've kissed me. You can't deny it anymore, Mark Hansen. You have feelings for me. And *I* have feelings for *you*. Come with me now, right this minute, to the hotel across the street. Spend the night with me."

God, was that her sounding so bold? She'd never propositioned a man in her life. And yet here she stood, heart pounding, as if she were some buckle bunny out to snag the attention of one of the nation's best cowboys.

"Nicki—" he began.

But she touched his lips and silenced him, knowing

that if she let him walk out now, she'd never get another shot at this. Well, okay, maybe that wasn't true. Maybe one day he might actually feel worthy of her. That was what this was about. He didn't think he was good enough for her, but she hoped to prove him wrong.

"Come on, Mark," she said softly.

She thought he might resist when she turned and led him from the saloon. He didn't, and when she looked back at him in question, she could tell by the light in his eyes that she had won.

"Make it quick," he said, his brown eyes full of fire. "Before I change my mind."

CHAPTER SIX

HER HANDS SHOOK as she signed for a room. Nicki could hear Mark behind her, shuffling his feet on the hardwood floor. He was pacing the tiny lobby of the authentically re-created 1800s hotel.

"Room twenty-one," the pleasant-faced receptionist said. "You'll love it. It's got a balcony with a view of the Black Hills."

"Thanks," Nicki said.

She was about to sleep with Mark Hansen.

When put that way, it seemed so unreal. She wasn't the type to jump into bed with a man. Not ever. Yet here she was.

It didn't help that Mark looked as if he was on his way to having a root canal as they climbed the sweeping stairway to the second floor. She almost said something, then thought better of it. If he wanted to back out now all he had to do was say the word. Yet he remained ominously silent as they hit the landing. Nicki tried to distract herself by studying their surroundings. The Wild West theme had been used here, too. More of the same wood paneling. Ceiling fans slicing the air. Music tinkled, compliments of a player piano tucked into one corner.

What are you doing?

Taking a chance, she told herself. Taking a huge

leap of faith. Hoping for the best…and that she wasn't making a mistake.

Their room was on the left, ten doors down. Frankly, she was surprised they hadn't needed reservations, given the limited space available.

Fate.

Or was it? Was this a disaster in the making? Her pulse escalated with every step she took. She felt on the verge of hyperventilating by the time they stopped in front of their door.

"Mark, if you've—"

He jerked her toward him, cutting her off. She gasped in surprise until her gasp was swallowed by his mouth. In that instant any doubt wafted away like rose petals in the wind. *This* was why she'd been so bold. When she'd kissed him earlier she'd experienced the same roller-coaster sensation she did now. She couldn't breathe for a moment, had to clutch his arms to keep herself from falling, and then she kissed him back, and it was like plunging down a precipice all over again.

He pressed her against the door. The feather in her hair poked her scalp. She turned her head but his lips never left her own.

"Mark," she finally had to gasp. "Door."

He needed no further urging. Nicki took a few deep breaths as he slid the card through the electronic lock.

Slow down.

But she'd been fantasizing about this moment for too long to hold back now. So once the door was open, *she* was the one who pulled him inside. She thought she might have heard him laugh as the latch clicked shut. She wasn't sure and didn't bother to check because she was too busy eyeing the bed and their distance from it.

And now you really are acting like a hussy.

But she didn't care. She just didn't care. She had Mark Hansen. Alone. In a hotel room.

"You're mine, cowboy."

Cripes. Was that her? Could she sound more harlotlike?

Mark didn't appear to notice. Apparently he was just as anxious to reach the bed as she was, because he scooped her up in his arms and carried her there.

"Mark." She half gasped, half laughed. She expected him to set her down. He didn't. She looked up at him in surprise.

The expression on his face took her breath away.

"I've been waiting for this moment half my life," he said softly.

She didn't know why, but she suddenly felt misty-eyed. "I think I have been, too."

He set her down on the bed. Nicki's breath caught as he towered over her for a moment. He was so damn good-looking. She'd been lusting after him for years now, but to be suddenly faced with making love to him caused her to feel incredibly inadequate.

"That outfit you're wearing is driving me nuts," he said, his lids lowering as he eyed her. "I've been wanting to tear it off you from the moment I saw you emerge from the costume area."

"You look pretty good yourself," she said. Out of the corner of her eye she glimpsed herself in the mirror, saw her chest rise and fall. Her breasts looked about ready to spill out. She propped herself up on her elbows, wondering if he wanted to her to undress him, or if he would undress her first.

"You should have been born a hundred years ago. You'd have made a fortune plying the trade."

"Thanks," she said softly. "I think."

He smiled, a wicked, boyish grin that made her heart melt. "I'm going to peel those tiny little straps off your shoulder first, then shove down that vest you're wearing."

His comment sent a delicious thrill through her.

"It's called a corset," she said, a burst of warmth causing her legs to clamp together—a perverse reaction, given that all she wanted to do was open up for him....

Jeez, Nicki.

Maybe she *should* have been a lady of the night, because she couldn't deny that as he leaned close to her, she felt her body arch toward his.

"Well, this damn corset is in my way."

He did exactly as promised, only there was nothing slow and measured about his movements. He pulled the edge of the garment down at the same moment his lips found her breasts.

And then...

And then...

She could do nothing but gasp, because seeing Mark Hansen kissing her so intimately, well, it did things to her insides that caused her to cry out in pleasure. He'd taken his hat off. When, she had no idea. All she knew was that she could see his mouth on her flesh, watch as his tongue tasted her. Her hands clutched the bedspread as he slowly peeled her costume down.

His head popped up, his brown eyes wickedly hot. "How the hell do you get this damn dress off?"

She smiled. "It laces up in the back."

"Well, you better help me untie it before I tear the thing off."

She rolled to the side, then glanced over her shoulder. "Undo the ties."

But her movement had exposed her shoulders, and he lingered there for a moment. Somehow, he managed to untie the dress and nibble her with his lips at the same time. Her hair had begun to break free of its bonds. She shook it loose, the feather falling to the bed by her arm.

How could a man who rode bulls for a living touch her so tenderly? He should have rough hands. Work-hardened hands. But he didn't. They were soft, and as they worked her laces, she was mesmerized by what he did to her. She felt the dress shift, his fingers sliding the costume down.

"Thong underwear," he murmured as he pulled the fabric over her hips. "I should have figured as much."

"What about you?" she asked, rolling onto her back. "Boxers or briefs?"

She wasn't really curious, just felt the need to say something, anything, to keep her nerves steady.

"You'll have to undress me to find out."

She was almost completely naked now, her underwear the only thing that kept them from touching flesh to flesh. He made no secret of the fact that he was studying her, his eyes heating in a way that made her swallow hard.

"Damn. If I'd known what was waiting for me beneath those tight jeans you wear, I'd have done this a long time ago."

"Tight jeans? I don't wear—"

He kissed her. Her protests faded away under the pressure of his lips, and when she felt his tongue swipe against her flesh, she opened her mouth and did the same. They touched, the taste of him strangely sweet, as if he'd had a slice of fruit—an orange—when she wasn't looking.

"My turn," he said, rearing back so he could toss his gunslinger's coat aside. He set to work on the buttons of his shirt, at the same time driving her mad with his intermittent kisses. Nicki helped him undress, batting his hands away at one point, suddenly impatient.

"Slow down," he said.

"I can't," she murmured.

Boxers.

She almost smiled. But he jerked her to him, leaving that last little article of clothing on. Her hands found his shoulders. He had solid arms, every ridge of muscle sculpted to help him hold on to a bull. She ran her palms down them as his chest pressed against her own, until they were belly to belly, thigh to thigh.

She wanted to part her thighs, especially when he deepened the kiss. His own hand lowered, touching her side, then dropping lower.

His mouth shifted, then he kissed the tip of her jaw, her neck. She moaned because he was going to do it again, going to kiss her there. Sure enough, his lips traveled the same path as before. He hovered for a moment over the swell of her breasts for half a heartbeat before moving lower. But he didn't linger there for long. To her shock he moved past her breasts, preferring instead to suckle the sensitive skin of her belly. Her whole body quivered at the first warm touch of his tongue. She waited, robbed of breath, for him to move lower still, and when he did, she groaned in delight. His fingers found the thin edges of her underwear. He slid them down, a centimeter at a time. Every nerve ending buzzed. There was a moment, right before her undies slide free, when she felt shyness overtake her again, but it disappeared as quickly as it came. He kissed her hip bone, then her inner thigh....

"Mark!"

She couldn't take it anymore. Frankly, she was tired of waiting. This was it, the moment she'd both anticipated and fantasized about for years and years, and she refused to wait another instant for him. She clutched his upper arms, urged him toward her. His breath found her hot center and she lost herself for a moment.

It felt *so good*.

But she wanted more. She wanted *all* of him.

She slid out from under him, knocking him off balance. He rolled onto his back to keep from falling off the bed. She straddled him before he could right himself.

"Hey," he cried. "Slow down."

She smiled in delight. "No more Ms. Nice Guy," she said softly.

"Ms. Nice—"

She jerked his boxers down and leaned toward him at the same instant. She could tell by the way his eyes widened that she'd caught him off guard.

"Where's your condom?" she asked.

"I don't have one," he all but groaned.

Uh-oh. Although to be honest she'd have been a little worried if he always carried one around. But this meant taking a risk. She knew it might not be wise, but she was beyond caring. Besides, Mark would never do something to hurt her, or put her life at risk.

"That's okay," she said, whispering the words against his lips. "We don't need one."

"Nicki—"

She cut him off, kissing him and mounting him all in one motion.

"Holy—"

That was all he had time to say because she was moving now and he was moaning into her mouth.

Yes.

This was what she'd wanted. Sex. Hot, wicked sex with Mark Hansen. It might not be wise, she might regret it in the morning, but for now he was hers.

She increased their tempo, Nicki releasing her own gasp when he rolled her onto her back in a move that would have done a steer wrestler proud.

"Hey."

He took her.

Her protest faded. This was no gentle lovemaking. This was a physical branding. A man staking his claim on a woman in a manner common throughout time. His kisses were greedy, his thrusting frenetic. Their bodies moved faster and faster. Nicki felt that pressure, that wonderful, heavenly pressure that was nearly painful in its intensity, and yet oh so sweet. She wouldn't last long. Not now. But she didn't mind. Soon she'd slip over the edge of a precipice that might change her life forever.

"Mark," she cried as the pleasure began to crest.

She clutched him, held on for dear life because suddenly she was there, jumping off the cliff.

"Oh, Mark," she cried again, as her body tightened around him, then tightened some more, pleasure coiling in on itself in a way that made her back arch toward him. It should hurt, this climax that was so violent she screamed in release. But it didn't hurt. It was the sweetest sort of ecstasy, a pleasure she would never forget.

He gasped. His body went rigid. He'd fallen, too; she could feel the moment he slipped off the edge. Waves of pleasure rippled through her anew, a second climax even more brilliant in intensity than the first.

"Nicki," she heard him gasp. "Nicki, Nicki, Nicki."

She held him. He held her, too. Together they rode the final waves, and it was a long time before Nicki's breathing returned to normal.

"That," he whispered, "was incredible."

"As good as riding bulls?" she heard herself ask, her voice still husky from desire.

"Better," he said, slowly drawing back. "Jesse might have won the rodeo today, but I've got the bigger prize."

CHAPTER SEVEN

"WHAT IN THE *hell* have you done?"

The voice on the other end of her cell phone caused Nicki to sit straight up in bed. Mark barely stirred beside her.

"Dad?"

"When you didn't come home last night I started asking around. Guess what I heard?"

She closed her eyes, scooted up against the headboard and drew the sheet up to protect herself. Silly to feel self-conscious while Mark was asleep, but she did.

"I left you a message about where I was going," she said softly, trying not to wake him up. She glanced toward the hotel-room window. The curtains were drawn, but she could see a bright glow emanating from a tiny crack. A new day had dawned. A quick glance at the bedside alarm clock confirmed her guess: 7:30 a.m.

"You told me you were taking the scenic route home. That you might stay overnight at a hotel. Not that you'd be sharing a bed with Mark Hansen."

So he did know, although how he'd found out she had no idea. "What makes you think I'm with Mark Hansen?"

"Chuck Rogers told me this morning he saw him get into your truck."

She had a choice then. She could lie and soothe things over with some excuse about giving Mark a ride into town, or she could be brazen and tell her father the truth.

"That doesn't mean he's with me now," she hedged.

She heard her dad draw a deep breath before asking, "Is he?"

"Yes," she said because to deny it would mean an out-and-out lie, and she didn't have that in her.

Her father said nothing for a moment. And then she heard a low rumble that she knew was the predecessor for a string of curses. "Son of a—"

She winced and held the phone away. Mark stirred, and she glanced at him with concern. When she put the phone back to her ear, her dad was still going at it. "Tell him he's not—"

She held the phone away again. Only when she heard silence did she dare to speak. "Dad," she said softly, "I'm a grown woman. And Mark is a grown man. You knew he liked me. He told me he asked for your permission to date me."

"And I said *no*."

"So I took matters into my own hands. I asked *him* out."

The silence was momentary. "Then he can find himself another job."

"No," she cried, a little too loudly, as it turned out. As Mark opened his eyes, she covered her cell phone with her hand and whispered, "Sorry."

"Who is it?" he asked sleepily.

And for a moment she forgot all about her father on the other end of the phone. Mark looked like an underwear model lying there, the sheet draped around his waist, a slight sprinkling of hair covering his chest. He was the type of man who needed to shave every day, or else razor stubble would dot his chin. But the five-o'clock shadow combined with his rumpled hair and mocha-brown eyes made him look very, *very* sexy.

"It's my dad," she finally admitted.

Mark grimaced.

"Is that him?" Jonathan's voice was perfectly audible as he'd yelled the words and they both glanced at the phone.

"Is that him?" they heard again, this time even louder.

"Call you later, Dad," Nicki said quickly, closing the phone before Mark heard something else—such as the fact that he'd been fired.

"How the hell did he find out I was here?" he asked, sitting up.

So much for a good-morning kiss. "Someone told him you got in my truck yesterday."

"And you didn't deny it?"

She wrinkled her nose. "No. Why would I?"

Mark leaned back in bed and covered his head with his hands, a long groan vibrating from his chest. "This isn't good."

She leaned over him and ran a hand down his body. "I know how I can make you feel better."

He propped himself on one of his elbows, his dark brows dipping low. "I don't think you understand, Nicki. This is bad, real bad. I was hoping to keep our relationship under wraps. At least at first, but now…"

He'd be fired. Although that wasn't necessarily true. She was good at sweet-talking her dad.

"Look," she said. "You don't have to report to work

until Monday. Until then, let's hang out together. Give my dad some time to cool down."

Mark looked about ready to argue the point, but then his face softened.

"Good," she said. "That's settled." She tried to pull him toward her again.

He resisted. "Nicki, wait. Maybe we should talk."

"About what?"

"Us. We both knew this would be complicated. I'm making a run for the NFR, my mom's health is failing. You've got a full-time job, I've got a full-time job, plus a second career riding bulls."

She couldn't believe it, felt so complexly poleaxed by his words that she found herself slumping back. "Are you telling me this was a one-night stand?"

"No," he said quickly, lifting one hand in protest. To his credit, his eyes had gotten wide. "I'm not saying that at all. I just think we should take a step back. Slow down a little. This thing between you and me isn't going to go away. We have all the time in the world."

Which appeared, on the outset, to be a very sincere speech, Nicki thought. But she'd been around rough stock riders too long not to wonder, at least a little, if he wasn't just saying that.

Mark's not a player.

She tried to reassure herself with the words.

"Hey," he said. "Don't look so scared. We can work this out."

Could they? Why, then, did she suddenly feel so panicked?

"I'm not scared," she lied. "I'm just hungry."

"Then let's get something to eat."

She forced a smile. "That sounds good to me."

IF MARK WAS honest with himself, he'd have to admit he felt a twinge of anxiety. He knew Nicki's dad, and knew Jon Sable wouldn't be happy with the two of them jumping into bed. That might present a problem on Monday. Or not. Honestly, Mark didn't know what to think.

"You look distracted," Nicki said, her stunning green eyes peering at him from across a plate of eggs and bacon. They'd had to dress in their costumes again, and Nicki looked just as stunning as she had the day before.

"No, no," he said quickly. If he was distracted, it was because of her—not her conversation with her dad. Light from a nearby window set her blond hair aglow. Her eyes were as green as a spring meadow and all he wanted to do was take her back to their room. "Let's enjoy the rest of the day."

Never mind that he had a million things to do at home. He had only one day a week off, sometimes not even that, depending on his rodeo schedule. Sunday was his day to catch up on paying bills or doing laundry or running errands. It was also his day to keep an eye on his mom. Janie wouldn't be happy if he stood her up.

"We won't be enjoying much of anything if you continue to look like a man sitting atop a rosebush."

Mark jerked his head sharply, mad at himself for being unable to relax. "Sorry," he said.

"What were you thinking about?"

"Nothing."

"Baloney," she said. "You have the same look on your face as my father the morning of a big rodeo. You're thinking about work. But don't worry about losing your job. I can handle my dad."

"No," Mark said quickly. "It's not that. I was thinking about all the stuff I need to do today. Next week

I'm up in Prineville. That's a long drive, so if I don't get things handled today, I'll be paying for it later. But that's okay. I want to spend the day with you."

"Yeah, but things would be easier for you if we got an early start back home," she said. Yet she didn't want the day to end, either. Mark could tell.

"Not necessarily. I could wake up early tomorrow to catch up." As in three o'clock in the morning, since his workday typically started at six.

Nicki knew that, too. "Come on," she said. "Let's go. We can make plans to see each other later this week."

"Are you sure?" he asked. "I don't want you to think I'm blowing you off or something."

He was joking, of course, but she took his words seriously. "Are you?" she asked.

He shook his head and reached for her hands. "Hell, no."

"Then let's get you back to civilization. Our time together can wait."

THREE HOURS LATER Mark was wishing they'd stayed in South Dakota.

"Where have you been?" Janie asked him the moment he stepped through the front door, Nicki's kiss goodbye still imprinted on his lips. "I've been waiting all morning for you to get home. When you told me you were catching a ride with a friend I didn't think that meant staying out all night and partying."

Mark winced, hanging his cowboy hat on a nail by the front door. The Hansens lived simply, in a twelve-hundred-square-foot modular home that was painted buttercup-yellow. Just inside there were two bedrooms off to the right, one for him and one for Janie, with the master bedroom to the left. Kitchen straight ahead, with rose-colored drapes on either side of a sliding glass door.

Janie sat at the old dining-room table. Her brown eyes narrowed as she slowly rose. "Mom's been seeing things again and so I'm afraid to leave her. God forbid she should get out a shotgun and start shooting at phantom intruders."

"Where is she now?" Mark asked.

"In her room, resting. She's been more tired than usual."

He nodded as Janie stopped in front of him.

"Seriously, Mark, where have you been? I hope she was worth the money you spent on dinner and a hotel room."

"She was," Mark said. "And who she was is none of your business, although I am sorry for leaving you in the lurch. I tried to call earlier, but the phone just rang and rang."

"It did?" Janie turned to look at the cradle that held the cordless handset. It was empty.

"Son of a…" Janie shook her head. "She's done it again."

"It" meaning their mother had misplaced the phone. Last time, they'd found it in the freezer, a lump of shaved ice stuck to its side.

Janie glanced over her shoulder at him. "You could have tried my cell," she said, going straight to the refrigerator and opening the door.

"I did," he replied. "No answer there, either."

"Impossible. I must have used my phone at least a half-dozen times to leave you a message." She fished it out of her pocket, her shoulders slumping at what she saw. "And used up the batteries doing so. Damn."

Mark went to the oven and opened the door. "Not here, either," he said. "And that explains why you didn't get my message."

"My phone was on all morning, though, Mark," she said, opening the bread box. She slammed it closed just as quickly.

"I know, I know," he said. "I was busy, is all." He looked inside the cabinet that held the pots and pans. Empty except for skillets.

"Busy my ass," Janie muttered. She was opening the upper cabinets, searching among the glasses and dishes and spices. "Damn it," she said. "What the heck did she do with it this time?"

Mark stopped his sister from charging past him on her way to the laundry room, their mother's second favorite place to stash the phone. She'd run it through an entire rinse cycle once upon a time. They'd had to buy a new one.

"Janie," he said, placing his hands on her shoulders. "I'm sorry I didn't get here any sooner. It was rude and irresponsible of me. I know you have things to do, too, but I'm here now. Go on out and do something fun."

His sister snorted.

"Go ride Chica."

"Our arena's washed out."

It had rained heavily the week before. Mark had forgotten. "Take her over to the Codys," he suggested, even though he hated Janie having to rely on the Codys for anything. "I'm sure Elly wouldn't mind your popping over."

His sister, the one person who helped to keep him

sane when things got to rough, as it had when their father died, eyed him intently. He could tell she was battling her need for personal time over her loyalty to their mom. Janie might complain about having to sit with Abigail in order to keep her out of trouble, but the truth was she loved their mother with a fierceness no one could deny.

"Go on," he urged again.

"Okay, fine," she said at last, flicking her long braid over one shoulder.

CHAPTER EIGHT

Janie hated to leave.

"Come on, Chica," she said, sliding open the latch on the pasture gate. She already had her truck and trailer hooked up—she'd been too tired to unhook it last night—and at least she didn't have to do that. Chica was a cinch to load, though she had to be tired after yesterday's performance. But that was the name of the game. Even when you felt as if your legs were going to fall off, you still rode. That was what it took to be a top rodeo performer. Sure, Janie didn't get to ride as often as Mark, but she made damn sure she didn't embarrass herself whenever she *did* get to compete.

"Sorry, girl," she said, patting Chica's cheek after attaching the trailer tie to her halter. "I promise. No barrels today."

Just a nice easy ride at the Cottonwood Ranch. She'd already called Elly. Her friend had been excited about her coming out to the ranch, even though Janie hated to impose. Elly was her best friend, and yet she didn't like to take advantage of that friendship. They were friends because Elly was the nicest person Janie had ever met, *not* because she was a Cody.

The town of Markton was to the east of the Shoshone National Forest—God's country, Janie thought, a land so beautiful that every time she returned from a rodeo she couldn't help but think how lucky they were to live among such splendor. To her right, on the west side of town, stood the Rockies, their craggy, tooth-like edges still covered by snow at higher elevations. Markton stood on the edge of a vast plain, level ground stretching to the east as far as the eye could see. In the spring those flatlands were covered by grass, but now they were bare. However, one didn't need to look far to spy lofty green spires and scenic mountaintops. Pine trees were in abundance on the slopes, clearly visible from town.

The closer she got to the Cottonwood Ranch, the more scenic the view became. The Codys' land bordered the national forest. That meant gently rolling hills, grassy valleys and meandering rivers for much of the drive, most of it belonging to the Cody family.

The entrance to the ranch was in one of the low-lying valleys. Two stone pillars held up an iron gate with the Cody family brand in the middle of it. Nicki pressed the keypad that would open it, having long since been given the pass code. She followed white fencing until the road forked, her vehicle ducking off the edge of the asphalt road for a second as she rounded a turn, and the trailer hit gravel with a thud.

"Sorry, Chica," she called, even though she knew her horse couldn't hear her. Janie always did that. Maybe one of these days she'd remember to swing the trailer a little wider around that curve.

"Hey, hey, hey," Elly called as Janie exited the truck. "You ready to get to work?" Her friend was on a horse Janie had never seen before.

"Who's that?" she asked, just as Chica neighed from inside the trailer.

"This is Baylee," Elly said, her blond ponytail swinging forward as she patted her mount's neck. "One of my dad's reining horses. She's been a bit of a handful in recent weeks so he asked me to get on her."

Janie went up to the mare, placing a hand against her muzzle and allowing her to inhale her scent. The soft breath of the horse tickled her palm. Janie smiled. She took a step closer.

"There you go again," Elly said, her green eyes twinkling. "Working your voodoo magic."

Janie had a way with animals. A gift, her mother used to call it. Something she'd inherited from her Lakota ancestors. She could usually soothe the most fractious of horses, and Baylee was no different. Within seconds Janie was right up next to her, their eyes meeting.

"What's wrong, honey?" she crooned.

"She's fine on the lunge line or when we turn her out," Elly interjected. "It's when we get on her back that she balks. She acts like she's scared of her own shadow."

"You've checked the fit of the saddle," Janie said, running her hands along the mare's jaw. She wore a leather bridle, and Janie absently scratched at a spot beneath it. The mare leaned into her hands in delight.

"That's the first thing we did," Elly agreed. "It's fine. And she doesn't really buck or anything. She's just terrified."

"Why don't I watch you while you ride?"

Elly grinned. "I was hoping you'd say that. I swear, Janie, nobody can diagnose a horse like you can."

Janie smiled. That was high praise, indeed, coming from Elly. She just wished she could find the time to finish her undergraduate work. One of these days, she'd get her degree in veterinary medicine. When that happened, she'd be the first vet in the state of Wyoming to mix holistic healing with modern-day medicine.

One day.

They passed by the massive barn that housed Cottonwood Ranch's stallions, more than a few lusty males calling out to the mare they could smell, but not see. And while Janie had been to the Cody homestead many times, it was difficult not to feel a pang of envy as she stared around her. As far as the eye could see was Cody land. Six hundred thousand acres. But what Janie really envied was the horse facility. Beyond the stallion barn was a covered arena, with stalls lining one side. Behind that was an outdoor rodeo arena. Both featured synthetic footing—rubber-coated pellets mixed with sand—that helped prevent equine injuries, and she supposed human injuries, too, if a rider fell off. Everything was surrounded by acres and acres of white fence that outlined horse pastures where mares grazed along with their foals in the spring.

Breathtaking.

"Dusty is inside, training one of the horses, so we'll have to work around him."

Sure enough, the moment they entered the barn, Janie could spy Elly's brother inside. The entrance to the arena was on the right, a pipe panel fence separating the work area from the stalls along the left side of the building. Dusty was riding a sorrel gelding, and Janie took a moment to admire the animal, whose coat glistened brightly under the fluorescent lights above.

"Can you get the gate?" Elly asked.

But Janie was already moving toward the latch.

"Hey, Janie," Dusty called as he rode by.

She waved. She liked Elly's brother. Actually, she liked all the Cody siblings, with the possible exception of Jesse. That man was entirely too self-confident for his own good, and it drove Janie nuts.

"Here we go," Elly said, trotting the mare forward.

Janie crossed to the center of the ring and watched. The minute Elly got to the rail, the mare took two steps, planted her feet, then darted right.

"Whoa, whoa, whoa!" Elly cried. Only her expert horsemanship kept her in the saddle. She nearly ran Dusty over in her bid to bring the animal under control. "Easy there, girl."

"You okay?" her brother asked, blond hair peeking out from beneath his cowboy hat.

"Wow," Janie said. "That was close."

"You see what I'm talking about?" Elly asked. "I thought at first she might be spooking at the horses in their stalls, but that's not it. She does it on both sides of the arena, and for the life of me I can't figure it out."

"Bring her here."

Elly nodded, then did so. Janie gave the horse a once-over, but couldn't see anything wrong with the saddle and bridle she wore—nothing that would cause such an extreme reaction, like a cinch strap slapping her on the flank or a long rein hitting her shoulder.

"Go on back out, but circle around me." Maybe she could spot something while the horse was moving.

Oddly, the mare didn't spook once as she did laps around Janie.

"Is it only at the rail that she balks?" Janie asked.

"Yup," Dusty answered, coming to a stop nearby, and grinning at her in such a way that the scar on his chin caught the light. "She's a barrel of fun."

"Go on out to the rail again," Janie instructed.

Elly complied, and once again the mare reacted.

"Whoa!" Elly immediately cried.

The mare headed straight for Dusty and his brown gelding. *Herd instinct,* Janie thought. The horse was seeking the comfort of her own kind.

"She's definitely scared," Janie murmured. "The question is, of what?"

She walked toward the rail, her eyes scanning the ground. But just as Elly said, there was nothing.

She turned back to Dusty, and that was when she saw it: his shadow.

"No way," she muttered.

"What?" he asked.

She turned back to the rail, scanned the ground. Sure enough, there was a black bar lying on the dirt—or what would look like a black bar to a horse's eyes.

"She really *is* scared of her own shadow."

"What?" Elly said in surprise.

"Check it out." Janie waved at the ground with a smile. "Take her to the rail again and watch what happens when she gets near the shadows."

Sure enough, the moment the mare got close to the fence, she cocked her head and tried to dart off again. Janie laughed. Elly had her hands full bringing Baylee to a stop.

"When you're near the center of the ring the light fixtures are overhead, and there's no shadow. But toward the rail, there are shadows. That's what's scaring her."

"Janie," Elly said, chuckled, "you're a genius!"

"Well, well, well," someone said. "Well done, Janie." She stiffened.

"Isn't she great, Dad?" Elly asked, turning the mare toward her father.

"I owe you a steak dinner," J.W. said.

Why, oh, why was it always so hard to be around the man? "That's okay, Mr. Cody," Janie said. "Elly will make it up to me."

Elly's dad was grinning from ear to ear. "Nah," he said. "Come on up to the house for dinner tonight."

"Yeah," Elly insisted. "Join us for dinner."

Janie looked into her friend's eyes and tried not to wince. She had no idea of the secret Janie held, a secret that involved her father. And she never would know, either. Janie had vowed to go to her grave with what she knew.

"Really, Mr. Cody, it's okay. Elly can buy me a drink the next time we go out."

J.W. repositioned his beige cowboy hat. "You sure?"

"Positive," Janie said.

"You make certain you do that, Elly girl," Mr. Cody told her.

"You know I will," she replied.

"And put a shadow roll on that mare," J.W. said to his son. "We have one of those around, don't we?"

"I'm pretty sure we do," Dusty said. "I'll go get it."

Elly jumped off Baylee. "Seriously, Janie, it'd be great to have you over for dinner."

Janie glanced toward the rail, where J.W. was talking to his son. She watched as they both headed toward the tack room.

"You know I don't like to impose."

"Yeah, but you heard my dad," Elly said, her green eyes pleading. "He *wants* you to come over."

Janie shook her head. "I have too much to do, but I'll take you up on that drink later this week."

Elly rolled her eyes. "I swear, Janie, sometimes you're a stubborn cuss. You're not an imposition."

"I know. But just the same…" She left the rest of her words unspoken.

Elly looked disappointed, but they were soon interrupted by Dusty, who was back in record time, thankfully without J.W. The fuzzy nosepiece that prevented a horse from seeing the ground worked out beautifully, so much so that Janie went and saddled up Chica. But Elly was still going on about her staying for dinner even after they finished riding.

"Honestly, Elly," Janie said, giving her a hug goodbye once everything was loaded up. The sun was starting to go down, and the sky was a shade of deep purple that took Janie's breath away. "It's no big deal."

"I know," Elly said, gazing at her sadly. "But it'd be fun to have you over. You never come to dinner. My whole family's starting to get a complex."

Janie doubted that. "Thanks just the same, but I'll see you soon. We're supposed to go to the Spotted Horse on Thursday night, remember? You can buy me that drink."

"Deal," Elly said.

But as Janie drove home she worried her bottom lip. Sooner or later Elly was going to figure out that Janie didn't like to be around J.W. And she prayed Elly would never find out why.

That would be a nightmare.

"Damn it," Mark said, slamming the door of the dryer closed. Where the hell was the damn phone? He'd been looking for it for hours now.

"Mark," a voice called.

"I'm right here, Mom," he yelled back, closing the washing machine. Nothing in there but damp clothes. He'd take care of them later.

"Those people are back, Mark. I can hear them on the rear lawn."

Mark slumped his shoulders for a moment. An odd thing about this disease was that some days were better than others. On those good days, he and Janie always got their hopes up. Maybe she was snapping out of it, they would think. Perhaps she'd go back to the way she'd been before. Unfortunately, that never seemed to happen, and lately she only seemed to get worse, especially around dusk. Sunsetting—that was the technical term for it. Alzheimer's researchers thought it was connected to the brain's serotonin. But for whatever reason, their mom was always worse around dinnertime. It killed Mark, because he knew she was proud, a trait she got from her Lakota heritage. But every once in a while, when she was deep in the disease's grasp, he would catch a glimpse of something in her eyes. Bewilderment, sometimes even panic, as if she knew something was wrong with her, and she was terrified.

It tore at his heart.

"I'll go out and chase them off," he called back. They'd been told to humor her during times like these. In Abigail Hansen's mind, there really *were* people outside.

So he made a great pretense of checking things out. The sun was going down, the tops of the mountains outlined by the waning rays. He slammed the screen door extrahard so she would hear him, then cupped his hands over his mouth and yelled out. He felt like an idiot. The back of their property had been cleared for horses and cattle to graze, and as expected, all he could see were acres and acres of grassland between them and the Big Horn Mountains.

No trespassers.

"All clear," he announced a moment later. It was definitely warmer inside the house. Life in the mountains meant the days were warm and the nights were chilly. "I think they drove off in a car," he added, stepping into his mother's room. It was dark. She liked the lights turned down.

"Are you sure?" she asked, her voice sounding almost feeble.

"I'm sure, Momma," he said softly.

She looked old. Drawn. Worn-out. He drew up short at the sight of her. It wasn't that she'd aged in recent months; her brown hair had sprouted gray a decade ago. And her skin had always looked weathered. Too many years of watching Tomas Hansen drink himself to death. In that instant Mark saw her as a stranger might. As Nicki might see her.

Sad.

And...scared?

"Hey, relax," he said, resting a hand on her arm. "Nobody's there."

"It's that damn J. W. Cody, come to get you."

Mark resisted the urge to let his spirits sink even more. And though he'd been told to humor her, he couldn't stop himself from saying, "Mom, there's no reason for J. W. Cody to come and visit us."

"Yes, there is."

"No—"

"After all these years," she said quickly, "he might have changed his mind."

"Changed his mind about what, Mom?" Mark asked, trying to hold on to his patience.

His mother's gaze came to rest on him. "My poor baby boy," she said. "You could have had so much more if I'd played my cards right."

CHAPTER NINE

"MOM, ENOUGH OF THIS." Obviously, she'd heard the rumors around town. Mark had heard them, too, though he'd never put any stock in them.

He was *not* J. W. Cody's son.

"You could have been a Cody," his mother said.

Okay. That did it. "Mom. Stop. J. W. Cody doesn't even know I exist."

His mother shook her head, her loose hair rustling on the pillow. Janie usually kept it braided—like mother, like daughter—but their mom was forever pulling the plaited strands apart.

"Oh, he *knows*," Abigail said, emphasizing her words with a knowing nod.

"Come on," Mark told her. He turned toward the room's only window, lit by the last of the sun's rays. "You can watch me make dinner."

When he glanced back his mother had the saddest expression on her face. "I did wrong by you," she said. "I should have *made* him take you."

Mark couldn't handle it anymore. "I'm going to go get you some tea while I make dinner," he said. Maybe the caffeine would snap her out of whatever fantasyland she'd sunk into.

J. W. Cody's son.

Yeah, right. He had a better shot at being related to royalty.

"No," Abigail said, shaking her head. "Don't leave me alone. Not with J.W. lurking around. He's never forgiven me for what happened. Every time I see him in town, I can tell by the look in his eyes. He blames *me* for some reason."

And here was all the proof Mark needed that this was some kind of Alzheimer's delusion. J.W. was *not* outside.

"I'll be right back."

His mom called out again, but Mark ignored her. He had nothing to worry about. Sure, there'd been talk in town, but it was just gossip. His mom hadn't even *lived* in Markton when he'd been conceived.

But what if it were true?

Mark shook his head as he went back to the kitchen and got out the tea his mom liked.

Still, later that night, when the house had gotten quiet and Janie and his mom were asleep in their rooms, he found himself surfing the internet. He'd never poked around the Cottonwood Ranch website, but he knew they had one. It stood to reason there'd be a picture of J.W. there. Not that he believed for one second that there was a chance he really was J.W.'s son. Mark was just curious. He'd seen the man around town and at rodeos, but he'd never really taken the time to study him in detail. They didn't look a thing alike.

The ranch Web site came up almost immediately, though individual pages took a while to load. He saw why the instant the screen began to fill with frames. There was an aerial shot of the ranch in all its glory. Mark was taken aback at just how big the place was.

"Holy…"

He'd known the Codys were rich—who in town didn't?—but even he was surprised at how lavish their facility was. Judging by the photo he studied, there were numerous homes and a state-of-the-art horse facility, the scope of which left him stunned. And, all right, maybe even a little jealous. No wonder the Cody brothers did so well at rodeo. They could practice their fool heads off. He scrolled down farther.

And there he was.

J.W.

"WHY AREN'T YOU in bed?" Janie asked, pulling her robe tighter.

The glow of the computer screen illuminated Mark's face. "Not tired," he answered shortly.

"What are you looking at?" She moved closer.

"Nothing." Before she could find out, he shut off the monitor, swiveled his seat and faced her. "Have you ever heard any rumors about Mom and J. W. Cody having an affair?"

Janie's heart stopped. "Mom?" she repeated. "And J.W.? Uh…no."

"Or that I might be J.W.'s son?"

Dear God.

Don't panic, Janie. He couldn't possibly have found the letter.

"Okay, what's this about?" she asked, pulling up a chair.

"Nothing. Maybe something. Shit, I don't know." He ran a hand through his dark hair.

"Spill it," she said, trying to stay calm. She couldn't

lose Mark. Not so soon after losing their father. Her brother was all she had.

"Mom mentioned something tonight. Something about J. W. Cody coming to claim me."

Janie relaxed. *Okay. Whew.* "Mark," she said softly, "you know Mom. She probably heard the rumors around town sometime in the past, and now believes they're real."

"So you've heard the gossip, too?" he queried.

"Of course I have."

"But you've never discussed it with me."

"Why, when it was just harmless gossip?"

Mark looked away.

Please, God, let him drop it.

"Harmless gossip," he murmured. "That's what I keep telling myself. There's nothing to it. A million times tonight I've told myself the same thing. But then I remember all the fuss about testing my blood back when Dad was sick. Remember? He wouldn't let me do it." Mark shook his head. "Said there was nothing I could do to help him. I never understood why. But now, with what Mom's saying…"

"You're wondering if there was another reason," Janie finished for him.

"I am."

She shook her head. "Mark. Go to bed. This'll all blow over by morning. It's nothing. Really."

He sighed deeply. "Maybe you're right."

The relief she felt caused her to close her eyes. "Go back to bed."

"I wish I could."

"You should," she said. "You need your rest. We need

you to make it into the NFR, remember. That's what's important now."

She left him sitting there, but it was Janie who didn't get any sleep the rest of the night.

THE NEXT MORNING Mark was still on edge. Unfortunately, he had reason to forget about the whole debacle when he arrived for work. The moment he pulled into the yard at the Sable ranch, his boss came running out. It was a pretty small operation compared to the Codys'. House to the left, barns and corrals to the right. Today Mark was supposed to take some steers to the local auction yard, but Jon Sable's "What the hell are you doing here?" had him drawing up short.

"Excuse me?" he asked.

"Mark," Nicki called, hurrying from the house. "I tried calling you this morning."

"Oh, yeah?" he asked, his gaze resting on her father.

Jon Sable crossed his arms in front of him. He was a short man with a wide girth. Mark often found himself thinking he resembled a garden gnome.

"I need to talk to you," Nicki said, coming to a stop in front of him, panic on her face.

"About what?" Mark asked.

"About the fact that you no longer have a job!" her father yelled.

HER DAD WAS LIVID. Nicki winced at the look on Mark's face.

"So go to the barn and get your damn saddle and whatever other crap you have in there and get the hell out."

"Dad," she said, "you don't really mean that."

Her father turned on her like an angry bull. "The hell I don't," he said. "I told you yesterday, Nicki, I have no patience for a man who doesn't keep his word."

"I never promised to stay away from Nicki," Mark stated, taking a step toward Jon Sable. "You were the one who put those words in my mouth, but I never promised. Over the past several years I've stayed away out of respect for you." He turned to Nicki and slipped an arm around her waist. "But now I see I was wrong. I should have done what was best for us, not for you."

The words made Nicki's heart feel as light as a feather. "Do you mean that?" she asked softly.

"I do," Mark admitted, smiling down at her.

"All right, that's enough," her father said. "Nicki, tell your boyfriend to leave before I get my shotgun."

"Dad," she cried, horrified that he would dare say such a thing. "You're being ridiculous. I'm old enough to know what I want, and I want Mark."

"Oh, yeah?" Jon asked, his face abnormally red—a sure sign that his blood pressure was on the rise. "And what about him? You think he's going to want you when he's out on the road all by himself, flush with victory, and some bimbo throws herself at him?"

"I'm not like that," Mark said.

"No?" Jon asked, before turning his gaze on his daughter. "Are you certain of that?"

"I am," Nicki said.

"Then have at him." Her father waved his hand in disgust. "But don't come crying to me when he leaves you high and dry." He turned and stormed away.

Nicki couldn't believe this was happening. Her father was acting like a complete jerk. "What are you doing?"

she asked, running to catch up to him. "You aren't seriously going to fire him for daring to date me, are you?"

He was. She could tell by the look on his face. Not only that, but he'd dug in his heels, and she knew that once her father did that, it was nearly impossible to get him to change his mind. "He didn't just date you, Nicki. He *slept* with you."

Nicki winced. She might be a grown woman, but Jonathan Sable was still her father.

"Did you use protection?"

Nicki's cheeks flamed.

"Dear God," Jonathan said. "If you get her pregnant—"

"What?" Mark asked. "I'll have to marry her? Gladly."

"Mark," Nicki said, her heart seeming to flip over in her chest.

"Over my dead body." Jonathan turned and stormed off.

"Mark, I'm so sorry," Nicki exclaimed.

He glanced at her, his eyes having gone dark with anger. "You have nothing to be sorry about. And I mean it, Nicki. You come up pregnant—"

"I won't get pregnant." She hoped. Or maybe she didn't hope that. God, she didn't know what to think.

"But if you do…"

"I know, I know." Lord, would he really marry her? "And don't worry about my father. He'll get over it. Give him a week or two to cool down."

"And in the meantime I'm out of a job." Mark took his hat off and scrubbed a hand over his face, his gaze glued to her father's back until Jonathan disappeared inside the house, slamming the front door behind him.

"Look at it like a vacation," Nicki suggested, grabbing his hand and trying to regain his attention. "Once he cools down, he'll change his mind. You're one of his best workers. He knows that."

They both turned as someone else drove down the road. It was Todd Miller, another of her dad's ranch hands.

"I better go get my stuff," Mark said, turning toward the barn.

"I'll go with you."

"Don't you have to head off to work?" he asked.

So he knew her routine. Nicki almost smiled. She worked at Spurling Natural Gas Company, but she was close to the owners so she could be late. "Not for another half hour."

"Yeah, but you have to change first," he said.

Wow. He really *did* know. "Are you trying to get rid of me?" she asked, as Todd's tires came skidding to a halt on the gravel drive.

"Just making sure you haven't forgotten," Mark said, nodding to his coworker when he got out of his truck. His ex-coworker. But that was only temporary, she reminded herself. Still, when Mark met her gaze, she could tell he was trying hard not to let her see how upset he was.

"C'mon," she said, tugging on his hand. "I'll walk you to the barn."

But he didn't budge. "Nicki, maybe we should back off a bit. Just until things get smoothed over with your father," he quickly added. "We both know it's going to take a while for him to come around to the notion that I'm dating his daughter."

Yeah, she did know.

"Just go on back inside. Tell him you feel bad. That

you'll consider his words. Whatever. Just try to calm him down. I'll call you tomorrow," he said.

"You're probably right. But I just hate the fact that you have to take your stuff. You want me to bring it to you later?"

"No," he said.

"Then I'm not taking no for an answer. I'm going to help you carry your things."

He glanced toward the barn again, then the house. "Up to you," he said. "Although I'm sure your dad's counting every second you stay out here."

She was sure he was, too. But to hell with him. It was time her father realized she was old enough to take care of herself.

"My dad can wait," she said firmly.

But Mark was quiet as they walked. She didn't really blame him. He'd just been fired by the father of the woman he was dating. That had to sting.

"Mark, I'm sorry," she said again.

"Don't worry about it. Honestly, I think I might have bigger fish to fry."

Nicki drew up short. They were in front of the main barn. Todd was already inside, loading bales of hay onto a trailer attached to the back of an ATV. "What do you mean?"

"Nothing," he said.

"Mark, what happened?"

He shook his head. She thought at first he might brush her off again, but he didn't. "My mom said something last night."

"What?"

"Have you ever heard the rumors that I might be J. W. Cody's son?"

Nicki's eyes widened. "You've heard those rumors, too?"

"So obviously you have," Mark said.

"Well, sure, but I never put much stock in them. You might have J.W.'s eyes, but that doesn't mean anything. Lots of people have the same color eyes."

"I have J.W.'s eyes?"

Nicki swallowed. "Uh, yeah." She'd noticed that a long time ago.

"Unreal," Mark said.

"What brought this on?" Nicki asked, glancing toward the house again. Was her father standing at a window? Probably, although he'd be far enough away from the glass that they couldn't see him.

"My mom," Mark said. "Last night she was convinced that J.W. was coming to get me. Told me I could have had a better life if she'd played her cards right."

Nicki felt her pulse skip a beat.

"There was some other stuff, too, words that got me to thinking." He glanced down at the ground for a moment, then shrugged. "Never mind. Like my sister said, it's all a bunch of nothing. I don't know why I mentioned it now except I think I'm in shock that I no longer have a job." He turned away.

"You'll get your job back," she reassured him, running to catch up. But as they entered the barn, Nicki's mind reeled. More than once she'd wondered if there was anything to the rumors.

"I sure hope so," Mark said, grabbing his saddle.

"I'll make certain of it."

He swung his saddle across his back. "I'll call you later on."

"All right."

He leaned down and kissed her, and Nicki watched as, a few minutes later, he drove off.

"You'll be lucky if he ever calls you again," a voice said.

Nicki turned on her dad. "You're wrong."

"Am I?" her father asked. "We'll see."

"No," Nicki said. "*You'll* see."

CHAPTER TEN

HE DIDN'T CALL HER that day.

Mark spent all morning and afternoon looking for work, with no success. By the time he returned home he was disappointed and disheartened. In a small town, jobs were hard to come by. That meant going to Cody, the next nearest town, to find work. The prospect of driving nearly an hour each day to earn money made him sick to his stomach, but he had to do whatever it took.

The next day he drove into Cody. Through word of mouth he discovered one of the bigger cattle operations needed some help. Even better, the ranch was located halfway between Markton and Cody, which meant a shorter commute. When Mark pulled into his drive-way he felt a sense of relief. Sure, it was only part-time, but the ranch owner was willing to schedule his hours around his rodeo performances. He'd even been told the job might evolve into a management position.

Nicki was sitting on the front steps.

Mark turned off the ignition and gazed at her for a moment, the joy he felt upon seeing her something he couldn't deny. Damn. What was it about the woman that made him feel like a teenager all over again? He'd been hoping to give her some space. Maybe give her dad a few days to cool off. But all day long he'd wanted to call her. He probably would have, too, if cell service hadn't been so spotty out in the hills.

"Hey, stranger," she said as he climbed from his truck.

He could smell her. Roses. Even from twenty feet away he caught a whiff of it. He'd been dreaming about that unique scent from the moment he'd left her standing in front of her father's house.

"What are you doing here?"

He hadn't meant the words to come out sounding so terse. But, hell, he'd planned to spend some time away from her. Sure, he had every intention of calling her, but hadn't wanted to actually see her.

Hadn't wanted to be tempted by her.

"I was in the neighborhood," she said, standing up to greet him with a smile.

He paused for a moment to gather his wits. She wore blue jeans and a green cotton T-shirt that clung to every curve. She looked so terrific that he couldn't deny he'd missed her.

"Damn," he found himself saying. "I'm glad to see you."

Her green eyes lit up like spring grass in sunlight. "I'm happy to see you, too."

He didn't know why he tried to fight it. He'd adored her from afar for too many years. He just wished the timing was better. And that her dad didn't hate him. And that there wasn't this question of his parentage suddenly looming over his head.

She walked over to him and slipped into his arms.

Mark saw the curtains jerk open. It wasn't dark yet— wouldn't be sunset for a couple more hours—but they had a huge picture window overlooking the front yard.

He saw Janie's face appear in it for a moment. Her brows lifted in surprise before she stepped back out of view.

"Let's go for a walk," he said.

"Sure," Nicki agreed, grabbing his hand.

Mark almost didn't take it, not because he didn't want to, but because he knew his sister was watching and she'd pounce on him the moment he returned, demanding what the heck he was doing with Nicki Sable.

"I thought you were mad at me," she said. "For showing up like this. Unannounced."

"No," he replied, a part of him wondering how they'd gotten to this point, walking hand in hand down the street. He and his family lived on the outskirts of town, away from residential areas with houses built side-by-side. That was one thing Mark had to give his dad credit for. Somehow he'd scrimped and saved until he'd bought the ranch, small as it was compared to a place like the Cottonwood.

But thinking about the Cody family and his father in practically the same breath had Mark's hands clenching.

Nicki must have felt it. "What's wrong?" she asked. He noticed then that when she was worried about something, the skin above the bridge of her nose wrinkled. "Still worried about finding a job?"

"Actually," he said, "that's why I didn't call you today. I think I found something. It's nothing much, but it could turn into a management position if I work hard enough."

"That's *great,* Mark," she said gently. "But I really think whatever you find will be temporary. You'll see. My dad will come around."

Maybe. But he didn't say the word aloud.

"So if it's not that, what has you looking so glum?"

Glum. The word summed up his mood perfectly. "Just thinking."

"About that thing with your mom?"

His gaze shifted to hers in surprise. "Not really." He shook his head. "Okay, I guess in a way I am."

Nicki squeezed his hand. He didn't know how she'd done it, but she'd managed to find a shirt that exactly matched her eyes. It made them appear more green. Or maybe that was compassion he saw lighting her eyes. "If it makes you feel any better, I did some poking around today."

"You did?" he asked, his heart suddenly lurching in his chest.

"I cornered Chet Prater in between customers."

If there was one place in Markton where you were certain to unearth any gossip, Chet's barbershop was it. "And what'd he say?" Mark heard himself ask, even though his whole body tensed the moment the words were out of his mouth.

"He said he'd never heard such a silly thing."

Mark started to breathe again.

"But that his dad had mentioned something to him a few years back, too."

The adrenaline started pumping again.

"Apparently, the rumors stem from the annual rodeo in Cody. Years ago, your mom and J.W. were seen together. Together together—like a couple. This was before your mom was married to Tomas."

"So?" Mark said. "I've been 'seen' at rodeos with plenty of women. It doesn't mean they were together."

"But you're not married."

He stopped suddenly. Nicki nodded. "J.W. was married at the time. It was right after Anne Cody miscarried their first child that your mom and J.W. were seen together. Suffice it to say the timing is suspect. I think that's why people talked. J.W. should have been at home with his grieving wife, not wrapping his arms around another woman."

"They were holding each other?"

"So the story goes," she said, her blond hair blowing around her face in the wind. "Of course, it might have been nothing. Maybe they were just friends. J.W.'s first-born had just died, so maybe she was consoling him."

"Maybe," Mark echoed.

Or maybe not.

"Of course, all of this could be completely wrong. You know how gossip starts. Someone sees something that perhaps they didn't really see. Maybe it was just someone who looked like J.W., you know?"

But there was always a kernel of truth to rumors. That was one thing nobody could deny. Just how much truth, however, was anybody's guess. Mark's mom's mind was too far gone to be deemed reliable, and he refused to ask J.W. about it.

"Honestly, Mark, I don't know what to think. But there's one sure way to find out."

He knew where she was going. Just the same, he found himself asking, "And what's that?"

"Have your blood tested."

Yup. Just as he'd thought. "No," he said. "I'm not going to do a paternity test. In the end it doesn't matter if J.W.'s my dad or not."

She turned to face him. "Mark, I know you better than that."

"What do you mean?"

"This is bugging you. I can tell."

"Maybe. But I'll get over it."

"Will you?"

Honestly, he didn't know. And he didn't understand why he was so fixated on the subject. Except…except maybe he did. There'd been snippets of conversations he'd heard when his parents didn't know he was around. Nothing he could recall exactly, but there'd been looks exchanged, too. Glances passed between them whenever the Cody name came up in conversation.

Or had he imagined them?

"Go to the Cody hospital," she said. "Your dad was treated there, wasn't he? They'd have his blood work on file. You could start with that. Have your blood tested against his."

"No," he said. "If I did that I'd feel…"

Like a jerk. Like he was somehow betraying his father by questioning his paternity. Sure, his dad hadn't been the best father in the world, but that didn't mean he hadn't cared about Mark. And poking around his parentage would make Mark feel as if he were forgetting everything his dad had done for him.

"You'd feel what?" she asked.

He turned to her. "Like a real ass…especially if Janie found out."

Nicki nodded. "What does she say about all this?"

He shrugged. "That it's all nothing. I should just forget about it. Focus on riding in Oklahoma at the end of the month. The purse there is huge. If I win, it's almost a guarantee that I'll make it onto the PRCA's list of top money earners." And into the NFR. But she knew that.

"She has a point."

"I know."

But there was a part of Mark that just couldn't seem

to let it go. What did it all mean? What if it was true? Should he look into it?

He was scared.

Scared that his whole life had been a lie. He couldn't focus on the NFR with such a huge weight on his mind.

Nicki broke his train of thought when she reached up on tiptoe and kissed him, gently at first and then more and more intimately. He could have lost himself in that kiss for hours, but they were standing on the side of a street, out in the open, and he knew Janie was back at the house, no doubt anxious to get over to Dr. Bill's, where they let her help out in the off hours.

"Mark," Nicki murmured.

But he started to pull back, though not before dipping down to suckle the side of her neck. Just a light kiss, nothing too serious, but he was immediately tempted to do more.

"Okay, that's enough," he said, impatient with himself. Edgy about the whole situation. Mark wanted to take Nicki back to his bedroom and kiss her until he forgot himself and all the stress he was under.

"What's the matter?" she asked.

"Nothing," he said quickly. "I just need to get back to the house. My sister volunteers over at Dr. Bill's for a couple of hours each evening. She'll be anxious to leave, and I don't want to hold her up."

"Is your mom that bad off then? Unable to take care of herself?"

"Actually, the problem is she thinks she's okay. She'll still try to cook if you're not watching her. We had to put a stop to that when she forgot to use a fork to turn over some fried chicken. Second-degree burns on all her fingers. And after the doctor wrapped them up, she kept trying to remove all the bandages."

"That's so sad."

"I know. It wasn't much fun. Then there's the water she forgets to turn off. The gas stove she can never quite turn on. I thought the house might explode one day." He pretended to laugh. "It's a full-time job trying to keep her out of trouble."

"Which you split with your sister."

"Somewhat. We hire someone to sit with her in the mornings. My sister gets off work in the early afternoon. Markton General Store has always been good about working around her schedule. Since I work nine to five, I try to take over her care in the evenings, which is why Janie does her part-time work for Dr. Bill then."

"She told me once she wants to be a veterinarian."

He nodded. "One of these days, God willing, she can transfer to vet school. She's done her AA work already. She's working on her bachelor's degree in between work and rodeos. She's one of the hardest working people I know, and I don't doubt for a minute that one day she'll succeed."

"Just like one day you'll be one of the best bull riders in the world."

He tipped his head in dismissal. "Maybe."

"Definitely," she said.

He couldn't help himself; he pulled her into his arms for another kiss. "Let's head back to the house," he said long minutes later.

"Did you want me to make you dinner?"

She had no idea how tempting that sounded. "Maybe another day," he said, stopping before they were in sight of the front window. "For now I should say goodbye."

"Aren't you going to invite me in?"

"Probably not a good idea with my sister there."

"But you said she was leaving."

"Yeah, but my mom's still inside and she gets upset whenever we invite in strangers." That wasn't precisely true; she didn't get out of control or anything, but she did become agitated. "The doctor told us it would be best if we kept visitors to a minimum." Which *was* true, but he'd never let that stop him from inviting friends over before.

"Too bad," Nicki said.

He almost changed his mind when he saw the disappointment on her face. Because that was just it: they weren't *friends*. They were more than that, and it scared the hell out of him, given everything going on in his life. How in the heck could they possibly make this work, between his mom, his new job and, most important of all, his commitment to making the NFR?

"Then I guess this is goodbye." Nicki tilted her face up to him.

"For now," he said gently, because he hated the look of sadness on her face. "I'll see you later this week."

"Promise?" she asked.

"Promise." And at the time, he meant it.

CHAPTER ELEVEN

"YOU'RE HOME EARLY," Janie said.

"I know," Mark replied.

"Did you get fired?" Janie asked.

Mark just shook his head again.

"You did, didn't you?" Janie said. "Because of Nicki."

"Doesn't matter if I did or not. I've found another job."

Janie spun to face him, her braid nearly hitting him in the face. "Where?"

"Just outside of Cody."

"Mark, the gas…"

"I know, I know." He lifted his hands. "It means a little less in our pockets at the end of the week, but we can still make ends meet."

"And what if it doesn't work out?"

"We'll cross that bridge when we come to it."

It was Janie's turn to shake her head. "I hope she's worth it."

"She says I should get my blood tested."

His sister's eyes widened. *"What?"*

"You know, compare it against Dad's blood type."

Janie hooked an arm through his, tugging him into the kitchen as if she was afraid their mother might over-hear them. As if Abigail Hansen might comprehend what was going on around her.

"Mark, don't do this."

"Why not?" he asked, even though five minutes ago he'd half convinced himself to let sleeping dogs lie.

"What does it matter? What does any of this matter? Damn it, Mark."

Something about his sister's attitude had started to alarm him. "Janie, what do you know that you're not telling me?"

He could have sworn she flinched. "What do you mean?"

"You're so vehement. It's not like you."

She took a deep breath, held it for moment before letting it go in a rush. "I'm just worried about you," she said. "First you start freaking out over something Mom said. Then you go and jump into bed with Nicki Sable when you can ill afford to be distracted, and now you're talking about getting your blood tested, all this when you have the weight of making it to the NFR hanging over you. Oh, and let's not forget a new job."

Mark lifted his hat and ran a hand through his hair. She had a point.

"Please," she said. "Don't listen to Nicki."

"Fine," he replied, putting an arm around Janie's shoulders. "I won't."

She leaned back, studying him. She must have been satisfied with what she saw because she reached up and kissed him on the cheek. "Watch yourself, big brother."

"I will," he said.

But as he watched her walk away he knew he'd just lied to her. Now more than ever he was determined to get to the heart of the matter. Something about the look in his sister's eyes worried him. But Janie would never keep a secret from him.

Would she?

HE GOT HIS HANDS on a copy of his dad's blood work the next day. The following morning he had his own blood drawn, but went out of town to do it, as Nicki had suggested. He didn't expect the result to come back right away. The doctor told him it'd take at least a week. So the news that would change his life forever came quickly, and completely out of the blue.

"I need to talk to you," Janie said the moment he entered the house four days later. He'd been out of town, his new boss having sprung an unexpected road trip on him. Mark had had to deliver some calves to Idaho, a trip that had meant limited contact with Nicki. And damn it all to hell, he'd missed her.

"What is it?" he asked.

Janie pointed to the couch beneath the window. It was an overcast day, so a gray glow seeped through the printed curtain fabric. It was Friday. Mark was hoping to run over and see Nicki before Janie had to leave for Dr. Bill's.

"Where's Mom?"

"At the seniors' center," Janie said.

One of the rare times they got a break. The local YMCA offered a special class for seniors with disabilities.

"What's up?" he asked, taking a seat.

"You had your blood drawn."

Mark's heart nearly stopped beating for a moment. "How'd you find out?"

But she looked so dismayed that Mark knew there was more to her reaction than being upset that he'd lied to her.

"What?" he asked quickly. "What'd it say?"

She didn't answer and Mark realized she was on the verge of tears.

"Janie. Tell me. Tell me now."

"I thought it was a bill for Mom, didn't even look to see who it was addressed to, but once I opened it, I should have just burned the damn thing," she said, wiping her eyes. "But I knew you'd just follow up with the hospital. One way or another you'd have gotten to the bottom of it. You're such a stubborn cuss."

"The bottom of *what?*" he all but shouted.

"I'm so sorry, Mark."

"Goddamn it," he said, shooting up from the couch, his heart beating so hard it felt as if it might pop out of his chest. "What did the test say?"

She couldn't look him in the eye. "Dad's blood was type O. Mom's is AB. Yours is AB, too."

"So? What does that mean?" he asked, the words seeming to come from a distance. For the first time in his life he felt as if he might pass out.

Janie shook her head, then met his gaze. "Mark," she said gently, "what that means is that it would be nearly impossible for Tomas Hansen to be your father."

CHAPTER TWELVE

"THAT CAN'T BE RIGHT," Mark said with a shake of his head.

"Trust me, Mark," Janie replied. "You got the answer you were looking for. I just wish you would have told me you were going to do it."

He crossed to the kitchen table and sank into a chair.

"Are you absolutely sure the blood work is right?" he heard himself ask.

"No. I'm not certain about anything," she said, taking a seat next to him. "That's why I didn't want you to do it this way. To be absolutely sure, you'd have to have a DNA test done, because there's a possibility there might be some weird mutation in Dad's blood that the doctor hasn't taken into consideration."

"But do *you* think it's a weird mutation?"

Her expression grew pained. Once again she couldn't look him in the eye. That was such a rare occurrence that it alarmed Mark all the more.

"You don't, do you?"

She nibbled her lip, shook her head. "But you should do a DNA test to be sure."

DNA testing. He scrubbed his face with his hands, the hairs on his arms standing on end. "This feels like a weird dream."

Tears glittered on her lashes again. "Why, oh why, didn't you tell me you were going to do this?"

"Because I didn't think you needed to know," he said.

"I'm your sister, Mark. No matter what that piece of paper says, I'm still your sister."

He reached out to pat her shoulder. "I know that," he said quietly, and was startled to realize his hands shook.

Janie didn't say anything, just sat there.

"How hard is it to get a DNA test done?" he asked, still rubbing her back.

She tipped her head, looking pained. "Simple from your perspective. Not so easy from the dad's perspective. It requires blood. Or a hair sample. Or saliva. Something they can test. And since I know you're going to ask, yes, there's a chance one of the labs might still have some of his blood to test, but it's a long shot. That means you'd have to use one of the other methods."

"Like what?"

She looked even more uncomfortable. "Like scouring the house for one of Dad's hairs. I mean *my* dad's hairs." She blinked, then looked away for a moment. "Damn it, Mark. I wish you would have told me."

He got up from the chair, still feeling a bit light-headed, but not as bad. "I know," he said. "And I'm sorry, but it was something I needed to do for myself. Besides, I honestly didn't think…"

"I know," she said. She looked up, her lashes wet from tears. "Mark…"

"I'm going to need a DNA test."

She started to shake her head, slowly at first, but then faster. "This is going to end in a disaster."

"Will it?" he asked.

It was her turn to stand up. "I truly suspect it will.

But I'll do what I can to help you. I know a college professor who's affiliated with one of the local hospitals. I'll see if he can pull some strings and help to expedite a test."

"Thanks, Janie." He tried to smile. "Maybe we're all worked up over nothing. Maybe there really *is* some kind of genetic mutation. But the truth is, no matter who Tomas Hansen is to me genetically, he's still the man who raised me."

She nodded. "I know."

But she suddenly looked even more sad. Mark went to her, pulled her into his arms.

"I love you, kiddo," he murmured. "Remember, I'm your brother...no matter what."

"I know," she repeated, her words muffled because she said them into his shirt.

"You'll see," he said. "This will all work out."

He just wished he believed his own damn words.

CHAPTER THIRTEEN

HE WASN'T RETURNING her calls.

Nicki tried not to panic. There was a reason for the sudden silence. Maybe Mark had to go out of town again. Perhaps his answering machine was broken. There was a chance he wasn't getting any of her messages.

But deep in the crevices of her soul, Nicki knew something was wrong.

The weekend rolled around. Her father had stock going to the Stampede Days in Lewiston, Idaho, and even though he didn't need her help and told her to stay home, Nicki took matters into her own hands and drove to the event by herself. She knew Mark would be competing there. He'd told her that during one of their phone conversations, back when he'd been speaking to her.

It was a long drive through the mountains of Wyoming and Montana, but Nicki didn't mind. She left before dawn, so that by sunrise she was within sight of the Big Belt Range. The view was stunning when experienced in dawn's early light, and the winding roads kept her on her toes. When she entered the northern tip of Idaho nearly eight hours later, in the Clearwater National Forest, she rolled down the windows and allowed the wind to whip through her hair. For a couple of hours at least she was able to forget her troubles. But eventually the mountains began to give way to rolling hills, and then to Lewis and Clark Valley, where Lewiston sat next to a fat, winding river.

The rodeo grounds were on the outskirts of town. The arena was huge by most standards, with the grandstands five stories tall. This was a relatively small town and the rodeo was one of the premier events of the year. Nicki had trouble finding a parking spot out back where the livestock trailers were parked, so many passenger vehicles were sandwiched in between.

"I thought I told you to stay away."

They were the first words Nicki heard as she slid out of her car, and they almost caused her to curse in frustration. Of all the rotten luck, running into her father the instant she arrived.

"Hey, Dad," she said, turning and pasting a smile on her face. He stood next to a stock trailer, talking to an old cowboy who looked vaguely familiar. "Fancy seeing you here."

"Nicki," he said in a low growl, his face more crimson than usual. "You better not be here to see that good for nothin' Mark Hansen ride."

And what if she was?

The retort was on the tip of her tongue, but she held it in.

"What?" the old cowboy said. "You letting her date rough stock riders these days?"

"Actually," Nicki said, "I haven't talked to Mark in a few days." Which was true. "I'm here to watch Jesse ride." Which was true, too, in a way.

Her words had the desired effect. The bloom in her father's cheeks faded a bit. "Really?" he drawled. Her father was no fool. Suspicion clouded his gaze. "Why didn't you tell me that earlier?"

"Because I thought I might have to work this weekend, and I wasn't sure I could come until you'd already pulled out last night."

Both her father and his friend were silent for a moment. "Long way to drive just to watch a man ride," her dad said.

Nicki let out an inward sigh of frustration. "It's not the first time I've driven a long way to see a rodeo."

"It's the first time you've driven when you could have ridden in a private plane with Jesse."

"I didn't want to impose."

Her dad obviously smelled a rat, and she wasn't surprised. It *was* a long drive, but she *had* driven long distances before, so he couldn't exactly call her a liar.

"Fine," he said, adjusting his hat. "Go on, then, but I hope you know what you're doing."

Which was his way of saying he didn't buy her excuses, not for a minute. Terrific. She'd hear about this later. "See you, Dad," she said with a smile.

Her father turned his back on her.

Double terrific.

In for a penny, in for a pound. The first order of business was to find Mark. She'd deal with the fallout from her dad later.

It was a beautiful day, with low humidity and clear skies. Nicki's spirits lifted as she headed toward the rodeo chutes, where more than a few cowboys smiled in greeting. She was a familiar face to most of them, having grown up among them on the circuit. In fact, the only cowboy to greet her with something resembling a frown was Mark, who she finally found hanging out by the grandstand, to the right of the rodeo chutes. He was watching team roping, and as fate would have it, he glanced in her direction at the exact same moment she spotted him.

He didn't look happy to see her.

Nicki's heart fell.

Sure, she understood he was like most cowboys—tense before a performance. But this was something more. She could tell.

This was something bad.

"Hey, there," she said with a bright smile. She went up and tried to kiss him, but he pulled back before she could get close.

"Hey," he replied, using his black hat to shield his eyes. He did that on purpose, Nicki realized.

"You up in slack?" she asked, trying to soothe her frayed nerves with conversation.

"No," he said. "I'm in the main."

She nodded, her attention momentarily diverted when she heard a familiar name: Dusty Cody. This time of day there was no colorful narration by a professional rodeo commentator. Not even close. Information was kept to a bare minimum, the announcements delivered in a near monotone, sometimes so fast they were hard to follow. Last names of contestants were given, along with the names of those on deck. When a team completed their run, a time was announced, but that was it.

Nicki watched as her friend's brother entered the header box, the bridle on the sorrel horse he rode twinkling in the afternoon sun. She didn't recognize the quarter horse. Probably one he'd "rented" for the day. Team ropers often swapped horses, the owner of the animal getting a portion of the winning purse if the time was good enough.

"Whose horse is that?" she asked Mark, more in an attempt to keep the conversation going than from any real interest.

He shrugged, his eyes focused on Jesse's brother. There was something strange about his expression, and it put Nicki on instant alert.

"Mark," she said softly, "what's wrong?"

But he kept his gaze on the competitors inside the ring. She glanced back, too, in time to see Dusty nod. With a clank and a loud squeak the roping chute opened. A brown-and-white steer ran for the opposite of the ring as if his tail was on fire, but Dusty was on his game, the sorrel horse putting him exactly where he needed to be so that all he had to do was swing once, twice, his rope sailing free on the third twirl. The loop caught on one horn, then the other, and Nicki's breath escaped in a rush as Dusty turned his horse, pulling the calf around so his roping partner—a man Nicki didn't recognize— could catch the heels. He did so in record time, despite Dusty never having ridden with the catch rider before.

"Four-point-one-eight-one," the announcer said. "That's fast time so far, boys. Next up is Burton and Hicks…"

The rest of the words were lost to Nicki because she was busy staring at Mark. The man's jaw was so tense his chin jutted out.

"Mark," she said, clutching his hand before he could pull away again. "What is it?"

He turned to face her at last. "Nothing," he said with a flick of his head, but she noticed he wouldn't look her in the eyes.

"Bull," she said. "Something's up, Mark Hansen." She lowered her voice. "And as someone who's been intimate with you, someone who really cares about you, I think the least you can do is to tell me. Have you decided to break things off with me? If so, just tell me now and I'll gladly walk away."

By now anger had begun to burn inside, so that when he didn't immediately answer, she let go, took a step backward. "Fine," she snapped. "I can take a hint. See you around," she called over her shoulder.

And he let her go.

The frickin' jerk of a man just watched her walk away.

Nicki found herself wiping away tears before she could stop herself.

"Nicki," someone called, "wait up."

Nicki kept on walking. She recognized that voice. Janie, Mark's sister.

But Nicki didn't want to wait up. Even though she and Janie were friends, she wanted to go back to her car. To drive away.

She couldn't believe her father had been right.

"Nicki," Janie said, sliding in front of her. "Look. Don't hate him."

That brought her up short. "You *heard* that?"

"I was standing by the rail, although I'm not surprised you didn't see me. You made a beeline for Mark."

For some reason it was getting harder and harder for Nicki to maintain her composure. She'd always liked Janie a lot, but when the other woman stared at her with so much pity in her eyes it made Nicki feel sick. She didn't want anybody's pity. What she wanted was to beat Mark up with his own cowboy hat.

"Sorry, Janie. I know you love your brother, but right now I think he's a real ass."

"Yes, but he didn't dump you for the reason you think," she said quickly.

"No?"

Janie glanced toward the grandstands, frowned, then hooked an arm through hers. Nicki almost dug in her heels, but felt so raw she didn't know which direction to turn.

"Lord, Nicki," Janie said, when they were a safe distance away. "Heaven knows I have concerns about you and Mark dating."

"Excuse me?"

"*Not* because I don't like you. And quit looking at me like that. You know how I like you. It's just the timing is wrong. I wouldn't have any problem with you and Mark hooking up if it happened after the NFR."

"Why not before?" Nicki asked.

"Because Mark needs to focus, and he's not going to do that with you around. Crap, Nicki, he's been half in love with you for too long for that to happen."

Nick felt herself straighten. "Well, he's got a funny way of showing it."

"I know," his sister said, swiping her brown bangs away from her eyes. She was a pretty woman, and unlike Nicki, she had curves. Nicki had watched more than a few cowboys focus their sights on her, never with any success. She'd heard Janie described as aloof, but that wasn't it at all.

"But you need to cut him some slack," Mark's sister finished. "He's had a bad week."

Despite telling herself that she didn't care, Nicki

found herself asking, "Is it his new job? Is it not working out?"

"No," Janie said, her dark braid flopping over one shoulder as she shook her head. "It's nothing like that, although it sure would have made things easier if your father hadn't gone and fired him like he did."

"I know," Nicki said, her stomach turning when she thought about that again. "I think we were both hoping Dad would change his mind. Now that Mark's..."

Lord, she couldn't even finish her sentence.

He'd broken up with her. Suddenly, she was horribly angry. "Damn it, Janie, your brother just dumped me."

"Did he?" she asked, her eyes instantly filling with compassion. They'd known each other for forever and Nicki didn't doubt Janie felt bad about the situation. "Did he say he didn't want to see you again? Or did he let you walk away because he needs some space?"

Nicki glanced back at Mark. He hadn't even turned to look at them, at least not that she'd noticed. "Is that what he just did?"

Janie rested a hand on her shoulder. "I don't know, Nicki. But he's got a lot on his mind right now. I know he's being an ass, but trust me when I say he has reason to be on edge."

And suddenly Nicki knew.

She clutched Janie's arm. "He had the blood test, didn't he?"

Janie drew back so fast Nicki's hand fell away. "What?" she said. "What blood test?"

"Don't hand me that, Janie. I can tell by your eyes that he did. Good Lord, the rumors are true, aren't they?"

"Nicki—"

But she was turning back to the grandstands. She'd taken only two steps when Janie stopped her. "Nicki, don't. Not right now."

"It *is* true then, isn't it?"

Janie looked truly torn. She even closed her eyes for a moment. "Please," she said, her brown eyes imploring. "Don't add to Mark's stress."

It was the plea she heard in Janie's voice that stopped Nicki. That and the fact that she had no idea what she'd even say to him.

"Give him some time," Janie repeated.

Nicki peered toward the grandstands again. Between the slats of the bleachers she could see Mark's back, and even from a distance she could tell how stressed he was.

"I'll try," she said at last.

BUT IT PROVED to be hard.

The rest of the day she watched him…from a distance. And even if she didn't suspect what was going on she would have known something terrible had happened. She'd seen him tense before a performance, but nothing like he was now. If he didn't get his head screwed on straight he'd end up killing himself during his bull ride.

But an hour later, when someone bumped into him by accident, and Mark turned toward the man looking as if he might rip the poor guy's head off, Nicki decided enough was enough.

"Mark, wait up," she called.

He was storming toward goodness knew where, the man who'd bumped into him staring after him in shock.

"Mark," she ordered, touching his arm.

He stopped suddenly. "I thought you'd left," he snapped.

"Not yet."

He wore a purple button-down—his bull riding shirt, she noted absently. And she could feel the heat of him through the cotton fabric.

"Not once I figured out *why* you're so upset," she added.

"Oh?" he said. "And why's that?"

"I know about your blood work."

She could tell she'd shocked him.

"I was talking to Janie and, well, one thing led to another. I figured it out on my own, by the way, so don't think for a moment your sister betrayed you, because she didn't."

Which was exactly what he *had* been thinking. Nicki could tell from his expression.

"It doesn't matter," he said, stepping around her.

She wouldn't let him. "Mark, I'm so sorry," she whispered. She could tell the situation was tearing him apart, and that went a long way toward soothing the anger she felt toward him. He was lashing out at everyone right now, and she didn't really blame him. Lord, she couldn't imagine suddenly discovering your father might be someone other than the man you grew up with. Her own dad might be difficult at times, but she loved him dearly.

"I honestly don't know what to say," she added, because Mark kept looking away from her, his jaw clenching as he ground his teeth together.

She took a deep breath to collect herself. "Are you certain J.W.'s your father?"

"No," he snapped.

"Then maybe you're worried about nothing."

"I'm not worried about nothing!"

"No?" she asked, trying to peer under his hat. He'd lowered the brim so she couldn't see his eyes. "What makes you say that?"

She didn't think he would answer, but suddenly his jaw relaxed. "Things," she heard him say so softly she thought she might have misheard him. Or that maybe he hadn't meant to say the word out loud.

"What things?" she asked.

He took his time responding again. When he finally faced her, the look in his eyes sent a jab through her heart.

"Little clues here and there," he said.

"Like what?"

He shrugged. "My dad's attitude while growing up. The way he flatly refused to let me test my liver when he was sick. I could have saved his life."

"Yeah, but it wasn't just you he refused, right?" she said. "Your sister was a potential donor, too, wasn't she? So he said no to both of you, maybe because he didn't want you at risk. You know. Put you under the knife to save his life."

Mark was quiet for a moment, but when she finally caught a glimpse of the emotions in his eyes she understood why. He didn't buy any of her excuses. Didn't want to hear any more of her theories. Didn't want to listen to another word she said, because in his heart of hearts, Mark knew Tomas Hansen wasn't his father.

CHAPTER FOURTEEN

"WHAT CAN I DO to help?" Nicki asked.

"Nothing," he said sharply.

"Are you sure?"

He looked away, then turned to her. "Talk to Jesse for me."

"What?"

"Ask him what he knows," he demanded.

"Mark, no. I mean, you know I'll do whatever I can do to help, but I'm not really comfortable talking to Jesse about this. I'm not really comfortable talking to *anyone* about this, except your sister, of course."

"Why not?"

She shrugged. "It's just none of my business. This is between you and the Codys."

"Me and the Codys," he repeated.

She could tell he was getting upset all over again. "Mark, please, don't take this the wrong way—"

"There you are."

They both turned, Nicki resisting the urge to groan when she spotted her father walking toward them.

"I thought you'd gone to see Jesse," he said, the glare he shot Mark about as friendly as snake venom.

"I was…I mean…I was about to, but I ran into Mark on the way."

Which wasn't precisely true, but she had to say *some-*

thing to defuse the situation. Mark was gazing at her with a combination of dismay and indignation. And her father looked about ready to say something derogatory and confrontational. Knowing her dad, whatever he came up with wouldn't be nice. Given Mark's frame of mind, Nicki worried he might say something back. Things would escalate from there.

"Come on," she said to her dad. "Let's go find Jesse now." She turned to Mark. "We can finish this conversation later."

But if she thought she'd done the right thing by agreeing to walk away, she could tell by the look on Mark's face that she hadn't. He was furious. Or maybe he was angry because she refused to spy. Either way, she tried to tell him with her eyes to be patient, that everything—including the question of his paternity—would work itself out. He just needed to stop himself from going off half-cocked.

But all he said was, "Fine, then. See you." He'd turned away before she could say another word. When he walked off, she would bet she could bounce a ball on his back, he looked so tense.

Damn it.

She contemplated going after him, but sensed it would do no good. He needed time to cool down. Time get his head on straight. Lord knew, she was the one who should be angry with him for ignoring her for the past week. Instead he'd somehow managed to turn things around so that *she* felt bad.

Men.

"I know you think you're old enough to know what's good for you," her dad said, obviously following her gaze. He took his hat off and smacked against his thigh.

"But you're wrong, at least where Mark Hansen is concerned."

"Dad—"

"No, no," he said with a lift of his hand. "Just hear me out."

They walked a distance away, toward the bucking chutes, where the sounds of anxious livestock filled the air. Amid the calls of calves and the neighs of horses, her dad said, "It's a dead end, Nicki. No rough stock rider is ever faithful. You ought to know that better than anyone."

She flinched, knowing exactly what her father meant. "Dad. This is nothing like what happened between you and Mom. Don't even go there with me."

"The hell it isn't," he said. "This has everything to do with your mom. Look what happened to her after she ran off with that man."

A bull rider. God. Nicki hated even thinking about it. Granted, it'd happened years and years ago, but Nicki remembered it as if it was yesterday. And, yes, she knew the risks, but with Mark things were…different. That's all she could think. That was all she'd *allow* herself to think.

"And if Mark makes it to the NFR, there'll be even more women hanging off his chaps. Now's the absolute worst time to get involved with a man like that." Her dad pointed over his shoulder.

"I'm not like Mom," Nicki said. Or was she? She'd always been attracted to Mark. For years and years she'd wanted to date him. Was it because she liked the challenge of dating a man in the public spotlight?

"Then steer clear of Mark Hansen."

"He's not like other bull riders. If he was, I wouldn't have come here to see him today."

"So you admit you came here specifically to see Mark?"

She rested a hand on the top rail of a wooden fence. On the other side a half-dozen black steers stared at her mournfully. "Yes," she said. "I did. Okay? I've admitted it. I was chasing after Mark. And, yes, it might have been a huge mistake to get involved with him, but you know what? It's *my* mistake to make. I'm not Mom. I'm not bitterly unhappy. Oh, yes," she said when her father flinched. "I remember how miserable she was before she ran off. And so I think I'm in a better position than most women to know just how crazy it can be to date a rough stock rider. Maybe that's why I stayed away from him all these years. I know, Dad. But there's something between Mark and me. At least I think there is. I can't explain. So, please, leave it be."

Her father crammed his hat down on his head. "I can't do that. Not when I think you're making a mistake."

"What's she making a mistake about?"

Nicki turned. Jesse was walking up behind her.

"You getting into trouble again?" he asked as he came to a halt.

"She's trying to," her father answered. "She wants to date Mark Hansen."

"You're dating Mark?" Jesse asked with a slowly lifted brow, even though he knew well and good she was.

"That's the plan," Nicki said, although after today's event who knew what would happen?

Jesse looked from her to her dad. "This sounds serious."

"It better not be," Jon warned.

"It's *not* serious," Nicki said. Or maybe it was. Whatever. She was fed up with both of them. "I'll talk to you two later." She needed to find Mark. "Good luck today, Jesse," she said with a nod.

But her longtime friend followed her, and her dad, ever the matchmaker, left them alone.

Typical.

Nicki tried to hold on to her patience. And that was the crux of the issue. Her dad had no problems with her and Jesse getting together, something that smacked of a complete double standard, given that Jesse rode bulls, too.

"Seriously, Nicki," Jesse said, hooking his arm through hers. "You should tread carefully."

That did it. "What is it with you men?" she asked. "First my dad, now you. Just what the hell is so wrong with Mark Hansen? He does a pretty good job going toe to toe with you."

Jesse jerked upright, as if her words were a physical blow.

"Is that it?" she asked. "Has he beaten you one too many times, so you have a grudge? Or is it something more? Something deeper?"

Jesse stepped back from her and lifted his hands. His white cowboy hat a stood out against the backdrop of horses and riders, a sea of tan and black. "Jeez," he said. "I'm just worried you might get hurt, that's all. That Mark Hansen doesn't have the best reputation in town."

"Says who?" Nicki demanded, suddenly on edge.

Jesse shrugged. "I don't know. It's just something I've heard. He's a real ladies' man."

"And who told you *that?*" she said, crossing her arms and tapping her foot.

"I don't know," he repeated. "I just seem to recall hearing it."

"And have you heard he might be your half brother, too?"

She regretted the words the moment she said them. Crap. She could tell by the look on Jesse's face that not only had he heard the rumors, but that he was outraged she would dare to bring it up to him.

"Where the hell did you hear that?" he asked.

"Like *you,* I don't recall." To heck with it. She might as well do as Mark asked and feel Jesse out. Maybe that would soothe Mark's ruffled feathers. "But the point is I *have* heard something about it—more than once."

Jesse was shaking his head now, his outrage having faded. "I'll tell you what I told the last person who mentioned that rumor to me—it's *ridiculous.*"

Which was precisely what she'd thought he'd say. "And so is the rumor that Mark is a ladies' man."

He stared down at her for long seconds, his eyes never wavering. "Touché," he said. "I guess you can't believe everything you hear."

"No," she said. But sometimes there was a kernel of truth to *some* of the rumors circulating around town. She didn't say that, however. She had her answer. She'd done as Mark had asked, despite telling him she wouldn't. Jesse didn't know a thing about the situation.

"You sticking around for the dance tonight?"

"Yeah." Although she suspected that might depend on Mark. But first, she needed to go find him. He was angry with her and that would only escalate as the day went on. The man shouldn't be strapping himself to a two-thousand-pound bull with his mind so distracted.

Jesse nodded, and Nicki waved as she turned to move around him.

"Nicki," he said, causing her to draw up. "Just be careful," he told her once their gazes met. "I really would hate to see my best friend get hurt."

"Don't worry. You have nothing to fear." She stepped forward and kissed Jesse on the cheek.

At least she hoped not.

"But thanks for your concern," she said. "I consider you my best friend, too."

CHAPTER FIFTEEN

WHAT THE HELL was Nicki doing, kissing Jesse Cody?

First she refused to speak to the guy about Mark's paternity, then she trotted off with her dad in search of the bastard, and now she was kissing him.

Mark turned and walked off. The more he thought about it, the more angry he got. He was supposed to be concentrating, preparing both mentally and physically for his coming bull ride. Instead he'd done exactly what he'd warned himself *not* to do: he'd let Nicki Sable get into his head.

He headed toward his truck, determined to put some distance between himself and Nicki. To hell with it—with the whole damn situation.

When he found his vehicle, he rested his forearms against the hood, head tucked between them.

Focus.

"Mark," Nicki said softly.

"Damn it!" he shouted, pulling himself upright as he tried to control his temper. "Can't everyone just leave me alone?"

He almost—almost—said he was sorry. There was such a look of hurt in her eyes that it was all he could do not to pull her toward him.

"I talked to Jesse."

He took a step toward her, surprise prompting him to say, "You asked him?"

"I did," she said, crossing her arms in front of her. "For what it's worth, he's heard the rumors, too, but he thinks they're ridiculous, and so now it's time for you to do something for me. Take that paternity test, Mark. Find out what the hell is going on, because until then, I'm keeping my distance."

She turned and started to walk away.

"Nicki," he said, rushing around to stand in her way, "don't go."

"Too late," she said. "I'm gone, and you better not get upset if you see me rooting for Jesse during the bull riding, either, Mark. Whatever the history between you and the Codys, they're still my friends. Annie's like a mom to me. And so if it turns out there's some truth to the rumors that J.W. had an affair, you better tread carefully, Mark Hansen. I won't see any of the Codys hurt."

"No?" he asked.

"No," she repeated. "I will not have you tear that family apart."

"Even if it turns out I'm entitled to a portion of the Cody wealth?"

God knew where the words came from. To be honest, he hadn't given the Codys' vast fortune a serious thought since he'd visited their website.

"Is that what this is about?" she asked. "You want their money?"

"No," he said, taking his hat off and shoving a hand through his hair. And just as quickly as it had come, his temper faded. "Crap, Nicki. I don't know what I want. I just know I'm not myself."

When she started to walk away again, he stopped

her once more. "I'm sorry, I shouldn't be snapping at you. And I don't want you to leave, either. Well, maybe I do. I need to focus, Nicki. You know that. I can't ride a bull and not have my head in the game. Please try to understand."

He took a deep breath, closed the distance between them and pulled her into his arms. She didn't respond. Mark nuzzled her hair with his chin. She tried to wiggle away. He nipped the side of the neck...and all became right with his world. Holding her like this, trying to make her smile, that was what was important, he admitted.

And that scared the hell out of him.

"Stop it," she said.

Mark released her, though his whole body buzzed after touching her. "Forgive me?" he asked.

Her green eyes met his for long seconds. "I'll think about it," she said.

He almost chuckled. "Okay. I suppose I deserve that."

"You do."

He liked that she wasn't afraid to stand up to him. "I'll see you after."

"If you're lucky," she said.

But was it luck that after all these years they'd finally hooked up? He kissed her. Quickly, because he didn't trust himself to do more than give her a quick peck on the cheek. "Maybe we'll both get lucky later on."

"Maybe," she said, but she didn't sound convinced, and that had Mark doubting himself all over again.

Damn it, he thought as he stepped away. He'd better get it together before he got himself hurt.

He just hoped he didn't hurt Nicki again in the process.

FIVE HOURS LATER Nicki watched, heart in her throat, as Mark climbed aboard a bull named Terminator. It wasn't the name of the animal that frightened her. Stock contractors were notorious for handing out monikers meant to send chills through an audience. No. What surprised her was the fact that she was suddenly terrified Mark might get hurt. She'd never felt that way while watching Jesse. Then again, she hadn't slept with Jesse.

"You talked to him, didn't you?"

Nicki was in the spectators' stand, a spot not exactly conducive for observing the rodeo, since it was situated off to the side of the arena, not directly opposite it, like the main grandstands.

"I did," she admitted, peering up the side of the arena to see Mark. "I know you'd rather I kept my distance, but I'm sorry, Janie. I just can't."

And it scared Nicki to death. They'd come so close to breaking up today. If he hadn't apologized earlier…

"Actually," his sister said, "I think I do understand."

They exchanged a glance, and Nicki was relieved to see the compassion in her eyes.

Nicki looked back in the direction of the chutes. Gathered around Mark were a number of cowboys whose job it was to help him mount.

"I'm surprised at how anxious I am," she admitted, as Janie took a seat next to her, her long braid dangling down her back.

"I'm not surprised at all," Janie murmured.

And then they both saw Mark nod. Nicki stood. So did Janie.

The chute opened up.

"Go, Mark!" Janie cried, but her words were lost in the sudden roar of the crowd.

The bull he rode, a speckled gray Brahman, immediately ducked left. Nicki gasped as Mark tipped right. Somehow he managed to hang on.

"Ride, ride, ride!" Janie yelled as the bull began to spin, Mark's free arm swinging in dizzy circles above his head.

"Hang on," Nicki called, although the words were barely audible. God. This was a million times more terrifying than watching Jesse ride. No. A *billion*.

The bull lurched right, changing directions with the speed of a thunderstorm. Mark tipped left this time, his legs beginning to lose purchase.

"Sit up!" Nicki cried.

It was as if he heard her words. With a superhuman effort he managed to jerk himself toward the middle.

"That's it!" Janie said.

The crowd went wild. Nicki shielded her gaze from the sun with her hand. Her fingers trembled as the seconds ticked down. Five. Six. Seven...

The buzzer rang.

"Right on!" Janie screamed. "Good job, Mark!"

Nicki wilted onto the bleacher like an old piece of lettuce. She couldn't have taken it much longer.

"And the score for Mark Hansen," the announcer said. "Seventy-five!"

"Seventy-five?" Janie echoed. "That's all? That bull was switching it up left and right. Mark should have scored *way* higher than that."

Maybe. Maybe not. It was hard to tell from their angle just how hard Mark's bull had bucked, and that was worth half the points. Mark had looked good, however.

"He's going to have to do better than that to beat that damn Jesse Cody," Janie grumbled.

A few minutes later, they saw for themselves that Jesse had a better bull. The moment the chute opened, Jesse was flung forward as the black animal he rode leaped through the air. Miraculously, Jesse stayed on, but not for long. Four seconds later he started to tip right, but unlike Mark, was unable to pull himself up again. Sensing victory, the bull changed direction. That was all it took.

"Oh!" Janie cried. "Too bad."

Which had Nicki glancing at her in confusion. Did she want Jesse to win? Or Mark?

"Two more to go," Janie said. "I don't know if Mark's score will hold up for the whole weekend, but he should win some day money. And, boy, we could sure use an influx of cash."

In the end, his score was the best of the day until a high-stomping, loud-snorting bull charged from the chute with its rider grimly hanging on, the very last competitor. But you wouldn't know Mark had been beaten by the way Janie rooted the guy on.

It struck Nicki then that Janie genuinely enjoyed the sport of bull riding. She didn't seem worked up about her brother's score, but appeared impressed by the other competitor's ride, so much so that she clapped wildly when he was announced as the winner.

"Well, at least we were second today. That's a nice paycheck Mark will be bringing home," she said. "Too bad about Jesse, though."

Something about the woman's words captured Nicki's attention. "Do you like Jesse?" she asked, studying her friend's eyes.

"Well, I... Of course I *like* him. He's my best friend's brother."

But there was more to it than that, Nicki could tell. "Hmm," Nicki drawled teasingly. "Maybe we'll see the two of you at the dance tonight."

"Fat chance," Janie muttered.

Nicki decided to drop it. She'd clearly made Janie uncomfortable. She got up and said, "I'd better go. I'll see you later." She started to head for the exit.

"Nicki," Janie called.

She turned. "Yeah?"

"Take care of my brother."

Nicki smiled. "I'll try."

Her smile faded as she walked away. The question was would Mark *let* her care for him?

CHAPTER SIXTEEN

TAKE CARE OF my brother.

Nicki had every intention of doing exactly that.

"You headed back to your hotel?" Jesse asked.

"Hey, Jesse. Tough luck in the bull riding today. And no, I'm not. Truth is, I didn't book a hotel before I left."

She correctly interpreted the dismayed expression on his face and said, "I know. But I figured, worst case, I could drive to the next town to find something."

Hotel rooms were notoriously difficult to find during a rodeo weekend, even in the current economy. People were looking for cheap entertainment and rodeo appeared to be it. There'd been no drop in ticket sales. None at all.

"You can stay in our rig. Slim drove the truck and trailer over with a few of our horses, but he won't be leaving until tomorrow. We did a day lease on two of our animals for tomorrow's performance. Slim's about to take off to go visit some friends in Twin Falls, so he won't be using it tonight and my brothers and I are all flying home in about an hour, so our trailer will be sitting empty for nearly twenty-four hours."

"Are you certain Slim's not driving back tonight?"

"I'm sure, but I'll tell him you're using it if you're worried."

"Well, I don't want to impose…"

"Nicki, you wouldn't be imposing. It's just sitting empty. My parents are staying at the hotel in town. Actually, you'd be doing us a favor. I hate leaving it unattended. All our tack's in the back, and you know how many trailers have been broken into this year."

"I do," she said, with a sad shake of her head.

"Will you do it?"

"Sure."

"Terrific. Let's go get the keys from Slim."

They walked toward the camper area. Most rodeo competitors had horse trailers with living quarters in the front. The Codys' rig was a deluxe version, with the name of their ranch spelled out in black letters on the side. The diesel truck that pulled the rig was darn near the size of a semi, and the trailer just as tall and wide. Nicki had been inside it a time or two, but not for a while. Long enough that she'd forgotten it looked like a hotel room when you stepped inside, with burnished oak cabinets and tables, a master bedroom at the front, a bathroom to the right. In between was a deluxe kitchen and living room, complete with an entertainment center.

"You want me to activate the sliders? It'll double the size of the living quarters."

"I know," she said. "But honestly, Jesse, all I need is the couch. No need to go to any trouble."

"You sure?" he asked, handing her the key.

"Positive."

"Feel free to use the master bedroom then. Unless, of course, you plan to bring that damn Mark Hansen here."

She stiffened at the mention of his name. Jesse must have seen it.

"What's the matter?" he asked.

She nibbled her lip before answering, "Nothing."

"Bullshit," he said, tipping back his cowboy hat. "What'd that son of a bitch do to you now?"

"*Jesse!* He hasn't done anything to me."

"Then why do you look as dejected as a cattle dog without steers to chase around?"

"It's nothing," she said, hooking an arm through his and steering him toward the front door. "Everything's just peachy. Have a safe flight home. Tell Slim I'll leave the key at the rodeo office."

Jesse allowed himself to be guided to the entrance, but it was obvious he didn't buy her everything's-coming-up-roses speech. He opened the door and stood there for a moment. "He better not hurt you."

"Go," she said, shooing him away. "I don't want you to be late meeting your brothers for your flight home."

"They can wait."

"Go!" she insisted. "I'll see you later."

She was left in silence, wondering if she should fetch her suitcase from her car. Instead she plopped down on the couch in the living room. The cushions were covered in real leather, and as she glanced around she could see why her dad wanted her to marry a Cody. Put simply, they were loaded. But their wealth had never impressed Nicki. What mattered to her was the person inside. Of course, the Codys were some of the nicest people on earth, but she just didn't think of Jesse as more than a friend.

"Nicki!"

She jerked, stunned to hear someone call her name outside the Codys' trailer. She was even more stunned when she saw who it was.

Mark.

"IS THIS WHY YOU wanted to catch up with me later?" Mark asked the moment she opened the door. "So you could spend time with your 'best friend'?"

Nicki stood there for what felt like an eternity, staring down at him, emotions flickering across her face like the payout bars on a slot machine.

"How did you know I was here?"

"Someone saw you." And she ought to have known better than to sneak around behind his back. After getting her text message to meet him at the dance later, he'd asked people if they'd seen her. It had taken only a matter of moments to discover she'd gone off with Jesse Cody.

"Is he in there now?" Mark asked.

She crossed her arms in front of her, and to be honest, her reaction kind of surprised him. She no longer looked stunned. Instead, he would call her expression one of disdain.

"Why don't you check for yourself?" she asked, stepping inside.

He needed no second invitation. But instead of spotting a chagrined Jesse Cody, what he saw was an empty trailer.

"He's gone," she said. "On his way to the airport. I'm keeping an eye on the rig for them, since Slim's not heading back until after the rodeo tomorrow, and he's off staying with friends tonight."

Mark spun back to face her, and in that instant he knew she was telling the truth. He was so instantly relieved that he could no longer deny how deeply he cared for her. God. On his way over he'd been filled with unmistakable rage. And now, looking at her, he could tell *she* was pissed that he'd thought she might be messing around with Jesse. Well, there was only one way to rectify the matter. He pulled her into his arms.

"Hey!" she cried.

If he was honest with himself, he'd admit he'd been dying to do that since the moment he'd spotted her on the rodeo grounds. "I'm an idiot," he said as his head dipped down.

"You are that—" He cut off the rest of her words with his mouth. She was tense in his arms and so he dropped his head to the side of her neck, nibbling the spot he knew would drive her wild. Had it only been a week? It felt like an eternity.

"Mark," she whispered, her whole body going slack.

That was more like it. She wore a button-down shirt and he wasted no time in undoing the first few catches. He owed her an apology, and knew just the way to show her how sorry he was.

"Mark," she gasped as he abandoned the buttons, picking her up and turning so he could set her down on the bed.

"You have no idea how hard it was for me to stay away from you today."

"You could have fooled me."

"I kept telling myself to keep away." When she was reclining on the bedspread, he resumed working on her shirt, after tossing his cowboy hat on the floor. He smelled like leather and livestock, but he didn't think she'd mind. "I needed to focus, but you're like a damn drug." His fingers were shaking, he wanted her so badly.

"Mark," she said yet again.

"Shh," he soothed, leaning down to kiss her. He'd undone her shirt by now, pulled the ends from her jeans. "I'm going to show you how you make me feel."

"If it's anything like the way I feel…" But her words faded away when his palm found her center. His tongue slipped into her mouth at the same time his hand slid into her pants, making Nicki's hips arch. She tasted so good, like peaches and cream. He could have knelt there and lapped up her essence all day, and would have, too, except there was something else he craved the taste of.

He broke off the kiss, slipped a hand beneath her back and undid the catch of her bra. She had beautiful breasts. They were perfectly formed, with dusky-rose nipples he couldn't resist tasting.

"Mmm," she moaned.

She tasted sweet all over, he realized, and it was all he could do not to jerk her pants down, to cover her with his body, to *take* her. Possess her in the most primeval way. Here. In the Cody trailer, so that she would never be able to come here again without remembering what they'd done.

His hands slid her pants down before he knew what he was up to.

"Mark," she moaned, "maybe we shouldn't do this here."

"No?" he asked, pressing his palm against her.

She sucked in a deep breath.

"You sure?"

She didn't say anything. He stroked her one more time, and she leaned her head back and groaned.

That was more like it.

He undid his jeans, felt himself spring free. She wore that damn thong underwear, the tiny strands of material making him, if possible, even harder. He had them off her in record time, her thighs parting the instant her legs were free.

He was in too much of a hurry to take his shirt off and ended up almost ripping it off. Her eyes had gone dark. He gently touched her. Mark felt his throat tighten with the effort it took not to groan out loud at the look that came over her face, an expression of complete and utter ecstasy. That they could so quickly reach this point took his breath away.

"Nicki," he said, his voice a groan of frustration because he wanted to plunge into her, "I want to do way more than touch you."

"I know," she said.

He shifted to slowly move atop her.

She met his gaze. Instantly, he went on alert. There was a look in her eyes…but he was too far gone to wonder what it meant. Still, he was helpless to look away as they connected, and Mark took his time even though he trembled with the effort to hold back. Her eyes lost focus for a moment. He nearly shut his own, but he didn't, so that when her gaze became clear again, he was right there with her. It seemed they stared into the depths of each other's soul as he slowly moved in and out of her. They never looked away, never even blinked, it seemed, the two of them flying off to a place where they were the only two people in the world.

He felt her hand press against his cheek, and almost closed his eyes again. Instead, he increased the tempo. She met his every thrust, and still they held one another's gaze. His pleasure began to build and he knew he would climax soon. But not yet, he silently promised her with his eyes. He would wait for her.

He heard a moan, recognized that it came from deep within himself. Her body had begun to tighten around him and he knew she was nearing her own release. He thrust harder. She lifted up to meet him.

Were those tears?

A pool of moisture gathered near the corners of her eyes. She raised her other hand to caress the side of his face, and then she could hold on no more. He saw her eyes close, watched as she tossed her head back, the cry she released matched by his own soul. At last he let himself go, gave in to the urge to shut his own eyes. Still, she held his face between her hands as he thrust and thrust and thrust....

"Mark!"

Her cry of pleasure was all he needed to let loose his own. Her hands dropped to her sides and he pulled her to him at the same time he lost control.

"Nicki," he murmured, holding on to her. But as his heart rate began to slow and his breathing returned to normal, his hands began to shake for another reason.

Dear God, what had just happened?

When they were together it was like...

He shut his eyes, trying to put everything into words. Scary. Exhilarating. Soothing. Such a mass of contradictions that he didn't know what to think.

She nuzzled his neck, her hair tickling his nose. Mark rolled to the side and pulled her close, running his fingers through her silky hair as he tugged the bedspread over them.

"That feels nice," she murmured.

His pulse began to escalate even more. It *did* feel nice.

Was he in love with her?

He'd been halfway in love with her for most of his

life. It would take only a little nudge to push him over the edge.

"Mark?" she said, when all he did was continue to stroke her hair.

Did he love her?

"Mark?" she said again, tipping her head to look at him. "What's wrong?"

But whatever he'd been about to say was preempted by a knock on the door. Not just a knock, but a battering ram.

"Nicki Sable, you better get your damn ass out here."

They both jerked upright. The blanket slid down from Mark's shoulders.

"Holy—"

Nicki's words were cut off by another bang.

"You better get it," Mark said, reaching for his pants. "If you don't, your father's going to break down the damn door."

CHAPTER SEVENTEEN

"YOU SON OF a bitch."

Nicki winced as her father barged into the trailer. She almost tripped when forced to take a step backward.

"I didn't want to believe it when Hank Summers told me *he* was with you."

How in the hell had Hank spotted them? Damn the small-town world of rodeos.

"Dad," Nicki said, slipping between the two men. Her father seemed ready to lunge for Mark's throat. "Calm down."

"And you," he said, turning on her. "I can't believe you slept with him again."

It was her turn to flush crimson.

"Mr. Sable," Mark interjected. He'd managed to get his pants on, but his hair was mussed, his chest bare. "You don't need to worry about your daughter—"

"Get out of here," her father yelled, pointing toward the door.

"Dad—"

"No," Mark said, crossing his arms.

"I mean it, Hansen, get out."

"Or what?" he challenged.

"You think I don't know about your new job in Cody?" the older man said, his voice so menacing that Nicki reached out and touched his arm. He drew away from her. "I know every rancher within five hundred miles."

"So?" Mark said.

"Don't bother reporting to work on Monday. I've already called your new boss and told him what a lying, cheating piece of work you are."

"Dad!" Nicki said, sliding in front of him. "That's enough."

"Oh, no," her father said. "I'm not even close to being done. You think you're worthy of my daughter? Think again. You'll never be good enough to kiss the heels of her shoes."

"All right, that's enough," she cried.

"No," Mark said, thrusting his jaw forward. "Let him finish."

"Mark," Nicki implored.

"She deserves the best," Jonathan stated. "And you're not it. Not even if you win the NFR. Not if you win *ten* world titles. You're nothing but a two-bit cowboy whose father was a drunken alcoholic."

Silence fell. Nicki felt her temples begin to throb.

"Oh, Dad," she said softly. "How could you say such a thing?"

Why did he hate Mark so much?

"Get your shoes, Nicki, you're coming home with me."

"No, I'm not," she said, and it was her turn to cross her arms in front of her. "I'm staying with Mark."

"Go," Mark said, not even looking at her. He was engaged in a battle of wills with her father, one waged with their eyes.

"No," Nicki repeated. "I am not leaving. I'm not

doing anything either of you want me to do. Damn you both. Why do you *do* this to each other?"

"I haven't done a thing," Mark said. "My only sin is daring to think I was good enough to date Jonathan Sable's daughter."

"You *are* good enough," Nicki exclaimed.

"No, he's not," Jonathan insisted.

"That does it," she said. "Out."

"No," her dad snapped back.

"Out!" she cried. "Or I will never speak to you again. I mean it, Dad. Leave Mark alone or I'm packing my stuff and moving out of the house the minute I return."

"You wouldn't dare."

For the first time in her life Nicki found herself threatening her father. "Watch me," she said softly.

She grabbed his arm and tried to tug him toward the door. Once again he pulled away from her. "We're not through here, Hansen," he called back to Mark.

"Yes, you are," Nicki growled.

"And good luck finding another job in the state of Wyoming," Jonathan added.

"Stop it!" she ordered, opening the trailer door. "Go."

She didn't think he would respond. He and Mark stared at each other like two bulls in a stock pen, but to her amazement, her dad's shoulders slowly relaxed.

"I'll see you at home," he said to her as he left.

"Fine." She swung the door shut. "Mark," she said, when they were alone again, "I'm so sorry."

"Your old man's an ass," he said, uncrossing his arms.

"I know." She closed the distance between them.

"I mean, who the hell does he think he is?"

"My father," she said gently, trying to slip into his arms. He wouldn't let her. "Mark?"

He turned and picked his shirt up off the floor. "I'm getting out of here."

"No," she said. "You and I are going to discuss this like adults."

"You mean like your father did."

She winced. "He's just being my dad."

Mark found his shirt and pulled it on. "And that entails calling me a worthless piece of crap?"

"He didn't say that."

"He might as well have," Mark said, slipping buttons into their respective holes.

"He didn't mean it that way."

"No?" Mark asked. "I bet he meant every word about getting me fired."

She shook her head, feeling more and more miserable by the minute. "He can't do that."

Mark huffed, swooped down and scooped up his socks. "That's what you think."

"I'll talk to him."

"And tell him what? That you're sorry? That you don't care what he thinks? Damn it, Nicki, nothing you say is going to make me worthy of you. Don't you *get* that? *Nothing.*"

"Mark," she said, but the word was a near whisper. Her nose was suddenly clogged. Her eyes burned, it took so much effort to hold back her tears.

"This was a mistake."

Her head snapped up. She hadn't realized she'd looked away. "What do you mean?"

Mark's jaw flexed as he gritted his teeth. "You. Me. Us," he said.

She crossed to his side before she knew what she was doing. "Don't say that."

But he wouldn't touch her, wouldn't even look her in the eye. "There's too much at stake."

"We can work through this together."

"You going to find me a new job?" he asked, his gaze slamming into hers like a bullet.

"No. But I can make some calls."

He turned around. His hat hung from the corner of a cabinet although she had no idea when he'd put it there. "Don't bother," he said, cramming the thing on his head. "I can take care of myself."

"Damn it, Mark," she said, stepping in front of him. "Don't you dare walk away from me."

"Tell your father he's won."

"No," she said, even more emphatically.

Mark brushed past her, although she saw him hesitate by the door. "Goodbye, Nicki."

CHAPTER EIGHTEEN

She cried all night.

Why she didn't just leave for home, Nicki didn't know, except she didn't want to see her father. She didn't know how she could ever talk to him again after the horrible things he'd said to Mark. And that made her upset all over again. Why hadn't Mark stood by her side? Why had he left?

"You okay?"

Nicki gasped. She hadn't even heard the trailer door open.

"I knocked a few times," Anne Cody said, her silver bob set aglow by the early morning light. "But when you didn't answer, I got a little worried. Your dad asked me to check on you this morning."

"Well, you can tell him I'm fine," Nicki lied.

Anne came into the trailer, her blue eyes full of concern. "You don't look fine. Your dad said something about a fight."

Nicki resisted the urge to hide her face in her hands. She sat up on the couch, and Anne sat next to her.

"I'm just a little blue today. That's all," Nicki told her, responding to the question in her eyes.

"About what?" the older woman asked.

Anne Cody was the closest thing to a mother Nicki had, and she hated to lie. "Just things." Nicki picked up a leather pillow and hugged it to her. It had brown suede fringe that felt soft to the touch.

"Did you have a fight with your boyfriend?"

"What makes you say that?" Nicki asked.

"You have the look of a woman scorned and, *trust* me, I know what that's like."

"You do?"

Anne tipped her head so that her turquoise earrings caught the light from the window behind them. "Most women have been in your shoes once or twice before."

Nicki couldn't hold back the tears anymore. "He hurt me."

Anne's eyes grew soft. "I know. But you'll get over it."

"I will?" Nicki asked.

"You will."

"But it's all my dad's fault. He said some horrible things last night."

"Nicki, your father loves you."

"He has a funny way of showing it."

"Sometimes men do silly things. If your father disapproves of the man you're dating, I'm sure he has his reasons."

"But he likes Mark. I know he does. Mark worked for him for years."

"Mark Hansen?"

Nicki nodded.

Anne nibbled her bottom lip for a moment, the oddest look coming into her eyes. "Oh," she said softly. "Well, I'm sure your father only has your best interest at heart."

She stood up so suddenly Nicki drew back in surprise. "I better go see where they are with slack."

"Slack," Nicki echoed. "Yeah. I forgot there was another performance today."

"Some of our horses will be in the main event."

"I know. Jesse told me."

"Yes, well, I don't want to miss that." She placed a hand against Nicki's cheek, her three-carat marquise diamond flashing prisms of light. She studied her face so intently Nicki wondered if she'd missed something. "Take care of yourself, Nicki. Things will work out... if they're meant to."

"DAMN IT," NICKI SAID a week later. She was supposed to go into town and get her hair cut, but a glance at her watch showed her she was already fifteen minutes late.

She paused for a moment in the lobby of her office building. Outside, beyond the glass doors, hardly any cars remained in the Spurling Natural Gas parking lot. Everyone appeared to have left hours ago. Not surprising, since it was the weekend. Most people had someplace to go or something to do—unlike her.

She pushed on the door with more force than necessary.

"Nicki."

And there he was, the man she'd been thinking of incessantly since the weekend before. The man who'd broken up with her and left her crying in a trailer. Who'd driven a wedge between her and her father, despite the fact that Jonathan Sable had repeated his apologies over and over again. Nicki had made him promise he wouldn't call Mark's new boss and get him fired. As far as she knew, her father had kept his word.

"What are you doing here?" she said.

Mark stood near the walkway that stretched along the front of the three-story building, beneath the shade of a tree.

He looked terrible.

"I wanted to talk to you," he said.

He wore his black cowboy hat, but it didn't shield him from her gaze. She could see his bloodshot eyes. His ashen face. His tense jaw.

"Oh, yeah?" she asked, forcing herself not to run up to him and rest a consoling hand on his arm. He'd *broken up* with her. Sure, her father was partly to blame, but Mark could have stuck by her side…if he'd really wanted to.

"It's about my dad."

And she knew in an instant where this was going, felt her own heart race in anticipation of his words.

"I found a letter," he admitted.

"A letter?"

"In her jewelry box, stamped Return to Sender. It was addressed to J. W. Cody."

Holy crap. "Did you open it?"

He didn't reply right away. "Yes."

"What did it say?"

"Nothing much. My mom wanted to meet…to discuss *things*. She didn't mention what things, but I would think that's pretty obvious."

And the knowledge had shocked him. He didn't say the words out loud, but Nicki knew he was thinking them.

She almost went to him then. Almost… "What are you going to do?"

He shrugged. "I don't know. Live my life. Act as if nothing is wrong."

"Do you think you can do that?"

"I don't know," he repeated. "Maybe."

"Does Janie know about the letter?"

Mark took another breath. It'd gotten harder and harder to breathe. "No. Maybe. Heck. I don't know."

"Do you think you should tell her?"

He felt his eyes widen. "Are you kidding? Elly's always been a good friend to Janie. Heck, Elly's sort of like a little sister to me. I don't think I have it in me to maybe mess things up with Elly, or to tear the Cody family apart."

He watched as Nicki's face softened, the tension that'd been in her eyes fading. "No, you don't, do you?"

He shook his head.

"Even though you have so much to gain by claiming your birthright?"

"I don't care about the Cody wealth."

She smiled, a beautiful, blinding smile that had Mark staring down at her in wonder. She had the most extraordinary face.

Why had he let her father chase him away?

Because you're terrified of how she makes you feel.

When he'd found that letter, she was the first person he'd thought of telling. Staying away from her had been damn near impossible, and he'd found himself in front of her workplace before he'd known what he was doing.

"You're a remarkable man, Mark Hansen."

"Not really. I walked away from you."

He heard her breath catch, saw her hands clench, knew he'd hurt her terribly, wondered what to do about it.

"Have dinner with me?" he asked.

"Mark—"

"I want you, Nicki. I know your dad disapproves, but I don't give a crap. You're the one person on this earth

who knows what I'm going through. I don't have anyone else I can talk to about this. It's driving me crazy."

"You hurt me," she said, her eyes pooling with tears.

"I know, and I'm so sorry."

She looked away. He closed the distance between
them. "Dinner?" he asked again, daring to touch her.
She didn't pull back. "Please?"

"Just dinner," she said.

He would take what he could get.

THEY ENDED UP in bed together. Nicki told herself to resist.
But one touch led to another and then another, although
she wasn't really surprised. Every time she was around
Mark she couldn't keep her hands off him. They were
like the moon and the tides, connected somehow. And
just like a wave, she could feel her emotions building and
building. She tried to fight it, oh, how she tried. He'd hurt
her when he'd left her standing in that trailer all alone.
And yet she understood why he'd done it. Knew that deep
inside he didn't feel worthy of her. If she really wanted
to make this work it was up to her to prove him wrong.

She was following her heart.

"I'm falling in love with you, Nicki, in case you
hadn't noticed."

She felt her breath catch. They were lying in bed together, her head on his chest, his voice a deep rumble
beneath her ear.

"I know," she whispered, meeting his gaze. "I feel
the same way."

"Do you?" he asked, with such a priceless look of
wonder she could only smile.

"I do," she said softly, scooting up so she could kiss

him. But he wouldn't let things progress. Instead, he held her at bay, forcing her to look him in the eye.

"And do you mind the fact that I have no idea who my father is?"

"No," she said, trying to convey without words that she was surprised he would even ask that. "Why would it matter?"

"In case we have kids."

Okay, that threw her for a loop. Kids? He was thinking kids?

"If we had children there might come a day when knowing who their grandfather is might be important. You know, if they have health issues, or need a medical history?"

"I don't think we have to worry about that." They were a long way from having kids together...weren't they?

"But what if? I've been thinking about it all night," he said, bending so he could kiss her forehead. "Actually, you put the thought in my head." He drew back and smiled. "I can't help but wonder what it might be like to have kids with you. Not right now," he added quickly, obviously noting her surprise. "But maybe one day. And if we were to go down that road, wouldn't it be smart to figure out who my real father is? You know. For sure?"

"And how do you propose to do that?"

"There's only one way I can think of."

She frowned. "How?"

When he didn't answer, she shifted a bit so she could stare him in the eye.

And she knew.

"You want to test J.W.'s DNA, don't you? And you want me to help you do it."

CHAPTER NINETEEN

"HE WON'T EVEN NOTICE," he answered, angling away from her so he could better see her eyes. "Just filch a few hairs. From his hat or something." Although now that he said the words out loud, it sounded like a really bad idea.

"No," she said, with a sharp shake of her head that sent her hair cascading over one shoulder. "I could never do that."

He didn't blame her, and yet found himself asking, "Why not?"

"It would make me feel uncomfortable."

Of course it would. And yet from somewhere came the words, "Is it because of Jesse? Are you worried he might find out?"

"What's that supposed to mean?" she asked, shoving her hair back.

"Never mind," Mark muttered. "Just forget it. I should heed my sister's advice and focus on making my ride at Oklahoma, not who my father may or may not be."

"No," Nicki said. "I want to know what you meant by that."

"It was nothing," he insisted, sliding out of bed. He hadn't meant to goad her about Jesse. What was wrong with him?

"Mark, wait," she said. She was in front of him in an instant, a beige bedcover draped over one shoulder like a Grecian goddess. "You don't seriously think I would put Jesse's feelings over my feelings for you, do you?"

He reached down, picked up his jeans and pulled them on one leg. When he straightened, she was staring at him in concern.

Did he feel that way?

"No," he admitted. "Not really."

She relaxed.

"But it'd be nice to prove my paternity without involving the Codys," he said. "I wasn't asking you to do anything more than pick up a stray strand of hair—if you happened to come across one. But you're right. It's a bad idea. Forget I even mentioned it."

Although something about the whole situation left a bad taste in his mouth. He didn't really blame her for balking at his—all right, he could admit it—unethical method of investigation. But couldn't she have pretended to at least *consider* the idea? That was what stuck in his craw.

"You're upset," she said, her gaze all but pinning him to a wall.

"I'm just tired," he lied. He tried to calm down, even told himself he was overreacting. He would never have expected to go through with such an unscrupulous idea, but still...

"I didn't get much sleep last night," he said with a halfhearted attempt at a smile.

"Neither did I," she stated. "But I'm clearheaded enough to know you're still jealous of Jesse."

"No, I'm not," he said, bending down and picking up his shirt.

Yes, you are.

He silenced the voice. "Look, Nicki," he said, tugging on his boots. "I have to leave for a rodeo in a couple of hours. Maybe we can talk about this later, after I get back."

"Are you coming home tonight?"

That'd been the original plan, but now he wasn't so certain. "Maybe tomorrow. Depends on how I feel."

She thrust her jaw out. Mark could tell she didn't believe for a minute that he wasn't jealous of Jesse, and she was right. To be honest, her father had a point. Mark *wasn't* good enough for Nicki. He'd never be a Cody. Well, maybe he *was* a Cody.

God, he was so confused.

This was exactly the kind of messed-up mind scramble he'd hoped to avoid.

"I'll call you tonight," he told her, frustrated with himself.

"Fine," she said. "Good luck today."

He paused at the door for a moment. "You're welcome to come with me," he offered, suddenly aware that she might be misreading his frustration. He wasn't mad at *her*.

"No, thanks," she said. "The last thing I need is to be seen at a rodeo with you. That'll stir my dad up all over again."

That stung. Mark knew it shouldn't, but he couldn't stop himself from saying, "Sooner or later he's going to have to get used to the idea of us being together."

"I know, and I'm working on it," she said, running a hand through her blond hair. "I got him to back off the idea of getting you fired, didn't I?"

"Only because you threatened to move out and never talk to him again."

"True, but he'll come around."

"Yeah," Mark muttered. "Sure." In Jonathan Sable's eyes, he'd never be good enough for his daughter.

He straightened, wishing she'd stop looking at him like that. As if she was afraid she'd never see him again.

"I'll call you when I get there."

"Okay," she said.

He turned to go, then looked back at her. "I had a great time."

It was the wrong thing to say. He knew it the moment the words left his mouth. It sounded so flippant, like a cheap line.

Sure enough, her eyes cooled, the blanket around her midsection slipping a bit. "Yeah," she said. "I had a great time, too."

Terrific. And now she thought he was brushing her off. He'd made a mess of the whole thing.

"I'll call you," he said, stepping forward and caressing her face with his hand.

She didn't jerk away, but might as well have. "If you say so."

He almost shook his head, almost told her he was sorry he'd upset her. Instead he bent and kissed her nose. She didn't move. Next he kissed her cheek. She held herself still. He went for her ear then.

She tried to move away.

He held her close to him, nuzzling her neck.

"Stop it," he heard her say, but he was almost positive he heard laughter in her voice.

That was better.

Sure enough, when he looked into her eyes again, he could tell they'd softened. "I'll miss you," he said gently.

"You better," she said right back.

He almost smiled. "I will."

But as he walked out to his truck, he wondered if dating Nicki was a huge mistake.

SHE WANTED TO kill him.

Well, maybe not kill him, but she wanted to conk him over the head. Maybe that would knock some sense into him.

But as Nicki sat on the edge of the bed, with Mark's truck engine cranking to life outside, she wondered why she felt so disappointed. It wasn't as if he was pushing her to do anything. He'd even admitted that his "idea" was a bad one. So what was she upset about?

He was asking her to take sides.

That was what it felt like. No matter that he'd backtracked and reneged on his request, he'd still put the idea out there. And then, later, when he'd implied she didn't want to do it because of her friendship with Jesse.

Nicki pressed her lips together.

He was jealous.

A half hour later her temper had settled down. When the cloud of anger dissipated she could sort of understand his request. But there was one thing she *didn't* get, and for that she would have to go see Mark's sister.

Later that afternoon, Nicki pulled into the Hansens' driveway.

Janie was obviously surprised to see her arrive on her doorstep, but she was quick to regain her wits. "Hey, Nicki. What are you doing here?"

Nicki glanced past her. "May I come in?"

Janie seemed to hesitate for a moment, but in the end moved out of her way. "Of course."

Nicki glanced around for Mark's mom, but the woman must have been asleep or something.

"She's at the seniors' center," Janie said. "It's bingo night. They come and pick her up for free."

So they were alone. That was probably a good thing.

"Did Mark leave for the rodeo?" Of course he had. Nicki had timed her arrival so that she would miss him.

"Yeah. He did," Janie said. "Have a seat." She motioned toward the kitchen table.

Nicki looked around. She'd been to the Hansen house before, usually when she and Elly went to pick Janie up for a girls' night out, but she was always so surprised at how feminine it was. The place was really quaint with its rose-colored drapes and the pretty floral border around the kitchen walls.

"What's up?" Janie asked.

Nicki took a deep breath, figuring there was no better way to broach the subject than to just spit out the words. "How long have you known Mark was J.W.'s son?"

If she'd been hoping for some kind of dramatic denial, she was disappointed. Janie was as cool as a cucumber. "What do you mean?" she asked, taking a seat opposite her.

Nicki had always liked Mark's sister. Anyone who went to school, worked full-time and also managed to squeeze in the occasional rodeo was someone she could admire. Through it all, Janie always managed to smile.

"Janie," Nicki said, "you and I have known each other for a long time. Please don't play dumb. How long have you known?" she repeated.

Mark's sister looked away, which was really all the proof Nicki needed.

"It has to have been for a while," Nicki surmised. "Either that or you were sleeping in your advanced biology class, because it's pretty easy to figure out what blood types are genetically possible given the blood type of the parents. Heck, it's been a while, but even *I* remember how to do a Punnett square. So like I said, either you weren't paying attention or…"

She waited for Janie to say something. It took a moment before she did. "Maybe I never did the chart in class," Janie hedged.

"You're at the local college, right?"

Obviously, she knew where Nicki was going with this. "All right, fine," she said. "I've suspected for almost two years."

"I figured that," Nicki said, leaning back in her chair. "But why haven't you told Mark?"

"Are you kidding?" Janie said. "How do you tell someone you love that you suspect he's really not your brother?"

Nicki nodded. She had a point.

"And then my dad got sick. I figured Mark would find out then. I never expected my father to decline looking into a liver transplant. I thought at first it was because he feared Mark would find out the truth, so I confronted my dad. He told me then that J.W. was Mark's father," Janie said, the look on her face suddenly sad. "He swore me to secrecy."

"And that broke your heart," Nicki said softly.

She nodded. "Mark is all I've ever had. He's the only brother I've ever known. I don't want to lose him. Not now. Not ever."

"I know," Nicki said, clutching Janie's hands.

"But it's been so hard to keep this to myself," she said. "Our mom's Alzheimer's is getting so bad. It's only a matter of time before she forgets how to eat and drink. When that happens, she'll go quickly, and then it'll be just me and Mark. He's all I'll have left in the world."

"Oh, Janie," Nicki said. "I'm so sorry. No one should ever have to watch a loved one die."

Janie squeezed Nicki's hand. "You know firsthand what that's like, too, don't you?"

"I do," Nicki said. "But I was never very close to my mom. She ran off so long ago, and we didn't really have much of a relationship after that."

"And here you are, following in her footsteps, dating a bull rider."

It was Nicki's turn to smile wryly. "You sound like my dad."

Janie shook her head. "Poor Nicki. I can't imagine your dad approves of my brother."

"He'll get used to the idea."

"For your sake, I hope so," she said with a sympathetic smile.

Nicki took a deep breath, worried about how best to phrase her next question. "Janie, how do you feel about Mark proving he's J.W.'s son? Is that something you want?"

She looked away again.

"You don't, do you?" Nicki asked.

Janie shot up from her chair. "I know it's selfish of me, Nicki. I *know* that. I should want what's best for Mark, but honestly, I'm terrified of what will happen should Mark verify he's really a Cody."

"How so?"

"What if they take him away from me?"

The words stunned Nicki into silence.

"I know that sounds horrible. And I know I sound like a selfish brat, but they have so much. So damn much. I love Elly like a sister, but you know what? Every time I'm over there all I can think of is Mark. And how he deserves a portion of their wealth. And how easy it would be for him to handle part of the Cody empire. He's such a great guy. So smart. And then I get angry. It's all I can do not to pounce on J.W. every time I see him, and ask, how could you do that? How could you give up your son?"

"Janie, stop," Nicki said. "We don't even know if he really is Mark's father."

"My father wouldn't lie," Janie admitted morosely. "I just wish this whole thing would go away."

"Mark asked me to spy for him."

Janie jerked around to face her. "He what?"

"Not really spy. Just grab a strand of J.W.'s hair or something. As if it would be that easy."

"You can't be serious."

"I am." Nicki frowned. "And Mark was, too. Well, at first. But then he changed his mind. He seemed to recognize that it was a bad idea."

"It is."

"I know, but then I drove away, and I started to think what if? What if I were to help him? So I'm asking you, Janie, as one of my longtime friends. Should I do this for Mark?"

CHAPTER TWENTY

"I DON'T KNOW," Janie answered honestly.

"If I helped him prove this, he'd be set for life."

"Mark doesn't care about their money."

Nicki smiled. "He said the exact same thing to me not too long ago."

"I'm not surprised," Janie said. "But in the end, it's really not your secret to prove or disprove."

And Nicki knew she was right. "Thanks. That's what I needed to hear. But do me a favor. Don't mention to Mark that I came by."

"As long you don't tell Mark what *I* knew."

"I won't," Nicki said.

"And I really, truly hope things work out between you and Mark."

"I know," Nicki said, giving her a hug.

Nicki shook her head as she left the Hansen household. It was a bad situation all around. But maybe Mark would drop the matter. Maybe this whole thing could be swept under the carpet.

But for how long?

That was the question that kept repeating in her head. If Mark didn't go to the Codys now, what about later? What if it became necessary to approach them at some point in the future as he had said? Wouldn't it be best to do what they could now? Perhaps in a way where nobody but J.W. and Mark had to know?

It was a solution that had her sitting up in bed later that night. Maybe if she acted as mediator... She glanced at the clock. Midnight. She doubted Mark was even up. That meant calling him in the morning, something she was loath to do. But she was tempted to see if *he* would call *her*.

That's just insecurity talking, she told herself.

So she called him, even though she half expected he wouldn't pick up the phone.

"Hello," he said, after only a couple rings.

Her relief was instantaneous. "How was your ride?"

"I didn't make the whistle," he replied, his voice sounding so low and sexy she wished she was with him...wherever he was.

"No?"

"No," he said. "I was a little too distracted by how bad I felt for grilling you over Jesse."

Her whole body went slack. She hadn't realized how tense she was until that moment. "Oh, Mark. I hope that's not true."

She heard him sigh. "It's true. I was an ass and I'm sorry."

She smile into the phone. "Apology accepted."

"Let me take you out to breakfast?"

She found herself nodding, even though he couldn't see it. "You bet."

They agreed to meet at The Sagebrush, a local diner that had been around since the fifties. Located right in the heart of downtown, it blended in with the single-story buildings to the right and left of it. All the businesses on the main street of Markton looked alike: flat storefronts with wood shake roofs and a sidewalk-wide overhang that covered pedestrians. Customers had to park on the street, which sometimes presented a problem, but not this morning. Nicki zipped into a spot right by the Welcome sign.

"Hey," Mark said as he opened her door.

He looked so good.

Those damn jeans he wore clung to every hardened leg muscle. His shirt matched his eyes—coffee-bean brown—even though his black hat shielded them from the sun.

"Hey," she said, taking her keys from the ignition. As she did so, she glanced straight ahead. The Markton gossip mill would be whipped into a frenzy, she noted, because she could see familiar faces in The Sagebrush's window, more than a few of them staring in their direction. Oh, well. In for a penny, in for a pound.

"You look great," he said, pulling her into his arms.

"You do, too," she admitted. He smelled like…she tried to pin down the scent. He smelled like home, she realized, her body coming to life at his touch. What was it about the man that could have her thinking hotel rooms and sweaty sheets within seconds of being in his arms?

"Let's go inside," he said, tugging her toward the entrance. "Before I kiss you and forget about *eating* breakfast."

So he felt it, too? That was good to know, she thought, shooting him a smile.

Moments later they were shown to a booth by a waitress Nicki had gone to school with. Oh, yeah, she thought, word would be all around town by the end of the day, but that was okay. They sat on orange-colored cushions that Nicki knew for a fact were at least twenty years old. There were cracks on the surface from too many rear ends.

"I'll be back to take your order in a minute," Patty said, her blue eyes sweeping over Mark appreciatively. Then again, half the females in town had set their caps for Mark at one time or another.

"Take your time," Nicki answered, refusing to grab Mark's hand in a blatant display of possessiveness.

"I'm glad you called," Mark admitted the moment they were alone.

"Me, too." She examined his face. "Did you get any sleep last night?"

"Hardly any at all."

Patty came back with their coffee, and Mark took a sip the moment he poured some cream into it.

"So what are you going to do?" she asked, her stomach growling. The diner smelled like bacon and eggs. She hadn't eaten much yesterday—too stressed out—but suddenly she was starved.

"I'm going to go see J. W. Cody."

"What?" she gasped, her appetite fading.

"I have to, Nicki. This has to be resolved."

She looked out the window for a moment. Storm clouds gathered in the distance. There might be some thunder and lightning later on. How appropriate.

"When?" she asked.

"Today."

"Today?" she repeated. "Mark, don't you think you should wait a bit? You only learned Tomas wasn't your father on Friday. Maybe if you do a little more research you might find the name of someone else who could be your real dad."

It was a ridiculous thing to say and she knew it, especially given her conversation with Janie. She was the one who'd originally stated that Mark had J.W.'s eyes. Point of fact, she had no doubt Mark was a Cody. But what would J.W. say when confronted?

She didn't want to find out…didn't want *Mark* to find out.

"I want to hear what J.W. has to say before I start pointing a finger at someone else."

Nicki's appetite had disappeared completely. "I see."

"Do you?"

She took a deep breath. "Yes." Because in the end Mark had a right to find out for himself.

"I'm going to go see him after breakfast."

"So soon!"

People were glancing over at them, not surprising, since she kept gasping out words like an overwrought actress.

"The sooner the better," Mark said.

Nicki gulped. "I hope to God you're not making a mistake."

"I hope so, too."

AFTER HE LEFT the restaurant and climbed in his truck, Mark noticed his hands shook as he fumbled with his keys. Nicki had stayed behind, the both of them having hardly touched their food.

Of course, there was the chance that when he made it to Cottonwood Ranch, J.W. wouldn't be there. Mark almost hoped the man *was* away.

As he approached the Codys' place, he encountered an immediate obstacle. The front gate was closed.

He sat outside in his truck for an instant, trying to

figure out what to do. There was a keypad to his left. He decided to punch a button or two, maybe see what happened. His fingers were trembling when he pressed the 0 key. To his shock, someone answered almost immediately.

"Can I help you?" said a man's voice.

J.W.? Mark couldn't tell. "Yeah, hi," he said. "I was hoping to come inside. I'm looking for a cutting horse prospect and I know you guys have a great breeding program here. Sorry, but I don't have an appointment."

There was a pause and then, miracle of miracles, the person said, "Sure. Come on in. I'll have someone show you what we've got."

Mark closed his eyes, relieved that the excuse he'd come up with on the way over had worked. He didn't have to resort to plan B, although what that would have been he had no idea.

The gate took what felt like half an hour to open. He was impatient, fingers drumming the steering wheel. That might be why he gunned it the moment he had enough clearance, his tires chirping as a result. *Calm down.*

He drove for what seemed like forever down a smooth driveway, one with blacktop as dark as night. On either side were white fences, and Mark caught sight of the occasional herd of cows. Hereford pairs, by the looks of it, the newborn babies hanging back from their mother's side. It always amazed Mark how a young calf's hide was so white. He'd long ago figured out that they had yet to acquire the permanent stains that would eventually turn their coats a milky beige.

The road forked. He paused for a moment. A sign guided the way. Main residence to his right, horse barns to his left. For a split second he was tempted to jerk the wheel right. If J.W. was around, he was more than likely at his home, but Mark didn't want to confront the lion in his den. Best to try to lure J.W. to the barn, where Mark could speak to him privately, although how he would manage that, he had no idea.

He turned left.

More white fences guided his way and Mark slowed down for a moment to marvel at the wide expanse of property the Codys owned. Sure, he'd scanned their website, had discovered how big the place was. But the internet didn't do it justice. Acres and acres of rolling green hills surrounded him, with clusters of trees popping up at intervals. He knew the Codys owned something in the neighborhood of six hundred thousand acres. That was a lot of land by anybody's standards, and yet it wasn't until Mark was actually on the property that it really hit home. The Codys weren't just rich, they were *filthy* rich.

Up on a small hill to his right he spotted a massive barn, one that blended into its tree-studded surroundings. There were several other buildings, an outdoor practice ring and an arena, and for a moment he found himself wondering, what if?

What if it turned out J.W. really was his father? What if Mark had been allowed to grow up here? What if he'd been given the same opportunities as the other Cody children? Would he have made the NFR in his twenties? Maybe been a world champion bull rider by now?

Probably.

"Might have been nice," he found himself muttering, stepping on the accelerator. Tomas Hansen hadn't been the worst father, but Mark and Janie had grown up one rung above dirt poor. There were times in Mark's life when he would swear Tomas had taken out his frustration over their financial situation on Mark. His dad had never beaten him to a pulp, but he'd come damn close, especially when he'd been drinking.

Only he wasn't your dad.

That thought alone had him speeding up. If J.W. was his father, he had a right to know.

And by God, he was about to find out.

CHAPTER TWENTY-ONE

HE DROVE STRAIGHT up to the main horse barn, a massive wood-and-glass structure that looked as if it belonged on the pages of *Better Homes & Gardens* rather than a horse magazine.

"Good Lord," he muttered, jerking on the gearshift so hard his truck lurched in response. It looked like a spread owned by a country music star.

And—all right, he could admit—the place took his breath away. The exterior of the barn was covered in knotty pine, with large, multipaned windows set into the sides at odd intervals. It had a green metal roof, or was that the patina on a copper roof? Mark couldn't tell. The roofline looked as if it belonged in Kentucky. Square turrets sprouted up at both ends and the one in the center held an elaborate weathervane, the tip pointing south. Mark glanced in that direction and spotted the dark, rolling clouds he'd seen at breakfast. A storm was coming this way. He could feel the breeze that spun the wrought-iron arrow in his direction.

"You here to look at some horses?"

Mark turned to face the man who'd spoken, surprised to see Dexter Cody coming toward him, his leg still in a brace, crutches under his arms.

Uh-oh.

"Mark. What are you doing here?"

He should have figured something like this might happen. Nicki had told him each one of the Codys ran a portion of the ranch. Mark just hadn't planned on bumping into them.

"Well, I, um…" Damn. He should have planned this better.

Dex glanced toward one of the other outbuildings. "Dusty told me someone was coming to look at prospects."

"That'd be me," Mark said. "Only I'm not really here to look at horses."

"You're not?"

"Why aren't you in bed?" Mark asked, hoping the question would stop him from asking the obvious: Why had Mark lied?

"Doc told me I needed to exercise. Keep my other leg from going bad," Dex said. "Hey, why'd you tell my brother you were here to look at prospects?"

Dang. He should have known he wouldn't be able to distract him. Dex was smart, and one of the coolest customers in the business. "I'm actually here to see your dad." Mark's heart had started to pound. Did Dex know? Had he heard the rumors? "Is your father here?"

"Yes." Dex eyed him for a second. "But why'd you tell Dusty you were here to look at some horses?"

The kid was like a dog with a bone. "I didn't want you guys to know what I'm really here about."

"And what's that?" Dex asked, the wind picking up a strand of his hair and tossing it across his blue eyes.

"It's about my sister," Mark said, although where the lie had come from he had no idea. "I was hoping he might be interested in sponsoring her. You know how it is. She's too proud to ask herself and I didn't want you guys embarrassing her about it in case it came up in conversation."

Dex's face cleared. "Oh. Okay, although you might have to go through my mom for that. She's in charge of money around here."

"Oh, yeah?" Mark asked, trying not to panic. "Well, I guess we'll have to see. I'd still like to shake your father's hand, though, if that's okay. I've never really met the man."

"Sure," Dex said with a nod, hobbling toward him. "Come on into the office. I'll page him from there."

Office. That would explain the windows across the front. Still, Mark had a hard time keeping his mouth shut the closer he got to the barn. It was massive. A showplace. Something that demonstrated the Cody wealth in such a way that you were left to wonder just exactly how rich they were. When they reached the main entrance, two double doors made out of paned glass, Mark paused for a moment. He couldn't help himself. And when he stepped inside he was taken aback. It was a lobby. They had a damn lobby inside their horse barn. Two more double doors separated the lobby and office from the horse facility. He had a brief glimpse of stall fronts that looked more like dog kennels before Dex motioned him forward with the tip of a crutch.

"Have a seat," he said.

This man might be his half brother.

The thought came from out of the blue. Mark all but slumped into the chair to his left, one made out of mahogany and covered in brown-and-white-brindle-striped cowhide.

"Hey, Dad," Dex said, after leaning across a desk

and pressing a button on the phone. "You have some-one here to see you."

The words were broadcast through hidden speakers. Mark could hear them echo in the barn aisle outside.

The phone on Dex's desk buzzed just before Mark heard someone say, "He'll be right there." A woman's voice.

"Thanks, Mom," Dex said. He smiled in Mark's di-rection as he pulled his crutches to his side. "You want something to drink?"

Dex looked nothing like Dusty, since they were fra-ternal twins. If they really were brothers, Mark would be the ugly duckling of the family. Dusty had movie-star good looks. In fact, Dex's twin worked in the movie industry. He supplied horses for films. Of course, with the Cody wealth at his disposal, Dusty didn't really have to work for a living.

None of them did.

"Mark?" Dex repeated. Mark remembered the man had asked him a question.

"Ah, no. No, thanks," he said. *Unless you have a gin and tonic. Or a shot of whiskey.* But he kept his mouth shut.

"Saw you ride the other day," Dex said, wincing a bit as he settled onto the desk. "You just about had that bull covered. Think you'll make it to the NFR?"

"I sure hope so," Mark stated, thinking Dex was as different from Jesse Cody as ocean water was from fresh. There were some similarities, but for the most part the two were different. Dex appeared to be nice.

"I must say, I'm jealous. I wish I had the skill to do what you do. But who knows? Maybe one day I'll make it to the NFR." He patted his leg. "Got to wait until the leg heals, though."

"How's that going?" He'd heard Dex had injured it at a local jackpot. Tough luck.

"Fine," Dex said. "Slow process, but eventually I'll get there."

Where was J.W.?

As if his thoughts had summoned him, Mark caught motion out of the corner of his eyes. When he turned he spotted the great man himself crossing the parking area.

"Here he comes," Dexter said, positioning his crutches before sliding off the desk. "I'll leave the two of you alone."

"Who's here to see me?" Mark heard J.W. inquire.

"Mark Hansen."

Silence. Then, "Where are you going?" J.W. asked.

Mark wished there was a window along the front of the office. When he turned in his seat all he could see was an empty barn aisle.

"Gonna go rest my leg."

"Stay," J.W. ordered.

"Actually," Mark said, getting up from his chair so he could peer out the doorway, "I'd just as soon meet with you alone, if you don't—"

But whatever else he was going to say became lodged in his throat.

He had J.W.'s eyes.

Damn. He really did.

"I *do* mind," J.W. said, seeming to be just as thunderstruck as Mark. "Dex runs the horse business here. Whatever you have to say can be said to him, too."

"I'd rather keep this between you and me, if you don't mind."

"Dad," Dex said, "what's the matter?"

J.W. looked from Mark to his son, and Mark could tell he was debating whether or not to put his foot down. But he must have realized raising a fuss might look strange, so he turned to Mark and said, "Nothing."

Mark resisted the urge to wipe his hands on the front of his jeans. This was it. The moment of truth. He waited for J.W. to take a seat behind the massive oak desk that Dex had sat on earlier. When he'd settled in his chair, he clasped his hands on the desk. Mark took a moment to study the man who he now believed to be his father.

Power. It seemed to ooze from his pores. Money. It was on display, thanks to a heavy silver watch he wore around his left wrist, and the crispness of his clothes. He wore a rust-colored shirt and a beige hat. Mark would bet his last prize winnings that the latter was made of the finest beaver. Probably a 20X hat. Or maybe a 30.

"What can I do for you?" J.W. asked, his booming voice filling the room.

"I know you're my father."

Mark hadn't meant to say the words like that. God knew where'd they come from. But J.W.'s reaction was instantaneous and undeniable. Mark saw him blanch. Saw his eyes widen for a moment. Saw his hands jerk on the desk.

"Excuse me?" he said.

Mark leaned forward, suddenly feeling relieved. If he'd needed proof, he'd just witnessed it. "I said I know you're my father."

"Look, Mr. Hansen, I don't know what makes you think—"

"No," Mark said, shooting up from his chair. "Don't

deny it, *Mr.* Cody," he said, suddenly angry. "I'd have to be downright blind not to know the truth. I have your eyes."

"You do not," J.W. said.

Mark leaned toward him, his fingers splaying across the surface of the desk. "So you're going to deny it."

"I don't know what you're talking about," J.W. said brusquely.

Mark's temper flared like an oxygen-rich fire. "You damn liar," he said. "What do I need to do? Force you to submit to a DNA test?"

J.W. rocked back in his chair. A second later he was standing. "I think this meeting is over—"

"Coward."

Mark watched as the older man very obviously ran through his options on how best to deal with the situation. Mark could see the thoughts whirling through his mind.

"Look, Mark."

So it was Mark *now?*

"I know you've been through a difficult time what with your father dying—"

You're my father. But he didn't say the words aloud.

"—but I resent the fact that you think I might be your father simply because your mother was loose with her morals a few years back."

"My mother…" Mark couldn't finish the sentence. He was so incensed that words failed him. "You think she was *loose?*"

"Of course she was," J.W. said, but Mark could see a bead of sweat forming on the man's forehead. "It was common knowledge."

Mark leaned forward. "Listen, you sanctimonious

son of a bitch, the only stupid thing my mother did was get involved with *you*. Frankly, I'm half tempted to hire a lawyer to force a paternity test just to see you squirm."

But he was already squirming, Mark could tell.

"But you know what?" Mark said. "Forget it. I came here for answers, only I had them the moment I looked into your eyes. You're my father. I know it and you know it. I just wish you had the balls to admit it, too."

Mark turned away.

"Is it money you want? Is that what you're after?"

He started to shake his head.

"Because if it is, it'll be a cold day in hell before you see anything from me."

Slowly, Mark faced him again. He didn't know why the words had his temper flaring again. He couldn't give a shit about the Cody money. And yet he found himself squaring off, boldly staring J.W. in the eyes. "We'll see about that," Mark said.

And he left the office before the rancher could say another word.

CHAPTER TWENTY-TWO

NICKI WAITED WITH bated breath for her phone to ring.

"C'mon, Mark," she murmured. "Call me."

He didn't. Nicki waited two hours before taking matters into her own hands. She called Mark's cell phone and then, when he didn't answer, the Cottonwood Ranch.

"Hello," someone answered. Who it was, though, Nicki had no idea. The Codys employed so many people it could have been anyone.

"Hi," Nicki said. "I was just wondering if someone could tell me if Mark Hansen has left already."

There was a pause on the other end. "Nicki?" the person asked.

"Yeah."

"This is Dex," he said. "And I don't know what's going on around here, but Mark Hansen took off well over an hour ago, a trail of rubber in his wake. My dad's disappeared, too."

"Oh, crap," she muttered.

"What's going on?" Dex asked. "'Cause I have a feeling this doesn't have a thing to do with the Cottonwood Ranch sponsoring Mark's sister."

"Sponsoring who?" Nicki asked, before thinking better of it. "Never mind," she said. "It's nothing to worry about, Dex. Mark and your dad had a...a business deal they were trying to put together." Well, okay, that sounded lame, but it was the best she could do. "I suppose things didn't go well."

"Business deal—"

"Gotta go," she said, cutting him off. "I'll see you at the rodeo this weekend." She hung up before he could say another word.

Damn, damn, damn. If Mark had left mad, that didn't bode well. Without another thought, Nicki headed for her car.

"Where are you going?" her dad asked when she paused at the bottom of the stairwell to scan the entry table for her keys.

"Out," Nicki said.

"To go see that damn Mark Hansen?"

She turned. Her father stood near the entrance to the family room, a monstrously large area done in Western decor. He had had the floral drapes and froufrou couches taken away less than a week after her mom had left them.

"I have absolutely had it with you," Nicki said, catching sight of her keys. She made a dive for them, the metal jingling in her grasp. "You either get used to the idea of my dating Mark Hansen, or I move out this weekend."

"Nicki."

"I mean it, Dad. You're trying to control my life and I won't put up with it." She was stressed out enough as it was without her dad adding to the mix.

"I'm just trying to save you from heartache."

She drew up short and released a sigh of frustration. It was dark outside, far more so than it should be. The storm clouds had finally rolled in.

"So what if he does break my heart?" she asked. "As I recall, you were warned away from Mom by Grandma and Grandpa, and did you listen?"

"No," he said, and even though it'd grown dark in the house, she could still see the anger in his eyes. "And look what it got me."

"A wound as wide as the Grand Canyon," Nicki answered for him, softening her stance a bit. She understood where his bitterness came from even if she didn't like it. "One that's never healed. *That's* why you don't want me near Mark. You think I'm following in dear old Dad's footsteps. But I'm not. And I'm tired of you constantly trying to interfere in my life." She took a deep breath. "It ends now."

Where was Mark?

"Look," she said, closing the distance between them. "I love you, Pops," she said, using the nickname she'd given him years and years ago. And though he was reluctant at first, she managed to slide into his arms. "Trust me to make my own decisions. I'm older and way wiser than you were when you married Mom."

And *that* he couldn't deny. She leaned back, then placed a hand on the side of his face. "I love Mark Hansen."

Her hand dropped to her side.

Holy crap.

But as she looked into her father's eyes, she realized she did. In Mark she'd found a man just like her dad. A man full of honor. Who would always try to do the right thing. And who loved her right back.

"Nicki," her father said, "don't say that. You've only been dating him, what? A week."

She all but snorted. "Longer than that," she said.

"But I've known him my entire life…and I'm not about to give him up."

She saw her father's gaze flicker, as if he was wincing deep inside. "You wouldn't really move out, would you?"

"I would, Dad. If it came right down to it, I would. I'm sorry, 'cause I know that hurts. You're losing Daddy's little girl and I know that stings, but it was bound to happen sooner or later. Trust me when I tell you Mark is a *good* man. Far better than you might ever know." She glanced away for a second. "I wish I could tell you some of the stuff going on in his life right now, but I can't. Yet I promise you he's the best man in the world for me. One day soon I hope you'll see that for yourself."

Her dad didn't say anything, which she supposed was a good thing.

"Fine," he said, stepping back. "Go. I'm gonna take your word that you know what you're doing."

Her smile must have been brilliant. She jumped up on tiptoe, gave him a kiss, then spun away. "You'll see," she called over her shoulder. "This will all work out."

But her smile faded as she headed toward the car. Thunder boomed in the distance. The storm had finally moved in. Was it a portent of things to come?

Why hadn't Mark called?

And where *was* he?

She tried his cell phone again when she got in her car. No answer. No response at the house, either.

"Dang it."

Out of the corner of her eye, she caught a flash of lightning. Ten seconds later she heard thunder. The sky had turned a deeply ominous gray, a few of the clouds almost black.

"To hell with it," she muttered, cranking the engine to life. She was going to his house.

The Hansens lived down a long gravel road, one that left a dirt trail in a vehicle's wake. That was how she originally spotted him. His truck kicked up a rooster tail that was easily visible despite the winds tugging it away. Nicki steered her vehicle toward the center of the road just in case...

Just in case what?

He decided to run, she admitted to herself. Because he wasn't slowing down even though he had to know she was approaching. Finally, he stopped his truck and sat there, waiting.

"Mark," she called as she slipped out of the car, the wind whipping her words away.

He didn't move as she ran toward his truck.

"Where are you going?" she asked, even though she knew he couldn't hear her words. He still hadn't moved. Hadn't even rolled down a window. Hadn't so much as smiled.

"Mark," she said again, trying his door. It opened, but the wind tried to push it closed.

"Leave it shut," she heard him say as she lost her grip on it.

Without a moment's hesitation she ran around the truck, wondering if the idiot would lock the doors on her. Her hair, pulled back into a ponytail, whipped against her cheeks. She shoved it away impatiently. Much to her surprise, he didn't press down the door latch, so she slipped inside the warm interior of his truck just as rain started pouring down.

"You shouldn't leave your car there," he said.

She watched the drops for a moment, each bead of

water landing with a fat plop. "Where were you going?" she asked again.

He didn't respond. The rain began to fall harder. Rhythmic *tink-tink-tinks* turned into a machine gun staccato.

Mark shrugged at last. "My new boss called. Said he has some cattle for me to haul out of state. I'm leaving tonight."

She felt her teeth grind together. "Without saying goodbye?"

"I was going to call," he said, finally—*finally*—meeting her gaze.

She saw guilt in his eyes then. And pain. And a deep cauldron of boiling rage that took her breath away.

"Mark," she said quickly, "what in the hell happened?"

"Nothing," he said, turning away from her. He pulled his cowboy hat down low, as if trying to conceal his face from her eyes.

She licked her lips, tried to think of something to say, something neutral and nonconfrontational that wouldn't upset him.

"He denied everything, didn't he?" she asked.

She saw Mark's Adam's apple bob as he swallowed. Saw his hands clench in his lap. He'd shut off the motor, although when he'd done that she couldn't recall. All she heard was the cacophony of rain.

"What do you think?" he asked, and she could hear anger tinge his voice.

Lightning flashed, and Nicki flinched. "I think he probably said some things he shouldn't have in the process, too."

Mark turned on her as thunder boomed, making

the interior of the truck rattle. "He called my mom a whore," he said when the sound had faded.

Nicki drew back. "He didn't."

"Not in so many words, no," Mark admitted, lifting his hat, smoothing his hair and then jamming the hat back down again. "But he may as well have."

She placed a hand on his arm. Mark's truck had a bench seat so it was an easy matter for her to slide closer to him. "He's just scared," she said.

"Scared of what?" Mark asked. "That I'm going to expose him for the asshole he really is?"

"You're not going to do that," Nicki said softly.

"No?" Mark all but snarled. "Watch me."

"Mark, I know you better than you think. You're just mad. And I don't blame you," she quickly added. "But give the man time. It couldn't have been easy for him to have you show up on his doorstep."

"He's my father, Nicki."

Nicki glanced away for a second, fiddled with her car keys which she suddenly realized she still held. "Are you certain about that?" she asked.

When she met his gaze, she could see the answer in his eyes. J.W.'s eyes.

How had nobody noticed over the years?

She didn't know. Didn't care. Just ached for the man sitting beside her. "What convinced you?"

"I could see it in his eyes," Mark admitted. "Not in the way you think," he added. "Although it was like looking in a damn mirror when I finally stood in front of him."

Nicki nodded.

"It was what I saw in his gaze when he first caught sight of me standing there. I've bumped into him before at rodeos, but I guess I never paid him much attention. This time I was looking...really looking. And what I saw, Nicki. I can't describe it except to say that I know...I absolutely know that the man is fully aware I'm his son."

And deep inside, Nicki knew it, too.

CHAPTER TWENTY-THREE

MARK KNEW HE SHOULD calm down, but he couldn't seem to quell the rage that ran through his body like a seismic shock. His hands shook. His quickened breaths seemed to erupt from his chest. His heart pounded to the point that he could feel every beat.

"So what are you going to do?" Nicki asked.

"I'm going to make him squirm."

She touched his arm again. "Mark, don't."

He turned to face her, concealing little of the wrath he felt. "I'm going to have a lawyer call him up tomorrow. Demand a paternity test. And money. Lots and lots of money."

She gasped. "You can't do that."

"No?" he said, leaning toward her. "Tell me why not?"

"Because if you do, it'll all be exposed. His whole family will find out."

"And what's wrong with that?" he asked, trying—and failing—to keep his temper in check. "Tell me why the hell I should care what his family might go through."

He saw her gaze dim. "Because *I* care," she said softly.

"About that damn Jesse."

"No," she said. "About them all. Jesse's mom, Anne, has been like a mother to me, Mark. When you left me in Idaho, *she* was the one who came by and comforted me. She's *always* been there for me. When my own mom ran off, she was all I had. I can't imagine what this news will do to her. Jesse told me once that she's fragile…mentally, that is, or she was once upon a time. A while back, things got really tough for her. She's been fine ever since, but Jesse still worries about her." She squeezed his arm. "Please, Mark, don't do this to her."

"Fine," he said. "I'll keep it between J.W. and me."

"Can't you just let it go?"

"Let it go?" Mark said, hating the fact that he made her wince, he shouted the words so loudly. "Why the hell should I let it go? For thirty-one years he's ignored me. Thirty-one years, and he's known of my existence the whole time. Did he ever once try to contact me? Did he ever once try to make amends? Did he ever call to check on me? Hell, I wouldn't be surprised if he isn't half the reason my mom lost her mind."

"Mark," Nicki said in a near whisper, "don't say that. Your mom has Alzheimer's. J. W. Cody didn't give her that."

"To hell he didn't," he muttered, knowing he sounded unreasonable and maybe a little insane.

He didn't care.

He just didn't care.

Everything he'd been carrying inside, all the anger he'd felt since first learning J.W. might be his father, came boiling to the surface and spilling out on Nicki.

"They don't know what causes Alzheimer's. Maybe it *is* stress related. Maybe it's brought on by traumatic events. Maybe it's caused by deep emotional pain."

No. That was him experiencing pain.

He gripped the steering wheel, trying to keep his body from shaking.

"Mark," she whispered, trying to slip into his arms.

He wouldn't let her. "Don't," he said. "Don't touch me."

She drew back as if he'd hit her with a lunge whip.

"J. W. Cody should be made to pay, and you're the last person on this earth I would have ever expected to take his side."

"I'm not taking his side," she said. "I'm just trying to make you see reason."

"Like he's been reasonable?" Mark snarled. "I'm sorry, Nicki, but when I do this you're either for it or against it, and if you're against it, you're against me."

She sucked in a breath. Or maybe that was the rain on the window. He couldn't tell. Didn't care.

"Don't say that," she said.

"I mean it," he said, ignoring her words. "Either you stand by my side or it's over between us."

"Mark," she said, the horror she felt upon hearing his words evident in the timbre of her voice. "You don't mean that."

"I do, too," he said, even though a part of him screamed, *No, I don't. I don't mean it at all, Nicki. Stay. Stay by my side.*

Only he couldn't bring himself to say the words. He'd just listened to the man who'd sired him call his mother a whore, and all Nicki could think of was protecting that same man's goddamn family.

"Then I guess this is it," she said. "Again."

He glanced over at her, his jaw so tense it ached. "You do what you have to do."

"My dad was right. You did end up breaking my heart."

"Your choice."

She shook her head, tears falling on her cheeks now. *No. Do not say you're sorry. Do not apologize.* She needed to pick a side. Now. His side. If she loved him, she'd stand beside him, not in his way.

"It is," she said, opening the door.

With the sheerest force of will he stopped himself from reaching for her.

"Goodbye, Mark," she said, sitting there for a moment even though he was positive the rain had to be dousing her right arm.

"I'm going to hire that lawyer, Nicki. If you leave me, that'll be the first thing I do when I get back to town."

"That's up to you," she said as she quickly slipped from the truck—almost as if she was afraid she might change her mind. "Do what you have to do," she said, rain and tears mixing on her face. "Just don't ask me to watch you do it."

"Nicki," he said, the anguish he felt suddenly breaking free, "don't go."

"I have to, Mark," she retorted, her chin tipped up with pride. "I can't stand by and watch you hurt the people I love." He saw her take a deep breath. "Even if one of those people I love is you."

What?

The door slammed. He jumped out before giving it a second's thought. "Nicki, wait!"

She was running toward her car, her head bowed against the rain. He tried to follow, but she was inside and starting up the engine before he could stop her.

"Don't," he told her through the windshield.

I have to, she mouthed, the sobs she'd been holding back breaking free.

"Nicki!"

But she was backing up, and Mark watched as she drove away.

"WHY HAVEN'T YOU answered your cell phone?"

Mark flinched at the words, turning to hang his hat next to the door before facing his sister. "I turned it off," he admitted.

He'd called his new boss, told him he had some unfinished business to attend to, and then shut off his phone. Of course, the excuse had gotten him fired, but Mark didn't care. He couldn't stomach the thought of leaving town, not with everything he had going in his life. And he'd be up in Oklahoma this weekend. Just what he needed. One of the biggest purses of the year and he was a damn emotional wreck.

"Nicki called," his sister announced.

Mark faced her at last. "Oh, yeah?"

"Don't give me that I-have-no-idea-why-she-would-have-called-you look. She told me something had happened today. Something that made you upset. And that she was worried about you, and you were supposed to go on an overnight trip someplace, but she didn't think you should be driving. She wouldn't tell my *why* you were upset, so I've been trying to reach you for hours. Between the two of you I was scared to death."

"Where's Mom?" Mark asked, glancing around.

"I dropped her off at the seniors' center," Janie said, crossing her arms. She had her hair in its ever-present braid, but it looked damp. As if she'd been outside earlier and it hadn't completely dried yet. The rain had stopped, but occasional thunder rumbled off in the distance.

"Why'd you take her there?" he asked. "It's Sunday. We're supposed to have dinner together."

"And don't try to change the subject," she said. "I dropped her off so she wouldn't hear what I have to say to you."

"And what's that?" Mark asked, tempted to cross his arms.

"That you're being an ass," Janie said. "Nicki told me that whatever had you in an uproar, you broke up with her over it. I can only assume this has something to do with the Codys."

His sister had always been the smart one. "I don't want to talk about it."

"You went and saw him, didn't you?"

"Him, who?" Mark asked.

Janie came toward him, her eyes flashing. "You know who." But when he remained quiet she all but shouted, "J. W. Cody."

He shrugged, turning toward his room.

She was in front of him in a flash. "What'd he say?"

He paused a beat before leaning toward her. "None of your business."

"He denied it, didn't he? That's what has you so upset."

And suddenly the fight drained out of him. "Does it really matter?" he asked. "The man's got more money than God. I doubt he'll lose a wink of sleep thinking about whether or not he's really my father."

"Mark."

"Let's just drop it, Janie, okay?"

But she wouldn't let him slip past. "I have a confession to make."

He drew up short.

"I've known for some time now that you're my half brother."

"What!"

"I know about the letter, too. The one Mom wrote to J.W. and he returned unopened."

"Why didn't you tell me?"

Her face crumpled. "Because I was so afraid of losing you," she admitted. "So afraid you'd pick the Cody family over our own."

Mark felt his anger fade away. "I'd never do that."

"No?" she asked, her brown braid falling over one shoulder as she looked him in the eye.

"Of course not."

"Oh, Mark."

He pulled his sister into his arms. And knew in that instant that, despite what he'd told Nicki, he had no intention of pushing the matter with J.W. As far as Mark was concerned, Tomas Hansen was his father. Maybe not genetically, but by thoughts and deeds he'd assumed that right a long time ago. To hell with J.W.

"I'm going to take a shower," Mark said.

"Not until you tell me what you're going to do."

"I'm going to focus on making it to the NFR, Janie. That's what's important right now. To hell with the Cody family."

She nodded, her relief evident.

"Promise me, though, that you won't tell Nicki or Elly."

"Why not?"

"Because it's better this way."

His sister looked torn.

"Promise?" he asked again.

He could see in her eyes the battle being waged. But one thing about Janie, in the end she had a streak of loyalty a mile wide. "If that's what you really want."

"I do."

His sister just shook her head and turned away. "Okay. But I think you're making a mistake. Nicki's probably the only woman in the world who could put up with you. Good thing she loves you."

He huffed. "She has a funny way of showing it."

"She does, Mark. I'm certain of it."

"Then *she* can patch things up with *me*."

"You're such a stubborn ass."

He was. He could admit it. Because no matter how he tried to excuse her actions, it still burned him up that Nicki would take the Codys' side.

NICKI READ JANIE'S text and breathed a sigh of relief. Mark was home. Safe.

So? she asked herself.

She shouldn't care. She was through with the idiot. Somewhere between his house and hers she'd gotten angry. If the man refused to understand how important the Codys were to her, then it would have never worked out.

She just wished her heart hadn't broken when he'd forced her to walk away.

Those were her thoughts as she drove into town later that week on an errand for her father. Markton Feed was situated on the outskirts, close enough to the edge of the city that the ranching community could easily stop by without having to go through town. The single-story brown building had a roof just like the other historic buildings surrounding it. One of those flat-fronted overhangs that looked as if it belonged in the Old West.

Just like the hotel in Dakota Town.

No, Nicki thought as she pulled up in front of the store. She would not think of her first night with Mark. Not now. Not ever. It was over. As much as it killed her to admit it, he wasn't the person she'd thought he was.

With a jerk of the door handle she stepped outside. She'd taken only two steps when she was brought up short by the words, "Hello, Nicki."

Mark.

She didn't need to look up to know, and yet she found her gaze drawn to his eyes. "Mark," she answered. She would not cave in and smile, even though, ridiculous as it might seem, that was what she'd wanted to do when she'd first heard that voice.

They were over. Remember?

"I thought you had to drive a load of cattle to the feedlot," she said.

Jeez, and now you're making conversation with him. What's wrong with you?

She couldn't help herself, because he looked so damn good standing there. The anger that had colored his Cody eyes was gone. He seemed…at peace, she thought. Maybe a little sad.

And worried.

"I quit my job."

"Quit?" she repeated in shock.

"All right, maybe not quit," he amended. "When I explained that I had some stuff to take care of this week my boss didn't like that I couldn't work. So I got fired."

Some stuff to take care of. He meant hiring an attorney, of course. "And how's that 'stuff' going?" she asked. In vain she'd tried to find out, as indirectly as possible, if there was anything going on. That meant talking to Jesse, but her best friend hadn't said a word.

"It's not going," Mark said.

"No?" she asked, surprised.

"I've decided to think about it for a while. To maybe go another route."

"Really? So you're not going to hire an attorney?"

"No," he said. "What would be the point? It's not like I don't already know the truth." He glanced around, lowering his voice. "J.W. is my father. But for whatever reason, probably because of the damage it'd do to his family, he doesn't want to admit it. Okay. Fine. I can understand that. Doesn't make me happy, but if that's the way he wants it to be, I'll respect his wishes."

"Oh, Mark," she said, taking a step toward him.

He retreated the exact same distance. That drew her up short.

"You should have trusted me to do the right thing, Nicki. If you truly loved me. If you had any sense at all of the kind of man I am, you'd have understood it was just anger talking the other day."

"I do know." But did she? Did she really? Had all her father's dire warnings soured her mind? Had she been too quick to jump to conclusions?

"I've got to go," he said, stepping away.

"Mark, wait."

He turned back to her, but she could tell it was reluctantly. "I'm sorry," she said.

He nodded. "See you around, Nicki."

The words made her want to cry. But she would not break down into tears. Not here, at least. Though it was hard. Damn hard. Her hands shook as she went inside, the smells of horse feed and leather instantly filling her nose.

"What'd my brother have to say?"

And now she would have to hold it together in front of Janie. "Nothing," Nicki said quickly.

It was dim inside, the tall shelves filled with animal supplements and horse tack. They kept the light from reaching the floor on certain aisles.

"I was hoping he'd have patched things up with you."

Nicki couldn't take the sympathy she saw in Janie's eyes. It made her want to bury her head in her hands and cry. But her dad had sent her over to pick up some three-way. That meant going over to the refrigeration aisle where they stored the animal vaccinations.

"He barely acknowledged my apology."

"You hurt him," Janie said softly.

"I know," she said, turning away. "And I don't think he can forgive me for it."

"I think he's in love with you," Janie called after her.

Nicki couldn't move. Couldn't turn around. If Janie saw how close she was to tears she'd pull her into her arms, and if that happened Nicki knew she'd lose control.

"Talk to him," his sister urged.

"He won't listen." Nicki lifted her chin before turning to face Janie.

"Don't be silly. Of course he'll listen."

Oh, God. Were those tears falling on her cheeks? Nicki brushed them away.

Janie moved toward her, but she waved her off. "Don't touch me, Janie. If you do, I'll lose it. I swear.

I'll mess up your work shirt, and I'm supposed to be buying vaccines."

"So?" her friend said, tugging her into her arms.

Nicki hugged her back, but didn't break down. Instead she sank into her friends arms, allowing herself to be comforted, thanking the good Lord above for her.

"He's so angry at me," Nicki admitted, sucking in a breath.

"I know. But he'll get over it."

She drew back. "You think?"

"I know."

Someone else came into the store, setting the bell above the door tinkling. Janie pulled away. "Be right there," she called out before trotting off. She came back a second later with a vial of three-way and thrust the tiny bottle in Nicki's direction. "Here."

She actually needed more than one bottle, but Nicki didn't say anything. She just took the glass vial from Janie's hand. "Thanks," she said with a sniff.

"It's on the house."

"No. I can pay for it."

"That's okay," Janie said, patting her shoulder.

"Thanks, Janie."

"He's up in Oklahoma this weekend."

"I know."

"See you there?" Janie asked.

Oklahoma. Mark's big rodeo. The one he had to win.

"I don't know," Nicki said past the tears lodged in her throat. "I don't want to distract him."

"I think he'd be more distracted if you weren't there."

"Really?"

"I do, Nicki. So think about it."

But as Nicki left, she wondered if Janie was right.

Would Mark really want her there? Could he ever for-give her for letting him down?

She pushed on the door with more force than neces-sary. What if he could? Didn't she owe it to him to at least try? He was a good man. She knew that now more than ever. Despite his threats, he hadn't blown the whis-tle. Hadn't been spreading nasty gossip around town. Hadn't done anything but tuck his head down and work hard at making the NFR.

She drew up short out front.

"Oh, Mark. I've been such a fool."

But she said the words to an empty walkway, be-cause Mark was gone.

CHAPTER TWENTY-FOUR

OKLAHOMA CITY. IT WAS one of the biggest rodeos on the circuit and Mark knew he needed to concentrate.

But he couldn't get her off his frickin' mind.

"Mark, you're doing it again," Janie said.

They were outside the Jim Norick State Fair Arena, in an adjoining equestrian complex where the cowboys competing in the timed events were warming up. The place was huge and Mark was feeling way out of his depth. It was his first time at the Oklahoma State Fairgrounds—and the first time in his career where he'd been high enough in the world standings to enter such a competitive event.

Everything—*everything*—hinged on his ride in a couple hours.

"Doing what?" he asked, trying to keep his head down so his little sister couldn't look in his eyes.

"Zoning out on me."

They stood alongside one of the pipe-panel rails, near where team ropers were swinging their lassos with rhythmic *woosh-woosh-woosh* that sang through the air. Mark watched them absently. Or maybe not so absently, because he'd spotted one of the Cody brothers riding around in there.

One of his half brothers.

"You're watching Dusty, aren't you?" Janie asked.

Mark shrugged. He didn't feel like talking.

"Is it hard being around them now?" she pressed.

He should have insisted Janie stay home, but there'd been no keeping her from *this* rodeo. She hadn't brought her horse to ride—the competition was too stiff for her to waste her money on entry fees—but she blended in with the crowd in her black cowboy hat and turquoise shirt.

"Not really," Mark said, watching as Dusty swung his rope, the animal he rode a prime example of what a quarter horse should be. It wore the famous Cottonwood Ranch brand, but it wasn't a patch of bare skin like traditional brands. The Codys applied freeze brands; using cold instead of heat to mark their animals. Mark could see the CR on the horse's right shoulder perfectly.

"Mark, it's okay to be angry. No one blames you for that."

"I'm not angry," he said. "I told you. I don't feel anything."

Except for Nicki. No matter how many times he told himself not to, he kept looking for her.

"Is it Nicki then?"

"Enough," he said quickly. "Stop hounding me." He turned away from the rail pulled his hat down low. "I'm going to go get my rigging bag out of the truck."

"Is it time?" Janie asked, her eyebrows lifted in surprise. She glanced at her watch and Mark knew what she'd see. It wasn't time. He had at least another hour before he was due to ride.

"No, but I want to get a good spot."

The bull riders had been given a room to set up in, one that probably doubled as dressing quarters for rock stars during concerts. It was on the main floor, and Mark had no idea if it'd be crowded in there or not.

Janie's eyes narrowed. She recognized his response for the excuse it was.

"Okay. I guess I'll head on up to the grandstands."

Mark didn't comment, just said, "See you after."

"Mark, wait," she said, tugging on his hand and turning him back. "Good luck."

"Won't need it," he quipped.

"I know," Janie said, her brown eyes full of pride and understanding. "But I'm saying the words just the same." She reached up and kissed him.

It should be Nicki wishing him good luck, Mark thought. Nicki walking with him to get his rigging bag. Damn it all.

He missed her.

He barely remembered going to his truck and jerking his bag from the back of the cab. Would never recall walking into the arena and heading toward the bull riders' dressing room. It was the first time he'd prepped his gear in an indoor facility, so it seemed strange to walk into a room with four white walls. Surprisingly, he wasn't alone. A few of his competitors were already there...including Jesse Cody.

Terrific.

"Mark," the bull rider said.

"Jesse," he answered back, equally deadpan.

The two of them knew what needed to be done. But while Jesse could get away with missing today's ride, Mark could not. He was lower in the world standings.

Because you can't afford to fly to all the big rodeos.

Stop it, he silently ordered. He would not be distracted with a game of what if. Such as, what if J.W.

had claimed Mark as his own? What if he'd been raised as a Cody? What if—

No, he told himself. He would not go there. His life was his own, make it or break it. The Cody money might have helped him get to the NFR a little sooner, if he made it that far, but what it boiled down to was talent.

"Good luck today," he heard himself say.

Jesse turned to him in shock. "Uh, yeah," he said. "You, too."

Mark nodded, then started to unpack his bag.

"You know, Nicki's here."

Mark looked up sharply, but try as he might he saw no animosity in the man's eyes. Jesse wasn't taunting him. He wasn't trying to put him off his game by mentioning the name of the woman he loved.

Yes, loved.

"Oh, yeah?"

Jesse nodded. "Gave her a ride down. All she could talk about was you. I had no idea things had gotten so serious."

In that moment Mark realized he'd been an idiot. A stupid, ridiculous idiot. There wasn't an ounce of jealousy in Jesse Cody's eyes, just the good-natured curiosity of a man who wished his best friend—*Nicki*—well.

"Yeah, well, I'd be a fool not to snatch her up."

"You won't get any arguments from me," Jesse said. "Even if she did spend most of the flight reading me the riot act for all the times I've tried to get under your skin."

"She did?" Mark asked, pulling out his bull rope, the cowbell clanging loudly. Someone had installed hooks on the wall. He stood and hung up his rope.

"Told me if I did that today, she'd never speak to me again."

That sounded like Nicki. She was nothing if not loyal to her friends.

But in this instance, her loyalty was with him. Suddenly, Mark felt about ten feet tall.

"And that I needed to tell you good luck. I mean, *she* wishes you good luck. And while I'm on the subject, I should probably point out that she told me she hopes I land on my butt."

Mark couldn't keep the smile from his face. "That's my girl."

They both smiled, and it was the first time Mark could ever recall grinning in Jesse's direction.

"I'll tell you what," Mark felt compelled to say. "I'll make you a deal. From here on out I'll stay out of your head if you stay out of mine." He held out his hand.

Jesse stared at the extended palm for a moment before saying, "Fine. But you better tell that woman of yours to be nice to me. Next time I'll make her walk."

They shook hands, and was it Mark's imagination or did Jesse stiffen a bit? They were close to each other, probably closer than they'd ever been. Did Jesse see the resemblance? Did he recognize his father's eyes? Mark didn't know, didn't care. He released the man, going back to work.

Nicki was here.

That was all that mattered. Of course, Mark had no idea if she was really here to see him. No idea if she planned on talking to him. Mark didn't care. All that mattered was that Nicki would be in the grandstands. She would watch him ride. And by God, Mark would show her without words that he was the man for her. She might not know it yet, but he planned on telling her that to her face…just as soon as eight seconds were over.

NICKI WANTED TO throw up.

The grandstands were packed, the tight quarters adding to her sense of claustrophobia. Inside the arena a horse galloped toward the last barrel, its rider's blond hair streaming out behind her.

"And that's fast ride, ladies and gentlemen. With a time of seventeen-two-sixty-eight she'll take the first spot, and with only two more riders to go, that just about guarantees Tonya Mason a paycheck."

Nicki covered her face with her hands.

Two more riders to go.

After that bull riding. In approximately five minutes—time enough for the last few riders and for the Dodge Pro Rodeo truck to clear the arena of the barrels.

"You look ready to puke."

Nicki straightened. The Codys had bought an entire box, most of which was empty. J.W. stood near the entrance, his gray head covered by a black hat.

"Hello, Mr. Cody."

He entered the box. "Hope you're not worried about Jesse. He'll be fine."

Nicki glanced around as J.W. took a seat near to her. They were alone. Well, as alone as it was possible to be at a rodeo competition, but nobody was within earshot.

"I'm not worried about Jesse. I'm nervous for Mark."

If she hadn't been watching him closely, she wouldn't have seen his lashes flicker. "I heard the two of you had been dating," he said.

She nodded.

"But I also heard he called things off."

"Actually, I broke up with him," she said. "We got back together again after Idaho, but then something happened and things went south."

"Oh, yeah?" he asked, shifting in his seat. He was a big man, surprisingly fit. Nicki knew for a fact that he routinely bulldogged cows, despite his age.

"And I think you know why," she added.

"Why what?" J.W. asked.

The crowd went wild. Nicki looked down in time to see a rider fly toward the first barrel, her purple shirt dotted by sequins that caught the light.

"Why Mark felt he couldn't see me anymore."

The rider rounded the next barrel, and J.W. shot her a glance. "Why would I know anything about that?"

Nicki waited until the rider on the course was finished, the crowd growing quiet as they waited for the next rider to appear.

"Because he confronted you about being his father."

J.W.'s eyes bored into hers.

"I know all about it, Mr. Cody."

He inhaled sharply before looking toward the arena again, as if he had a hard time meeting her gaze.

"You need to make this right, Mr. Cody."

"Nicki—"

"No, no," she said, lifting her hands in protest. "I don't want to hear another word. This is between you and Mark."

She saw J.W.'s jaw clench. Nicki took pity on him then. "You're a good man, Mr. Cody. I know that. Whatever happened all those years ago, I'm sure it was a mistake. But it's not too late to make amends."

"I'm going to go check on Jesse," he said, shooting up suddenly.

Nicki just nodded goodbye, watching as he all but ran from the box.

"Uh-oh," someone said. Nicki turned and saw Janie outside the box. "That didn't look good."

"He left because I confronted him about Mark."

"You didn't!" Janie said, staring at the older man's retreating back. "What'd he say?"

"I told him that he needed to make it right with Mark."

"I'll be damned," Janie said, her hands clenching the rail in front of her. "Wow." But anything she might have added was preempted by applause. The last rider had ridden into the arena.

"You think he'll get in touch with Mark?" she asked over the sound of cheering.

"I don't know, but I've done what I can from my end."

Janie pulled her gaze away from the arena, a tremulous smile on her face as she leaned over the rail. "Thanks," she said.

Nicki smiled right back. "You're welcome." When she faced forward again the barrel racer had rounded the turn, the audience inside the stadium yelling wildly.

"Seventeen-nine-oh-eight," the announcer called. "Not good enough to be in the money today. Tough break for the Missouri cowgirl…"

But the rest of his words were lost because across the arena Nicki had spotted Mark.

"There he is," Janie said, obviously following the direction of her gaze.

Nicki's hands clenched in her lap. She felt sick all over again. Dear Lord, this was hard. She wasn't afraid for Mark. Well, okay, maybe she was a little. But only a little. What had her stomach curdling was the fear that Mark wouldn't make his ride. That he'd fall off with two seconds to go. Or get left behind in the chutes. Or—

"Relax," Janie said, clasping Nicki's knee. "He's going to do okay."

He was standing on the walkway above the chutes, his gaze scanning the crowd. Inside the arena a silver truck headed toward the barrels. Racing was over. Bull riding next.

"He's trying to find me," Janie said.

Or maybe he was trying to find *her*. Had Jesse delivered Nicki's message? Did Mark know she was rooting for him? Just him. Only him.

She saw his head turn in their direction, saw him jerk upright. Janie waved. Mark's smile could be seen all the way across the arena, and Nicki knew, she just knew, he'd spotted her, not his sister.

"Look, he's waving back."

To her. Nicki felt tears come to her eyes. He was waving to *her*. She was certain of it. She found herself lifting her hand. She had no idea if he understood sign language, or if he could even see her hand from that distance. But that didn't stop her from lowering her two middle fingers and giving him the universal sign of love.

To her surprise he lifted his own hand, his fingers moving until he'd done the same thing right back.

I love you, too.

Janie leaned toward her and whispered in her ear, "Looks like the two of you made up."

"I guess we did," Nicki said with a smile.

Janie's eyes crinkled near the corners, her smile was so big. *"Thank God."*

CHAPTER TWENTY-FIVE

THIS WAS IT, Mark knew, looking away from Nicki for a moment. Make it or break it time.

Get your head in the game, Mark. You have something to prove tonight. Something to show the woman you love.

He was worthy of her love.

Had that been why he'd resisted asking her out? Had he been secretly afraid he wasn't good enough for her?

He had, he admitted. Jonathan Sable had managed to do something very few cowboys could do—psych him out.

But not tonight. Oh, no. Not tonight.

He hardly remembered the last barrel racer completing her pattern. Couldn't recall the bulls being loaded into the chute. He'd gotten an early draw. Second to go. That was good, meant he wouldn't be forced to watch everyone ride. Wouldn't have the added pressure of knowing what he had to score in order to top the leaderboard.

"You need someone to help you pull your rope?"

Jesse. His half brother—strange how easily the words came to mind—stood next to him.

"Sure," Mark said. "If you've got time."

"I don't go until dead last, so I've got all the time in the world."

Mark grimaced. "Tough luck. And, yeah, I'd be grateful for your help."

They waited until Mark's bull had settled into the chute before stringing his rope around its belly. It was not an easy task. Sometimes you could be injured before you even got onboard. Not tonight, however. Tonight things went smoothly. Mark hardly heard the first chute open. Didn't register the roar of the crowd as the bull that'd just been freed bucked off a cowboy less than two seconds into the ride. Mark's bull didn't appear to be paying attention, either. It stared straight ahead, didn't move when the rope was pulled taut around its abdomen, first by Mark, and then, as Mark gingerly settled on its back, by Jesse.

"Tighter," Mark grimly ordered his former rival.

"How's that?" Jesse asked.

"Good," Mark said.

And the world settled into silence. He heard nothing but his own breathing as he wrapped his legs around the bull's sides. Nothing but his own heart as he gave the nod. Nothing but his own grunts as the bull leaped into the air once, twice…three times.

You're off center!

He waited until the bull's next jump before thrusting himself to the left.

Don't slap him.

Mark lifted his free hand higher.

Gonna spin right.

As if the bull heard his thought, the massive beast dipped to the right. Mark lifted his outside leg, showed the judges just how good a rider he was by spurring his bull every chance he got. Inside his head a clock ticked off.

Four seconds.

The bull changed directions. Mark stuck with him.

Five seconds.

Don't blow it. Just ride!

Six seconds.

Show Nicki what you can do.

Seven seconds.

Show J. W. Cody just how well you can ride.

Eight seconds.

Mark let go. He landed on his feet. The crowd roared. He turned, keeping a lookout for the bull. But the giant Brahman was already headed out.

Mark turned and found Nicki.

She stood in the grandstands, her hands covering her cheeks, and if he wasn't mistaken, there were tears in her eyes.

He took off his hat and pointed at her. She started to clap. Slowly at first, then faster and faster.

Mark's smile was ear to ear as he turned back to the chutes.

"And there's your first eight-second ride," he heard the announcer say. "Let's wait a moment for the score… eighty-eight!" the man cried. "Wow. I don't know about you, folks, but I think that's going to be hard to beat."

"Good ride," Mark heard as he climbed over the chute.

Jesse stood there, hat in hand—that silly white hat he wore in honor of the woman he'd once loved.

"Thanks." *Bro.* The word was on the tip of Mark's tongue, but he held it back. "Thanks a lot," he said instead. "Means a lot coming from you."

Jesse clapped him on the back. "Think nothing of it, especially since I'm going to mark a higher ride."

Mark laughed. He sincerely hoped the cowboy did, because Mark knew he would finish in the rodeo. Not many cowboys were capable of beating a score of eighty-eight. One of the things about bull riding was that you were only as good as the bulls you were slated to ride. Mark had drawn one of the best. That meant he would most certainly have one of the top scores.

His spirits were high as he left the chutes behind. He accepted the congratulations of fellow riders on his way out. They knew which way the wind would blow.

He'd made it into the NFR.

Mark paused for a moment, suddenly all emotional. Shit. He was gonna cry like a damn baby if he didn't watch it.

"Congratulations," someone else said.

"Thanks," Mark replied, head down.

He was going to Vegas. Las frickin' Vegas.

Damn it, Mom. I wish you were here to see this.

But his mom wouldn't have had a clue what Mark had just accomplished.

"Good ride."

Mark drew up short. J.W. stood in front of him.

"That was a hard bull to cover," the man added.

It felt as if Mark was in a dream, as if this wasn't real. He was walking out of the rodeo arena after marking an eighty-eight…and accepting congratulations from his father.

Wow.

"Thanks," he said.

J.W. held out his hand. Mark felt the world tip sideways for a moment. Then he was clasping the big man's hand right back. Eyes so like his own softened for a moment. For a second Mark wondered if the burly old cowboy might pull him into his arms. But, no, he wasn't ready to go that far.

Instead J.W. let him go, but he patted Mark on the back on his way by. Mark stared after him, wondering what it all meant.

"That was nice of you."

Mark drew up short, the adrenaline rushing through his veins still causing everything to feel surreal.

"Nicki," he said softly.

He turned toward her without thought, almost jerked her into his arms. Inside the arena another competitor must have been bucked off, because following the sound of cheers he heard groans.

"I was worried you might spit in his face," she admitted, her hair sliding over one shoulder as she tipped her head to look up at him.

"Nah," he said, thinking there could be no other woman in the world as beautiful as she was.

"I'm glad you didn't."

He took a step forward. She did the same. The breath was knocked from him as he pulled her into his arms. "Nicki," he murmured, his lips finding hers before he could stop himself.

She groaned his name, too. At least Mark was pretty certain she did. Nothing else mattered except that she was here. In his arms. At last.

"I love you," he said, drawing back. "I hope you saw me signal that to you before my ride."

"Of course I saw," she said, and Mark was surprised to see tears in her eyes. "Just like you saw me."

"I did," he stated. "Although I felt it here—" he placed a hand over his heart "—before I saw you."

"You got my message then?"

"About wishing me good luck?"

She nodded.

Mark smiled. "Yeah. And I heard you hoped Jesse would fall on his butt."

"Well," she said, "not really. But I figured you'd understand the meaning behind the words."

"That you were choosing me," he said softly.

"It was never about choice," she admitted. "It was about trust."

He drew back a bit. "Trust?"

She nodded again. "You needed to trust that I would stand by your side…no matter what, and no matter who might try to drive a wedge between us."

"Your dad."

Her eyes dimmed for a moment. "I think he's finally coming around."

"I hope so," Mark murmured.

The crowd went wild. Someone had covered their bull. The two of them paused for a moment, listening for the score.

"Seventy-five," the announcer called, sounding as excited as when Mark's score had been posted.

Nicki smiled. "Still in first place."

"But I've already won," Mark said simply.

"Have you?" she asked with a smile.

"You know I have," he answered, closing the distance between them.

"I love you, Mark Hansen," Nicki said, just before their lips connected.

He didn't say it back. Didn't need to. He showed her without words how he felt. And later, when they called him to the arena as this year's winner, Nicki was by his side. He showed her then how he felt, too, in front of thirty thousand people, as he kissed her senseless one more time and then, to the amazement of all, got down on a knee and proposed.

She said yes, much to the crowd's delight.

EPILOGUE

"WHERE IS THAT damn Mark Hansen?"

The two men in the tiny church annex turned toward the voice, and Mark had a hard time keeping a straight face when he saw who stood there.

"I'm here to make sure he makes my Nicki an honest woman."

Mark smiled. The pastor hired to preside over the ceremony eyed the new arrival nervously.

"I'm right here, Mr. Sable," Mark said, glancing down to make sure the white rose in his lapel was pinned on straight. There was only one window in the tiny room, but enough light shone through to tinge his black tux with a gray sheen.

"And a damn good thing, too," his former boss grumbled, his own tuxedo firmly in place.

"Is everything all right?" the pastor asked, clutching his Bible so tightly, his knuckles turned white. Mark wondered if the man worried he might have to beat Jonathan Sable off with the word of God.

"It's fine," Mark said, patting the pastor on the back.

"Well, if we're ready then, I'll just take my place," the bespectacled man said quickly. "You should probably take yours, too. I would imagine the bride will be ready to walk down the aisle any moment now."

The clergyman dashed off, the door of the old church

squeaking as he slipped outside. Mark smiled again, the scent of flowers reaching him where he stood. Today he would marry Nicki.

Mark couldn't keep the smile off his face.

"So you're really going to do it?" Mr. Sable said when they were alone.

Mark made sure to look him right in the eye. "Did you think I wouldn't?"

He was only half kidding. While his future father-in-law hadn't exactly welcomed the news of his little girl's impending nuptials with a shout of glee, he hadn't blustered about it, either.

"No. But I wish you'd wait a little while longer."

They *couldn't* wait.

Nicki was pregnant.

They hadn't shared the news with her father. Not yet. They'd used the excuse that they wanted to get married before the NFR, and Jonathan Sable had seemed to accept that. But Mark wondered if Nicki's father didn't already suspect the impending news. Not that it mattered. Mark was marrying Nicki because she was the only woman he'd ever loved. The fact that she would soon bear him a child was icing on the cake.

"Truth be told, Mr. Sable, I don't think I could have waited another day to make her mine."

Nicki's father nodded, then glanced away for a quick second. "Look, about what happened—"

"Don't say it," Mark interrupted. "There's no need to apologize. I know you had Nicki's best interest at heart, but I hope you realize by now that I do, too."

Jonathan peered out the tiny window to Mark's right for a moment, his lashes lowering. "I do," he said, finally meeting his gaze. "And I'm sorry for making things difficult for you."

Mark smiled. "That's okay, Mr. Sable. I'm sure you'll make it up to me. I expect you to give me my job back and up my salary by a dollar or two once I slip the ring on your daughter's finger." He was only joking, of course, and his former boss seemed to recognize that.

"Actually, I'd be happy to have you back, Mark." And to Mark's complete shock, he held out his hand.

Mark took it, and to his further surprise found himself tugged forward. The hug he received was of the brief variety—almost as if Jonathan was embarrassed by his actions—but it was a start.

"I'll take good care of her," Mark said as he drew back.

"I'm sure you will."

"Excuse me," the church's pianist said, a smile on her ancient face. "The bride is ready."

Mark's heart quickened.

"I'll see you at the altar." Nicki's father made a quick exit.

Ten minutes later, Jonathan Sable handed off his daughter with tears in his eyes. "Treat her right," he said softly, his voice sounding more hoarse than usual.

"You know I will," Mark told him. He glanced at Nicki. "Your dad and I have an understanding. He's allowed to shoot me if I ever mistreat you in any way."

He smiled down at his bride, the sunlight that poured through the church windows on their right and left setting her white gown aglow. She glistened like snow on a winter morning in her strapless dress with pearls and rhinestones across the bodice. Stunning didn't begin to describe her, and it was all Mark could do not to scoop her up in his arms and run out of the church so he could begin the process of peeling that dress off her....

"Someone better shoot *me* if I have to stand in these heels another moment."

They all looked toward Janie, whose light blue dress matched the tiny turquoise earrings she wore, a gift from Nicki. She was Nicki's maid of honor.

"Can we get the show on the road?" Janie asked, much to the amusement of those sitting in the closest pew. The Cody family. It seemed as if half the town had showed up for their shotgun wedding. The only person among the masses who appeared out of sorts was Jesse, but he'd been that way for days—probably because despite what he told everyone else, he really *had* wanted Nicki for himself.

"Come on," Mark said, taking his bride's hand.

And as they turned toward the minister, he squeezed it. She looked up at him then, all the love in the world shining from her eyes. They faced the pastor together, the two of them hand and hand, which was exactly how they faced the rest of their lives...together.

* * * * *

RANCHER AND PROTECTOR

To the lawman who saved our homestead. Chris Ashworth, we couldn't have done it without you. All the words in this book couldn't express how grateful we are.

CHAPTER ONE

"ALL RIGHT, HORSE. We can do this the hard way or the easy way."

Amber Brooks stared at the animal in question, a tiny window placed high in the wall giving her a perfect view of the brown horse as it cocked its head in her direction. The look it gave her clearly indicated disdain.

"Okay, the hard way." Her hands tightened around the nylon strap someone had told her was a halter—although she had no idea how it worked.

"Just go play with a horse," she murmured under her breath, mimicking the camp director. "You'll do fine."

As if handling an animal as big as a bookcase would be "easy." What if it bolted out of the stall? Or charged in her direction? Or, God forbid, tried to bite her?

"Nice horsey horsey," she said. The animal's black mane seemed more of a dark gray in the stall's ambient light—like the color of a snake. She shivered. Her feet felt heavy in the thick bed of pine shavings. "I'm not going to hurt you."

She stopped by its head and looked down at the halter. Now what? Obviously, the smaller hole went around the horse's nose. Or maybe its ear? But there was only one hole and so that didn't make sense. Nose, she decided.

A soft breath wafted across her crotch.

"Whoa," she cried, jumping back. "We don't know each other well enough for you to be doing that."

Someone coughed.

Amber turned in surprise to see John Wayne standing outside the stall.

Well, okay, it wasn't really John Wayne, but it sure was a cowboy. Black hat. Checkered beige shirt. *Cool blue eyes.*

"He's just trying to get to know you," the man said, his deep baritone splashed with a Southern accent. "He doesn't mean anything by it."

Easy for the cowboy to say. Amber couldn't take her eyes off her unexpected visitor. He was *gorgeous.* A hunk-o-hunk of burning love, as her friend Rachel would say. And just what was it about cowboys? They all looked the same. Five o'clock shadows. Square jaws. The smell of outdoors clinging to them. Was it part of the cowboy genome?

"I don't mean to be rude," she said. "But do I know you?"

He shook his head. "Colton Sheridan. I was hired on Thursday."

Just as she'd been, Amber thought. Well, she didn't get hired on Thursday, but she was new to Camp Cowboy, too.

"Gil sent me in here to help you out," he said.

Gil. The camp director. Gil and Buck had been looking for some additional help since the moment they'd realized their enrollment numbers were nearly triple what they'd been the previous year. Buck was off buying more horses, which left Gil in charge. Not many horses in the heart of San Francisco, but that's where the camp was. Amber once again marveled at their location—smack-dab in the middle of Golden Gate National Recreation Area. Step outside the barn and the high-rises were clearly visible in the distance.

"Nice to meet you, Colton, but I'd rather tackle this on my own."

That's what she was supposed to be doing: learning about horses. She'd come to Camp Cowboy committed to the idea of becoming a hippotherapist. Therapy was her thing. She specialized in speech therapy now, but she'd heard of some remarkable breakthroughs when children were exposed to horses. She might not like the animals, but she would get over that.

Anything for Dee.

She turned back to the horse. Its name was Flash, or so she'd read outside the stall. She hoped that didn't mean it'd trample her in a flash.

"It goes the other way," he told her when she held up the halter.

Oh, yeah. That was right. She'd been told that by Jarrod, the man who was supposed to mentor her through the process. He'd shown her how to halter a horse yesterday. Obviously, she hadn't been paying attention too well. She flipped the thing around.

"Not that way," Colton said with a small shake of his handsome head. She hated overly attractive men. They always made her feel so...so uncomfortable.

"The hole goes over the nose," he added. "The long strap buckles behind the horse's ears."

"Right..." she murmured.

"Here." The stall gate, which was on rollers, whooshed open like supermarket doors. "I'll do it for you."

"No, no," she said quickly, her feet bogged down in

wood chips once again. He was tall. That was another thing she didn't like. Tall men intimidated the hell out of her. Jarrod, the registered hippotherapist she was working with, was short and blond. She could deal with short and blond.

She could deal with *this,* too. "I can do it."

She heard the stall door close with a bang just the same, and the sound startled Flash.

What followed was not Amber's proudest moment.

She shrieked; the horse turned away from her. The back end of the animal bashed into the wall with a boom, sending dust and debris down from the rafters. Her feet became entangled in the wood chips again. She started to fall....

He kept her from going down with a hand against her shoulder.

"Sorry about that," he told her. "I didn't think it would close so easily."

You idiot, she wanted to say. But he wasn't paying attention to her, anyway. Flash was now dancing around the stall as if Amber was a monster.

"Don't move," Colton told her. "Easy there."

Easy? There was nothing easy about this horse. The iron-shod animal had to be at least six feet tall.

"You okay?" he asked.

"I don't mean to sound panicked, but shouldn't we get out of here while the getting's good?"

He appeared to be sizing her up. "We'll be fine," he said, stepping toward the horse.

Over her shoulder, she could see that the brown beast was back to eyeing her nervously. Its swishing tail sounded like a jump rope in motion.

"No offense," she said, "but are you sure you're qualified to give direction to nonhorsey people?" After all, it was his fault the animal was acting up.

She saw Colton's eyebrows rise. They were a little too thick for her taste. "I've spent a lot of time on ranches."

"And I've spent a lot of time in a city. Doesn't mean I know how to teach people to drive."

One side of his mouth lifted in a cowboy smile—which was more of a smirk. "Point taken. I've ridden horses my entire life. I'm comfortable sharing what I know."

"In that case," she said. "I'm really glad to meet you, Colton. I'm Amber Brooks."

"Colt," he quickly corrected. "And I know. You're an intern here. You're learning to become a hippotherapist."

"I'm actually one of the camp's speech therapists, too. Hippotherapy is just something I'm hoping to study while I'm here."

He was giving her that look again. The one that made her want to wiggle like a worm on a hook. "Don't take this wrong, but you sure you want to work with horses?"

"No."

"No?"

She turned toward Flash, releasing a sigh. How to explain her life? How to explain about Dee, the nephew she loved so much? How to explain the situation with Dee's dad? That Sharron was dead, and that Dee's father was in jail…because he'd killed her sister. Not intentionally, but just about.

"It's complicated," she said.

And she shouldn't explain, anyway. The fact was Dee had been enrolled in Camp Cowboy this season, and the only one who knew that was the camp director, Gil. Amber planned to keep it that way, too.

"Try me," he said.

She shook her head. "No, seriously, it's not worth getting into. I just want to learn about horses. Hippotherapy intrigues me."

And there he went, staring at her again. It was the oddest sort of look. As if he was trying to peel back the rind of a pomegranate, to get to the ruby-red seeds beneath. "You don't look like *any* kind of therapist," he mused.

"That's because I left my thick-framed glasses in my room."

He smirked again. "So you mind me asking why someone who doesn't know a thing about horses, and who doesn't want to become a hippotherapist, is trying to put a halter on one?"

She had to turn away.

"I'm an equine intern. That means I'll be lending a hand with the kids throughout the next few weeks. That means working with horses, obviously, so I need to get used to them. The horses, I mean."

She sneezed before she could stop herself. The horse's head popped up, and she braced herself for impact.

Nothing happened.

Flash returned to nuzzling the ground, apparently intrigued with something it found there. Ah. Food.

"Should I bother it while it's eating?"

"Nope. Horses are always looking for something to munch. If you wait for him to stop, you'll be standing there all day."

Damn, but his accent was really Southern. "If you

say so." She gave Flash the same look she used when dealing with a petulant child. "Horse, prepare to be haltered."

COLT ALMOST LAUGHED.

Almost.

He hadn't laughed in years, or so it seemed. Not since…well, a lifetime ago.

"Easy there," said the woman he'd been told was the most dishonest piece of work this side of the Mississippi.

Standing in a beam of sunlight, she looked like an angel. One of those made-in-Taiwan Christmas tree toppers, the kind with masses and masses of fake blond ringlets. Except her hair was real. He took in the bloom of color across her cheeks. Her tipped up nose. Plump lower lip.

Gorgeous.

"Shit."

"What?" she asked, turning toward him. "Am I doing something wrong?"

"No," he said. *Get a grip, Colt. You've seen beautiful women before.* "Just walk on up to him. Trust me, he knows what you want to do."

She didn't look like a criminal.

But Logan, his best friend, swore up and down that she'd stolen his son. Hidden the boy—her nephew—away in some kind of boarding school, and she wouldn't tell Logan where he was. Didn't *have* to tell him because she had full custody of the child, thanks to Logan's brush with the law and her sister's death. From what Colt knew of her, she was a deceitful city dweller with the morals of a snake. And so Colt had built up an idea of what Amber Brooks would look like—and this wasn't it.

She was just about to put the halter on the horse when she sneezed again. The gelding started; Amber darted away. "Okay, that does it," she said. "I'll never make it as an intern if this keeps up."

"You can't back off now," he said. "The horse will think he's won."

It might have been a few years since he'd worked his father's ranch, and he might have been young back then, but when you were dealing with animals, you wanted to be in control.

"I'm scared," she admitted. "Seriously, I think I should wait for Jarrod. He's the person I'm interning with, and when he helped me out yesterday, I wasn't half as scared."

"That's because he was standing right behind you," Colt said, moving up next to her and urging her forward with his hand. "And I can, too."

She was short, no more than five-three, with enough curves to fill a road map. But his buddy had warned him that Amber Brooks was a real piece of work. He'd known Logan since high school and was inclined to believe his friend. She might look heaven sent, but she was no angel.

"Here," he said. *Damn it.* "It goes like this." He demonstrated how to hold the halter, how to put the horse's nose in first, than how to slip the crown piece through the brass buckle. "See?"

"Oh, yeah, that's right," she said. "I remember now. It's like the harness that people use for bondage."

Colt froze.

"Not that I'm into bondage or anything!" she quickly

exclaimed, and if he read her body language right, she couldn't believe she'd said the words. "I did a paper on fetishes when I was working on my masters."

"Uh-huh."

So. She was highly educated. Probably thought she was better than everyone else.

"Thanks," she said, wry amusement on her face. "Honestly, I feel like an idiot."

"You'll do fine next time," he found himself saying. "Let's go."

"Where?" she asked.

"I was told to help you saddle up the horse. That you were wanting to learn how to ride."

"Ride?" she repeated, her blue eyes suddenly huge. "Oh, I—uh…"

He waited, wondering what the deal was with her. Why was she at this camp if she didn't know anything about horses? *She* was the reason *he'd* taken the job. It was a deal he couldn't refuse. In exchange for locating Logan's son, Colt would receive the papers on his buddy's best roping horse—an animal that'd been sitting around for a few years, sure, but a damn good horse all the same. The gelding was just the ticket Colt needed. A tie-down roper was only as good as the animal he rode, and for the past few years, Colt hadn't been that good.

"Well," he said, "the only way to learn is by working with them. Go get me a lead rope."

"Is that the long cord thingy?" she asked.

He nodded. He needed to get to know her better. To put her at ease. To become her friend.

She came back into the stall, lead rope in hand.

He snapped the rope to the horse's halter.

She was temptation wrapped in denim, and that presented a hell of a problem. He planned on betraying this pretty little package one day soon.

CHAPTER TWO

RIDE, AMBER THOUGHT with a gulp.

She realized in that instant that it was one thing to decide to become a hippotherapist, quite another to actually do it…especially when horses were involved.

"Go on," Colt said, motioning her ahead of him.

He didn't look happy. She wondered if men like him found it tedious to teach newbies like her. His expression was as dour as a thundercloud.

"Where should I take her?" She glanced up at Flash.

"It's a him," the cowboy said. "There's a rack out in front of the stable. Tie him out there."

It was as if a really scary monster was following on her heels; that's what leading a horse felt like.

Get used to it, Amber. A horse might be just what Dee needs. And if that proved true, well, she'd buy him ten horses.

Colt appeared unfazed by his surroundings. How nice to have been born on a ranch. Maybe if she'd been born on one, too, she wouldn't feel so dang scared.

"How long have you been in the horse business?"

"Long time," he said.

They stepped out of the shelter of the barn, and after being inside for so long, Amber had to blink in the glaring sunlight. It was bright outside, but so beautiful. Tall trees framed a parklike setting. She was pretty sure the trees were redwoods, they were so huge. In the distance she could see the empty army barracks. It seemed sad that up until last year the place had been abandoned. Well, now the Golden State Therapeutic Center, aka Camp Cowboy, made good use of it.

"No," Colt said. "Not like that."

Amber glanced down at the cord she'd wrapped around a pole.

She'd been so deep in thought she hadn't given a second thought to how she tied it. "Not like what?"

"You need to use a quick-release knot."

"Uh…how do I do that?" Jarrod hadn't taught her that yesterday. The good-looking blond staffer had simply taken the lead from her and done it himself.

"Like this." Colt stepped toward her. Surely some football team in the South was lamenting the loss of such an athletic looking guy. "See?"

No, Amber hadn't seen. They stood in front of a hitching post that looked a lot like the ones in Western movies. Apparently, there hadn't been a lot of technological advances in horse hitching recently. But what he did with that rope might as well have been cat's cradle. "Can you do that again?"

"Wrap it around once," he said. "Then cross over, then make a loop, then pull the end through the loop. See?"

"I think I do," she said. But it quickly became apparent that she didn't see at all.

"Here," he said, taking her hands in his. He had a really huge one. Ginormous. She felt like Fay Wray in King Kong's palm.

"Wrap it around once, cross the two strands, slip the

loop through the V here." He demonstrated, then slid the loose end through the resulting loop.

"Oh!" At last she got it. Though why they needed a special way to tie horses was anybody's guess.

"It's so you can release the rope quickly if he pulls back."

Had she really been that easy to read?

"Got it," she said. "Although I'm not sure I want to know what 'pulling back' means in horseydom."

"I don't expect that to happen with any of the animals here. As I understand it, they've all been therapy horses for at least a year."

"That's a relief. I was thinking I might need to update my life insurance policy."

There he went, staring at her again. "You'll be fine," he stated simply.

"Good to know," she murmured. "Now what?"

"Well, I assume there are some grooming brushes around here?"

"Oh, yeah. Jarrod showed me where they were. They're in the tack room."

Colt nodded, his hat tipping low over his eyes. He reminded her of a cardsharp from an old Western, the kind that sidled up to a bar and growled, "Whiskey. Straight up." A lot of men wouldn't be able to carry off such a look. He could.

A moment or two later, he came out with a bucket of brushes and a saddle slung over his shoulder. She felt her jaw drop, because honestly, it was as if he were trying to look like some kind of commercial cowboy. The kind that sold aftershave. All he needed was a pair of chaps.

"Here." He handed her the dark green tote.

"Thanks," she said. "I think." Because once he set that saddle down, something else struck her. This was real. She was about to get on a horse.

Shit.

"Should I wait for Jarrod or something?"

"Why?" Colt asked.

"Well, he's the...the—" She'd been about to say horse expert, but realized how ludicrous that might sound, given Colt's background. "He told me he would teach me everything I needed to know." And he'd said it with such a gleam in his eyes that he seemed to promise other things, too. Things she had no interest in.

"Well, Jarrod isn't here right now."

"Yes, I am."

Amber felt her heart thump. "Jeez," she said, turning away from the hitching post. "I didn't even hear you come up."

"Gil wants to see you," he said, eyeing Colt curiously.

"Have you two met?" she asked.

Colt shook his head. Jarrod stared at the cowboy for a long moment. The two were like sunshine and darkness. Jarrod, with his light blond hair and loose T-shirt, looked more like an engineer than a horse handler beside Colt's tall frame and dark-tanned body.

"Jarrod James," he said, shaking Colt's hand.

"Colt Sheridan."

But Amber could tell Jarrod took an instant dislike to Colt. There was something about the way Jarrod's shoulders were set. Something about the way his arms hung at his sides. And he didn't smile.

"Colt's a rancher."

She didn't know why she said it, except maybe she was trying to make conversation.

"Actually, I'm a rodeo cowboy," Colt said. "I only work on ranches part-time."

He was a rodeo man? Amber thought. That explained the aloof attitude. Her brother-in-law had ridden in rodeos. Back before he'd been arrested for drunk driving and vehicular manslaughter. She knew the type. Cocky. Arrogant. Womanizers... Too bad.

"Oh, yeah? You ever make it to the NFR?" Jarrod asked.

Frankly, Amber was amazed Jarrod even knew what the National Finals Rodeo was. She did because Logan had almost made it one year. In hindsight things had started to fall apart when he'd failed to make the mark.

"Not yet," Colt said. "Next year."

Jarrod huffed, conveying all too clearly, *Yeah, that's what they all say.*

"Well, I better head up to Gil's office," Amber said.

"I'll walk with you," Jarrod announced.

"You coming back?" Colt asked before she could turn away.

"Depends on what Gil wants."

Colt's eyes narrowed. Amber knew exactly what he was thinking.

Chicken.

"You needed to see me?" Amber said, entering Gil's office tentatively. The way he was bent over his massive oak desk, she could see the horseshoe of hair around his shiny pate.

"Amber," he said, pushing his wire-rimmed glasses back up his nose. "Come on in."

They were in a centuries-old lodge, one that had been erected to house cavalry offices well over a hundred years ago. Frankly, it amazed Amber that the place was still standing, but it had been crafted in an era when things were made to last. Vaulted ceilings. Crown molding. Wood-paneled walls. The four-story building had been meticulously maintained by the County of San Francisco, and that was a good thing. It would have been a shame to let such a treasure go to waste. That had been Camp Cowboy's selling point to the county when they'd wanted to lease the building. Apparently. As a newbie, she was still piecing together this business and how it could exist on the Presidio grounds.

"What's up?" she asked.

"Have a seat," he said.

Gil's office was on the bottom floor, to the left of the entrance, in a room Amber suspected had been occupied by the base commander years and years ago—or whatever the cavalry equivalent of that was. Wood-framed windows offered a stunning view of the park outside. Off in the distance was a grove of trees, and just above that, barely noticeably unless you knew what you were looking for, the tall spires of the Golden Gate Bridge.

"I received a call today," Gil said, leaning back and making a steeple out of his fingers.

There was a chair in front of his desk. Amber sank into it. "Oh, yeah?" But she knew.

"It was from Pelican Bay."

Her shoulders slumped. "He *phoned* here?"

"Care to tell me what's going on?"

She hadn't told Gil about Dee's father. Hadn't wanted to tell him. It was her own personal skeleton. All the camp director knew was that she had sole custody of her nephew. That Dee's father was out of the picture.

"Who is *he?*" Gil asked.

"My nephew's father," Amber admitted.

The edges of Gil's eyes crinkled as he gave that some thought. "So this is what you meant by out of the picture?"

She nodded. "He was incarcerated for involuntary manslaughter."

Of her sister. Sharron.

And it made her physically ill to think about it. To be pulled back to that night. The call from the police. The drive to the hospital. The doctor gently breaking the news.

Frankly, jail had been too kind a punishment for her ex-brother-in-law.

"When will he get out?" Gil asked.

"He was given a five year sentence. He has two years left to serve." But he had a parole hearing in another month. They might actually let the bastard out. And then he would fight her for custody of Dee. He'd already told her that. But she would never let that happen. She would not allow the man who killed her sister to kill her sister's child, too.

"Okay," Gil said. "So I should expect calls from him?"

"I told him not to phone me," she said. "But he's been demanding to know where Dee is."

"You mean he doesn't know?"

She shook her head. "Early on, he would call Dee. When Dee wouldn't talk to him, he would get belligerent, start yelling." And her poor nephew didn't do well with that. Not at all. "It would upset Dee," she explained. "I told the facility not to take his calls anymore, but when Dee's father started making threats against the workers there..." Gosh, she hated airing her dirty laundry. "It was just easier to move Dee to a new home, especially once we figured out he was nonverbal. He's been at Little Voices ever since, and he's doing well. His father doesn't need to know anything more than that."

But one day he would be out of jail.

She closed her eyes, refusing to think of that.

"This is hard on you, isn't it?" Gil asked.

She shrugged, trying to make light of the situation, but it was a sham. "It kills me some days," she admitted. "But I have to have Dee's best interest at heart."

Gil seemed satisfied with the answer. "Well, I'll tell the switchboard to put all calls through to you."

"Thank you," she said. "And if you could please make sure nobody knows Dee is my nephew…"

"Confidentiality is the policy of this facility," Gil said sternly.

"Yes, of course." She was counting on that.

"But I do wonder if telling his father that Dee is here with you might be a good thing. Surely he would settle down if you told him the lengths you've gone though to help his son."

"No," she said. "I tried that route before. Dee's father doesn't trust me. He thinks I hate him."

And she did…didn't she?

No. She didn't hate anybody. She just didn't trust him. He might make claims that he'd changed, but she knew that wasn't true. A leopard didn't change its spots.

"Well then," Gil said, "I'll respect your need for privacy."

"Thank you."

"But if this doesn't work out, if your nephew doesn't respond to therapy like you hope, what will you do then?"

She'd thought about that at least a half-dozen times since taking a leave of absence from work to train at Camp Cowboy. What if this was a mistake? What if Dee didn't respond to horse therapy as she hoped?

"Either way, learning a little about hippotherapy is a good thing," she said. "Who knows where it might take me?" She glanced down at her lap for a moment. "And I'll do whatever it takes to help my nephew. If this doesn't work out…" She shrugged again. "Well, I'll just try something else."

Gil nodded, smiling. "Good. I'm glad you're not looking at this like it might be an answer to your prayers. One never knows how an autistic child will respond."

"I know."

"Then I wish you luck," he said, standing.

Luck. Yeah, she *would* need that.

CHAPTER THREE

SHE WAS IN a meeting, Colt thought, heart pounding, as he put Flash away. He would never have a better opportunity to search through her belongings than right now.

But the idea filled him with a sense of anxiety and dread.

His fingers shook as he unclipped Flash's halter. The camp wasn't fully staffed yet. He'd been told most of the live-ins would arrive tomorrow. That meant fewer people around today.

He had to investigate now.

His stomach roiled as he left the stables. "The lodge," as staffers called it, looked like it belonged on a dollar bill: Georgian-style roof, sash windows, wide steps leading up to the entrance. It had been built on a slight incline, with a pebbled road leading up to it. Those employees who would be driving in Monday would park around back, but for now, the place looked deserted.

Colt took the steps two at a time, feeling sick with trepidation. The lodge had double doors at the entrance, but only the right side worked. Colt saw movement on the other side of the frosted glass. He knew Gil's office was to the left, and when he stepped inside, that door was closed.

Good. Amber was still in her meeting.

"That was fast."

Colt jerked his gaze to the right, to find Jim or Jerry or whatever his name was sitting there. In the cafeteria, actually, although the spacious room with the hardwood floors looked more like a ballroom, except for the tables and chairs.

"No reason to stick around at the stables if there's nothing to do." The horse therapist Amber had introduced him to earlier looked skeptical.

"Don't you have to feed stock or something?"

The guy—Jarrod, he suddenly remembered—was obnoxious. Colt had no idea what he'd done to garner such animosity, but it was obvious they hadn't hit it off. "Not for another hour," he said, moving past the cafeteria without another word. There was an elevator in the left-hand corner of the foyer—a recent addition by the looks of it. He ignored it and took the steps directly ahead. The staff would all be living coed style, which, for all he knew, meant Amber could be bunking right next to him.

She wasn't.

He checked the room chart hanging at the end of the hall. Room seven. He was in room three, which meant he had to walk by his own room, which meant—

Woof!

"Mac," Colt warned. "Quiet."

But his dog had caught his scent. White-and-black paws scratched at the door. Colt could just make them out through the crack. Terrific. He'd insisted the animal wouldn't be a problem, but Gil had warned that if Mac disturbed any of the residents, Colt would have to board him at a kennel—an option he couldn't afford.

"Quiet!" He glanced left and right as he walked on. A few of the doors were open, but he didn't see anyone.

The place reminded him of a hospital ward. *Utilitarian* was the word. No frills here.

Her door was closed.

He peeked over his shoulder, grateful that nobody was around, but when it came time to actually grasp the doorknob, he hesitated.

Woof.

"Mac," he called out. He opened the door and stepped inside before he could change his mind. If someone heard his dog and came to investigate, they'd see him standing there. Not good. But once inside her room, he froze.

He hated this.

Just do it.

Forcing himself to relax, he scanned her room. Bed to his left. Table and chairs to his right. There was a purse sitting on the brown seat, clearly open.

Go.

But he couldn't. He wasn't cut out for this, he realized. The idea of rummaging through her things…

He just couldn't do it. He swung around, and came face-to-face with Amber.

"What the heck are you doing in here?" she said, her blue eyes wide with surprise.

"I…uh…" Damn it. He couldn't think. "I wanted to apologize."

"Apologize? For what?"

"Earlier," he improvised. And he hated it. Lying wasn't in his nature. "For forcing you to get on Flash."

"You didn't force me," she said, crossing her arms. "I didn't ride at all." With the window behind him and the sunlight pouring over her, her eyes seemed to glow.

As did her hair. He found himself forgetting for a moment what he'd come here to do.

"You would have if we hadn't been interrupted. And I was pushy about the whole thing."

"I didn't notice," she said, but he knew she lied.

Colt shook his head, hoping she didn't see guilt on his face. "I, uh, I spend a lot of time working out of doors. With men. On ranches. I guess I just forgot you weren't one of my crew." That, at least, was true. So far he hadn't lied to her. Not really. And he hadn't rummaged through her belongings.

"You don't have a girlfriend?"

"No," he said quickly.

Her lips twitched, as if she was about to ask him a question, but she must have changed her mind.

"Do you have a boyfriend?" he asked, to fill the quiet.

Now why'd you go and say that?

"Boyfriend?" She laughed. "Hah. Who has time for that? Between my job and my…"

He waited for her to say the word *nephew*.

"…crazy life," she said instead, "I don't have time for sleep, much less a boyfriend."

"Your life's crazy?"

But she wasn't budging. He could see that. "It is," she said, swinging open the door pointedly. "Anyway, apology accepted."

"Can we try again tomorrow?"

She raised her eyebrows. "You mean ride?"

He nodded.

She licked her lips. And suddenly he found himself thinking less about subterfuge and more about the shape of those lips.

"Let me think about it," she said.

He didn't move, even though it was obvious she wanted him to leave. But he couldn't do that. If he couldn't bring himself to rummage through her belongings, he needed to come up with some other way to get the information out of her.

"Don't chew it over too long," he said, forcing himself to smile. "Tomorrow's Sunday. From what I hear, things are going to get crazy on Monday." He walked to the door, but didn't leave. He turned to face her, effectively imprisoning her between his body and the wall.

"I want to help you," he said.

"You do?"

Man, she was a pretty little thing. He couldn't keep from staring at her mouth. "Let me coach you some more."

She chewed the inside of her lip. She looked adorable when she did that. Like a kid trying to determine if she wanted vanilla ice cream or chocolate.

"What time were you thinking?" she asked.

"Maybe around ten or so?" he said, cursing inwardly. She was not to be trusted. "I'm supposed to do some things around the barn tomorrow. So after that?"

She seemed to think about it for a moment. "All right. Tomorrow."

"See you then," he said, because he knew if he didn't leave right then, he might do something he would regret. And that wouldn't be good. Logan had told him exactly how horrible this woman really was.

See you then.

Lord, her sister would be laughing her head off if she knew the direction of Amber's thoughts.

A cowboy.

"Brother," she murmured, dropping onto the bed.

But she didn't get much sleep that night. She told herself she could bug out on Colt, maybe go down and try to halter and work with Flash on her own. But that would be silly. She didn't want to get hurt. She wanted to learn.

The other option was asking Jarrod, but something about the guy's attitude really rubbed her the wrong way. At least Colt seemed genuine.

So she showed up in her jeans and a sweatshirt. While the day had dawned overcast and cold—typical January weather—the fog had burned off, leaving bright blue skies behind, although it was still a bit chilly. When she arrived at the stables, she was startled to see Flash already tied out front, and that Colt wasn't alone.

"Mac," he called to the dog, which stood up when he saw her.

"You have a *dog?*" she asked in shock.

"I do."

"Hey, there," she said, squatting.

"Mac!"

But the dog didn't listen. As if he'd been waiting for just such an invitation, he charged.

"Damn it, Mac!"

But Amber didn't mind. She held out her arms, thoroughly enchanted with the gray-black-and-brown animal. He had no tail. It'd been cropped at some point, but that didn't stop his rear end from swinging back and forth.

"What kind of dog is he?"

"Australian shepherd," Colt said. "And I'm about to deport him back to his homeland." He stomped forward.

"No, it's okay," she said, staving him off with a hand. "I love dogs."

"You do?"

"I do," she exclaimed, plunging her hands into the shepherd's thick fur and giving him a good scratch. Mac fairly moaned. "Such pretty eyes," she cooed. They were blue. Blue like the water in Crater Lake. "But where have you been keeping him?"

"In my room," he said. "Gil told me that was okay as long as he didn't cause trouble."

"What?" she said in mock surprise. "Mac, cause trouble? Nah." She smiled at the animal.

When she stood up, she found Colt staring at her, and she felt self-conscious all of a sudden. "I see you got Flash ready."

"Uh, yeah. Hope you don't mind. I didn't see any good reason to torture you by making you halter the animal. I want you to enjoy yourself today."

"Thanks," she said, her relief so great she almost hugged him.

"Come on, Mac."

"Where are you putting him?"

"In one of the empty stalls. I don't want him getting under your feet. Go on in and get some brushes," Colt added. "I'll be right back."

She did so, thinking *In for a penny, in for a pound.*

"Don't those hard bristles hurt?" she asked when he came back out.

"No, not like that." Colt took the brush from her hand. She felt the jolt of their fingers meeting like a static charge.

"And horses actually like it," he said.

As he moved closer, Amber found herself wanting to edge away.

"Use long strokes," Colt instructed, his gaze hooking her own. "Start at his neck and work your way back. Sometimes it's easier to use a currycomb first. That'll knock the hair loose."

"And a currycomb looks like…what, exactly?"

Colt bent and pulled something out of the bucket that caused her to say, "Ouch. Now *that* can't feel good." It looked like a lollipop, only the "pop" part was made of metal. And it had teeth. Sharp, pointed teeth.

"You'd be surprised what feels good to a horse."

She eyed the animal. "Actually, given that I know absolutely nothing about them, I don't think anything would surprise me. How do I use the currycomb?"

"Move it in circular patterns."

She nodded. "Wax on. Wax off."

"Excuse me?"

"*Karate Kid.* Haven't you ever seen that movie?"

Colt stared down at her as if he'd never heard of anything remotely related to karate—movies or otherwise—in his life, but that didn't dissuade her.

"Sensei tell you to wax on, wax off," she said.

But all Colt did was stare. The man was about as warm and as friendly as Mount Everest.

"Once you're done," he said, "follow up with the brush. I'm going to go get the tack."

She gave the brush a hard flick, and was immediately rewarded by a cloud of dust and dander. She coughed, waving a hand in front of her face, although the smell of horse wasn't all that unpleasant. And the animal seemed to have calmed down. His head hung low, his brown eyes half-closed, as if he was falling asleep at the hitching post. Hmm. Maybe this wouldn't be as scary as she thought.

"You done?"

"No," Amber said in exasperation. "And please don't sneak up on me like that."

Colt dropped the saddle and hung the bridle on the end of the post Flash was tied to. "Here," he said, "I'll do the other side."

And that was how Amber found herself quietly grooming a horse—because Mr. Colt Sheridan appeared to be the tall, dark and *silent* type. But that was okay. It gave her time to think.

Dee would be arriving soon, although no one could make the connection. Her nephew's birth certificate said Rudolph, a result of Sharron's twisted sense of humor, when he'd been born on Christmas Day. But everybody, including his father, called him Rudy, and that suited Amber just fine. Logan had been begging to see him again, and Amber just couldn't do that to her nephew. The last time they'd been to visit it had been so horrible. Dee had gone into meltdown. Logan had grown irate. The supervising officer had had to intervene.... Horrible. All the proof she needed that her brother-in-law hadn't changed, not one whit.

"So what made you want to work with special needs children?"

She again waved a hand in front of her face as dust tickled her nose. "It's a long story."

Colt continued grooming Flash, although she could swear he was trying to denude the beast. Dander and hair were flying. Thank goodness she wasn't allergic to horses.

"I've got all the time in the world," he said, his eyes meeting hers for a moment.

"No, really," she said.

"You like kids, don't you?"

"Of course I do," she answered quickly.

"Do you want any of your own?"

He hadn't stopped brushing, but she could feel him glancing at her. Every time he did, it was like warm flashes of sunlight touched her—which, honestly, was a strange thing to think.

"Someday," she said. "How about you? What made you want to work for Camp Cowboy?"

"I didn't."

That made her stop brushing for a second. "Excuse me?"

"I heard about this place from a friend. He told me I should apply. So I did."

She didn't know why that stunned her, but it did. She'd just assumed everyone who worked at Camp Cowboy had done so out of a need to serve. To make the world a better place. To reach out and maybe help a child.

Her life's mission, thanks to Dee.

"So if your friend hadn't suggested you apply, you'd have…what?"

He shrugged. "I don't know what I would have done for cash. Found something else."

"But you wanted to work with special needs kids, didn't you?"

She could tell he didn't want to answer her question because his eyes flicked over Flash as he groomed, then to her, then back again. "My first love is rodeo," he admitted.

Of course. She should have known.

Just like her sister's husband.

Amber was certain the rodeo lifestyle had corrupted Logan to the point of no return. Cowboys boozed it up and chased women. That's what her sister said, and Amber believed it. "I know someone who used to do that."

"Yeah?" Colt asked.

But she wasn't ready to answer questions about Dee's father, even though she was curious if the two knew each other. The man was better off gone from their lives, something that was hard to explain to strangers.

"Please tell me you at least *like* kids?" she replied, trying to change the subject.

He paused. "Kids and I don't get along."

Her body turned into a pillar of salt—or so it felt. "What the heck are you doing here then?"

He looked her right in the eye. She watched as he tried to find the words. In the end he simply shrugged and said, "Searching for something."

CHAPTER FOUR

NOW WHY THE HECK had he gone and said that? he wondered, flicking the brush over Flash's back harder than necessary. Flash pinned his ears, and Cold patted his rump in apology.

"Searching for what?" she asked, clearly curious.

"I don't know," he hedged, then shrugged. "But the rodeo life, it's getting hard."

That's why he *had* to do this. Time was running out—and she was his ticket to the big leagues.

"So quit," she suggested.

"No," he said. "Not yet."

Because he could still do this thing. He just needed to figure out a way to discover where Rudy was without feeling like a complete jerk in the process.

You are *a jerk*.

Amber was shaking her head, and he could tell she didn't like his answer. Not only that, but she almost appeared disappointed.

"Okay," she said brightly—too brightly. "What's next?"

He wondered if he should push the issue. Ask her about the guy she knew on the rodeo circuit. Logan. It had to be Logan. It was the perfect way to get her to talk. That's what he *should* do. Instead, he found himself gesturing with his chin. "Saddle first, then bridle."

"And how do you do that?"

"Here." He scooped up the saddle blanket. "This goes on first." He made sure it was placed squarely. "Then the saddle," he said, swinging it onto the horse's back.

"How come I have this feeling it's a lot harder than it looks?"

He pulled the saddle off and demonstrated again. But the whole time he worked with her, he found himself wondering if Logan might be wrong about her. Was that possible? Was there more to the story than met the eye? And why the hell did Colt keep thinking about his ranch all of a sudden? He hadn't been back to Texas in years, not since he was seventeen....

Don't go down that road again, buddy.

"Is that thing going in there?" she asked.

They'd reached the part where it was time to bridle the horse. Colt realized it was the bit she was staring at.

"It is," he said, telling himself to smile. Except he couldn't bring himself to do much more than say, "Don't worry. Doesn't hurt. He knows the deal. Watch." He showed her how Flash had been taught to take the bit.

Could Logan be wrong? Or worse, lying?

Damn it. Colt wished he could just ask.

"Doesn't that hurt?" she asked when the metal clunked against the gelding's teeth.

"Only if you don't know what you're doing," he said. *Just focus on what you're here to do.* "But you will," he quickly reassured her. "Here. I'll show you." Because that's what he'd been hired to do—help out with the horses.

"Can I try?" she asked.

"Sure." He slipped the bridle off again and handed it to her.

Just tough it out.

When the camp closed in eight weeks, it was back to rodeo—with his pockets full and a new horse to ride.

"Hold it from the top," he instructed when she looked at the bridle, baffled. She moved the bit close to Flash's mouth, but when the gelding jerked his head back, she jumped as if he'd tried to bite her.

"You know, I'm starting to think you don't like horses," Colt said.

"I don't."

He thought he misheard her. "Excuse me?"

"They intimidate the hell out of me."

"Then what the heck are *you* doing here?" he found himself asking.

She looked at the animal, then at the stable where he'd come from. "This is the wave of the future," she said. "Or at least that's what research shows. There have been studies recently, really amazing studies, that prove an animal can connect with special needs children in a way that defies explanation. I *have* to do this."

"Why?"

She flicked her chin up. "Because."

Was it because of her nephew? Logan had admitted his son wasn't quite "normal," but said he just had a learning disability. Was that what drove Amber's passion?

"If you don't want to be afraid of horses, you need to realize something."

"What's that?" she asked, the bridle in her hand forgotten.

"They're like dogs."

"Excuse me?"

"Like a gigantic Mac," Colt amended. "Really. Most

horses are just as smart as Mac in there—sometimes
smarter."

As if his dog had been listening, Amber heard him
yelp.

"Is he okay?"

"He's fine. He just wants to be out with us."

"That'd be okay with me."

"No," Colt said. "You need to focus on what I'm
saying."

"I am paying attention," she said, eyeing the horse.
"What you just told me was not to worry. That if a horse
wants to kill me, it's smart enough to know the best way
to accomplish that goal."

Against his better judgment, he smiled, but only for
a moment. "Horses don't want to kill humans. I've seen
half a dozen jump over a rider unfortunate enough to
land in front of them."

She tipped her head sideways, her ringlets hanging
over her shoulder like a bunch of grapes. "Yes, but how
did that rider get in front of those horses in the first
place?"

"At rodeos cowboys fall off all the time. As a matter of fact, it's what I do for a living—jump off horses."

"What do you mean?"

"I'm a tie-down roper."

"What's that?"

"Someone who jumps off a running horse and wres-
tles steers to the ground."

"And you do that why?"

It's a living.

They were the first words to come to mind, even
though he knew well and good there were easier ways
to do that. Hell, he worked ranches during the off-

season. He *owned* a ranch. But full-time ranching? Nah. That'd been his dad's deal. And his mom's. And his baby sister's—

Colt snatched the bridle from Amber. "Sorry," he said when she looked up at him in surprise. "Let's just get you mounted. That way you can see for yourself there's nothing to fear."

And he could get out of here.

"Find yourself a helmet," he snapped.

"Helmet? You think I might fall off?"

"No," he said. "It's a safety precaution. I was told everyone here rides with a helmet."

He wasn't cut out for this, he decided. Dealing with her while trying to keep quiet about why he was actually at Camp Cowboy. And then there was this…this whatever it was that reminded him of his family and the life he used to live.

"Do you know where the helmets are?" she asked.

"Never mind," he said. "I'll go get one."

He thrust the reins at her. But as he walked into the barn, blinking in the sudden dimness, he wondered if maybe it wouldn't have to be so difficult. And maybe he wouldn't have to lie to her. Maybe he could discover some other way to unearth her nephew's location.

Because even though he wanted to help his buddy, he wasn't at all convinced he had what it took to do. *She* might be a deceitful you-know-what, but *he* wasn't. And that might present a problem.

HE'D GONE ALL QUIET on her. Since they'd walked to the arena together, helmet in hand, he'd said hardly two words to her.

"Climb on board," he said.

Okay, make that four. "Sure," she said. "If you tell me how."

He looked at her as if butterflies were spitting out of her mouth. "Haven't you ever seen someone getting on a horse before?"

He seemed angry. Or frustrated. Or...something. "Haven't you ever worked with beginners before?" she retorted.

He didn't answer her.

"Haven't you?" she pressed.

"No," he finally admitted.

That got her attention. "Then how the heck did you get this job?"

"Frankly, I don't know. Luck, I guess."

"No way," she said.

"I faxed in a résumé last Monday, had a phone interview on Tuesday. They did a background check and verified my references by Thursday and here I am today."

Today being Sunday. But she'd known Gil and Buck had been desperate to find someone to help out. Scuttlebutt was that finding qualified horse personnel in the middle of San Francisco had been a challenge, especially someone willing to work with special needs children.

"So this is your first time teaching people to ride?"

He nodded. "And so I guess we *all* have something to learn."

She squared off with Flash. "Well, all right then. Tell me what to do, cowboy."

He crossed his arms, the motion highlighting the muscular bulge of his biceps. She liked the way his shirt hugged him, emphasizing how fit he was.

"Okay," he said after a moment's pause, as if he'd

been mentally gearing himself up for the task, too. "Put your left foot in the stirrup."

"And my right foot out?"

She could have sworn he fought back a smile.

"So after the left foot, then what?"

"Grab the saddle horn and pull yourself up."

He made it sound sooo easy.

It was not.

She felt as if she was playing a game of Twister. Once she managed to get her foot into the stirrup, it slipped out the minute she went to grab the saddle horn. Forget about pulling herself up.

"This is impossible," she said. "You'd have to be double-jointed to get close enough to drag yourself onto a horse's back."

"Try facing the front of the animal," he said.

Amazingly, that seemed to do the trick. But even after getting her foot into the stirrup and taking a firm hold of the saddle, she couldn't pull herself up.

"I'm too fat," she muttered.

"You are *not* fat," she heard him pronounce.

"Easy for you to say. You're not the one trying to pull it all up."

"You are not fat," he said again.

She turned to look at him, drawing back instantly. He was right behind her. "You're the perfect weight," he stated.

Amber wondered if he was attracted to her, too.

"Thanks."

"I'll help lift you up," he said.

"If that involves putting your hands on my rump, forget it."

He had an amazing smile when he chose to use it. "Just try and swing yourself up. I'll do the rest."

She thrust her foot in the stirrup, grabbed the saddle...

He did the rest.

He clasped his hands around her waist as if she were a figure skater and he was her partner. She didn't need to use the stirrup so much as clutch at the saddle. The end result was less than graceful, but before she knew it she found herself sitting on the worn leather.

Amber sighed loudly, out of breath. She could still feel where his hands had been. "And they make it look so easy on TV."

"It'll get easier," he said.

She kept clutching the saddle horn, even though she knew she should be looking around for the leather strap thingy. What did they call them? The reins. She should be holding on to the reins in case the animal beneath her—a very *big* animal—decided to bolt, or to charge, or to buck and twist to throw her off.

"Maybe it's nothing to you," she said. "But it's a big deal to me. I feel like I've conquered the world." She smiled.

"You're right. No big deal." He turned on his booted heel and began to leave.

"Hey!" she cried.

But he didn't turn back.

"Hey!" she called again, louder.

He walked away.

CHAPTER FIVE

IT HAD HAPPENED AGAIN, Colt thought, practically running ahead of Amber.

Something about her reminded him of his mom. Or maybe his sister. One of them. So? That didn't mean anything.

"Hey," Colt heard her call again.

He told himself to walk straight past the arena gate. Hell, he should head to the parking area and get in his truck. Amber Brooks was the worst sort of woman to be attracted to. The only reason he'd met her was because he'd been sent to find out where her nephew was. She'd stolen a man's son away. Okay, so maybe not stolen. She had legal custody of the child, but the fact remained that she refused to bring Rudy by to visit his father. Refused to let Logan see his son. Refused to let Logan even talk to him on the phone.

"Okay, fine," she said. "Leave me here. But I want you to know that you're the worst damn riding instructor I've ever met."

And he was angry, he admitted. That's why he wanted to walk out.

"And that's saying a lot, since you're the only riding instructor I know."

"Crap," he muttered under his breath.

He couldn't leave her there.

He slowly swung around to face her. She had the same joy of spirit that his sister had. That's why she reminded him of Maggie.

Crap.

"Follow me," he said.

She sat on the horse like an abandoned child. "I would love to 'follow you,'" she said, "if you would only tell me how, exactly, to do that."

Get it together, Colt.

"Okay." He took a deep breath. He could quit at any moment.

And go back to day-leasing pathetic horses next year.

"First thing you need to do is pick up the reins."

She glanced down. "Reins," she said, scooping them up as if she was scooping out ice cream. "Check."

Damn it. He would have to touch her again. "Not like that," he said. "Both of them in one hand."

She looked at them, clearly confused, then switched the reins to one hand, but they were all wadded up wrong.

"No," he said. "Leave the ends hanging out." Against his better judgment, he went over to her. "Like this."

She had petite hands. And nice nails. They weren't painted, but were well-shaped. He couldn't stand bright colors on a woman's nails. Made them look cheap.

He almost forgot to let go of her hand holding the reins until she said, "Oh, I see."

Colt stepped back, grateful for a little distance. He forced himself to remember she wasn't as sweet as she looked. Even panthers were beautiful.

"Now what?" she asked.

Mean. Arrogant. Self-righteous. Those were the words Logan had used to describe her.

"Go ahead and squeeze Flash's sides with your legs," he said.

But she didn't seem evil.

"Like this?" she asked.

Not at all.

"Harder," he said.

Her face was turning red. Colt realized she was squeezing the horse as if trying to make juice out of him.

"It's not working," she huffed.

"Try a kick."

She tapped her heels.

"Harder."

That seemed to do the trick. Flash took a step. Colt almost laughed when he caught the look on Amber's face. She couldn't have appeared more stunned, if she'd been shot off in a rocket.

"That's working better," she said, kicking harder.

The gelding flung his head up in response. "Not too hard," Colt said. "We don't want to get him upset, especially when he's moving along just fine now."

She looked pleased. And excited. And…happy.

"Lay your reins on his neck to guide him to the arena."

"What are you going to do?"

"I'll be right next to you in case you need me, but you won't."

"How do you know that?"

"That's a good horse you've got there," Colt said. He'd met Buck only once, but had been impressed with the old cowboy's horse sense.

"How do I apply the brakes?"

"Pull and lean back at the same time."

She started to do as instructed. "Not now," Colt said quickly. "Wait until you get into the arena before learning to use the control stick."

"Leave it to a man to call the reins a control stick," he heard her mutter.

Eucalyptus trees towered overhead, their shade and pungent smell pleasant. He kicked at the fallen leaves. Beyond them lay the arena, and beyond that, an open field that seemed out of place given all the trees around them. Then he remembered what it was. He'd read about it online. That was the cavalry field, where officers had practiced maneuvers on horseback. The arena had been added later, and the wood fence that surrounded the perimeter painted a brilliant white.

"Here." He moved ahead of her to open the gate. "Pull him to a stop when I get inside."

"Okeydokey."

It was a nice arena, Colt thought. Someone had spent major bucks on the place. He would give his right eye for an arena like this to use for practice. As things stood, he was forced to mooch off his friends. Drove him nuts. But the only way he could afford something like this was if he got his hands on Logan's horse, which meant getting his head out of his ass.

Colt took a deep breath.

"You have any family?" he asked, coming to a stop next to her.

If she was startled by his question, she didn't show it. "Some."

"Were you ever married?" he asked, even though he knew she wasn't. But he was trying to draw her out, get her to talk.

"No."

Too late he realized his question might be misinterpreted as interest on his part. He scanned her face, searching for evidence that she might have taken it the wrong way. She wouldn't look him in the eye.

"Any brothers or sisters?"

He'd have to have been blind not to notice the way she winced. Her sister had died in a car crash, he knew. That was how Amber had gotten custody of her nephew…when Logan had gone to jail.

"No," she said again. "Nobody."

He couldn't very well call her a liar. Although, technically, she wasn't really lying.

Kinda like you.

One step at a time. He moved back and crossed his arms. "Try a circle."

"And how does one turn?" she asked pointedly.

"Move your arm in the direction you want to go."

And that was that. Flash must have been very well trained because he listened to the halfhearted directions she gave him.

"Can I go faster?" she asked.

"Wow! First day on a horse and already she wants to go faster."

They both turned to see Gil approaching with a young couple and a child. The balding camp director looked especially out of place in such a countrylike setting, in his polyester black pants and a button-down white shirt, Colt decided. The woman with him held the hand of a little boy, who looked to be six or seven years old.

"Good to see you're having so much fun," Gil said.

"Fun?" Amber smiled widely. "This isn't fun, this

is *work*. My arms are sore from brushing and my legs are weak from squeezing."

Gil smiled back at her. "Hear that, Eric? This isn't going to be all fun and games."

But the little boy didn't move. He didn't do much of anything besides look at the ground. Colt noticed that he had a prosthetic leg, and his arm was curled up against his belly.

Colt felt as if he'd been punched.

Car crash. What else would have caused these kinds of injuries?

"Amber and Colt, this is Mr. and Mrs. Peery. Despite your experience, Amber, the Peerys are hoping their son, Eric, might have fun learning to ride."

Colt turned just in time to catch Amber jumping down from her horse like a member of the Pony Express. He marveled for a moment, wondering where she'd learned that move. Her curls tumbled around her shoulders, as bright as her smile. He couldn't take his eyes off of her as she dashed forward, only to draw up abruptly when Flash didn't immediately follow.

"Come on," she told the gelding.

But the big bay was moving at his own pace. Colt interceded. "Here, I'll lead him forward."

His gaze slid to the parents. Both of them had their eyes on their child, and if Colt wasn't mistaken, the mother looked disappointed by her son's lack of interest. He watched as she lifted her free hand to touch her blond hair, then dropped it again. Her husband seemed just as on edge.

"Hi, Eric," Amber said as they drew close to Camp Cowboy's newest student. She squatted low. "My name is Amber."

He wouldn't look at her, but that didn't faze her. "Would you like to meet Flash?" she asked.

Eric edged nearer to his mom, his expression pained.

"Don't worry, he's not going to hurt you," his mother said softly. Then she glanced at Colt, telling him without words he could bring the horse closer.

"It's okay to be afraid," Amber said. "I was scared of horses at first, too. But I've learned they're really nice."

Colt led the gelding as far as he could without actually bumping into the child. Flash seemed curious, pricking his ears up and dropping his head. Colt watched as the gelding's nostrils flared, a sure sign he was trying to catch Eric's scent.

"See?" Amber said gently, reaching up to pat Flash's neck.

"Go ahead, son," the father said. "You can pet him, too."

Tentatively, the kid reached out with his good arm. Colt saw the scars there—multiple angry red lines that could only result from deep gashes.

He had to force himself not to turn away.

"Hey, horsey." Eric glanced up at his parents, wonder in his face.

"Would you like to ride him?" Amber asked.

Eric looked from his dad to his mom.

"I don't have a problem with that," Mrs. Peery said. "If you think it's safe."

"It's an excellent idea," Gil said. "Colt here can help him up."

"I'll get him a child-size helmet," Amber said, dashing off eagerly.

Colt stared at those scars.

"Drunk driver," Eric's mom said in a low voice, next

to him. Her son was busy stroking the horse, her husband squatting down behind him. "We were on our way to a baseball game."

She shook her head, her eyes red.

"Three in the afternoon and the man's triple the legal limit."

"I'm sorry," Colt said, but he was frozen inside. He wanted to leave.

"Here we go," Amber said breathlessly, handing over the helmet.

Mr. Peery took it from her and helped his son put it on.

"You ready?" Amber asked in a bright voice.

Eric nodded.

"Okay, here we go." She took the reins from Colt, who guided the child to the horse's side. He weighed next to nothing when Colt swung him into the saddle.

Drunk driver.

Had the driver lived? If so, did he suffer from the crushing burden of his guilt?

"You okay up there?" the little boy's mother asked him.

The child wore a grin on his face that stretched across his entire face.

Colt busied himself adjusting the stirrups.

"Mom, Dad," Amber said, "can you take up a position on either side?"

Then Colt stepped away, and Amber began to lead the horse forward. Eric's grin went supernova. He clutched the saddle horn with his good hand, his giggle causing everyone around him to smile.

Except Colt.

"You okay?" Gil asked.

Colt hadn't realized he'd stopped moving and that the director had come up next to him. "I'm fine," he forced himself to say. "Just watching."

But he was far from fine.

CHAPTER SIX

SOMETHING WAS WRONG with Colt, Amber thought as she led Flash around.

It took every ounce of her resolve not to turn and ask him what was up, but her focus had to be on Eric and helping him to stay on the horse. And it was funny, too, because she didn't feel half as uncomfortable around Flash today as she had yesterday.

"You're doing great, Eric," his father said.

"I can't believe it," Mrs. Peery added. "You're riding. I didn't think you'd do that for at least a week."

"Normally he wouldn't," Amber said, glancing at Colt again. "Usually, we spend a week or more just getting kids used to being around horses, but I've never heard of a pony ride hurting someone. Not," she added quickly, "that I'm an expert. Yet."

"What the heck are you doing?"

The three of them froze.

"That child shouldn't be riding yet," Jarrod called.

Gil and Colt both stepped forward, preventing the distraught therapist from getting any closer to Eric. *Good.* Amber was worried he'd startle the horse.

"Excuse me?" Colt was saying.

"Gil, I'm sorry," Jarrod practically snapped. "But—"

"Is everything okay?" Mrs. Peery asked Amber in a worried voice.

"It's fine," she answered as calmly as she could.

"He shouldn't be up there without some basics first," Jarrod was arguing. "That's especially important for children with—" he lowered his voice "—disabilities."

"That child is having fun," Colt said.

"It won't be fun if he falls off," the other man retorted.

"He's not going to fall off."

"Oh, yeah?" Jarrod countered. "And how would you know that, cowboy? You ever work with disabled kids before?"

"No," he said. "But I've grown up on horses. No one's going to fall off a plug like Flash."

Jarrod leaned in, saying very quietly but intensely, "He has no lower leg."

Amber quickly glanced at the Peerys to see if they'd also heard. They had.

Colt's response was equally low and ferocious. "He doesn't need one to ride." The Peerys looked over the horse at each other, clearly confused.

"Okay, that's enough, you two," Gil said. "Amber. Bring Flash on over here. We'll let Eric finish his ride some other time."

"Yeah, like when *I'm* in charge," Jarrod muttered.

"Jarrod," Gil said quickly.

"You ready to get down?" Colt asked, clearly forcing a smile as he stepped forward.

"Do I have to?" Eric asked.

His mother patted his thigh. "It's time, honey," she said softly.

"You need any help?" asked Mr. Peery.

"Nope," Colt said, moving to Eric's side. "We're good."

But Amber could tell he was furious.

"Come on down, buddy," he said, gently lifting the child off Flash's back.

"Aww, drag," Eric said.

But Eric's mother was beaming. "I've never seen him so excited," she whispered to Amber. Her smile faltered a bit. "After the accident…"

Amber gently touched the woman's arm. "I know. They withdraw into themselves. But something about horses…"

Mrs. Peery watched as her son went up to Flash's head.

"Thanks, horse," he exclaimed, his eyes bright.

"He loves it," she said in a low voice. "I haven't seen him smile like that in…well, a long time."

"His reaction is the reason I'm here," Amber confessed.

Colt was squatting next to the child, showing him how to touch Flash's nose. The cowboy had calmed down somewhat, but Amber could tell he was still mad as all get-out.

"Actually, it's the second reason I'm here." She turned to Mrs. Peery. "I'm doubling as a speech therapist for the next eight weeks, but I'm interning as a hippotherapist at Camp Cowboy."

"You mean you don't work here permanently?"

"No. I joined up for the first session of the year."

"I was so glad we got in," Eric's mom declared. "We've been trying for six months now."

"Gil—" Amber pointed her chin to where her boss stood "—said if I like doing this, I'm welcome to join them for the session in March." She watched as Gil looked from Colt to Jarrod, who appeared to be arguing.

"I'm hoping we'll be allowed to return in March, too," Mrs. Peery said with a glance at her son. "We were put on a waiting list for this session, and even then they didn't call until after the Christmas break. Just before New Year's." She frowned. "Someone needs to open up a place like this year-round instead of for eight-week sessions."

"I agree." But Amber knew Camp Cowboy operated in eight week segments for a reason. To help more children in need.

"Hippotherapy seems so promising," Mrs. Peery said.

"And Camp Cowboy has some of the best hippotherapists in the business. I'm hoping they'll give me their insights—you know, teach me how to work with children and horses. Become more than a speech therapist."

Mrs. Peery's eyes were bright. "I think you're going to do *great*."

"I hope so."

"Here," Colt said, reaching for Flash's reins, "I'll take him back to his stall."

Amber hadn't heard him come up, even though she'd had one eye on his argument with Jarrod this whole time. "Can I help?"

"No." She and the Peerys trailed him as he led the horse from the arena.

"He doesn't look happy," Mrs. Peery whispered as they stopped by the gate.

"I think he's mad at Jarrod for telling him he shouldn't have put Eric on Flash."

"Oh, I hope not. Eric loved it so much."

But as she watched Colt head back to the barn,

Amber heard Jarrod say to Gil, "He has no business working with special needs kids."

The director nodded.

"He's not trained," Jarrod added.

"I'll talk to him," she heard Gil reply before pasting a bright smile on his face and turning to Eric.

"Did you have fun?"

"Yup."

"Just wait until you get better at it," Gil said.

Colt disappeared with Flash into the barn.

"I hope he doesn't get in trouble," Mrs. Peery murmured.

"Me, too."

Amber wondered if she should follow Colt.

"Oh, the helmet," Mrs. Peery said.

"I'll take it back," she said quickly.

"I can do that," Jarrod offered.

"No, thanks," she snapped.

What a jerk.

But before she could dash after Colt, Mrs. Peery stopped her. "Thank you," she said. Amber noticed the woman had tears in her eyes. "I mean, really, thank you. It was wonderful to see Eric smile again."

One day, she hoped to say the same about her nephew.

"You're welcome." Amber turned away and vowed that, yes, one day she would.

But first she had to see what was up with Colt.

Dirty rotten bastard. He should have clocked the guy in the face. Who did he think he was?

Have you ever worked with disabled children before?

"As if you need a degree to ride," Colt muttered under his breath.

Flash snorted.

"I know," he said. "Pompous ass."

"You okay?"

He turned, stunned to see Amber behind him in the stall.

"Fine," he said curtly.

"Liar."

He just shook his head. Where was Flash's halter? He spotted it in the shavings.

"I'll get that," she said, obviously following his gaze. She handed it to him the proper way—crown piece up.

She was learning.

"Thanks."

"For the record, I think putting Eric on Flash was the right thing to do."

"For the record—" Colt slipped Flash's bridle off, then slid on the halter "—I have more experience with horses than every hippotherapist at this camp combined."

"I know," she said, even though she didn't really know any such thing. She just didn't think now was the time to argue.

"Eric was having a great time until Bozo came along."

"He was." She watched as Colt flipped the stirrup up, hooking it on the saddle horn.

"All you need are your knees to hang on."

"I can attest to that," she said. Her own knees felt chaffed where the saddle had rubbed against them.

"Eric's prosthetic was on his lower leg," Colt said. "I could tell."

She could, too.

He undid the leather strap that attached to a wide rubber piece. The girth, she thought it was called. But before he could jerk the saddle from Flash's back, she rested a hand on his arm.

"I know Eric was in no danger."

Colt's hands were shaking, she noted in surprise.

"I did *not* put that child in danger."

Was he stricken by guilt? Why did he seem so devastated? So disappointed?

"I know you didn't," she said, gently rubbing his arm. A man's arm. The hard cord of muscle beneath his shirt sent a static charge up her fingers. Or was that from something else?

"I would never intentionally put someone in danger."

"Of course not." She slid her hand up to his shoulder. So hard. So masculine. So tempting to touch.

He shook his head and pulled the saddle off, heading toward the tack room before she could say another word.

She almost leaned against Flash.

Amber crossed her arms in front of her, disgusted with herself. Had she learned nothing from watching her sister fall head over heels for a cowboy? A man like the one who'd just walked away. A man who didn't know the meaning of the word *commitment*.

"I must be losing my mind."

She felt something nudge her leg.

Mac stared up at her.

"Hey, boy." She reached down and stroked his fur.

It took a while before Colt returned, snatching up a brush.

"Um, you want to get a bite to eat after this?" she said, still rubbing Mac. "The cafeteria is open."

"No."

Colt's tone was as impersonal as a doctor's.

"Okay, sure. Yeah. I understand. No problem." She gave Mac one last rub and turned away.

"Amber, wait."

She forced herself to keep walking, Mac following behind her.

"Amber."

She kept moving.

Catching up, Colt blocked her path. "Mac, get back to the barn." His dog glanced first at her, then at him, then reluctantly—or so it seemed—returned the way he had come.

"I'm sorry," Colt said. She watched as he tipped his head back for a moment, releasing a breath. "I didn't mean to snap. I'm just pissed. And...sad."

"Sad?" she asked, forgetting for a moment how prickly he'd been acting.

"For Eric. That kid will have to go through the rest of his life feeling different. And if he doesn't know that now, I'm sure other kids will remind him of it. It upset me." Colt shook his head. "And then the horse whisperer came along and got me angry."

"I've got to go," Amber said, pulling away from him.

"What?" he asked.

"I just remembered I have to do something."

It was one thing to be physically attracted to a man, quite another thing to be attracted to the person he was inside.

CHAPTER SEVEN

SHE DIDN'T SEE HIM the rest of the day.

Thank God for that.

Amber didn't want to like Colt. Not when she was so damn attracted to him. That way lay danger.

So she suffered through a restless night. When she finally dragged herself out of bed she told herself not to worry. Yesterday had been a fluke. An aberration. She was over it now.

Still, when he wasn't around at breakfast, she wasn't disappointed, although she did wonder where his dog was.

Two hours after sunrise Camp Cowboy became a bustling hub of activity.

Her nephew arrived today.

Heading back to her room after breakfast, she tugged on a black turtleneck. She'd learned that San Francisco was cold in the morning, far different from Sacramento, where she lived. Once that early morning fog rolled in, the temperature dropped by a good twenty degrees. That meant jeans and a thick pair of socks.

"You ready?" one of her coworkers asked, exiting her room at practically the same moment as Amber.

The woman—one of the live-in volunteers—smiled. Melissa. Long, brown hair. Matching brown eyes. Pretty smile. Friendly. Amber had liked her right off the bat.

"As ready as I'll ever be," she answered.

They walked together down the stairs to where the staff was meeting in the lobby, the area between Gil's office and the cafeteria.

"Thank you, everyone, for coming," said the director, taking center stage in yet another polyester suit, this one gray. "I don't know about you, but I'm excited."

The words stood as a reminder of what Amber had come here to do. Learn. To get over her fear of horses. Help Dee.

"As you all know," Gil added, the light fixture above his head shining on his bald scalp, "the schedule will remain the same every day."

Against her better judgment, she looked around.

And there he was.

In his black jacket and cowboy hat, he was hard to miss…and he was staring right at her.

"Who's *that?*" her neighbor whispered.

"One of the horse wranglers," Amber answered in an aside.

"Well, he can sure wrangle me."

Amber just shook her head. Gil was speaking again.

"The kids will be down at the barn right after breakfast. I expect the kitchen staff to help in this endeavor." He glanced behind him, toward the food prep area. At least ten white-clad people stood behind a glass partition. Amber could smell the eggs and bacon that had been on today's menu.

"Those of you who've been here before know the drill. We'll need a full slate of therapists ready and waiting at the barn every morning to supervise the kids."

Colt was still looking at Amber. She could feel it. But why? Hadn't he gotten the message last night?

"Horse personnel," Gil went on. "Your animals will need to be saddled and ready by 8:00 a.m. You'll need to be on hand at all times. We'll break for lunch at noon."

Amber tuned him out. She'd already seen the schedule Gil was talking about. It'd been in her new-hire packet.

"At one o'clock, we'll resume working with the horses."

Colt didn't appear to be listening, either. At least he wasn't staring at her anymore.

"I'd like to remind everyone," Gil said firmly, "that the children at this camp are our first priority."

Children. Dee.

"Last year," he continued, "we had a few hitches, but this year I expect perfection from everyone, even the new hires. I want this to be the best facility in the nation for challenged children."

Someone began to clap, then another person. Soon the room was filled with applause and whoops of excitement. Amber knew she should be equally inspired, but she was too busy looking around for Colt.

He'd disappeared. And she felt…abandoned. Silly. It wasn't as if they were friends. Or as if she should befriend him at all.

She forced her thoughts elsewhere, because she would be dealing with Colt soon enough. Gil appeared to be wrapping things up.

"All right. The first bus arrives in—" he checked his watch "—any minute now. Go upstairs, grab your jackets or whatever you need to get. Do me proud, people. Above all else, let's help the children."

Those were words she should live by, Amber thought, pushing away from the wall.

"You look sad."

Her heart leaped at the sound of the male voice, but it wasn't Colt who'd spoken. A man she'd never met stood behind her.

"I'm just wishing the weather would change," she said with a smile. "Amber Brooks." She offered her hand.

"Steven Simpson," he said back. Blue eyes and black hair. Cute in a noncowboy, completely normal sort of way.

Why can't you be attracted to him?

"Do you have a brother named Bart?"

He seemed to appreciate her lame attempt at humor. "No, but I have a sister named Jessica."

That made Amber laugh. "Obviously, you've been asked that question before," she said.

"Once or twice."

To her excitement, he turned out to be another of the certified hippotherapists. Thank God. Maybe she wouldn't have to work with Jarrod anymore. She spotted the pompous blond talking to Gil. Not surprising. Probably kissing the camp director's ass.

"You ready for this?" Steven asked.

"I think so," she said.

"I am, too," Melissa exclaimed, leaning into the conversation. The young intern's expression was filled with excitement. "And who's this?"

"Melissa, Steven. Steven, Melissa."

The two of them started talking eagerly, which was okay by Amber because she was abruptly dealing with self-doubt. Wondering if she should have driven up to the Sonoma care facility where Dee had been a resident for the past few years, maybe taken him down to San Francisco herself. But Dee was…difficult. He required round-the-clock attention. She'd found it impossible to take care of him and hold down a full-time job. So she'd done the next best thing. Enrolled him at one of the best facilities in the state of California and then driven in from Sacramento to visit him every weekend. But that had done little good. Her nephew was so disconnected from the world he acted as if she wasn't even there.

Maybe horses would provide the breakthrough she'd been looking for. Lord knows she'd tried everything else.

She followed the crowd outside. Still no sign of Colt. But a giant diesel pusher that looked almost like a tour bus was headed up the road, its motor growling like a grizzly. Somewhere behind her she heard a rooster crow, but she focused all her attention on the black bus. Like Dee, all the children lived in the area, but he'd been on the bus the longest, since he came from Sonoma. His caretakers had put him on at five this morning. Poor pumpkin was probably tired—not that any staff here would know it.

"Okay," Gil said. "Once the kids are unloaded, we'll take them down to the barn one by one. Tomorrow we'll start doing things in groups, but today I just want the children to see the horses, maybe touch one—nothing more. They won't be riding until next week, so no need to rush things."

Amber found herself wondering if that had been for Colt's benefit. She hoped not.

Where had he gone?

"Those of you not working down at the barn will be responsible for bringing the kids' luggage up to their rooms."

"Oh, man," someone grumbled.

"First ones down to the barn will be Amber and Melissa, with Jarrod as the hippotherapist."

"Right on," Melissa said.

Son of a— Oh, well. Amber would *not* let this spoil her mood.

"The child you two will be working with is Dee." Gil met her gaze, all but giving her a wink at their little secret. "Just speech therapy today, Amber. Don't worry. You won't be riding any horses." He glanced at the crowd. "And while Dee is down at the barn, someone will need to bring his bags up."

"I'll do it," a young woman offered.

"Terrific. Thanks. We'll need all hands on deck today while the kids settle in," the director added, his ring of gray hair nearly the same color as the fog above them. "Have fun, people."

Fun.

That seemed impossible. She'd be dealing with a man who made her heart do funny things and another man she couldn't stand.

And then there was Dee.

She was nervous, she admitted. Keyed up. She did her best to peer through the tinted windows of the bus, but all she saw was the white reflection of the lodge in the shiny surface. She hoped he wasn't fidgety from his long ride. He could become difficult when he wasn't allowed to move around a lot.

The sound of the engine grew louder, the crunch of gravel filling the air. Her heart rate increased every foot it traveled, until at last the bus pulled to a stop in front of them. Amber jumped when the hydraulic brake hissed. All she could make out were dark shapes inside.

She knew they had nurses and caretakers on board, too. The vehicle looked packed.

"Here we go," she heard someone say. She glanced back.

Jarrod. Lovely.

The door opened with another gust of hydraulic fluid.

"I had them put Dee in the very front," Gil said, giving her a secret smile.

"Okay, thanks," Amber said, consumed by the urge to hug him for his thoughtfulness.

"You know someone on the bus?" Jarrod asked.

"No," Amber lied. And she didn't feel bad doing it. This was none of his business.

"Well, as lead therapist, I'll go in and get the child."

"Actually," Gil said, "Amber can manage. Down at the barn, you take over."

Jarrod looked confused, maybe even a little perturbed, but he was smart enough not to say a word.

She scooted forward, her heart pounding so hard she would bet people could hear it.

At the door, she smiled at the driver.

And there he was, his dark hair mussed up as usual. Dee's button nose was a little red, probably because he'd been rubbing it, a nervous affectation of his. Surprisingly, however, his big brown eyes were alert. He was clearly intrigued by his surroundings, his head turning to take everything in.

Her heart swelled.

This was why she was here. To help her nephew, and with any luck, other kids just like him.

She wasn't here to kiss cowboys.

CHAPTER EIGHT

"DEE," AMBER CALLED, hoping he'd look in her direction. He didn't.

"Did you need my help getting him off the bus?" Melissa asked from behind her. One of the other volunteers brushed past to keep unloading the other kids.

"Sure." Now Melissa's help, she didn't mind.

It was darker inside the bus. The driver, who sat in the front seat, was engrossed in his paperwork.

"Dee," she said again, softer this time. Loud noises upset autistic children, as did touching. She took care not to reach out and startle him.

"It's time to leave the bus."

He knew she was near, knew she wanted his attention. She glanced around at the other children. Some were autistic, like Dee. Some had other afflictions such as Down syndrome. Some were physically handicapped. Most got up without much prompting and followed a camp worker off the bus.

"Dee?" she said again.

And though she'd had years to get used to his condition, it always broke her heart to see him like this. She'd been by her sister's side at his birth, back when Logan had been a nice guy and her sister had been filled with pride. But then it'd all fallen apart. They'd suspected something wasn't right with Dee when he was three.

By four he'd been diagnosed. By five Logan was out on the rodeo trail, ostensibly to make more money. But they'd all known the truth. He couldn't stand the sight of his son. And then he'd caused the car crash that had taken her sister's life, and he'd gone to jail.

Everything had happened so fast. One minute Amber had been holding her sister's hand, the next she'd been helping to bury her. And Logan? Well, he was better off out of their lives. Forever.

"We might need to help him up," one of the nurses who'd accompanied the kids said.

"I just hate to do that. He doesn't take to physical contact very well."

"Yeah, but sometimes there's no other way."

She was an older woman with kindly gray eyes, and Amber knew she was right. It was part of the reason she'd put him in a full-time care facility. She'd needed help with him—and hadn't been too proud to admit it.

"All right, let's go."

But before she reached for him, she bent her head close to him and said, "Dee, I'm dying to show you something."

And the nurse, bless her heart, waited patiently, children squeezing past them.

"There are horses outside." Amber dared to move her hand closer to his. "Horses," she said again, louder. "You want to see them?"

Her heart stilled as she gently made contact.

He didn't pull away. Didn't do anything, just continued to stare out the window. She followed his gaze.

He could see the horses.

Colt was down there, grooming Flash, and Dee was transfixed.

"Let's go see," she said, clasping his hand.

He didn't resist. She thanked the good Lord above for that. Of all the types of autism, Dee's was the most severe. She knew that, tried to prepare herself for their visits. Oftentimes, it didn't work.

"Come on," she said, guiding him up.

Did he understand? Sometimes she could swear he did. But as she'd explained to Colt, an autistic child's wiring seemed to be scrambled. Sometimes it worked, sometimes it didn't.

"Nnnn," he said, squinting against the foggy sky. At least that's what it would look like to most laymen, but Amber knew he was squinting because of all the new information his brain was processing. At times it would be too much for him to handle and he would stem, but not today. Thank God, not today.

"Over here," she said.

This was why she hadn't worried someone would figure out they were aunt and nephew. He acted as if she was a stranger; he'd *always* acted that way.

And it broke her heart.

"I'll walk down with you," Melissa said, bending down near Dee's ear. "Hi, Dee, I'm Melissa."

Jarrod just stood there, arms crossed. He didn't even move forward to meet Dee. What a jerk.

"Come on," Amber said gently.

Each child—thirty of them—would be working in groups with other therapists. Dee was first on the list for this morning. They'd do this for eight weeks. And all the kids had dossiers—diagnosis, prognosis, method of therapy. So Amber knew Melissa wouldn't touch Dee, just as she knew Melissa would follow her lead when it came to dealing with her nephew.

"Here we go," Amber said.

Dee seemed to know where they were headed. Or maybe he was just drawn to the horses. Once again Amber felt herself wondering what it was about the beasts that attracted kids. She could feel her own heart beat just a little faster as they approached.

Or was that because of Colt?

What would he think of her nephew?

She would never know, she reminded herself firmly, because he would never find out who Dee was to her. And yet she wanted to tell him everything. It frightened her how badly she wanted to do that.

Dee, however, seemed impervious to anything other than the animal in front of the barn. He couldn't take his eyes off Flash.

"Nnnn," he said again, pointing.

"He's nonverbal," Jarrod observed.

"Yup." Amber wondered if Jarrod had read Dee's dossier.

"Horse," she repeated, enunciating the word carefully. It was like double therapy at the camp. She would work with the children's verbal skills while someone like Jarrod worked to make a breakthrough via the horses.

"That's Flash," Amber said, noticing the direction of her nephew's stare. "And that's Colt standing by his head."

Woof.

Amber straightened suddenly.

"What was that?" Jarrod asked. "Sounded like a dog."

From inside the barn came a streak of gray, white and

brown. Amber froze. Dee and Melissa did, too. "That's Mac, Colt's dog."

"Dog?" Jarrod said. "He has a *dog* here?"

"Mac!" Colt shouted. "Mac, stop."

The dog ignored him.

"He likes people," Amber said. And he was headed straight for Dee.

"Son of a—" Jarrod jumped in front of Dee. She had to give the therapist credit for reacting so quickly. Dee had never been around dogs before, and who knew how he'd react?

"Mac," she warned. But the dog was on a mission. "Mac, no!"

The animal darted to the left around the adults, his tailless rear end seeming to make him more agile than normal dogs. Amber tensed, knowing her nephew could take this wrong, expecting a shriek of terror as the dog jumped. His scream would be followed by body tremors and then "the crash," as she'd dubbed it over the years.

But Dee giggled.

"Mac," Colt called, coming up behind him. "Gosh darn you, dog."

"Get him off of the child," Jarrod ordered.

"No, wait," Amber said, as Colt moved to do so. "I think Dee likes him."

The boy giggled again, and Colt stepped back.

"I can't believe you let your dog run free," Jarrod snapped.

"He's usually well-behaved," Colt said.

"Obviously not anymore."

"Shh, you two," Amber ordered. "Quiet."

They watched as Mac stretched up, his front paws resting on Dee's chest. The little boy giggled yet again.

"Easy, Mac," Colt told him.

Dog and child had eyes only for each other. The little boy reached down. Mac went still.

Well, that wasn't exactly true. His entire back end swung left and right. If he'd had a tail, it would have been wagging. But his front end? That didn't move.

"Go ahead, Dee," Amber encouraged.

Tentatively, her nephew lowered his hand. When he buried his fingers in the animal's fur, he cooed. Amber knew exactly how he felt. She'd been intrigued by that fur, too.

"Has he ever been around dogs before?" Colt asked softly.

"Not around— I don't think so." *Damn it.* Five minutes in her nephew's company and already she'd almost blown it.

Dee looked around, his brown eyes seeking out and finding hers. He smiled.

"I think he likes you," Colt said.

He recognized her. Amber had wondered if he would. It was one thing to visit a child on weekends in his own home, another to take him out of it and have him recognize you. Sure, she'd known him his entire life, but who knew what went on in his mind?

"I still think you should kennel the dog," Jarrod said.

Amber inhaled deeply. Her eyes burned. He'd smiled! When had she ever seen him do that? Once, maybe? When he'd been younger. Much younger. Back before he'd gone quiet.

"I don't think he needs to be kenneled," said Melissa. "I think having a dog around is a good idea."

"Do you like him?" Amber asked.

"I'll be talking to Gil about this," Jarrod said.

"You do that," Colt retorted.

Amber ignored them.

"He's not upset by the dog," Melissa said.

No. Her nephew seemed completely enchanted by the animal in front of him. Dee's smile turned into more giggles and his hands began to move faster and faster. It was typical autistic behavior. They didn't do things halfway, but all out.

"Easy," Amber said.

But Mac took it all in stride. And when Dee sought her out again, she wanted to cry. That was definitely a smile. It'd been so long.... So damn long.

"If he reacts like this to Mac, I wonder what he'll do around the horses," Melissa said.

"Well," Amber sniffed. "Let's find out. Come on, Mac."

"Maybe you should put the dog away," Jarrod suggested, glancing toward the lodge. A few more kids were headed toward them.

"No," Amber said. "He's fine."

"For now," the therapist snapped.

"If something happens, I'll take full responsibility."

"If you say so."

COLT WANTED TO throttle the man. Then again, he'd been short-tempered all morning.

All night.

All damn night he'd thought about her.

"Hi," the dark-haired girl said. "I'm Melissa."

"Colt Sheridan," he said, shaking her hand.

"Nice to meet you, Colt. I'm a volunteer here. Anything you need me to do, you just ask."

"Thanks," he said gruffly, glancing back at Amber.

Clearly, what had just happened had affected her deeply, just as his own interaction with Eric had touched *him* deeply.

"Dee," she said, "slow down."

The little boy had spotted the horse tied at the front of the barn. It didn't help that Mac seemed to be guiding him toward the animal.

"Don't let him rush up to the horse," Jarrod said.

"It'll be okay." Colt stepped in front of the child nonetheless.

"Don't touch him," Amber warned, but he could tell she didn't mean it harshly. "He doesn't like physical contact."

"Unless it's with a dog." Melissa smiled.

"I don't want him rushing up to the horse," Jarrod repeated. "One wrong move could upset this child seriously."

Who was this clown? He might be a certified therapist, but he had a lot to learn about kids and horses.

"Mac, down," Colt ordered, instantly rewarded by Mac dropping his front paws to the ground. Dee stopped, too.

"Okay, good," Jarrod said, as if he'd orchestrated the whole scenario. "I'm going to take the lead. You all just stand back and watch."

"Uh, don't you think this should be more of a group effort?" Amber asked.

He ignored her. "Hey," he said, squatting next to Dee. "My name's Jarrod and I'm going to introduce you to a friend of mine."

"Don't talk to him like he's an infant," Colt said.

Jarrod's eyes all but stabbed him. "Excuse me?"

"He's a child," Colt said. "He might be a special

needs child, but he's still human. He can hear. You're talking to him like he's three years old."

"He is three," Jarrod said. "Mentally."

"Okay, you two." Amber stepped between them. "That's enough. Not in front of this child."

Dee didn't appear to care, but Colt respected Amber's request. Jarrod looked ready to pop a seam.

"Am I running the show or not?" he demanded.

"We *both* are," Amber said. "I respect that you're a hippotherapist. I'm here to learn from you. But I'm a therapist, too. This is a team effort, and if you have a problem with that, I suggest we both talk to Gil."

Jarrod didn't say anything.

"Now," she added.

Colt wanted to clap Amber on the back.

"Fine," Jarrod said. "Amber, bring him on up to the front of the horse and we'll see what happens."

Colt stepped back. "I love this part," Melissa said as the two therapists stood side by side. "It's always so exciting."

He'd gotten a glimpse of that yesterday with Eric, but today wasn't anything like that. Dee refused to get close to Flash. He stopped about three feet away, and didn't even look at the horse. He was fascinated by Mac.

"Would you like to see the horse?" Jarrod asked the boy. He'd lost the preschool voice.

Colt glanced at Amber. She was staring at Dee so intently it appeared she'd forgotten to blink.

"I don't think he wants to move," she said.

"I think you're right," Jarrod replied. "I'll bring the horse to him."

That's what they'd done yesterday. For Eric. Colt had learned, while during research last night, that today would be all about introducing the children to the horses, nothing more. Before each child was allowed to ride, he or she would go through basic instructions on a pommel horse. That wasn't scheduled to happen until next week. According to Gil, Colt's job was to simply lead the horses up to a child and keep an eye on things while the therapists went to work.

"Dee," Jarrod said. Mac stood meekly in front of them. "This is Flash."

Amber had knelt next to the boy, and Colt was transfixed by the way all her energy seemed to be focused on the child.

"Dee," she said. "Flash is a horse." She tipped down so that she interrupted his line of sight. Dee was so intrigued by Mac that he leaned to the right to keep his eyes on the dog.

But Amber was patient. "Dee, I need you to focus on the horse." She moved into his line of sight again.

"Do you want me to put Mac away?" Colt asked.

"Hmm. Maybe." Colt admired the way she devoted her entire self to this. She never looked away from the little boy she was trying to help.

And this was a woman who'd kept a child from his father?

Why? Why would she do such a thing?

"Let's try it," Melissa said. "I'll grab Mac's collar." The intern met Colt's gaze. "Will he mind that?"

"No." He shook his head. "But he'll come if I call him."

"I don't think that's a good idea," Amber said quickly.

"I think it's a *great* idea," Jarrod countered. "The dog's a distraction. No doubt about it." He shot Colt a look that conveyed his disgust.

He's a cattle dog, buddy. He's better with horses than you are.

"He'll move off too fast and that will upset Dee," Amber said. "We need to avoid making sudden movements. Best to do this slowly."

"I say ditch the dog," Jarrod insisted.

"If that's possible." Melissa gently tugged the dog away, her eyes darting between the boy and the animal and another group fast approaching.

"Nnnn," Dee began to moan, his hands beginning to flail.

"It's agitating him," Amber announced.

"Yeah." Melissa released Mac's collar.

"Don't give up *now*," Jarrod prompted.

"Darn it," Amber said. "I want him to be aware of the horse. That's why he's here."

"He's too in love with Mac," Jarrod said, shooting Colt yet another glare. "You should never have let that dog loose."

"He's part of the team," Colt said firmly. "That dog can herd an animal faster than any human."

"Great, if we ever farm cows he'll be perfect."

"You don't *farm* cows."

"Colt," Amber interjected.

"You might think about putting Mac up next to the horse's head," Colt offered after a moment's pause.

Amber looked up quickly. "Will Mac mind that?"

"He's a ranch dog," Colt explained. "Horses are part of the program."

Amber turned back to the little boy, clearly torn. "I don't know. The last thing we want is a stimming episode."

"No." Melissa's brown eyes widened. "We don't want that."

"Stimming?" Colt asked.

"It's when a child goes into a sort of meltdown," Amber explained.

"It's common with autistic children." Jarrod made a sound as if that was something Colt should know.

Putz.

"But the whole purpose of this initial meeting is to get him used to horses," Amber added. "So let's put Mac by the horse."

Melissa reached for him again. The gray dog moved willingly enough, but it was clear Dee didn't like it. Colt had never been around a special needs child. Their reactions were just so physical. Dee didn't only moan, it seemed as if every limb went into action. Every single one of his nerve endings.

"Mmmmn," he moaned.

"It's okay, Dee. We're just moving the dog," Amber said. "The *dog*. Can you say *dog*?"

Melissa stopped Mac right in front of the horse. "Can you drop Flash's head down?" she asked.

In response, Colt pulled on the gelding's lead. Mac eyed Flash's big head warily. The dog was used to chasing horses, not sniffing their noses. Colt would swear Australian shepherds had a love-hate relationship with the animals. This was one of those hate moments, but to do Mac credit, he didn't growl or show his teeth. He held still, all the while giving the horse a look that said, *One wrong move, buddy, and you're dead.*

"I don't think your dog likes this very much," Amber commented.

But it was working. Dee stopped moving. They all watched as the little boy looked up.

"Horse," Amber said. "This is a horse, Dee. Can you say horse?"

The horse, as Dee had earlier, had discovered Mac's fur. It buried its muzzle in the hair behind Mac's collar. The dog shot Flash another look, one that clearly said *not a good idea.*

"Stay," Colt ordered.

Mac glanced over at him, then at Flash again. Flash lipped Mac's fur.

"What a good dog Mac is," Melissa said, amused.

"I know," Amber said. "Poor Mac."

"Poor Mac."

Everyone froze.

Amber stared at the child in disbelief. "He spoke," she said softly.

Melissa stood up. "Aww, Amber," she said. "You're crying."

"I am," she admitted.

And it shocked Colt how much he wanted to pull her into his arms, to comfort her and tell her the real reason he was at Camp Cowboy. Because as he'd watched Amber work with Dee, and as he'd observed Eric the day before, Colt was beginning to wonder if Logan was wrong.

Or had lied to him.

CHAPTER NINE

HER ELATION LASTED all day.

As Amber let herself into her room that evening she was exhausted yet happy. It helped that working with the rest of the kids had gone equally well. Sure, there were a few less than stellar moments; some of the kids were like Dee, refusing to focus on the horse. But for the most part each child was intrigued by the big animals that had been led before them. Eric, the boy Amber had met the day before, was the biggest star of all. He'd taken to working with horses like a pro.

"Amber?"

It was Colt on the other side of the door.

"You in there?"

She debated whether or not to respond. All day she'd been forced to work with him. To stare at him. He was remarkably gentle with the kids.

She loved men with a soft touch.

She opened the door. "Hi, Colt," she said brightly.

Mac was at his feet. During the day, the dog had become Camp Cowboy's unofficial mascot, much to Jarrod's dismay. Everyone loved Colt's dog.

"Mac, no," Colt said when the dog darted into her room.

"It's okay." She opened the door wider. "Do you want to come in?"

He wore his black cowboy hat. Amber wondered if he slept with the thing on. The thought caused her to blush, because she couldn't imagine ever sleeping with him.

Oh, yes, you could.

"I was just wondering if you'd eaten."

"Yup. Had the chocolate mousse for dessert. Yum."

He stepped inside. She watched as he looked around, as if looking for something. As usual, she felt dwarfed by his size. She'd never met a man who made her feel so…so aware of herself and her femininity.

"What's up?" she asked when it became apparent he had something to say.

"Do you have a family member that's autistic?"

She gasped. How did he know? "I, well, I…"

"You do, don't you?"

How to answer? Would he realize Dee was her nephew? Had he already guessed? Had her emotional response to Dee's success that day given her away? Or maybe he'd seen her check in with Nancy on how Dee was settling in.

"Never mind," Colt said. "I can tell by your face that you do."

She gulped. "I don't know what to say."

"Whose child is it?"

"What do you mean?" she hedged.

"Well, obviously it's not your own child."

"What makes you say that?" she asked. "Many special needs children require full-time care. It wouldn't be implausible for me to have a child, one in an assisted living facility somewhere."

"But you don't, do you?"

Really, what would it hurt to tell him the truth? Except she didn't want him to know.

Dee was her secret. Her sister's son. The nephew she loved. "I don't think that's any of your business."

But to her surprise, Colt didn't look disappointed by her answer. He seemed relieved. She had a moment to consider the strangeness of that reaction before he threw her another curveball.

"You're not at all what I expected. I thought you'd be stuck up. Arrogant."

"Why?"

He seemed flummoxed by her question. "Your vocation," he said. "I thought only stodgy academics had therapy degrees."

Relieved that he'd dropped his interrogation, she laughed. "So all educated therapists are stodgy, huh?"

"I shouldn't be in your room."

"Colt," she said softly. She wasn't laughing anymore.

Because Colt wasn't exactly trying to leave. In fact, he was advancing. "All day, I watched you, thought about you," he murmured. "I can't seem to help myself. I don't like women who value careers over everything else."

"What makes you think I value a career over everything?"

"This," he said, splaying his hands. "The way you've thrown yourself into learning something new—all so you can help children. Or the child in your life who's such an awful lot like Dee."

"I think you should leave now."

"No," he said. "Not until I get to the bottom of this."

He was inches away, so close she could smell him. He didn't wear a cologne. He didn't need to. The man smelled like a potent combination of sweat and pine shavings, and she realized it was a scent that turned her on.

He turned her on.

"I want to know if this will get any better if I kiss you."

"Colt—"

"So I'm—" he slowly reached for her, his eyes almost black beneath his cowboy hat "—going to kiss you."

"I don't think—"

He bent his head and she knew, just *knew* she'd been kidding herself. She could have thrown him out...if she'd wanted to. Trouble was, she didn't want to. And so when his lips connected with hers, she held still. And when his hands drew her closer, she leaned toward him. And when his teeth grazed her lower lip, she sighed.

That sigh was all the invitation he needed.

His tongue touched hers and she moaned.

He plunged deeper. His hands touched her through her shirt, and his tongue withdrew from her mouth, only to thrust back inside again. His big, manly hands made her ache.

He lifted the edge of her shirt from her waistband. She arched to give him better access, and when his fingers found her bare flesh, her skin acted as a conductor of electricity to various parts of her body.

But one part in particular.

An area that warmed and tingled and reminded her that she hadn't had sex in...well...a long, long time.

"Colt," she gasped, coming up for air. "We shouldn't."

"I know." His hands pressed against her abdomen. He was trying to guide her toward her bed.

"We're all wrong for each other."

"I don't care."

You know what? She didn't, either. Then he was kissing her again and she wanted, even if only briefly, to feel that delicious desire that only a man's touch could bring.

"Lie down," he ordered.

She shook her head. They were about to make a huge mistake. Huge.

"Fine." He scooped her up.

"Colt!"

He tossed her onto the bed, and the headboard rattling against the wall. She bounced a few times, the mattress springs squeaking, but then he was on the bed with her.

"Take off your shirt."

"No."

He drew back and lifted the hem.

And for some reason, she found the whole thing amusing. Her first official day on the job and she had a man in her bed and coworkers on the other side of the wall.

She should be ashamed.

"Sit up."

She did.

He tugged her shirt off so quickly she didn't have time to think, and when his hands reached behind her and unsnapped her bra, she instinctively covered herself.

"No, don't." With his big hands he clasped her upper arms and guided her back. "No," he repeated softly. He took a moment to study her before jerking his hat from his head and tossing it onto her dresser.

"You have beautiful breasts."

She didn't. They were too big. And they sagged.

They weren't fake and perky and tight like the breasts of rodeo groupies.

"I'm going to kiss them."

Her nipples hardened instantly. She wanted that, wanted his mouth on her. She really did. Her body arched in anticipation again as he leaned toward her. She could feel his hot breath against one of her breasts.

"Hey," someone called out in the hall. A male someone.

The both froze. Had they been found out? If Gil had been told there were two employees in a room together...

"Did you get the health report on the kid in number one?" the guy asked. One of the interns. Or caregivers. Clearly *not* talking to them. Thank God.

"Colt," Amber said, ready to stop this insanity. But he was looking at her, his gaze so heated she couldn't move.

"This is crazy."

"I know," she said.

"I don't care."

"I don't, either."

He kissed her again, hard. Then he was moving down, his tongue finding her nipple again. She closed her eyes and, arching, sighed, "Oh, Colt."

There was a thump on the other side of the wall, but it didn't deter him and in fact seemed to heighten the sexual intensity. The suckling sounds he was making at her breast were erotic. The knowledge that someone might hear them, might figure out what they were up to... She should care about that, she really should. His hand began to move down her bare skin. His fingertips glided toward her belly button, and her stomach muscles contracted. She moaned. His mouth. That wonderful mouth…

He shifted to her other breast, not quite distracting her from what else he was doing.

Unhooking the snap of her jeans.

Her hands found his shoulders. She meant to push him off, to stop him from doing what she knew he was going to do.

Touch her. *There.*

But she lacked the willpower to do more than run her palms up and down his arms, to shift a little so that when he finally did slide his hand toward her center, he had easy access to her—

Her gasp was so loud she was sure her neighbor heard. She tried to bite her lips, but the feel of him suckling her nipple at the same time his hand stroked her soft folds…

"Colt," she said again. "Oh, Colt."

She would lose it if this kept up much longer. She could feel the tremors begin to build, those sweet tremors that she hadn't felt in so, so long and that caused her willpower to fly out the window.

What was wrong with this?

His mouth began to follow the path of his hand.

They were two consenting adults.

His tongue circled her belly button.

There was nothing bad about—

She gasped.

Her orgasm came so quickly, so unexpectedly, that she cried out in shock.

"Shh," he soothed.

"Shit," she muttered as her whole body seemed to burst outward, then contract, then burst all over again.

"Oh, goodness," she moaned. She wanted it to last. Wanted the feeling to go on and on and on.

She barely heard the knock on the door.

"Hey," a man called. "You okay in there?"

Amber's body continued its erotic beat.

"I'm fine," she managed to gasp weakly.

Colt nuzzled her belly.

"Just fine," she called again, softer this time.

God, she was fine.

CHAPTER TEN

"WAS THAT GOOD?" he asked, admiring the way her hair fanned out on the pillow behind her.

Colt watched as her eyes opened wide. "Yeah. It was good."

He wanted it, too. Wanted to rip open his jeans and plunge inside her. But shit, if that person hadn't just knocked on the door, but come into the room...they'd have been fired for sure. There was a strict "no fraternizing" policy at the camp. Colt had been warned.

"I've got to go," he said, forcing himself up and off her.

"Colt. No. Don't leave."

She wouldn't say that if she knew what he was really doing here. "I need to take Mac for a walk," he offered by way of excuse.

She looked disappointed.

"I'll see you tomorrow." He scooped his hat from the dresser and crammed it on his head.

This had to stop.

This *had* to stop.

Damned if he knew of a way to control it, though.

HE IGNORED HER the rest of the week.

Actually, that turned out to be easy to do. There was a constant stream of children in and out of the barn, and more often than not, he didn't even get to see Amber. Frankly, he'd begun to wonder if she'd ditched the whole horse therapy thing. But then he'd catch a glimpse of her working with one of the hippotherapists on the pommel horse. She was just taking care to have no direct contact with him.

And then Logan called.

And it was just damn good luck that he called when Colt was on his way to lunch. One of his female coworkers waylaid him, saying, "Um, you have a call holding for you from a *prison*."

"Oh." Colt glanced behind him to make sure Amber wasn't around. "What line?"

"Three," the woman whose name he couldn't remember said.

"I'll take it up in my room."

Colt sprang into action, hoping against hope that Amber didn't find out about this somehow. What if the woman talked? Why hadn't Logan emailed him like he'd asked?

"Logan," he said after snatching the phone.

"What the hell is going on?" his friend cried. "I swear to God, Colt, I can't believe you're doing this to me."

"Wait, wait, wait," he answered. "I haven't done anything. I just asked if your sister-in-law was really as bad as you think."

"And what the hell kind of question is that?" Logan said. "You're supposed to be my friend. That woman stole my child. She's a selfish, arrogant control freak."

Which wasn't the same thing as the nasty child abductor he'd described the last time they'd spoken.

"She's not what I expected," Colt explained.

"You're kidding me. You aren't starting to like her, are you?"

"No," Colt said quickly. "She's just nothing like I expected."

Or you described.

"You crapping out on me?" Logan asked, a portion of his words interrupted by a long beep, followed by the message, "You are speaking to an inmate of the California Correctional Department. Please hang up if you have reached this number in error."

Colt wanted to hang up.

His stomach had congealed into a knot. This wasn't going how he'd expected.

Well, what did you expect?

Did you think Logan would tell you something that would change your mind about Amber?

Lord, Colt wished he would.

"I just think she might have changed," he admitted. "She's not the heartless bitch you described."

"Yes, she is! She won't let me talk to my son. She won't even bring him by for a visit."

Because maybe Logan's son couldn't talk.

Colt sat up suddenly. "How autistic is Rudy?"

"What?" Logan cried. "He's not autistic."

"Are you sure?"

"What the hell makes you ask that?"

"Just answer the question, Logan."

"He's not autistic," his friend said firmly. "Maybe he's a little different. The doctors called it a learning disability. But that's all."

He was lying. Or maybe not lying. Maybe Logan refused to accept the realities of his child's health.

"When was the last time you saw Rudy?"

There was silence, but only for a moment. It was interrupted by another long beep, followed by the warning message. But when Logan answered, Colt could hear the wariness in his voice. "A year ago. And before that, maybe another year. I've seen him maybe four times over five years."

"And what happened?"

"Nothing," he said.

"What happened?" Colt demanded.

Another pause. "The kid freaked out a little bit. So what? Most kids wig out when they see a parent in prison."

So what? After everything Colt had learned about dealing with disabled kids, he had a good idea. Rudy could be autistic. Could be severely autistic.

Was he at Camp Cowboy?

Was it possible? Was one of the kids at the camp Amber's nephew? He immediately thought of Dee.

"Do you have a picture of him?"

"Why?" Logan pounced. "Do you suspect where he might be?"

"I might," Logan admitted.

"Oh, man, Colt, I'd sign over the registration papers of Ronnie tomorrow if you could tell me where Rudy is. Crap. I should have given you a photo before now. The only one I have is from when he was younger."

"Send it anyway."

"You bet I will. Anything to find Rudy."

Why?

Colt had heard Logan might get parole soon. Was that why he wanted to find Rudy? So he could snatch him away from Amber? If it was his son, Colt would want to do the same. But Rudy wasn't...like normal kids. Colt was certain of it.

"Just email me the photo."

"I'll have to scan it in," Logan said. "That means I'll have to wait until I have access to a computer. Give me a few days."

A few days. That meant the weekend. Colt didn't think he could wait that long. But he had to.

"Whatever it takes," he said.

"Thanks, buddy," Logan said. "Thanks a lot."

Colt hung up, collapsing on the bed. There were thirty kids at the camp, half of them autistic. That would make it easy to narrow down.

He might find Rudy today.

And if he did? Then what?

He had no idea.

HE'D BEEN IGNORING HER for a week.

And Amber was hurt, she admitted, staring out her bedroom window.

It was stupid. Ridiculous, really. They were wrong for each other. He obviously thought the same thing. She should be grateful to him.

But she wasn't.

And now it was Saturday morning. The weekend, and even though the kids were in residence 24/7, she had them off, which meant she had nothing to do. And she was feeling sorry for herself.

Someone knocked on the door.

Amber's heart leaped.

"Amber? You in there?"

Melissa. Damn it.

"I'm here."

Melissa let herself in. "Come on," she said excitedly. "Let's go down to the barn."

"What? Why?"

"I just saw a horse trailer head that way," her new friend said. "I think we have some new horses arriving."

"Oh, well, I don't know…" Colt would be down there. Amber didn't think she could stomach seeing him.

"Come on," Melissa urged, grabbing her hand. "You look so glum. This'll be fun."

But as they left the shadow of the lodge, the sun already high enough in the clear blue sky to cast one, Amber told herself this was a mistake.

"Don't you think Colt is cute?" Melissa asked with a smile and a flick of her long brown hair as they walked toward the barn.

"Oh, um. I hadn't thought about it."

"Come on." She punched her in the arm. "You had to have noticed how hot he is."

Yes…yes, she had. "He's not my type."

"Really," Melissa drawled. "He sure is *my* type. Does he have a girlfriend, do you know?"

Yup. Just as Amber had thought. The man could attract women by the dozen. One more reason to stay away from him.

"Oooh, look. There he is," Melissa said.

They'd made it to the barn without Amber even noticing. And Melissa was right. There was a trailer in front, with CAMP COWBOY stenciled on the side, and beneath it, THERAPEUTIC RIDING RANCH, SAN FRANCISCO, CALIFORNIA. Colt was standing by the cab and talking to the ranch manager, whom Amber hadn't seen in a good week.

"Hi, Buck," Melissa called out. The grizzled old man

in the straw cowboy hat looked over and waved. Mac stopped dancing around and headed straight for Amber.

"Hey, Mac." She stroked his soft fur.

"Hi, Colt," Melissa added.

Amber gave her colleague credit; she didn't gush.

But Melissa's interest made her sick.

She wanted Colt.

"Hey," Colt said, his eyes seeking hers.

Amber gave Mac one last pat and walked toward him. "Hey," she answered.

"Have you met Buck?" Colt asked. "He's the ranch manager."

"Yes, of course." Amber shook the old cowboy's worn and work-hardened hand. "Last week. But you've been gone awhile."

Buck nodded, his stooped frame making him appear older than he was. "Out buying more horses." He hooked his fingers into his jeans. He was short and had a portly belly, but she'd heard he was one of the best at managing horses. "Too many kids, not enough rides," the stocky man said with a smile.

"Can I help unload them?" Melissa asked. Mac was begging for attention from her now.

Colt went to the rear of the trailer and opened the door without another word.

He's just doing his job, Amber thought.

Mac caught on to what was going on and raced after him. It amazed her how the dog knew exactly what to do. Mac backed up, his eyes on the trailer, ready to act the instant his human needed help.

"My dad had a rope horse," she heard Melissa say.

"Well, then," Buck said, "you can lead the horse Colt's about to unload to the third stall on the right."

Hooves banged inside the trailer. Mac's head tipped sideways. Amber moved to the right so she could see inside. Was Colt getting trampled? It sure sounded like—

He led a horse out.

Idiot! It was just hooves on the trailer floor. But for a minute she'd felt…she'd felt terrified. Worried about a man she liked.

She liked Colt.

"Give the lead to Melissa there," Buck ordered.

Colt didn't even look at her as he handed over the brown horse. Melissa's smile was wasted, for he simply headed back in.

So it wasn't just her, Amber thought.

"You can lead the next horse."

It took her a moment to realize Buck had spoken to her. "Me?"

"Nobody else standing next to you, is there?"

Amber heard the same banging and thumping as before, only this time Colt led out a spotted pony. "Oh, my gosh, he's adorable."

"It's a she," Colt said.

When she glanced up she found him staring at her in a way that made her heart beat faster and her mouth go dry. It was all she could do to remember to take the lead rope from him.

"Fourth stall on the right," Buck said.

"Okay." Amber took one last glance at Colt. "Come on, girl."

"Petal," Buck said. "The pony's name is Petal."

Despite the fact that she really didn't trust any horse, small or not, "Petal" amused her. "Let's go see your new home."

The little pony followed meekly behind. Mac trailed

them as if waiting for a chance to jump in and help. There was something about ponies that kids—and, apparently, adults—couldn't resist. She suspected the camp's autistic charges would be no more immune to their charms than any other child in the world.

"You're going to be such a pampered pony," Amber told Petal as she opened the stall door. Mac appeared to know that he needed to stay outside. She paused for a moment to get her bearings, and noticed that some-one—probably Colt—had taken the time to lower the horse feeder and the water inside. "And wait until you meet the kids," Amber added, leading the tiny animal forward. "You're going to love them."

"Oooh, that one is so cute," Melissa said, obviously done putting her horse away. She peered at them from near the doorway. "Look at those spots. It's like a mini-leopard appy."

"A miniature leopard what?"

"Appy," Melissa said. "An Appaloosa. They're the horses with spots. Not a big fan of them myself. They can be as stubborn as mules. And I've never been big on white around the eye. But this girl is adorable. Look at her big brown eyes." Melissa came in and wrapped her arms around the pony's neck. "She's just so tiny."

"She's going to be real good for the kids," Buck in-terjected. Behind him, Colt walked past with yet an-other horse in tow. "Picked her up for a song," Buck added. "Came from a carnival outfit down south. She was one of those pony ride horses. Bet she'll be happy not to have to walk in circles a million times a day."

"No kidding," Melissa said with a sympathetic shake of her head. "Poor thing. I've often wondered what kind of life that was for a pony. Tied up all day. But no more. Now you get to have kids love on you all day long."

"Anything else you need me to do?" Colt asked.

"Nope. That's the last. Just keep an eye on them tonight. Make sure they settle in good."

"I'd like to go riding," Melissa said. "If it's okay, Buck."

"'Course it's okay," the older cowboy said. "I would encourage all you therapists to ride."

He looked straight at Amber.

"Oh, um, I've got some stuff to do up at the lodge," she mumbled.

"Nonsense. That can wait. Colt, go and saddle up Flash for her."

"No, really," she said. "I have reports to write. Parents to call. I don't have time to ride. I'd just like to pet the pony for a little bit longer, if that's okay. She's more my size."

She couldn't look at Colt. Was worried that if she met his gaze he'd see how much she'd missed him all week. How every time she saw him she remembered what they'd done in her room.

"Suit yourself," Buck said. "Melissa, I take it you know how to saddle a horse?"

"Sure do."

Amber felt a pang of envy toward her friend.

"Great. You can take Flash then. I'll saddle up one of the other horses. I understand you can ride all the way to the beach from here. Let's see if that's true. Colt, why don't you park the truck and trailer out back for me and then keep on mucking stalls."

Amber focused on the pony. She wanted Colt to stay behind. To talk to her.

She heard a noise. Her heart leaped.

"You okay?" she heard him ask.

"Fine."

"You don't look fine."

He started to enter the stall, ordering Mac to stay outside.

"Colt…"

"Shh." He closed the door. "Just shh."

He touched her face. And Amber was lost.

CHAPTER ELEVEN

WHAT ARE YOU DOING?

He shouldn't touch her. What if Logan really understood this woman better than he did? After all, Colt had met her just a few days ago. But he couldn't seem to stop himself.

"Just shh," he warned her, glancing outside the stall to make sure they were alone.

Logan would skin him alive if he knew of the lascivious thoughts Colt was having about his ex-sister-in-law. And yet he couldn't seem to pull away.

He kissed her. He didn't care that Buck and Melissa were outside. Didn't care that Amber and he were in the middle of a stall. Didn't care about anything.

He could fall in love with this woman.

The thought came as a shock. He drew back.

"What's wrong?"

God, what a mess.

Logan was wrong about her, Colt was certain. Amber didn't keep his son away out of cruelty. She did it for Rudy's sake.

Colt had the little boy's picture in his pocket, had been checking it against the children in the camp ever since he'd received it last night. But Logan was right. It was too old. The child in the picture was too young, his face softened by baby fat. The kids at this camp were older. Colt had sent Logan an email advising him of the fact, but he had yet to hear back.

"Colt?"

He drew her toward him, so conflicted, so filled with longing. She was so incredibly lovely. "Amber," he said softly.

The moment their mouths connected, he couldn't seem to stop himself. His tongue slid across her lips and he tipped his head to the side for better access. He fitted his body to hers in such a way that she couldn't misunderstand his intentions.

"Colt," she moaned when he nibbled the shell of her ear. He felt her shift, and she captured his hand.

Brought it to her breast.

"Touch me," he heard her whisper. "Touch me *here*."

She pressed herself against him, then did some exploring of her own.

"Jeez," he murmured when she touched him, stroked his length.

She didn't let the fabric of his jeans deter her. He dropped his hand, his mouth finding the side of her neck. And then *he* found *her* center.

"Yes." She moaned again.

Their lips met once more and he almost lost himself. Here. In the middle of a damn stall.

"Amber," he murmured.

"Just grab the curb bit."

Buck. They sprang apart.

"They're all hanging on the wall to the left," the ranch manager was saying.

As she passed, Melissa glanced in the stall, saw them and stumbled.

"And this is the horse's fetlock," Colt pronounced loudly.

"Uh-huh," Amber said.

But Melissa wasn't stupid.

She gave them a look and kept on walking.

"Crap," Amber said, straightening. "Crap, crap, crap."

"Amber—"

She left him standing there, nearly colliding with Buck on her way out.

"Excuse me," she said, and then was gone.

Mac tried to follow, but Colt ordered him to stay.

"What happened?" Buck asked.

"Nothing," he said blandly.

It was a lie.

CHAPTER TWELVE

"DAMN IT, DAMN IT, damn it," Amber cursed as she closed her bedroom door behind her. She stripped off her clothes.

She smelled like Colt.

"There must be something wrong with me," she muttered.

Her room was on the utilitarian side, with off-white walls, white drapes at the window, a single bed against one of the walls. Wooden chair, a tiny desk, tiny closet... She sank into the chair.

Someone knocked on her door.

Colt?

"Amber, you have a phone call," one of her coworkers called. "Line two."

Not Colt. Disappointment sluiced through her.

"Hello?"

"Where's my son?"

"Logan," she said sharply.

"Why the hell haven't you returned my emails?"

She took a deep breath. "Logan, I can't put him on the phone. He can't talk to you. You know that."

"Because you won't *let* him talk to me."

She clenched the phone. "He's autistic."

"So he's got a learning disability," Logan said. "That's nothing."

Lord, she was tired of his denials. "I *have* tried, countless times, to put him on the phone. He won't do it. Something about the plastic against his face—"

"Liar."

"I'm going to hang up."

"Don't you dare."

This was how it always went. Logan would insult her. She would lose patience trying to explain things. He would call her a bitch, or worse. She would hang up.

She took another deep breath. Not this time. Time to take the bull by the horns. To settle the matter, because quite frankly, she couldn't take this anymore.

"Okay, look," she said. "I promise to arrange a visit next month." She could take Dee back to Sonoma herself, pop in to see Logan on the way there.

"Liar."

"Stop saying that! I'm not lying, Logan. I'll call the prison and arrange it right away."

"Why don't I believe you? Oh, wait, I know. Because then you would have done it before this. It's been more than a year."

She sighed. She didn't understand the animosity. She was doing the best she could with Dee. *She* was the one who'd been wronged. It was *her* sister who'd died. She should be the one yelling at him on the phone. For driving drunk.

"I promise, Logan," she finally said. "I'll set it all up next week."

She hung up before he could call her a liar again. But she sat there for a long time afterward, staring out the window. She could see the barn from her room, and occasionally Colt and Mac down there.

She got up to go visit Dee.

He was staying in a room on the next floor down.
Someone had come up with the idea of painting the hall
blue, with a rainbow snaking around the doorways and
walls. At the end of the rainbow closest to the stairs was
the nurse's station. The head nurse, Nancy, smiled and
waved. Amber had invented a cover story to explain
her visits. She'd let it slip that Dee was the subject of a
paper she was writing for her master's thesis. Nobody
had questioned her.

She found him in his room, staring outside, ironi-
cally, just as she had been.

"Hey, kiddo."

He didn't turn. Didn't look at her. Didn't acknowl-
edge her presence in any way, shape or form.

"How do you like your bedroom?"

As if he would answer. She almost laughed at herself. She sat on his bed. Like at his regular care facility,
Dee was pretty much left to himself here. He was su-
pervised, of course, but was usually in his room unless
it was time for one of his therapy sessions, or mealtime.

Amber wondered what that was like. Wondered what
he thought of all of it. But she had a feeling he preferred
to be left alone. Autistic children were the epitome of
antisocial.

"I think I'm going to take you to go see your dad in
a few weeks."

He blinked, sunlight softening the edges of his face.

"I really don't want to, but I think it's time to try
again."

Dee didn't seem to care. He was starting to look like
a young man, she noticed. Even his hair had darkened.

Where had the time gone?

Her eyes watered, and she wondered if she'd done the

right thing in keeping him away from his dad. Should she have given up her job, too? Gone on social welfare? Kept him with her? Or had it been the right choice to move him into a place that specialized in giving the care he needed? That kept him safe and away from things that might harm him? She honestly didn't know.

And she felt so alone.

She stood to see what he was staring at. He was looking toward the barn. Of course he was. His room faced the same direction as hers. She tried to spot Colt, but all she saw was Mac.

"Dog."

"What's that, sweetie?" she said, leaning toward him, wishing she could hug him.

Sis, I'm trying so hard.

But Sharron couldn't hear her. Neither could Dee, it seemed. The boy touched the window, his fingertips leaving smudgy circles on the glass.

"Dog," he said again.

Amber froze, then closed her eyes against more tears. She lifted a hand, wanting to touch him.

"His name is Mac," she said, gently resting a palm on his shoulder. Dee didn't move away. "And you're right, he's a dog."

"Dog."

"Mac," she enunciated.

"Dog," he said again.

She'd take it. At least he remembered dog. And it was a minor breakthrough. A word. His second in ages. Something more to build from.

She had no one to tell. No one to share the victory with.

"Maybe Colt will bring Mac by to see you later."

Dee didn't say anything.

"I'll ask him if you want."

He continued to stare toward the barn. And that was okay with Amber. There were so few moments like these. As he grew older, there would be even less. It would be just Dee and her. Although not if she allowed Logan back in their lives.... One day, she would have to give Dee up—at least part of the time. Logan would want him back, she'd begun to accept that. Even if Logan had pushed his child away at the onset of Dee's autism, escaping to the rodeo. He seemed to have come to terms with it....

She spotted Colt and pressed her hand against the glass, too, amusing herself for a moment by covering up his hat with her thumb.

"He's different," she said softly.

A rodeo cowboy. What irony.

She made a decision then, one that she knew in her heart was right. She was so weary. Sick of being alone.

"I love you, kiddo," she told her nephew.

She turned away, heading toward…well…she didn't know what she was heading toward.

But she wanted to find out.

HE NEEDED TO get off his ass, Colt thought, sweeping the floor more furiously. Needed to do a better job trying to match the photo in his pocket to the kids at the camp. To keep his mind off Amber.

"Hey there."

He almost dropped the broom.

"You look busy," she said.

"Hey." He forced himself to meet her gaze.

Her blond hair was illuminated by the light behind

her, the edges burnished gold. When he was younger he'd pictured his ideal woman. Amber was it. But that had been a long time ago, back before his life had fallen apart.

"You doing anything right now?" she said softly.

"Why? You need something?"

It seemed she might not answer, but then she squared her shoulders, looked him right in the eye. "I was hoping you'd take me for a ride," she said. "Next week's kind of crazy for me. I should get some time in the saddle before all hell breaks loose."

You want to find Rudy, don't you?

"Flash?" he asked.

"Uh, sure," she said, glancing toward the gelding's stall.

"You could always ride Petal."

"Aren't I too big for her?" she asked.

He felt his lips twitch. "I was kidding."

"Oh. Well, then, I guess I better go catch Flash."

"I can do it for you."

"No, I'll do it," she said, turning away. His dog tried to follow in her wake.

"Mac," he called.

The Australian shepherd obeyed his command, but Colt could tell he didn't want to. He'd taken a shine to Amber. Colt didn't blame him.

She picked up the halter, studying it for a moment. Flash was eating his dinner in a corner of his stall, his ears swiveling back and forth.

"This won't upset his stomach or anything, will it?" she asked.

"What?"

"Interrupting his meal."

"No." Colt stared at her from beneath the brim of his hat. "Horses in the wild are frequently startled by prey. They can graze for hours and then run for ten miles without any harm coming to them."

She slid the stall door open. He was pleased to see she held the halter the correct way this time, and that she walked right up to Flash. Since the horse was eating, it paid her hardly any attention. In a matter of minutes she'd buckled the headpiece and then stood back, proud of herself.

Colt couldn't help but smile. "Good job."

She tugged the horse away from his food. Flash wasn't exactly thrilled to have his dinner interrupted, but he followed her out. Colt hung back at a distance as she walked toward the front of the barn. It wouldn't be dark for a couple hours yet, but the eucalyptus trees shielded the barn from the sun. He had a feeling the people who'd built this place had planned it that way. Amber didn't seem to notice the waning light. She marched right up to the hitching post, wrapped the lead rope around it and executed a perfect slipknot.

"Wow," he said, pleased on her behalf. "Impressive."

"Thanks." She eyed the horse. "If only I didn't feel like jumping out of my skin."

"You'll get used to him."

But she frowned, her expression doubtful.

"Let me go get my horse," he added.

"Your horse?" she asked. "You have one here?"

He would if he played his cards right. The thought depressed him.

"No. Not my own. I meant one of the camp's horses. Oreo," he said. "Big paint."

"Paint?"

"It's a color," he explained. "And a breed. Here, I'll get him. You can start grooming if you want. Just grab one of the buckets out of the tack room. You know what you're doing now. I'll be back in a minute."

"Okay," she said warily. "But if you hear a scream, call 911."

What was it about her that could make him smile one minute and want to avoid her the next? He tried to reason that out as he haltered Oreo, Mac by his side again. By the time Colt tied the horse next to Flash he was still no closer to figuring her out.

"I'll saddle up if you brush Oreo," he offered.

He could see her relief. "Deal."

Mac hung back as he made short work of the task. Colt was looking forward to this.

Aside from today, it'd been a week since he'd spent any time with her. A whole week and not once had he gotten up the courage to go to her room...either to see her or to snoop around.

"You ready?" He led his saddled horse toward hers.

"I think so," she said, brushing back a strand of hair being tossed by a breeze. He smelled the pungent scent of the eucalyptus leaves and then her own unique smell. Sugar cookies, he thought.

"Use the mounting block," he suggested, pointing. They'd been schooling the kids on it all week.

"Wow," she said. "I wish I could have used that before."

"Better for you to learn how to pull yourself up," he said, wheeling Oreo around with a tweak of the reins while she positioned Flash to mount. "You never know when you might have to dismount out on the trail."

"Is it dangerous?" she said, wide-eyed.

"No, no. Sometimes you need to open gates and whatnot. Or I might need you to hold my horse. No big deal."

Mac followed them at a distance. Colt almost told the dog to stay behind, but the Australian shepherd needed a good run.

"This isn't working," he heard her say.

He glanced back. She stood on the plastic steps, contemplating the distance between herself and Flash. The horse had stepped away from her.

"Smart-ass," he said.

"Who, me?" she asked.

"No, Flash. He knows what you want him to do. He just doesn't want to do it."

He swung a leg over the front of Oreo and leaped down. "Jump off and reposition him."

She did as instructed, but Flash decided he didn't want to move. "You really are a smart-ass," she told the horse.

"Here. Hold mine."

Flash seemed to recognize authority when he saw it because he instantly did as asked.

Colt motioned for Amber to bring Oreo closer. "Climb aboard," he said, taking the reins from her.

But even with him holding Flash's reins, the gelding sidestepped again, and Amber, who'd chosen that moment to mount, ended up off balance.

"Grab the horn," Colt warned.

Too late. She teetered near the edge of the steps and he knew he would have to break her fall.

"Damn it," he muttered, lunging for her.

But he missed and she slipped off the steps and landed on her rear with a thud.

"Are you okay?" He tugged on Flash's reins to get his attention.

"I'm fine," she said, her brow wrinkling as she winced. "The only thing wounded is my pride."

He felt something strange then, something that took him a moment to identify.

Affection.

He *liked* this woman...*a lot*.

And given that he would soon betray her, that scared the living crap out of him.

CHAPTER THIRTEEN

SHE FELT LIKE an idiot.

Amber sat in the dirt, staring up at Colt. He must surely think her a dumb blonde. She couldn't even get on a damn horse.

Instead he appeared as if he wanted to console her. It filled her with warmth.

"Maybe this isn't meant to be," she said in resignation. "Maybe I should just stick to speech therapy."

"Nope," he said quickly. "Best thing to do is get back on the horse."

"I never actually got *on* the darn thing," she said. Mac sniffed at her, as if to offer sympathy. "Can you have a little talk with Flash?" she asked the pooch. "I don't think he understands I'm a beginner."

"Oh, he knows," Colt said. "That's why he's doing what he can get away with." He offered her a hand. She slid her fingers into his, so big compared to hers. She felt diminutive next to him.

Feminine.

She felt like a woman. And it was a feeling she discovered she really liked.

"Thanks," she said softly.

He let her go, but it seemed like he did it reluctantly. "Okay," he said, taking a deep breath. "Try it again."

She eyed the horse, her heart beating so loudly local seismographs likely picked up a reading.

"Hold still, Flash," she said as Colt brought the horse alongside the mounting block. "Mac, make him stay still."

Then she jumped on board so fast Flash didn't have time to pull away.

"Ha!" Her cheeks hurt, she was grinning so widely. "I did it."

"Yes, you did." Colt's brown eyes looked black beneath the brim of his hat. He turned away without a backward glance, swinging up on his horse like Jesse James fleeing the OK Corral. "Follow me."

She told the horse to go. Flash didn't.

"He's doing it again," she stated.

"Push him forward with your legs like you did the other day."

It worked.

Flash moved forward reluctantly, but at least he moved. He tossed his head as Colt led them toward the arena.

"What about Mac?" she asked.

"He'll come along."

Colt was getting farther ahead.

"Are you going to give me a lesson?" she called out. That would make her feel better.

"No."

No? "Then...where are we going?"

"On a trail."

"How do you know there's a trail out here?" she asked as they walked past the arena.

"Buck told me," he said. "It's all public land. If you ride long enough, you can get to the beach."

"I remember. I was there." The thought of riding near the ocean filled her with grim determination. It was something she'd always wanted to do despite not knowing anything about horses. Who hadn't seen beach resort brochures with a couple riding bareback among the waves? Sounded good to her.

At least in theory.

"How long will it take to get there?" she asked.

"Where?"

"The beach?"

He glanced back at her. "We don't have time. This'll just be a short ride."

"Oh," Amber said, disappointed. Maybe one day.

They rode along in silence, Amber marveling that in a few hours the fog would roll in and the entire peninsula would be shrouded in mist. She could feel the early warning of the weather change in the cold breeze that had begun to blow. It made her wonder if she shouldn't have grabbed a jacket. Mac didn't seem fazed. As they passed the arena, the dog ran toward a thick stand of trees that she'd been curious about—tall pines with low-lying scrub beneath. A path led right toward them.

"Hard to believe we're only a few miles from Fisherman's Wharf."

"It's more than a few miles," Colt replied, although it was hard to hear him because he was so far ahead of her. He'd already made it to the trees, and didn't seem inclined to turn around.

She debated trying to catch up to him, but had no idea how to put Flash into second gear. But maybe it was better this way. Maybe she should just hang back and enjoy the ride.

Heh. Enjoy. Yeah, right.

"Colt," she called, when she saw no sign of him slowing down.

Reluctantly, he pulled back on the reins. "What's up?"

She caught up to him. "Nothing."

His eyes had narrowed. "You're doing fine."

"Thanks," she said. Against a backdrop of pines and Douglas fir, he looked like something off a poster. It was still sunny out, but beneath the trees it was chilly. The earth smelled moist and rich. And *he* smelled wonderful. The combination of Colt and trees and the out-of-doors smelled…heavenly.

As they set off again, Mac wormed his way through the brush. He was panting now, his pink tongue hanging out. They entered a denser grove of trees, the tall pines closing in on them.

Amber was enjoying the rocking motion of her horse, just as her autistic charges would once they learned to ride, she decided. Something about it seemed to soothe her frazzled nerves.

"I am one with the horse."

"Good," Colt said curtly.

"But I think it'll be a while before I'm as comfortable around horses as you."

A long, *long* time.

He didn't reply.

"How long have you been riding, anyway?"

His hands twitched on the reins. "How about this," he said as they moved even deeper into the trees. "I tell you something about me and you tell me something about you."

She contemplated the idea. "Okay."

"Who in your family is autistic?"

"Excuse me? Why do you keep asking me that?"

He pulled his horse up so they were side by side. "Your passion for what you do comes from somewhere. I would bet it has to do with a family member."

She shook her head, but in the end, she supposed it wouldn't hurt if he knew.

"It's my nephew," she admitted.

"You have a nephew?"

She nodded. "I do."

"How old is he?"

"Your turn," she said instead. "Where did you grow up?"

He clearly didn't like the question, or maybe it was the game they were playing. But it had been his idea. "New Mexico."

That took her by surprise. For some reason she'd expected him to say Texas or Oklahoma or some other place known for cowboys with Southern accents.

"Your turn." His horse tossed its head. "How badly autistic is he?"

She gulped. It was hard not to come right out and tell him it was Dee. "Pretty bad." She smiled through the pain it caused her to admit that. "I didn't know they raised cattle in New Mexico."

"Some of the biggest cattle ranches in the world border the Texas and New Mexico state line. Is your nephew the reason you became a therapist?"

"Hey, I didn't get to ask my question."

"You asked me about raising cattle."

"I was merely thinking out loud."

He gave her a look.

"Honestly."

"Fine. Ask a question."

She resisted the urge to roll her eyes. "Do you have any family?"

"No."

It took a moment for his response to sink in. "Not even a cousin or an aunt?"

"No," he said. "And that's two questions."

"Nobody?" she pressed.

"Three," he said. "And no. Not a mom, dad, grand-parent or uncle."

She clutched the reins tighter, completely blown away. She'd had it in her head that he came from a big family. That he'd grown up on a ranch. Surely that meant lots of cousins.

Apparently not.

He was staring at her oddly, as if he wasn't certain what to make of her reaction. The only sound for a moment was the dog's panting. Colt kicked his horse forward. Flash kept in step with him.

"My turn," he said. "Do *you* have any family?"

"Yes." But her mind was still chewing on what he'd revealed. What would it be like to have nobody in the world? She at least had Dee. That was something.

"Where does your nephew live?"

Right now, with me.

"Wherever he gets the best care," she answered evasively.

"I meant what town?"

"That's three questions," she said. "Why do you want to know, anyway? And he lives up north."

"Just curious. And that's not a town."

"Near Sonoma," she said.

He leaned back in the saddle. "Sonoma. That's up north?"

"Is that a question?" she asked. "Because if it is, you're back up to three."

"No." His eyes searched hers, as if he wanted to ask her something else, but wasn't quite sure how to pose the question.

"And now it's my turn," she said, echoing his words from earlier. "How did your family die?"

It was a horrible thing to ask. Invasive. Rude. And *way* too personal, and yet she had to know.

But he wasn't going to answer. His expression had turned to stone, his eyes to slate.

"Ask your next question," he muttered.

The trees were starting to thin out. In between them, Amber spotting what looked to be apartment buildings or maybe homes. And was that the roar of the ocean in the distance? Or was that a freeway?

The path they were riding, shielded by trees and lined by shrubs, was beautiful.

"Was it an accident?"

He pulled up his horse again. "It's none of your business."

It wasn't. She knew that. "You asked me about my nephew. That was none of *your* business, but I answered."

"That's different."

She spotted something big and red to her left and stiffened. "Look!"

He didn't move.

"Over there," she added, "through the trees. It's the Golden Gate Bridge!"

She pushed her horse forward, proud of herself for making Flash walk past Colt's horse. Sure enough, the trees opened up farther ahead and a small clearing afforded her a more direct view of the bridge. It was in the distance, but not so far away that she couldn't hear the sound of cars traveling over it—that was the noise she'd heard.

"Check it out," she said when Colt came up beside her. "Isn't that amazing? We're so far away, and yet you can hear the cars."

"Neat."

He said it so harshly, she asked, "What is the matter with you?"

He didn't answer.

"Look, I know it was none of my business to ask about your family, but I thought it might help to talk about it. I'm a therapist. It's what I do. Push people to their limits."

"You're a speech pathologist," he said.

"Ooh, you've been paying attention," she teased, trying to draw a smile out of him.

"And I'm a cowboy," he said. "Me and therapists don't mix."

"That's not what it felt like the other day. Or should we both go back to ignoring the elephant in the room?"

"I'd rather ride." He kicked his horse forward and whistled for Mac.

"We can't ignore what's between us," she called out. As she'd sat there, watching him try to hide how he felt, something inside her had clicked. It all made sense. *This* was why she was attracted to him. What it was that drew her attention.

They were alike.

She'd lost everyone near and dear to her, too. Well, except for Dee. But her loss was still a fresh wound. She missed her sister terribly. They'd been everything to each other since their parents died in a commuter train accident years and years ago. They'd spent their early lives in and out of foster homes, and it had been terrible. Amber was a therapist because of that, too. She'd seen the effect having no family could have on children, the speech impediments it could cause. So she'd put herself through college. A year after she'd graduated, her sister had died and Logan had gone to prison. She'd been caring for her eight-year-old nephew ever since. For four years now...

She shook her head.

Colt missed his family. She missed her sister.

They weren't much different, after all.

CHAPTER FOURTEEN

COLT AND MAC kept ahead of Amber for the rest of the ride—close enough to keep an eye on her, far enough away that she couldn't ask any more probing questions.

Such as how his family had died.

That he wouldn't think about. Didn't *ever* want to think about.

It hurt too damn much.

The trail circled through the trees, and he pulled up when he spied an even better view of the bridge.

"It's so pretty," she called out.

It was. As golden as the name implied.

The sun had dipped even lower, making it feel like dusk in the forest. So when they emerged from the trees, it was almost a shock to see the sun still above them.

"How'd that happen?" Colt heard Amber call. "We're almost right back where we started."

He took off his hat, tilted his head back and absorbed the sun on his face. It felt good. He wished he could sit here all day. But there was too much to do. And Amber...

She wouldn't leave him alone.

When they got to the barn, Colt jumped down. "Use the mounting block to dismount," he ordered.

"Oh," she said. "You *can* speak."

He grabbed Oreo's halter, made quick work of slipping off his bridle and sliding the nylon harness on.

"Holy moly!" Amber cried.

He jerked around.

She was already off her horse. "I don't think I'll be able to walk for days."

"Damn it, Amber. I thought you'd fallen off."

"Surprisingly, no," she said with a smile. "Apparently Flash doesn't mind standing still while someone gets off."

Colt went back to work.

You're being an ass.

He was. He knew it. But he just wanted to get this over with. To get the horses unsaddled and Amber up to the lodge. That way he could have some privacy. Some time to figure out what the hell was wrong with him, because despite narrowing down where her nephew lived, Colt felt no elation.

"Can I help you take the saddle off?" she asked, after tying Flash.

"No."

When he glanced over at her as he pulled the saddle off Oreo's back, he saw the hurt in her eyes.

"I'll go hang up the bridle," she said.

"No need." He held out his free hand. "I'll take it."

"Colt…"

He grabbed the bridle from her even as he chastised himself for being so harsh. "See you up at the house."

"Uh, okay."

He didn't hang around to see if she had gone or not. After he tossed the heavy saddle on the rack, he rested his palms on the seat. Mac whined, his head tipped to the side, ears pricked.

"Crap," Colt muttered.

He had to get hold of himself. He'd scored a major victory in finding Logan's son. He knew where Rudy was.

How did your family die?

Colt closed his eyes as he thought back to that day, to the site of the accident...the broken railing. The branches near the base of the hill. The gouges in the asphalt.

"Colt."

Pulled from his memories, he straightened with a jerk, and spun around, planning to lash out at Amber. But he didn't have the heart. It wasn't her fault his memories caused so much pain.

He hadn't had a heart since his teens.

"What happened to you?" she asked gently.

He shook his head. "It's nothing." He drew a breath, then another. "I thought you went back to the lodge."

"I couldn't leave you like this."

"Like what?"

"Upset."

"I'm not upset," he lied.

She took a step closer. "This is about your parents, isn't it?"

"Don't you have something to do?" he asked, tempted to leave.

But she'd already closed the distance between them. Already lifted a hand and touched his cheek. "I've taken far too many psychology classes not to know when someone's lying."

Did she know his whole existence was a lie? That he had no business being here? That the day his parents and his little sister had died, he should have been with them?

"Colt," she said. "You shouldn't keep this bottled inside. It's eating you up."

"You don't know anything about me," he snapped. "Nothing at all."

"I don't," she agreed. "Despite what's happened between us, I don't know hardly anything about you."

Her eyes drew him in. He swore they could swallow his pain. How lucky the children were who had her on their side. How lucky Rudy was.

"Maybe it's better that way," he said, backing away.

But she followed him. "Keeping things inside is never better for you," she said softly.

She moved around him and somehow wedged herself between the saddle on the rack and his body.

"Sometimes, Colt," she said, her blue eyes as big as the compassion in her heart, "you need to let things out before life can get better."

He wanted to turn away. But her eyes held him.

For the first time ever, he found himself on the verge of making a confession. Of telling her what had happened all those years ago.

But he didn't deserve her pity…or her compassion.

"I need to go," he said, brushing past her.

This time she didn't follow him.

SHE DIDN'T SEE HIM for the rest of the day. Not at breakfast, either. It was Monday, and today would be the first time the children would actually ride the horses. A crowd of about twenty or so volunteers, physical therapists and interns—like herself—headed toward the barn.

"I'm freezing," Melissa said with an audible shudder.

"Me, too," Amber said, trying to spot Colt. He must be in the barn.

"Is the sun ever out in the morning here?" her friend asked.

It had dawned another foggy and overcast day, but the humidity made it seem particularly cold. "I don't know." Amber tried to draw further into her jacket, like a turtle.

Buck came out of the barn leading a horse, but so far no Colt. And no Mac, either.

Where were they?

She needed to apologize. To tell Colt she was sorry for pushing. She'd been born too pushy, and that was what made her a damn good speech therapist. She didn't give up. Didn't mind the repetition. She pushed her patients to get it right. Colt wasn't a patient.

"Okay, here's how it'll work," Jarrod said. "We'll break into four teams, each led by a hippotherapist. That means Jackie, Sam and Sarah will be in charge. Whatever they tell you guys to do, you do it. I'll run the other team."

"Who died and made him king of the universe?" Melissa said in an aside.

Amber smiled. "I think the horse-therapist experts need to take control at this point, don't you?"

She tried to avoid the man whenever possible, but the few times she'd bumped into Jarrod at the lodge he'd seemed just as bossy and, frankly, annoying. He'd asked her out last week. She'd said no. Amber hoped that would be the end of it.

"Melissa and Amber, you'll be on my team," he said.

"Oh, great," Melissa muttered.

"We'll need a fourth," Jarrod announced. "Any volunteers?"

An older woman with thick-framed glasses lifted her hand. Maybe Jarrod wouldn't hit on someone clearly over forty.

"Thanks," he said. "Jackie, Sam and Sarah, you want to pick your teams?"

Melissa stepped closer. "Is it just me, or is Jarrod really, really annoying?"

Drops of moisture were clinging to her friend's dark hair. Amber had no doubt the humidity was doing the same to hers. "Really, really, really annoying." She looked past her, to see Colt leading a horse out of the barn, Mac following behind. But the cowboy didn't look up.

Something inside Amber withered.

"The children are on their way down," Jarrod called out. "Let's get it together, guys. My team will go first. Any idea when you'll get the rest of the horses saddled?" Jarrod asked Colt, his tone on the verge of rude.

"They're tacked up in their stalls," Colt said. "Just let me know when you need the next one."

Hah, Amber wanted to say.

"Amber!" someone called. "Can I speak to you?"

She turned, startled to find Gil escorting the three children they'd be working with. Wait a minute…*three?* "Where's Dee?"

"He didn't want to leave his room," Gil explained. "We tried everything. We were thinking of just leaving him be. He could work with one of the physical therapists today, and then later, with you for speech, if that's okay."

Amber glanced to where Mac stood beside the horse.

"Actually," she mused, "I have an idea."

She turned back to her boss. Did he have an endless supply of polyester suits? He looked out of place among everyone else in their jeans and thick jackets. "I'd like to try a little experiment with Colt's dog."

A frown creased Gil's forehead above his glasses. "How so?"

"I think Camp Cowboy's focus should be expanded." When his expression grew even more puzzled, she added, "I think we should use *all* types of animals for therapy."

His eyes widened. "Colt's dog?"

"If Colt doesn't mind. I'm curious if my neph—" She caught herself. "If Dee will respond to Colt's dog. Honestly, it's been tough to get Dee to look at a horse. Mac, however—"

Gil had begun to nod. "Hmm. It's not something we ever considered."

"It's worth a shot," she said. "You can't tell me every child responds to horses."

"They don't," the program director agreed. "And it's always a disappointment. Colt?" Gil called when he came back out, leading a second horse. "We have a proposition for you."

Amber noticed that the moisture had turned Colt's black hat even darker.

"What's up?" He still wouldn't look at her.

"Amber here would like to borrow your dog, if that's okay."

Finally, their gazes connected. "What for?"

She pasted a smile on her face. It killed her to see him like this. Obviously, he was upset about yesterday. "I'd like to introduce him to the other children."

Colt glanced at Mac, then back at her. "I don't mind."

Gil clapped him on the upper arm. "Excellent. I suspect Amber might be on to something, especially after how Dee responded to the dog earlier." Her boss met her gaze. "But are you certain you don't want to wait until later? When you're done working with the children and horses?"

"I have weeks to work with the horses, Gil." Amber smiled. "Mac!"

The dog instantly turned. Amber decided she wanted a pet just like him one day. She loved the way Mac came running, tailless rear end wagging, tongue lolling, eyes shining. She wished his owner would be as happy to see her.

"Come on, Mac," she said. "Let's go up to the lodge."

She wondered if he'd follow her or if he'd want to stay with his master, but the canine didn't hesitate.

"Thanks, Colt," Amber said.

He held her gaze for a split second longer than before. "You're welcome."

And off she went, with Mac at her side. That gave her some comfort. At least his dog liked her.

And Mac loved children.

That became obvious the moment she hit the children's wing and found Eric standing in the long hallway there. He must have been on his way to one of his therapy sessions but paused in delight when he spotted her canine companion. Mac seemed just as happy to see Eric as he was every other child on the floor. They soon attracted a crowd of children. Nancy, the head nurse, tried to keep things under control. But it was a challenge. Amber squatted down at Mac's level, trying to shield him from small probing hands. You never knew what a special needs child might do. Some were like Dee, autistic and uncommunicative. Some had minds that just didn't work right, symptomatic of causes as varied as Down, fetal alcohol or genetic syndromes.

"Okay, guys," Amber called at last. "Time for us to go."

There were choruses of "Aww," from kids and adults alike. Amber smiled.

Yup. A dog was just what this place needed.

She straightened and headed toward Dee's room.

"Knock, knock," she said.

He was standing in the corner of his room, in the space between his bed and a closet. Just standing there. Examining the wood frame around the closet door as if fascinated by the way it connected to the wall. And maybe he was fascinated.

"Hey, buddy, I brought you a friend."

The dog looked around, sniffing, taking in the new surroundings. And then he spotted the little boy. It was funny, but Amber could swear the dog wanted to rush to him. Yet he didn't.

Mac didn't jump up on Dee. Didn't bump into him. Just stood there, waiting to be noticed. And when Dee didn't move, Mac touched the boy's hand with his nose.

Dee turned and looked down.

"Dog."

Amber was so delighted, her mouth dropped open. He remembered!

"That's right," she said, pleased that he remembered. "Dog."

That was the thing with autistic children. You could never be certain what they would retain. Heck, with Dee, they'd never been certain he was absorbing *any-*

thing. Off in his own world. He fed himself, for the most part, but only vegetables that were a certain color. And only if items on his plate didn't touch. And never meat. Dee couldn't stand meat.

Mac backed up a few steps. And to her surprise, Dee followed. Amber squatted down, encouraging Colt's dog to come to her.

"Come pet him, Dee," she urged.

She didn't expect him to comply. Honestly, there was a good chance he really didn't understand her, that he was just following the dog, but Amber didn't care. As long as he responded.

"Sit, Mac," she instructed.

From this angle, she could see her nephew's eyes, and as always happened, the loss of her sister came back in a wave of sorrow. He had her eyes. Who was she kidding? He had her entire face.

"Put your hand out," she told him softly. But her nephew's beautiful brown eyes were fixed on the dog. Amber held her breath as she reached for his hand.

He didn't pull away.

"Pet him," she said, burying his fingers in Mac's soft fur. The dog, bless his heart, held still, staring up at the boy.

"Remember, his name is Mac," she said. "He's an Australian shepherd." She showed her nephew how to stroke the dog. "Isn't he pretty?"

"Dog."

Amber smiled. "Yes, dog."

Mac swung around, poised to move, but waiting.

Amber sat back and watched. "He wants you to follow him," she said, although she had no idea where the dog was going. "Follow him, Dee."

And he did. Mac's rear end began to swing, his blue eyes wide. Tongue hanging out, ears pricked forward, he crouched and then lunged away. The dog was playing with Dee.

But Dee had never played with a dog before. He seemed confused about what to do.

He was engaged, however. Engaged!

Forget the horses. This dog seemed to be all the therapy Dee needed.

"He wants you to chase him," Amber said, going to sit in a chair in the opposite corner of the room.

Mac yapped, then darted toward the boy, only to quickly move away again. With a leap that would have done Superman proud, he jumped onto the bed.

Dee giggled.

He'd laughed.

"Oh, no," Amber said, springing out of the chair as Mac attacked the pillow on the bed. She lunged, but the dog got away from her, pillow in mouth.

"Mac, no!"

Dee giggled again.

Amber paused, turned back to her nephew. "You like that?"

The dog tossed the pillow in the air—or tried. Amber made a grab for it, but Mac snatched it away.

"Mac!"

Dee laughed, a sound so full of delight it brought tears to Amber's eyes.

"Oh, Dee," she said softly.

She'd never, ever, heard him laugh or seen him smile like that. Joyfully.

Mac tossed the pillow in the air again. Amber caught the motion out of the corner of her eye. Quick as a cat, she grabbed a corner, laughing herself when she out-smarted the dog.

"Got it."

Mac didn't let go, though, and jerked it back. Amber held on, and while Dee continued to laugh, she continued to pull. And then the most miraculous thing of all occurred: Dee reached for the pillow, grabbed a corner.

And actively participated.

Oh, dear Lord.

Amber wanted to sob in joy. Instead, she tugged on the pillow. Mac held on and so did Dee, and Amber laughed until she felt tears roll down her cheeks.

When she heard the sound of ripping, she instantly released the pillow. But not Dee and Mac. Oh, no, the two of them continued with their tug-of-war.

The pillow spewed an eruption of feathers that would have done Vesuvius proud.

"No...!" Bits of down flew everywhere—the bed, the floor, the windowsill to her right.

"Ooop." Dee held the empty pillowcase in his hands.

"Yes, Dee," Amber said, on the verge of laughter again. "Oops. Nancy is going to kill us."

"No," a masculine voice said. "But she'll probably make you clean it up."

Amber wasn't the least bit embarrassed to see Colt. She was glad he could witness this happy moment.

"Gil told me it was okay to come lend you a hand, since all the kids at the barn are riding right now with their therapy teams."

"I didn't do it," she declared, palms up.

She could see the evidence of contained mirth on his face. Spotted the telltale signs. Knew that he had a hard time fighting laughter.

Mac shook himself, sending feathers flying.

"What in the world?" Nancy cried, standing in the doorway.

Amber giggled.

Dee said, "Dog."

Mac barked.

And Colt...well, Colt finally gave in. He laughed, too.

CHAPTER FIFTEEN

"You know you're going to need to clean that up," Nancy said, hands on her hips. She peered at them from Dee's bedroom door.

Colt wanted to laugh at the nurse's expression.

"I know," Amber said.

"We'll take care of it," Colt interjected.

He'd come up here under the pretext of lending her a hand, when in reality he'd been curious about which child she'd gone to visit. But he should have known it would be Dee. She was always with Dee.

Her nephew.

He was certain of it. Dee. Rudy. The names were so similar he felt like a fool for not realizing it sooner.

He struggled to mask the grief this realization caused him. Yes, grief. He would have to call Logan. That meant betraying her, and he didn't want to do that.

He closed his eyes.

She wasn't a conniving witch. She didn't hate men. She was a brilliant, beautiful woman who put everyone else's needs before hers.

"You okay?" Amber asked.

"Uh, yeah, I'm fine." He forced himself to look at her.

Dee, her nephew, the little boy Amber cared so much

about, was standing next to Mac, his left hand stroking and stroking and stroking Mac's gray fur.

"We haven't been able to reach him before this," she said softly, following Colt's gaze.

"Why not?" He needed to know about this child she tried so hard to protect from the world. Even from his father.

"He's severely autistic," she explained. "He talks on occasion, but only to repeat something he's heard. Echolalia—that's what it's called. A bit of dialogue, something he's mimicking, but never actually conversing with anyone. Today he called Mac a dog, for the second time. He knew what the word was and used it in the right context. That's remarkable."

"So there's hope," Colt said. That's what she was doing here. To find hope for her nephew.

A child Logan wanted to take away from her. A child Logan said had minor social issues. Was his friend consciously misleading him or did he really not understand the extent of his son's condition?

"As long as he keeps responding," she said. "I'm hoping once he gets to ride he'll open up further. Vestibular stimulation has done remarkable things for some autistic children." She looked back at Dee. "There have been a few cases where the child has been cured." She tipped her head. "Well, as cured as possible."

"And if you can cure one child, you might be able to cure others."

Children like her nephew. Children who didn't have someone like her to look out for them.

"Yes. This facility is a model for future camps. The foundation that started it invested hundreds of thousands of dollars, all in the hope of proving this can work. So more children can find the help they need."

"Like Dee," Colt said.

"Yes, like Dee."

He would have to talk to Logan, convince him Amber deserved to be involved in Dee's life. Because no matter what she might have told herself, Logan would soon be out of jail. It seemed incredible to believe. Colt's friend had been convicted of vehicular manslaughter with gross negligence. He'd been sentenced to six years in prison, which meant he had two more years to serve. But with California prisons as overcrowded as they were, there was a shot—a really good shot—he'd be released early. Colt suspected that's why Logan was so determined to find his son. And Amber would be blindsided.

Amber. The woman who loved her nephew so much she would change careers for him.

"Do they always do that?" Colt asked.

She didn't need any explanation. "The stroking? Yes. It's part of their condition. Mac soothes him. I suspect there's a connection between special needs children and animals. All animals. I want to introduce Mac to some other kids next. Study what happens."

Colt wanted her to succeed. He hadn't come to Camp Cowboy looking for a cause, but he'd found one. He'd have to be inhuman not to be affected by what Amber was trying to do for children.

She was a remarkable woman.

"I'm sorry about yesterday," he found himself saying, although maybe he was apologizing for something else.

Her eyes dimmed. It was like watching someone pull down blinds. "That's okay."

"I was a jerk."

"And I was nosy," she admitted.

She looked so pretty. The sun had dipped behind the trees, but light still poured into the room, and into her eyes.

"Friends?" he said.

No. Not friends. He couldn't be her friend. Not with what he knew.

"Friends." She smiled.

It was hell, especially when she held out her hand and he took it, knowing that no matter how badly he wanted to keep on holding it, he couldn't.

He released her. "I better get going."

"You'll want to take Mac."

"No," he said. "Leave him here. Keep on doing what you're doing. See if he helps."

"Will he stay?"

"If I tell him to."

She startled Colt by stretching on tiptoe and kissing his cheek. "Thanks. I'm going to sit with Dee for a while and see if I can't coax more words out of him."

God, she was killing him. Colt knew in that instant that Logan had lied. She wasn't the horrible person he'd made her out to be.

She wasn't horrible at all.

HE HAD A hard time sleeping that night. When he woke up in the wee hours, he told himself to get up. He needed to send Logan an email through his cell phone. It was hard to figure out what to say, though.

Dear Logan. I quit.

That was certainly tempting. But Colt knew Logan would just find some other way to locate his son. And if he did that, Colt wouldn't know about it and then Amber would still be blindsided when Logan came for Dee.

Damn it.

Colt sat at the tiny table in his room, opened up the internet on his cell phone, then loaded his email. He was half hoping there was a message in there. Something from Logan, telling him he was off the hook. Of course, that meant losing out on Logan's horse. But that was okay.

No letter.

It was up to him to make contact.

Logan, he typed, using the tiny keys.

I've located Rudy.

It wouldn't hurt to tell him that, he thought.

He's somewhere near Santa Rosa.

That was close enough to Sonoma to be true, yet not an exact location.

But before I tell you exactly where, promise that you won't cut Amber out of Rudy's life when you get out of jail. That you'll continue to let her see him.

He thought hard over what to say next.

I've gotten to know Amber. She's not the evil person you think she is. She has Rudy's best interests at heart. She loves him. Please don't break her heart.

And what if Logan rejected his plea?

Colt ran his hands over his face. He honestly didn't know.

Begging you, Logan. Give her a chance.

He pressed Send before he could change his mind.

How long he sat there, he didn't know. At some point he crawled into bed. Mac woke him early in the morning by jumping onto the bed and curling up near his feet. Colt tossed and turned from that point on. When he finally got out of bed, he told himself he should be relieved that at least he'd done something to help Amber out.

He wasn't. If anything, he was even more confused. What would he do if Logan demanded to know where his son was? What if he told Colt to get lost? What if… what if…

Colt got up filled with anxiety. And when he caught sight of Amber walking toward the barn later that morning, her blond hair pulled back, blue jeans hugging her body, he felt dread on top of his anxiety. But maybe she wouldn't spot him standing inside the stall.

"Mac, stay," he ordered, because the dog noticed Dee at the entrance to the barn. Colt shook his head. He didn't know what it was about the boy that drew the dog's devotion, but it had been love at first sight.

Love.

He could never love a woman like Amber. He went back to tacking up the horses for the day's riding classes. They were opposites, from two different worlds—his filled with road trips and rodeos, hers with research and self-sacrifice. And then there was his past. Messed up, that's what he was. He knew it. Had figured out long ago why he avoided relationships like the plague.

He was afraid.

Afraid of losing something else he loved.

"You done?" Buck asked as he left the neighboring stall.

"Yup." Colt gave a girth one last tug.

"Okay, then. Let's lead the horses on out. We'll do the same thing as yesterday. Bring them one at a time, help the therapists get their charges mounted."

"Got it."

One at a time.

He should focus on the job at hand. Keep his mind off Amber.

"Hi," Amber said brightly.

He was in the stall, untying Oreo.

"Hey," he replied.

"I got Dee down here this morning."

"Oh, yeah? I'm surprised Mac hasn't run off to greet him."

Colt looked down. His dog was facing the door of the barn, his whole body tensed.

"Stay," Colt ordered.

"We might need Mac if this doesn't go as planned."

She was nervous. He could tell by the way her eyes darted over the horse. How she kept glancing back toward the group of people gathering outside.

"Relax," he said. "If this doesn't work, I promise to lend a hand."

His dog had started to whine.

"All right, fine," Colt said to him. "Go on. Say hello."

Mac needed no further urging. Like the herding dog he was, he ran full-tilt toward his human friend, to be greeted by Dee's cry of "Dog."

"You're right," Amber said. "I shouldn't worry. Things will work themselves out."

He ached for her.

There was no other way to describe how he felt. He ached with compassion for all she was going through. He also ached for the pressure of her body against his. To hold her. To kiss her.

"Let's get the show on the road," Jarrod called.

Colt led Oreo forward. His heart beat faster not just because of Amber, but because he, too, was anxious to see how Dee reacted.

"You better be good," he told the horse.

The little boy with the sunny smile was busy stroking Mac again.

"Oog," he said. "Oog, oog, oog."

His obvious delight caused those around them to smile. And if Mac could talk, Colt had no doubt he'd be saying, "Dee, Dee, Dee," in a rhythm that matched the beat of his back end.

"Okay, since this is his first time, let's not give him a chance to balk. Let's lead the horse right on over to the mounting block," Jarrod said. "We'll put him up straight away."

"Do you think he's ready?" Amber said. "He's only ever petted a horse before now."

"You'll never know until you try."

Colt wasn't so sure, but that might have been more to do with disliking Jarrod than his own instincts. He could read body language pretty well, and he would swear that came from working with horses. Dee was engrossed in Mac, but there was something about the child's stance that had seemed to change when Oreo was led out of the barn. He might not have glanced at the horse, but he was aware.

"How do we do this?" Amber asked.

"The same way we did the pommel horse," Jarrod answered.

Colt had watched them last week. Kids had been taught to walk up the wide steps of the mounting block and then get on. Still, this was a whole other ball of wax.

"Lead him on over," Jarrod said.

Buck stood watching from the entrance of the barn, Colt noticed, the cowboy squinting his rheumy blue eyes. Someone placed a helmet on Dee, though it was obvious he wasn't happy about it. He kept trying to tug the thing off. Fortunately, Mac distracted him. Before too long they had the child at the wooden steps. He didn't want to climb those, either, but once again Mac came to the rescue. Colt warily led Oreo up to the mounting block, but Dee had eyes only for Mac. He wasn't the least bit interested in the horse.

"Okay," Jarrod said. "Everyone take up your positions."

Colt had seen this before, too. There would be two therapists on each side. The other four, including Amber, would stand by Dee's legs—two on each side...if they got him in the saddle.

"Okay, Dee," Amber coaxed, and Colt marveled that he hadn't noticed the resemblance before. They had the same profile. "Time to climb on board—just like we practiced on the pommel horse the other day."

Dee kept stroking the dog, a lock of brown hair covering one eye, the white-and-gray-striped shirt he wore nearly the same color as Mac's fur.

"Go ahead and get up there next to him," Jarrod said impatiently.

Amber nodded, climbed the steps of the mounting block and tentatively laid her hands on Dee. Colt knew that was because of the boy's acute sensitivity. She was careful when she nudged him toward the horse, too.

"Nnnn," Dee groaned, his eyes still on Mac.

"Come on, kiddo. This'll be fun. Don't you want to ride the horse?"

"Nnn," Dee said.

"Just try for me, okay?"

But Dee would have none of it. Colt watched from in front of Oreo as the child's body language grew more and more pronounced, all but screaming, *Leave me alone.*

"Just slip one foot in the stirrup."

"Amber—" Colt warned.

"No, no," Jarrod said. "Keep going with him."

Colt shook his head. The guy might be trained to work with kids and horses, but he didn't know squat about reading body language.

"I'm not so sure this is a good idea," Colt said.

"I'm not so sure, either," Amber agreed.

"Do as I tell you and we won't have a problem."

Colt almost walked away. One thing held him there. Amber.

"Okay, Dee," Amber said softly. "I'm going to grab your hand."

Colt tensed. Amber reached for the boy.

All hell broke loose.

A sound unlike anything Colt had ever heard before erupted from the child's mouth. Dee flung himself from the mounting block. The therapists reached for him. Amber cried, "No!"

"Aaaahhhhh!" Dee lifted his head and banged it back down repeatedly, his legs thrashing, arms punching.

"Dee, calm down." Amber had followed him to the ground. "Calm down," she soothed over and over again. Colt's heart broke on her behalf. "Please, calm down."

But there was no getting through to the child. He rolled around on the ground, kicking and screaming and moaning and making noises unlike any Colt had heard before.

"He's stimming," Jarrod pronounced—as if he hadn't had a hand in causing it.

"I know." Colt thought Amber might smack him.

Nobody could do anything about Dee. That was clear by the looks on their faces. They were forced to stand back and watch.

It was Mac that came to the rescue.

He plopped himself down right next to Dee, his eyes clearly fixed on the child's.

Dee stopped moving.

Mac didn't move, either.

"That's incredible," Colt heard Melissa say softly.

How long they stayed that way, he wasn't sure. But then slowly, tentatively, Dee reached out. Mac nuzzled the boy, who laughed.

There were audible sighs of relief all around.

"I don't know where you got that dog, but I want one just like him," Melissa said.

"Me, too." Amber gave Colt a smile.

She could have one all the time if she wanted to, Colt thought. But then he chastised himself. As if they could ever have a future together, with all that he'd kept from her.

"Where'd you get him?" Melissa asked.

"Down south."

"I want that breeder's number."

"Let's get back to work, people," Jarrod said, glancing at his team. "We need to get him up on that horse."

"But…" Amber glanced at Colt helplessly.

"Let Mac help out."

"What do you mean?" she asked.

"Watch." He whistled. The dog instantly came to his side, and Dee sat up.

"Up, Mac," he ordered, pointing to Oreo.

"You're going to put him up on the horse?" Jarrod asked. "That's ridiculous. No dog will do that."

"He's done it before," Colt said, biting back what he *really* wanted to say.

Just be quiet, jerk-wad.

"Sometimes when we're out gathering cattle," Colt added, "I'll give Mac a ride back to the ranch." Granted, he'd always held the dog in his lap, but Mac probably wouldn't care. As it turned out, the Australian shepherd didn't. All Colt had to do was point to the saddle and the dog jumped up. Dee followed right on his heels. Oreo seemed to take it all in stride.

"Go on," Amber said. "Climb on board. Mac wants you to go for a ride."

Did the child understand? Amber had told him that autistic children understood far more than it might appear. For years psychologists had labeled them mentally retarded or developmentally slow. But, in fact, autistic children could have genius IQs.

Dee slipped into the saddle as if he'd been doing it all his life.

"I'll be damned," Jarrod said, clearly incredulous.

Of course, it took some twisting and turning before dog and child settled into the saddle together.

"I wish I had a camera," Melissa said.

Colt did, too. But the sight was something he'd never forget.

"Here." Jarrod held out his hand for the lead. "I'll take over."

Colt almost told him to get lost. But Jarrod was right. Colt was there to tend to the horses; it was the therapist's job to work with the children.

He handed the lead over.

"Ladies, take up your positions, please," Jarrod said.

"Be careful with my dog."

"Thanks, Colt," Amber said softly, glancing up at her nephew as they started the horse walking.

Colt watched them from a distance even though he should've gone back into the barn to lead the next horse out.

"Cluck, Dee," Amber said. "Like this." She made a clucking sound.

They walked away from the mounting block and toward the arena. Mac sat in front of the child as if he were the King of Pasha. And if someone had bet Colt six months ago that he'd be watching a child ride around while his dog sat shotgun, he'd have laughed all the way to the bank. He smiled as the pair coasted along.

"You done good," Buck said, coming up next to him.

"Thanks."

From a distance, Colt heard Amber say, "Do you see

the trees, Dee? Trees." She pointed. Ever the speech therapist.

Dee's little body swayed back and forth. He began to smile.

"Look at that," Buck said. "That's what makes it all worth it."

Dee let go of Mac, threw his arms up in the air.

"Dee ride," he said as clear as a bell.

Colt saw Amber stumble. He heard Melissa's gasp. Saw Jarrod glance around in self-satisfaction.

"And *that's* why we force them up," Jarrod said.

"Pompous ass," Colt muttered.

"He's like a bull with one horn," Buck drawled. "Swaggerin' around like he's something special with his lopsided head, when every cow in the pen can see he's just a bull with one horn."

Colt felt himself smile. "I'm surprised you put up with it."

Buck hooked his thumbs in the front of his jeans. "Well, son, I'd put up with a lot to watch what just happened over and over again." His rheumy eyes met Colt's. "I don't do this because of the money, that's for sure. Though it pays better than most ranching jobs, and you get a comfy bed to sleep in." He cocked his head. "But what are you doing here, Colt?"

Spying.

He would have thought that after a week his guilt would have faded. "It's a job," he admitted.

"Humph. I think you'll find it's a lot more than that."

Colt knew he was right. He'd already seen that. During the days he'd been at Camp Cowboy he'd watched numerous kids come out of their shells. He'd heard more than a few first words. He'd seen the delight of

therapists and children alike, and though he never figured himself to be the soft type, he couldn't deny he'd
been moved. Was even discovering a side of himself
he hadn't known existed.

"Is it always like this?" he asked.

"You mean chaotic? Rewarding? Loud?"

"That's it."

"You'll get used to it," Buck said. "And you'll find
the trouble is worth the price of admission." He winked.
"Especially when you have a pretty little distraction in
the mix."

Colt followed the man's gaze. Amber was laughing. Dee was smiling. Colt knew in that instant that he
didn't want to let her go. For the first time in his life he
felt more than mere attraction for a woman.

For the first time in a long time he was tempted to
care about somebody besides himself.

CHAPTER SIXTEEN

AMBER COULDN'T KEEP the smile from her face.

He'd used words. In the right context. At the correct moment. A *third* time!

"Did you have a good day?" Gil asked as she entered the lodge. She was tired, but looking forward to catching up with Dee's various therapists to see how the rest of his day went.

"Yeah," she said, pausing by the office door. "It was *great*."

She'd learned a lot. Dee hadn't been the only one to have a stellar time. Other children had been equally affected by the horses they'd ridden. Amber wished she could figure out why. Guess she'd have to crack the therapy textbooks Jarrod lent her.

"Look, Amber," Gil said, "Dee's father called again."

Her stomach dropped.

"I told him you were working and that you'd phone him back."

"Thanks."

"You really think we should add dogs to our therapy program?"

"I do," she said, remembering Mac up in the saddle.

"Okay, then." Gil's wire-rimmed glasses caught the light. "I'll look into it."

"Let me know if I can help." She moved away from

the door, lost in her thoughts, and nearly collided with Jarrod.

"You want to get a bite to eat?" the cocky blond asked.

Only if someone gave her a lobotomy beforehand.

"Actually—"

"She'll be with me tonight," Colt said, coming up behind her, Mac on his heels.

Jarrod glanced from one to the other in sudden understanding. "I see."

And when Amber's eyes met Colt's, she saw, too.

"Whatever," Jarrod muttered, turning away.

They were left standing there, together, in the main hall.

"Sooo," Amber drawled. "What's up?"

"I was wondering if you had a moment to talk," Colt drawled right back, in his Texan twang.

In my bedroom?

She almost asked out loud, but didn't have the courage.

"What about?" she said, although just the memory of what he'd done with her when they'd been in her bed together...

She wished he'd do that again.

"I hope you don't mind what I said to Jarrod." He hesitated.

Her heart fluttered like an anxious bird. Seeing him in his black hat and jeans, she was reminded of his innate masculinity, which never failed to excite her. Even now. Standing in a busy hallway, the two were forced to move out of the way as another therapist entered the lodge.

"I don't mind," she said. And then she swallowed back her bout of nerves. "If you meant it."

He looked away for a moment, took a deep breath.... He was nervous.

"I did," he said at last. And then he placed a hand on her lower arm. A big hand, the same hand that'd touched her intimately not so long ago. "There's something about you, Amber. I can't seem to get you out of my mind. I've tried." He rubbed his hand over his face. "Lord, how I've tried. But I can't."

"I know how you feel," she said.

"But there's something I need to tell you—"

"Amber!" Melissa raced down the steps, sounding out of breath. "Thank God. Nancy needs to see you right away. She's in Dee's room."

"Dee?" Amber repeated.

"Yes. Go."

The look in Melissa's eyes scared the hell out of Amber.

She took the stairs two at a time, not looking to see if Colt followed.

She knew the moment she hit the second floor landing that something major had happened. A group of people, including Nancy, stood outside Dee's room, staring in.

"What is it? What happened?" she asked the head nurse.

"Amber," Nancy said, turning toward her, "there's a problem with Dee, and when I looked at the emergency contact information, it listed *you*."

"What's wrong?" Amber pushed her way to the door. Her nephew lay on the floor, his body racked by convulsions.

"Dee," she cried, rushing to him.

"No, Amber, stay back." Nancy grabbed her by the

arm. "I know you want to go in there, but you need to keep away. I've got an ambulance coming. We need to keep the room clear for when the paramedics arrives."

Stay back? Not on her life.

"Let. Me. Go." She wrenched free and darted to Dee's side.

"Why are you listed as his emergency contact? Do you know his parents?"

"He's my nephew," Amber replied.

"Your what?" Nancy was clearly taken aback.

But Amber was too busy cradling Dee to care. She stared into his unfocused eyes. The world grew unfocused. Blurry. She felt dizzy. The room began to spin....

"Dee," she murmured, holding his head as tremors continued to rack his body. "It's auntie," she soothed. "Settle down."

"He can't hear you," Nancy said. "He's seizing."

"No kidding." Amber held him tightly. "Dee, it's me. Calm down, pumpkin. Don't fight it—"

Mac barked.

"Get the dog out of here," Nancy snapped. "I'm sorry, Colt, but he'll have to go."

"I'm not going anywhere, and neither is my dog."

Mac whined, raced to his friend.

And the convulsions stopped.

Dee's back settled onto the floor. His head stopped thrashing. His limbs still twitched, but it was as if someone had turned the power off.

"Oh, Dee," Amber said softly, tears trailing down her cheek. "That's it. Calm down."

Mac moved in even closer. Nancy, thankfully, didn't say a word. The other nurse, a male one Amber had met once before, took Dee's pulse.

"Coming through," someone said a moment later. Amber had been so fixated on Dee she hadn't even heard the sirens. "Everybody give us some space," one of the paramedics, a dark-haired man, ordered.

"I'm not budging," Amber said firmly. "I'm his aunt."

"Right." The guy set his medical kit down next to them. "Then give us some space to work."

Amber scooted back. She didn't know when Colt had knelt next to her. When he'd wrapped his arms around her. All she knew was that when she felt his comforting presence, all she wanted to do was cry. But she couldn't. She had to hold it together. For Dee's sake.

"Has this ever happened before?" one of the fire-fighters who'd arrived with the paramedics asked the room at large.

"No," Amber answered. Her voice hitched. "This is the first time."

She watched as the dark-haired man shone a light in Dee's eyes. Her nephew looked so pale beneath the beam's white light. So small and fragile.

"Dee," she murmured.

Colt's arms tightened around her. He was cradling her from behind, supporting her, and she was grateful for that. If he hadn't been in the room with her, she'd have collapsed in a heap, crying.

"Pupils normal," the man said to his companion, a woman, Amber finally noticed.

"Pulse 90 over 145," said the woman. A blonde.

"Let's get him on the board and out of here."

The blonde nodded, and the pair worked quickly to get Dee immobilized. While they did, another team arrived, from the ambulance company.

"Is he being transported?"

"Yup," said the male paramedic. "But he's stable."

Amber nearly collapsed. Only Colt's arms kept her upright.

"Is there room in the ambulance?" Colt asked as they lifted the child.

"Yeah, sure," a gray-haired man said. "You family?"

"She's his aunt," Colt stated.

"Works for me," he said. "I can get some info from you while we're on the way."

Things moved quickly from there. Colt asked if someone could watch Mac. Melissa volunteered. They got Dee down the steps and into the ambulance in a matter of minutes, Amber keeping a wary eye on him the whole way. One of the paramedics helped her into the back of the ambulance. Colt stayed behind.

"No," she said. "I need you to come with me."

"There might not be room."

"There's room," the blue-shirted paramedic said. He was busy starting an IV. "You'll need to sit over there, though." He pointed toward the front of the ambulance before poking a needle in Dee's arm.

Dee hated needles.

But he didn't even react to this one. Dear God. He didn't react at all.

She felt nausea building inside her, thought she might lose it then and there. Colt kept her grounded, his big hand holding hers, guiding her toward the padded seat. They would need to put her in a padded *jacket* by the time this was over, she thought morosely.

Dee had had *convulsions*. Why, damn it? *Why?*

"He's going to be all right," she heard Colt say as they started rolling, sirens blaring.

"I don't understand what could have happened." She

raised her voice over the keening wail of the ambulance. "He was fine this morning."

"You're certain this has never happened before?" one of the paramedics asked.

She tore her gaze away from Dee's prone body. "I'm positive."

But she couldn't keep her eyes off Dee for long. He still wore the same white-and-gray-striped shirt as before, his jeans somewhat dusty from his earlier collision with the ground. But in his stillness, he looked like a normal little boy. Except for being hooked up to the IV. The way his tiny body was strapped down...

"No," she said. "Never."

"Well," said one of the ambulance paramedics, his body swaying as they rounded a corner, "he's stable. And his vital signs have returned to normal. Pupils look good. He's just out of it from the seizure. Happens. Well, not necessarily seizures, but I swear the human body goes into some kind of deep sleep after something like this happens. I've seen it a million times." The man smiled reassuringly. "Can I get some information from you?"

Colt watched as Amber nodded, then grabbed a strap hanging by her head as they rounded yet another corner. She answered the paramedic's questions, looking as pale and as drawn as her nephew while they made their way through city streets.

Her nephew.

Colt had known it. Still, such an abrupt confirmation of the fact left him reeling.

He wondered if he should question her. Act surprised, maybe even angry. But in the end, he didn't have it in him.

They arrived at the hospital in minutes. A group of doctors was waiting once the doors opened. From that point forward, things got chaotic. Amber wanted to stay with Dee, but they took the boy into a room and told her to stay out. She didn't like that, but Colt wrapped her in his arms, his chin resting on her head as they waited. And if he wasn't mistaken, Amber cried. Gently and softly.

Dee was her nephew.

Back at Camp Cowboy, Colt had been about to tell her he knew that. Had been right on the verge of confessing everything.

Now wasn't the time.

One of these days he'd have to tell her the truth. The question was would she forgive him?

"Ms. Brooks?" Colt turned to find a nurse standing in the doorway. "The doctors will see you now."

CHAPTER SEVENTEEN

SHE HATED HOSPITALS. They reminded her of the worst day of her life—the day her sister had died....

"Ms. Brooks," said a Hispanic man with kind brown eyes and a light dusting of gray in his hair. "We'd like to take your nephew down for a CAT scan."

She nodded. "Of course."

"So far, from what we can tell, he suffered a grand mal seizure. He's autistic, isn't he?"

The name tag pinned to his white coat said Dr. Salazar. "He is," she said. She seemed to have lost the ability to project.

"Then I'm sure you know these kinds of seizures aren't unusual for a child with autism."

"He's never had one before."

"I know, and that's reason to be optimistic. This could be something simple. A deficiency in salt, perhaps. Then again, it might be something more serious. It's too early to tell."

She nodded.

He patted her on the back. "There's a waiting room down the hall. Why don't you and your husband stay there? I'll have someone come get you just as soon as we know anything more."

He's not my husband.

"Thanks," was all she managed to say.

Colt guided her to the waiting room then, his big hands so warm. He was such a comfort to her. She didn't know what she would have done without him. She'd never felt such a keen sense of loneliness.

"It'll be okay," he said softly.

"Will it?"

Nothing in her life was okay. She'd lost her parents when she was five. Her sister had died fifteen years later. She'd had to bury everyone who ever meant anything to her, except Dee. And now Dee was in the hospital....

"I promise you. It'll all be fine."

He'd sat next to her, tipped his hat back, then pulled her into his arms. How long he held her in silence, she didn't know. She sank against him willingly, and slowly allowed her stress to bleed into him.

"My parents and my sister died in a car accident," he said at last.

She gasped, leaning back. "How old were you?"

"Seventeen."

All she could do was shake her head. "I hardly knew mine," she whispered. "They died when my sister and I were really young."

"Yeah, but you didn't think you'd killed them."

She lifted her head. "What?"

She heard him swallow, watched his Adam's apple bob up and down. "I'd told my dad I could handle it."

"Handle what?"

"Changing the brakes. I'd been in auto shop since my freshman year. Rotors were simple. But…" His eyes had gone as dark as obsidian. "I blew it."

She clutched his arm.

"They never officially blamed me." He swallowed again. "But I knew."

"Oh, Colt. You don't really think—"

"Yeah," he said. "I do. I went to the accident scene. Saw the scars on the pavement. One of the tires came off. I must not have tightened the lug nuts all the way. And my family…"

He didn't finish the sentence. He didn't need to.

"But the police. They never said…"

"I was seventeen. About to graduate high school. I suspect they knew, too. They just didn't tell anyone. And why would they? From where they stood it was an accident. I've mulled this over long and hard. In the end I think they figured, why ruin my life? So they never said anything."

She couldn't imagine… No, that wasn't true. Actually, she *could* put herself in his shoes. She'd heard about her sister's accident from a cop at the door. She wondered what she would have done if they'd told her she'd been responsible for her death.

Like Logan.

She straightened suddenly, struck by how all this must have affected Dee's dad. Had she thought to ask him? Had she even cared?

She felt ashamed.

"What did you do?" she asked.

"Graduated high school. Managed to qualify for the high school rodeo finals, don't ask me how. One of my teachers took pity on me, encouraged me to go to college."

"Did you go?"

"I didn't want to, but, hell, it was a free ride, so I went."

A cowboy with a college degree. Who would have figured? "How old are you?"

"Thirty. You?"

"Twenty-nine."

"We're almost twins," he said with a small smile.

"You compete in rodeos," she said slowly.

He smirked. "You make it sound like I sell drugs."

With Logan as her single example of a rodeo performer was it any wonder? "I just wouldn't have figured a rodeo cowboy as the college type."

"I did what I had to do."

So he could make it through. She read the unspoken truth in his eyes.

"I'm sorry," she said gently.

"No," he said. "*I'm* sorry."

"What do you have to be sorry about?"

But he never had time to answer. "Ms. Brooks?"

"Yes?" She looked up.

Dr. Salazar smiled from the doorway. "CAT scan looks good. Potassium levels were so low we're treating him for dehydration. He's awake now if you want to see him."

"Yes, of course." She dived out of Colt's arms. "But, wait, you're telling me he's okay," she said as she and Colt followed him out of the room.

"I think so," the doctor said. "We'll need to keep him overnight to get him rehydrated. There's a facility across the way. Rainbow House. It's a place for families to stay during times like these. You'd be right across the street."

Good Lord, she hadn't even thought that far ahead.

"All right."

"I'll make the arrangements," Dr. Salazar offered.

And then they were in Dee's room, and Amber spotted him in the bed, awake and staring into his corner of the room. He seemed bewildered.

"Hey," she said softly.

"We're going to continue running tests," the doctor murmured. "But I'm leaning toward dehydration. Kids like these…"

He didn't finish. She knew the difficulty of caring for an autistic child.

"Is it possible to bring a dog in here?" Colt asked the doctor.

"No," Dr. Salazar said. "No dogs. I'm sorry."

Colt bent toward her and whispered in her ear, "Maybe we can sneak Mac in here by putting him in a bag."

Dee turned his head, looked up at Colt. "Dog."

What weight remained on her shoulders melted away. "Yes, dog." Amber took a seat next to the bed.

"That's a good sign," Dr. Salazar said. "He's remembering words."

Two weeks ago he'd never even used the word, and yet here he was, associating Colt with Mac. With time, perhaps Mac could help Dee's ability to focus. Perhaps Dee might learn even more words.

She reached out and blindly grabbed Colt's hand. Yes, Dee was in the hospital, but she had someone by her side to help her through it, and that meant so much to her. So very, *very* much.

"I'll go get the paperwork for the Rainbow House."

They stayed until midnight, when the nurse kicked them out and told them to get some rest. Dr. Salazar had given them everything they needed to use one of the rooms across the street. Amber didn't think anybody would be there to greet them, but she was wrong. The place was like a hotel, one staffed by volunteers. They were shown to a space that was more like an apartment.

"If you or your husband need anything, just let me know," said a perky brunette with thick, straight hair. "You can come and go as you like for as long as you need."

She started to correct her, but she was already gone.

"So, if I decide not to stay here with you, does that mean we're getting a divorce?" Colt asked.

Amber smiled, even laughed a little. "Don't be ridiculous."

But when she met his gaze, she saw something in them that made her catch her breath.

"I don't think I should stay, Amber. I really don't."

He was afraid...afraid of what might happen between them. But she wasn't. Not in the least. And even though ten minutes ago she would have sworn all she wanted was a pillow and a bed, now she found herself taking Colt's hand.

"Don't leave," she said, closing the distance between them. "Not yet."

"Amber—"

She wrapped her arms around his neck and pulled his head down. He was so much taller, making her feel feminine and small. She just loved that.

"I need you, Colt Sheridan."

She kissed him. He didn't move. She nuzzled his lips. He still didn't move. She ran her tongue across his mouth slowly.

"Damn you," he muttered, and pulled her to him.

Yes.

His lips had softened, but his body had done the opposite. She could feel the hard length of him nestled against her belly. Every sinewy ridge of his body was pressed up against her. And his mouth…his mouth was so very soft.

"I want to taste you," she said, not caring that she sounded brazen. She licked him again.

He jerked her against him even harder and gasped, "Amber. Jeez. You're killing me."

"I want you," she moaned.

And he wanted her, too, she could tell. His eyes were no longer obsidian, but more like warm amber….

She ran her hand up the front of his pants. He gasped again.

"I don't have any protection," he muttered between clenched teeth.

Well, she supposed that was better than him carrying around something 24/7. "That's okay," she said. "We can make it work."

When he scooped her up in his arms, she knew how this would end, and that was fine with her.

He found the bed, set her on a thick, brown comforter. But he didn't follow her down. She had to grab his hand, had to tug him toward her.

"Come here, cowboy."

CHAPTER EIGHTEEN

THIS WAS MADNESS.

Colt should walk away from the bed. At the very least he should tell her the truth about why he'd really come to Camp Cowboy. "If you still want me after I—"

She slipped her hand beneath the waistband of his jeans and cupped him, "You're going to kill me," he groaned. "I haven't been honest—"

"Honesty later," she said softly. "Unless it really is life and death."

She reached up with her free hand and knocked his hat off. He didn't care. If she wanted to feel him inside her, he was beyond resisting. Honesty could wait.

"Take your clothes off," he commanded.

He saw her eyes flare, saw the way they narrowed not with anger, but with passion. She drew away, then pulled the shirt she'd been wearing off in one quick jerk. She never hesitated, and suddenly he couldn't get undressed fast enough, given how her strip show was causing his body to harden.

She reached behind her, unclasped her bra. Her breasts sprang free, begging for a man's touch. Colt dropped the shirt he didn't even know he'd been holding.

She leaned back and undid the clasp of her jeans. He did the same. She slid the denim down her legs, slowly, erotically. He mimicked her actions, although he had to kick off his boots first. She'd lost her footwear somewhere, but he didn't have time to wonder where or how, because she'd hooked her thumbs on the sides of her sensible undies. No frilly G-strings for her. Watching her strip them off was just as much a tease as if they'd been lace.

"You're so beautiful," he said, sinking down next to her.

The most beautiful woman he'd ever seen, with her curly blond hair splayed around her head, her full breasts.... Her hips were tiny compared to the rest of her, and below those hips was an area he wanted to explore, was dying to taste.

"Come here, Colt," she said again.

What did this beautiful, compassionate creature with a heart as big as an ocean see in him?

He'd lied to her.

He didn't want to think about that now. All he wanted was Amber.

He stepped out of his own underwear. Sank down next to her and once again felt her naked body against his own.

"Colt?"

He reached up and captured her left breast.

"Colt," she repeated, this time with a sigh.

His hand dropped, and she lay there compliantly, even parted for him, as he slid his fingers toward her core.

"Colt," she whispered again, her eyes closing, her head tipping back as he swirled his tongue around her nipple, at the same time touching her intimately. He wanted to see her climax again. Wanted to hear her cries. Had never forgotten what it felt like to bring her pleasure.

But he wanted…

That was just it. He wanted, too. Wanted her. Shook from the effort it took not to cover her body with his own.

His tongue drifted in lazy circles before his teeth lightly nipped her nipple. Her back arched off the bed, and he trailed kisses downward.

"No," she said, clutching at his arms, trying to draw him back up.

He resisted, because he wanted to give her something first. Something she would remember even if she couldn't ever forgive him.

Please, God, let her forgive him.

He tasted her.

She moaned, her hips rising off the bed.

He suckled her.

She cried out in pleasure.

He flicked his tongue against her core.

"Colt." She groaned. "Oh, jeez, Colt."

He could feel her trembling, loved the way her movements became more frenetic, drew pleasure from her soft moans.

"Let go," he urged.

In the next moment she was crying out, her pleasure so sweet that he felt his own body spasm in response. Damn. What was it about her? Why did he feel the need to do it again, to stay there and make her cry out a second time, or a third, or a fourth?

"Now."

"Now?" he asked. Now *what?*

And since he needed instruction, she pulled him toward her, his body sliding up her own.

"Now," she said again, her eyes intense.

He had no protection. Neither did she, he suspected, but he covered her with his body just the same.

And yet he couldn't stop himself.

His knees nudged hers apart, and she was so soft and wet and warm beneath him that he had to grip the pillow near her head to keep himself from thrusting into her.

"Colt," she admonished as he lay poised at her entrance.

Slow, he told himself. *Enjoy it. Savor the moment.*

Because it might not happen again.

There was only right now, this instant, this one incredible moment when he became one with the most incredible woman he'd ever met.

I love you.

He froze.

"Goddamn it," he murmured.

She lifted her hips, wresting control away from him. The second he connected with her warm embrace, there was nothing he could do. He moved into her, closed his eyes, rested his head against the crook of her neck.

He loved her, he realized, pushing into her.

"Colt," she murmured.

He kissed her neck, drew out, slid in again.

He loved her.

He began to move faster. She welcomed every thrust. *He loved her.*

Tears rose to his eyes as, for the first time, he understood what it meant to make love to a woman. This wasn't just sex, he thought, kissing her neck, memorizing the taste of her. This was as different from sex as the sun was from the moon. She *was* sunlight. He basked in her warmth, absorbed her heat and energy, all the while thrusting and thrusting and thrusting....

"Colt!" she cried.

And this time he climaxed with her. This time he was the one who moaned in pleasure. He found her lips as he slowly, inexorably, became aware.

A door closed somewhere. The alarm clock next to the bed flashed 12:00 a.m. The room smelled of cinnamon. Or was that Amber?

"I don't think I can move," she said in amusement.

"I don't want to move." He sighed.

She clasped his head with her hands, forced him to look at her. "I don't want you to, either." By the light of the clock, he saw what he least expected.

Tears.

"Amber..."

She was falling for him. She might not love him yet, but it was there, right beneath the surface. He could see it.

And he'd lied to her.

THEY HARDLY SLEPT, but that was okay with Amber. She marveled at how quickly and...diversely he could bring her to pleasure.

In the early hours of the morning she finally drifted off to sleep, only to be woken by the shrill sound of her cell phone.

Dee.

She scrambled to find her pants, as Colt slept soundly beside her.

"Hello?" she said, heart pounding.

"So you *are* going to answer." She didn't recognize the voice.

"Excuse me?"

"Don't tell me you didn't recognize the number."

Her blood ran cold. "Logan," she said quietly.

"When were you going to tell me my son was in the hospital?"

"How did you find out?"

"I called the school to check in with you. Your boss told me."

Damn it. "He shouldn't have told you," she hissed. "I wanted to wait until the doctor was sure Dee was okay before I called. No point in upsetting you unnecessarily."

"That's not your decision to make. I'm his dad."

"*I've* got custody of Dee."

"You won't for long," he said grimly. "Or didn't you wonder why there've been no annoying beeps so far? No message that you're getting a call from an inmate?"

She hadn't thought about it. "Where are you?" she asked, her blood turning cold.

"All that matters is that soon I'll be San Francisco."

Oh, dear God, he was out. They'd set him free.

"How?"

"Early parole."

She clutched the phone.

"He's my son, Amber."

"And he's *my* nephew," she said. "And you should have thought about the consequences of your actions the night you… The day you…"

She couldn't finish the sentence, and damn it all to hell, she was on the verge of tears. She'd worried about this for so long, had thought there was no way he'd ever get out of jail before his six years were up. She should have known better.

"I *have* thought about it," he said. And much to her surprise, he sounded almost sad. "Every frickin' day of my life I've thought about it."

"It was a choice," she said. "One that cost my sister her life." *And custody of your son.*

"We had decided to get back together again," he stated. "I've told you before, we were celebrating."

"Yeah, right," she scoffed.

"I know you don't believe me," he said, and for a second she heard something in his voice, something she'd never heard before. Sorrow. Pain. Guilt. "You've never believed me, but I'm telling you the truth, Amber. Just like I'm telling you the God's honest truth now. I want my son back."

"We'll be gone."

"You told me you'd let me see him."

"That was before."

"Before you knew you'd be seeing me face-to-face? Without Plexiglas between us?"

"Something like that," she murmured.

"I knew you hadn't changed. He told me you had. That you weren't as horrible as I thought, but you are."

"Who told you I'd changed?"

"The friend who's done me a favor. He actually begged me to give you a chance. It's why I'm calling. Because I wanted to believe him."

She didn't think it was possible for her blood to turn colder, but it did. "Who?" she asked.

"Doesn't matter."

But she knew. She just *knew.*

"I swear to you, Logan, if you really want me to bring Dee to you, you'll tell me who it is."

"Dee? Is that what you call him?"

"It's what I've always called him."

"No wonder why he didn't put two and two together."

"Who?"

There was a momentary pause. "Colt Sheridan. Sound familiar?"

She squeezed her eyes closed. Clenched the cell phone. "Oh, yeah. It sounds familiar all right."

"I offered to give him one of my old rope horses in exchange for his help."

"Really?" she said. "What a deal."

And then she turned off the phone.

CHAPTER NINETEEN

"You *son* of a *bitch!*"

Colt's eyes snapped open, the room still dark though it was early morning.

"You lying sack of—"

He sat up in bed, shocked to see Amber standing over him, a look in her eyes unlike any he'd ever seen on a woman's face before.

"Get out," she snarled.

"What?" he asked, blinking the sleep from his eyes. "Amber, what's going on?"

"I can't believe you," she said. "You traded us off for a rope horse."

"Rope horse? What are you—" His spine snapped upright. *Holy...*

She knew.

"Amber, calm down."

"Calm down? You want me to *calm down?*"

Her usually pale skin was flushed red. "Get out," she repeated, pointing toward the door. But then she seemed to crumple. She lifted her hands to her mouth, tears pouring from her eyes. "Get out, you son of a bitch," she sobbed. "Now."

He pulled the covers off and went to her. "No. I'm not leaving. Not until I explain."

"Explain what?" She stepped away from him before he could touch her. "That you were spying on me. That two weeks you were at Camp Cowboy to report back to Logan. Logan!" she said, her mouth trembling. "The one man on earth I loathe." She hissed in a breath.

Colt tried to calm *himself* down, but there was no escaping the bitter truth. He'd done exactly as she accused.

"I didn't mean to hurt you," he said. "I…" God, he didn't know what to say. "When I started working at Camp Cowboy, I expected to meet a selfish, arrogant woman. That's how Logan made you sound. Instead I met you."

"And that's supposed to make me feel better?" she asked. "Well, it doesn't."

She had no reason to forgive him. "Yes, I got the job at Camp Cowboy as a way of getting close to you."

She wiped her eyes, and it broke his heart.

"As a way to find Dee." He swallowed. "In exchange for a rope horse."

She quietly sobbed.

"And I'm so sorry, Amber. I never meant for things to turn out like this. I never expected to fall in love with you."

She huffed out a laugh. "Love," she said. "Hah."

"I do love you."

"Then why didn't you tell me the truth?"

"I *tried* to," he said. "Just before Dee got sick, when we were in the hallway, I tried."

"Save it," she said, holding up a hand. He wanted to wipe away the tear tracks on her face.

"No," he said. "I'm not going to save it." He tried to touch her. "I love you, Amber. I don't know how it happened. Don't know how it's possible when we practically just met, but I do love you."

"I'm leaving," she said.

He realized then that she was dressed, and that her hair was brushed and her shoes were on.

"No," he said, darting in front of her. "Don't go."

"Get out of my way, Colt."

"Amber, please. Yes, I got hired at Camp Cowboy because of you, but then I started working with the kids. Watched what happened when you worked with them and it…touched me." And goddamn it all to hell, he felt tears come to his own eyes. "The past two weeks have meant more to me than the past many years," he said, reaching out a hand.

She flinched away from his touch.

"Yes, I was in contact with Logan, but it was to ask him not to take Dee away from you. And I didn't tell him where Dee was. I swear to you."

She'd stopped crying. From somewhere deep inside her she'd found strength. God, he wished he could, too. "I don't believe you." She stepped around him.

"Amber—"

But she was gone.

"Damn it!" Colt slammed his fist against the wall, only to collapse to the floor a moment later and cry… cry as he hadn't done since the day his family died.

SHE WENT BACK to the hospital, but not before alerting security that she had a stalker who had tracked her to the facility. It was the truth, or close enough to the truth that it must have shown in her eyes. She didn't want to see Colt, either, so she told them nobody was allowed inside. The black-clothed security guard didn't hesitate. "I'll get right on it."

Whatever the officer did, it must have worked. She

didn't see Colt. She went back to Dee's room and pasted a bright smile on her face.

"Everything looks good," Dr. Salazar reported an hour later. "He was dehydrated. Probably the new environment. You know how kids like this are. They'll spit stuff out when you're not looking. You might want to monitor his fluids for the next week or two. I'll send instructions along to the home he's in."

"Thanks," she said softly.

Dr. Salazar cocked his head. "You okay? You look worried."

"No, no," she said. "I'm fine. Just tired." She forced another smile. "Long night."

"I'm sure it was. But things will get better from here on out. You can take him back to this residence—" he glanced down at his paperwork "—Camp Cowboy."

"Thanks," she said.

"Good luck, Ms. Brooks. It's not easy dealing with a child like Dee. Get some rest. You look like you need it."

"Yeah," she huffed, holding back tears. "I think you're right."

He patted her on the arm and left the room. Amber sat in the chair to wait for the discharge papers. Dee sat in his bed, staring at the TV above it as if it held answers to all the questions in the universe…and maybe it did.

"Here we go," a nurse said eventually, startling her. "All ready." She was pushing a wheelchair, their discharge papers on the seat. "Will your nephew listen to instructions?"

"Not really," Amber said, getting up. "But it's always worth a try."

She sat on the edge of Dee's bed. "Dee, we're leaving."

No reaction.

She dipped her head in front of him, blocked his vision. "You ready to go, kiddo?"

He leaned away from her, eyes so much like her sister's staring upward.

I want to see my son.

And he'd sounded so sincere. Almost desperate. She'd never heard Logan talk like that.

"Come on," she said, slowly reaching for Dee's hand. He jerked when she touched him.

It was one thing too many.

"Please, Dee," she said. "Don't make this hard on me. I don't think I can take it today."

He didn't move.

"I love you, kiddo," she said, trying to keep from crying…again. Damn it. She couldn't lose him. Couldn't bear not being a part of his life. "Auntie loves you so much." She needed to hold on to that thought. That was all that mattered.

She stood, held out her hand.

"Come on."

Dee actually listened.

Gil had sent a car earlier that afternoon. It was a short ride back to Camp Cowboy, but it took every ounce of her resolve to get out when they arrived. What if she saw Colt? What would she do? What should she do? Should she tell Gil what he'd done?

But, as it turned out, she needn't have worried.

"Did you hear what happened?" Melissa asked. "Colt quit. Just up and packed his bags and left. Buck and Gil are beside themselves."

"I'm not surprised," Amber heard herself answer, though she wasn't certain if she was responding to Melissa's comments about Buck and Gil or the fact that Colt had quit. "I'm going to settle Dee into his room."

"You need any help?" Melissa called.

But they were halfway up the stairs. "No," she said. "I'll be fine."

But she wasn't fine. From the moment she'd first caught sight of the lodge, she thought she might be sick. Didn't think she would have the strength to climb the steps. Dee had darted ahead of her, obviously remembering the way to his room. By the time she caught up to him in the doorway, he was standing in his corner again, only this time facing out.

"Dog?" he asked, his head turning this way and that.

Amber caught her breath.

He turned around. "Dog?"

She lifted a hand to her mouth, tried to fight back even more damn tears. "No, Dee," she said softly. "No dog."

Her nephew continued to search his room. "Maaac," he called. "Mac!"

A sob broke free. "Oh, Dee."

"Mac!"

"He's gone, Dee. They're both gone."

And then she was on the floor, without knowing how she'd got there. She couldn't stop herself from crying. She didn't want to lose Dee. Didn't want to lose Colt.

"He's gone," she repeated.

"I love you, kiddo."

Amber looked up. Her mouth dropped open. Dee stood above her, his hand outstretched.

"Dee love you," he said, his brown eyes full of compassion.

CHAPTER TWENTY

SHE WOULDN'T TAKE his calls. Colt didn't blame her. If he'd been in her shoes he wouldn't have taken his calls, either.

He did something he hadn't done in a long time then. Something he never thought he'd do. He went back to his family's ranch in Texas. The place where he'd grown up.

The northern part of the state wasn't the dry desert everyone thought it was. There were areas of green. Valleys and canyons with landlocked lakes. It was beautiful country. Perfect for raising cattle.

He turned down the narrow, two-lane road that led to his parents' home. That's what it was—his parents' place. It had never been his. The two-story ranch house was deserted, as he'd known it would be.

Except for the extreme dust and spiderwebs, it was exactly as he'd left it.

Ten years ago he'd packed up and headed out on the rodeo trail. Occasionally he would come back, when a competition brought him nearby, but for the most part he'd stayed away. It was too painful to return. So he'd lived the life of a hobo, staying this place and that.

He tried calling her one last time, and when that failed, broke down and phoned Logan.

"So you finally decided to call me back?" his old friend asked, but he didn't sound angry.

"Had a hell of a time tracking you down," Colt admitted, sitting in one of his mother's kitchen chairs. They were old, with hollow aluminum legs and vinyl seats. Buttercup-yellow. The whole kitchen was yellow. He didn't have the heart to change it…not yet. "Last time we talked, you didn't have a cell phone."

"How'd you find me?" Logan asked.

"Rodeo crowd." Colt absently patted Mac's head.

"Ahh," Logan said. "Word of mouth."

Colt swallowed. "Have you seen her?"

There was a pause. "Next week, as a matter of fact," he said. "Amazingly, she actually called me and set up a time."

"So you're going to take him back?"

There was another pause. "I don't know what I'm going to do just yet."

And in the words Colt heard sorrow…and regret.

"Why'd you make her out to be a witch?" Colt asked.

"She was," Logan said. Colt pictured his friend. Dark hair. Dark eyes. So very like Dee. It was remarkable that Dee had so much of both parents in him. Yet again, Colt was shocked he hadn't put two and two together far sooner than he had. "Or she has been."

"She isn't now?" Colt asked, getting up and staring out the kitchen window. Rolling hills stretched as far as the eye could see.

A thousand acres.

It had been a bitch to keep current on the property taxes, but he had. The whole place was his. No mortgage. No liens. Just land. His father's land, and his father's father's before that.

"She's…different now," Logan said. "More willing to talk to me about Rudy."

Rudy. The name Logan would always call his son. Just like Amber would always call the boy Dee. Her pet name.

"How is he?" Colt asked, clutching the counter in front of him.

"Good. No more seizures. She's thinking it really was diet related."

"I hear that can happen with autistic children."

Another pause. "Yeah, I guess he really *is* autistic, isn't he? But Amber's staying on top of things now."

As she always had.

"Hey, listen," Colt said. "If you see her, will you give her a message?"

"I don't know," Logan said. "I have a feeling mentioning your name to Amber might ruin our newfound friendship."

But Colt could tell his friend was joking. Whatever had happened to him all those years ago, whatever had caused the drinking, the partying, the carousing, it was over now. Colt had no doubt Logan was ready to take on the duties of fatherhood.

"Tell her I'm sorry," he said. "And that I wish…I wish things could have been different."

"I'll do that," Logan promised. "You coming out to California again anytime soon?"

"No," Colt said. "I'm done with rodeo."

"You sure? I still got my old rope horse out in Morgan's pasture."

"No." Colt glanced out the window once more. "I'm going to try and make a go of it here."

Logan paused again. "Good for you."

"And good for you, too. Tell Dee that Mac says hello."
And that I miss him.
Miss them both.

SHE'D BEEN DREADING the meeting for weeks. But a deal
was a deal, Amber thought. She'd promised Logan she'd
give him a chance. That he could spend some time with
Dee…if for no other reason than to convince him that
keeping Dee in an institution was the right thing to do.

She'd chosen a neutral spot—Golden Gate Park, just
a little distance from Camp Cowboy. It had dawned a
beautiful day. The fog that had plagued the camp for
weeks had disappeared. So they'd spent the morning
walking to Baker Beach. It had been a bit of a hike,
but Amber didn't care. It was so green and peaceful.
The peninsula was on a slope, and she could see break-
ers rolling toward shore. The Golden Gate Bridge was
off in the distance, its shadow seeming to undulate on
the choppy sea. Dee hung back, his eyes firmly on the
crashing waves.

Rudy. Dee.

That's why Colt hadn't put two and two together.
Logan had confessed it all. How he'd sent Colt to find
Dee, since she wouldn't tell him where Dee was. How
Colt had begged him not to do it.

Colt hadn't been lying about that. She didn't know
what to think.

"Hello, Amber."

She stiffened. She'd been expecting the meeting. She
should be nice. This was, after all, Dee's father.

"Logan," she said, turning to face him.

He'd aged.

It shocked her, this first glimpse of him. His black

hair had gone gray around the edges, though he was barely in his thirties. Usually a little on the long side, it was close-cropped. His eyes were still the same warm brown, but they held the weight of the world.

"I didn't think you'd come."

She shrugged, returned to staring at the ocean. Sailboats were zigzagging through the channel. "We made a deal."

"Rudy?" Logan said gently, far more gently than Amber would have ever thought possible from him.

"He likes the waves," she found herself saying, even though the last thing she'd told herself to do was try to soften this meeting. Dee's autism was why Logan had left in the first place. Why her sister had called it quits all those years ago. He couldn't take living with an autistic child.

"Rudy?" he said again, stepping in front of him.

Amber was stunned. The old Logan would have made some ridiculous comment. Would have claimed, "I can fix him." Would have argued with her when she explained that Dee's condition couldn't be fixed.

This Logan squatted near Dee. "Hey, son." He didn't clutch his shoulder. Didn't force him to turn and look at him.

"It's me, Rudy...Dee," Logan corrected. "Dad." Amber watched as he swallowed. "I'm your dad."

Dee didn't look at him. Didn't even move. Just stared out at the ocean.

And Amber could see the hurt in Logan's eyes.

"It's nothing personal," she said. "He's like that with everyone, even me. But he's aware. I swear to you, Logan, he knows everything you say."

That had been illustrated to her perfectly on that day she'd been sobbing in the child's room.

Dee loves you.

Logan glanced up at her, his hair blowing in the breeze off the ocean. "Are you sure?"

"Positive."

Dee's father stood back up. And Amber noticed he was even dressing differently. No jeans this time out. He wore brown slacks. And a dark-brown, button down shirt instead of a T-shirt. But most impressive was that he didn't try to touch his son. Didn't try to hug him. Didn't do anything the old Logan would have done.

"Give it time," Amber said.

Logan nodded, then turned so he could follow where his son was looking. They stood there together for goodness knows how long. Amber was so completely transfixed by the sight. She'd always thought Dee looked like her sister. But that wasn't true.

Dee resembled his dad.

She swallowed hard. How she not seen that before?

She hadn't wanted to.

But this wasn't the man she remembered.

"He never told me where he was, you know," Logan said.

"Pardon?"

"Colt," Logan said. "He didn't betray you like you think he did. He'd already put it together, who Dee was. A week before Dee got sick, he knew. But he never told me where Dee was specifically. Instead, he begged me to give it a chance. To trust you. I have the email if you want to see it."

"No."

Logan came over and placed a hand on her shoulder.

Amber wanted to cry.

"He told me I owe you big time." He half turned. "For everything you've done. And I know I do, Amber. I really do." He looked down at the sand. "I messed up." And there were tears in his eyes. "I really messed up." The wind caught his hair again. "But I'm sorry. For everything, Amber. I'm so damn sorry, and I *swear* to you I'll make it up." She heard his voice hitch. "I don't know if I ever can. But I swear I'm going to try."

She couldn't breathe for a moment. How had this happened? How had a man who'd been so horrible, changed so much?

She couldn't deny that he had.

Sharron would have wanted her to move forward.

"You don't need to make it up to me."

"Yes, I do," he said. "I do. And I promise I'll be there for the both of you. I swear to you, Amber."

They both glanced at Dee. The little boy had turned. A second later he lifted his hand and pointed. "Mac!"

It was like a stab to the heart. "No, Dee, that's not—"

But it was.

A dog that looked just like Mac ran forward, a gray-and-white speeding bullet that hurled itself straight at Dee.

"This is step one of making it up to you," Logan said. "He loves you, Amber. I've never met a man so devoted to a woman. Your rejection is killing him. Please, give him a chance."

Because beyond Mac, walking along the edge of the beach toward her, was Colt, black cowboy hat firmly in place.

"Oh, damn," she muttered.

Through eyes suddenly filled with tears, she watched as Mac threw himself at Dee's feet.

"Mac!" Dee cried.

That was all the incentive the dog needed. Rear end swaying, tongue lolling, eyes wide and bright, Mac rubbed up against the little boy he loved so much.

"Mac," Dee repeated, squatting and burying his head in the dog's thick fur.

She had to look away. If she didn't she'd start bawling like a baby.

"Hello, Amber."

She still found herself dashing tears away, having to inhale deeply before facing him. She should be angry. She should tell both of them, Logan and Colt, to get lost.

"I hope you're not mad at Logan," Colt said.

The sound of the ocean was nothing compared to the roar in her ears. "I'm not," she said, uncertain what she felt. But it wasn't anger.

Colt blocked her view, so she had to look at him.

"I went back to Texas, Amber," he said. "I went back and faced my inner demons."

She inhaled deeply. "And?" Something inside her shifted as she looked into his blue eyes.

"All alone, surrounded by a thousand acres...all I wanted was you," he said, reaching out to brush a lock of her hair away from her eyes. "And I found I couldn't live without you."

"Colt..."

"I hated myself before I met you, Amber. I couldn't see the good in anything...or in anybody. And then you came along."

She tried again. "Colt..."

"And I realized that if a woman like you could like a man like me…"

She shook her head.

"That if someone who only saw the good in things could find some good in me… And if she wasn't afraid to put everything on the line, then I could do no less."

Her vision began to blur. He reached for her hands.

"I love you, Amber. I love you more than I've loved anything in my life."

Except his parents and his sister. But he didn't need to qualify it. His family that he'd loved so much, and that he blamed himself for killing. But he'd forgiven himself now. Amber had taught him how to do that. She'd forgiven the man who'd killed her sister. How could he do less? She could see it in his eyes.

"I love you," he repeated earnestly, cupping her face in his hands.

She loved him, too. Still. With him standing in front of her, there was no way she could deny it.

"You lied to me," she whispered.

"I might not have been honest about my reasons for coming to Camp Cowboy, but I never lied."

"But it was dishonest."

"Yes," he admitted, "it was. And I'm sorry. I'm so damn sorry."

He clutched her hands again. "I love you," he repeated. "Please tell me you forgive me."

She drew a deep breath, inhaled the scent of him and absorbed the feel of his body.

"Marry me?" he asked.

She looked past him, at Logan, who'd been kind enough to step away and give them some privacy. At

Dee, who sat stroking Colt's dog. And at the sky, so blue
and beautiful and so much like Colt's eyes.

"Marry me?" He tipped her chin up and forced her
to look at him.

He loved her.

"Marry me."

He kissed her. And the moment their lips touched,
she knew it was useless. She loved this man. He might
have met her under false pretenses, might not have been
exactly honest, but she loved him. And when he kissed
her, she couldn't doubt that he loved her right back.

"Marry me," he said a fourth time.

And this time when she looked him in the eyes she
answered, "Yes."

He jerked her to him so quickly and so suddenly that
she gasped. And then she was laughing. And crying.
And hugging him back.

"Dee love Mac."

They both glanced over in time to see Dee plop down
on the beach as he wrapped his arm around Colt's dog.

"Good dog," the little boy said.

And then they were both smiling and laughing, as
for the first time, Amber felt hope. Colt loved her. Dee
loved Colt's dog. Amber loved Colt. And if Dee continued to speak, that was a minor miracle in and of itself.

The *second* miracle of her life.

* * * * *

We hope you enjoyed reading this
special collection from Harlequin®.

If you liked reading these stories,
then you will love
Harlequin® American Romance® books!

You love small towns and cowboys!
Harlequin American Romance stories are
heartwarming contemporary tales of everyday
women finding love, becoming part of a
family or community—or maybe starting a
family of their own.

Enjoy four new stories from
Harlequin American Romance
every month!

Available wherever books and
ebooks are sold.

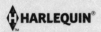

American Romance®

Romance the all-American way!

www.Harlequin.com

STEPHAl

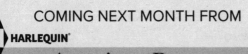

SPECIAL EXCERPT FROM

H HARLEQUIN®

American Romance®

*Rose McCabe wants to use Clint McCulloch's newly
acquired ranch for blackberry farming, but the sexy
cowboy wants it for pastureland for his herd. Can the
two come to a temporary agreement?*

Read on for a sneak preview of
LONE STAR DADDY
by *Cathy Gillen Thacker*,
part of her **MCCABE MULTIPLES** *miniseries.*

"You can ignore me as long as you want. I am not going
away." Rose McCabe followed Clint McCulloch around the
big farm tractor.

Wrench in one hand, a grimy cloth in another, the rodeo
cowboy turned rancher paused to give her a hostile glare.
"Suit yourself," he muttered beneath his breath. Then went
right back to working on the engine that had clearly seen
better days.

Aware she was taking a tiger by the tail, Rose stomped
closer. "Sooner or later you're going to have to hear me out."

"Actually, I won't." Sweat glistened on the suntanned
skin of his broad shoulders and muscular back, dripped
down the strip of dark hair that covered his chest, and
arrowed down into the fly of his faded jeans.

Still ignoring her, he moved around the wheel to turn the
key in the ignition.

It clicked. But did not catch.

He strode back to the engine once more, giving Rose
a good view of his ruggedly handsome face and the thick

chestnut hair that fell onto his brow and curled damply against the nape of his neck. At six foot four, there was no doubt Clint was every bit as much as stubborn—and breathtakingly masculine—as he had been when they were growing up.

"The point is—" he said "—I'm not interested in being a berry farmer. I'm a rancher. I want to restore the Double Creek Ranch to the way it was when my dad was alive. Run cattle and breed and train cutting horses here." He pointed to the blackberry patch up for debate. "And those thorn- and weed-infested bushes are sitting on the most fertile land on the entire ranch."

Rose's expression turned pleading. "Just let me help you out."

"No." He refused to be swayed by a sweet-talking woman, no matter how persuasive and beguiling. He had gone down that road once before, with a heartbreaking result.

A silence fell and Rose blinked. "No?" she repeated, as if she were sure she had heard wrong.

"No," he reiterated flatly. His days of being seduced or pressured into anything were long over. Then he picked up his wrench. "And now, if you don't mind, I really need to get back to work…"

Don't miss LONE STAR DADDY
by Cathy Gillen Thacker,
available June 2015 wherever
Harlequin® American Romance®
books and ebooks are sold.

www.Harlequin.com

Love the Harlequin book you just read?

Your opinion matters.

Review this book on your favorite book site, review site, blog or your own social media properties and share your opinion with other readers!